My Wild Highlander

Vonda Sinclair

My Wild Highlander

Copyright © 2012 Vonda Sinclair

ALL RIGHTS RESERVED

www.vondasinclair.com

ISBN-13: 978-1478337638

ISBN-10: 147833763X

DEDICATION

To my wonderful, supportive and amazing husband.

❦

ACKNOWLEDGMENTS

Special thanks to Sharron Gunn, Jody Allen, and Cindy Vallar for helping me translate Gaelic and French, answering difficult questions and assisting me with research.

ುಲ್ಲ ಲ್ಲ

CHAPTER ONE

London, England, 1618

"Lady Angelique! Come back, sweeting!" ancient Lord Chatsworth called.

Sacrebleu! Angelique Drummagan rushed down the corridor, eased open a door and slipped inside a dark drawing room, one of many within the maze of Whitehall Palace. She prayed Chatsworth would pass by. He fancied himself her suitor and did naught but drool on her hand every time he was near.

Heavy breathing and moans sounded from across the room. She turned and froze, her eyes searching the near darkness. Who was here? Only the shifting moonlight glinting off the Thames provided any illumination, revealing chair backs and settees.

A high-pitched giggle pierced the air from several yards away, in the vicinity of a sitting area near the cold hearth.

"Shh."A long moment of silence stretched out, broken by sounds of kissing.

"King James wishes her brought before him forthwith," a muffled male voice said outside the closed door.

"She vanished in this passage," Chatsworth said.

A pox upon the old lecher! And the king, too. Angelique crept across the Turkish carpet and slid behind the brocade window drapery.

"Ooh, I'm impressed with your swordplay skills, my laird."

1

Lady Eleanor's voice, breathy and excited, shattered the quiet of the room. She was the one moaning and giggling?

The harlot.

"I'm not a laird, but I do thank you for the compliment."

A Highlander? Angelique would recognize that tongue-rolling speech anywhere.

She had never known Eleanor, countess of Wexbury, to dally with anyone below a viscount. What was she doing with a barbarian? That's what her mother—God rest her soul—would've called him, or any Scot. And Maman should know; she'd been married to one.

Eleanor cried out with carnal pleasure. Angelique's face burned hot. She couldn't comprehend how a woman found pleasure in the act. Never again would she entrust her body and heart to any man. Since men were naught but faithless pigs, she knew she only had duty before her, not happiness. Not love. That had been a foolish child's dream.

Eleanor gasped for breath and the Scot made a growling noise. The height of pleasure, some said. Surely the French term *le petit mort*—the little death—was more accurate. Nausea gripped Angelique even as shocking excitement quickened her heart beat. A dark, hidden part of her wondered… No, never again. *I cannot marry and be subjected to a man's lust.* She pressed trembling fingers against her throat and found it damp with perspiration.

The door opened and lamplight reflected off the white walls.

"Lady Angelique?" Dryden's nasal voice echoed through the room. He was the most vexing of the king's courtiers.

The two lovers became silent.

"I know you're in here. I heard a noise."

From her position behind the draperies, she noticed the light moving across the floor.

A thump sounded, then rustling.

"Sir Lachlan? What in Hades are you…?"

"I was but…resting," the Scot said.

"Have you seen Lady Angelique?"

"Nay."

"Dryden, the lamp, if you please," Chatsworth said.

"What is it?"

In the silence, the light shifted again, growing brighter as it moved in her direction.

Mon Dieu, do not let them find me, s'il vous plaît. Angelique's pulse roared in her ears. She detested Chatsworth, and now, to be discovered lurking about in a dark room while a Scot coupled with a lady harlot would be exceedingly mortifying. They might even accuse her of spying on them.

Dryden yanked the drapery aside.

"Parbleu!" Angelique blurted and pressed a hand to her mouth.

Dryden sent her a vile grin. In the background, Chatsworth scowled, then shot a murderous glance at the man they'd called Sir Lachlan, who stood in a darkened corner.

Where had Eleanor crawled away to? Angelique couldn't see her beneath the carved furniture in the dimness.

"You and Sir Lachlan?" Dryden snickered. "His Majesty will likely find this interesting."

"Non! I was not—Lady Eleanor was—where did she go?" Embarrassment flamed over her. Now, they thought she'd been with the Scot? *Never.*

"No need to lie, *mademoiselle.* Come. The king wishes to see you." He ushered her toward the door. "You, too, Sir Lachlan."

"Me?"

"Indeed." Dryden waved him forward.

The Highlander stepped into the light. The giant was more than a foot taller than she, broad shouldered and wearing a belted plaid, leaving the bottom portion of his muscular legs bare. She'd seen few of these barbaric articles of clothing since she was nine years old and her mother had taken her from Scotland.

His face was ruggedly masculine with a square jaw and hard chin, enticing to a woman's baser instincts, but not refined. This was the same man she'd seen leaving Lady Catherine's bedchamber the night before. Then, he'd been wearing trews. Dallying with two women at court? Or perhaps more? *Lecher.*

Amusement sparkled in his eyes before he bowed. "M'lady."

"Sir." She curtsied.

The Scot's darkened eyes fixed upon her in a too-knowing way. To cover the heat rushing over her face, she strode from the room.

Feeling like a prisoner headed for the block, Angelique walked beside the Highlander through several rooms and dark-paneled corridors, taking two steps for his every one. Dryden and Chatsworth followed. She would not be surprised to feel the prick of a sword at her back. Glancing around, she found the men empty-handed.

They passed through four doors, guarded by numerous courtiers and royal servants before reaching the antechamber with its gleaming ebony furniture upholstered in the finest red velvets. Numerous candles lit the room and glimmered off the gold leaf.

What did the king want? He'd sent for her two days before at Hampton Court Palace, though he hadn't been ready to meet with her until now. She disliked leaving the comfort of the queen's household, but King James was her guardian and she must do as he bid. Chatsworth and Dryden had been searching for her before they found her in the room with this Highlander, so the summons could have naught to do with him. Why had they asked him to accompany them?

They neared the king's private rooms and an usher opened the carved door. "Lady Angelique Drummagan and Sir Lachlan MacGrath," he announced.

The four entered. The men bowed, and she curtsied deeply before the king.

The scrawny, aging monarch, wearing overblown clothing in colorful silks, occupied an ornate chair on an elevated platform. Buckingham, his favorite courtier, a regally handsome dark-haired man in his early twenties, stood next to him, along with several other members of the aristocracy.

"You have found her." King James turned his rheumy, unsteady gaze toward the tall man beside her. "And Sir Lachlan, I'm so glad you have joined us once again."

"Your Majesty, 'tis a supreme honor." Lachlan bowed.

Dryden whispered something to another courtier, who whispered to Buckingham. And he proceeded to murmur into the king's ear.

The frail monarch's eyes widened. "The two of you have… met?"

Angelique's face heated. "*Non*. Not in truth."

The king frowned at his courtiers but his expression lightened when he looked at Lachlan. "It matters not. This is my ward, Lady Angelique Drummagan, the new countess of Draughon in her own right." He motioned toward her. "My dear, meet Sir Lachlan MacGrath, a hero to whom we owe much."

The cursed MacGrath took her hand and kissed it. "'Tis my

great pleasure to make your acquaintance, m'lady." His rich baritone and the Scottish burr appealed more than it should have.

She stiffened.

In the bright candlelight, she saw he was a most visually interesting man. His tawny hair was too long by far and not of the current style. His eyes gleamed like a tiger's eye stone. It was not the color that arrested her, but the expression—assessing and sensual. She had come upon many a rogue like him in France, and barely escaped marrying one.

She jerked her hand away but remembered her manners just in time and curtsied. Not too deeply, because he didn't deserve even that. "An honor, Sir Lachlan."

A tiny grin lifted one corner of his full lips. Though she already loathed him because he was a Highlander and a debaucher, something about him defied her to look away.

"Through his cunning and sharp wits, Sir Lachlan has saved the life of our dear Marquess of Buckingham and broken up the den of conspirators," King James said. "We knighted Sir Lachlan a fortnight ago but we believe he deserves an even greater reward. Do we not, Steenie?"

Buckingham nodded.

"He will also receive a title." King James gave her a toothless grin. "Earl of Draughon."

What? Her late father's title?

The shock and silence threatened to render her senseless on the floor. What had the king meant?

"Yes, my dear, I have finally found you the perfect husband. He is Scottish, as you are. He is pleasing to look upon and..."

"Pray pardon...Majesty." Fearing she would faint, she quickly curtsied and fled the stateroom as if Lucifer himself chased her. She would die before she'd marry a Highlander whose favorite pastime was lifting skirts.

☙❧

Lachlan watched the lovely red-haired lass dash from the room. What the devil had just happened? Had the king said something about a husband? And the earl of something? He shouldn't have drunk so much sack earlier.

He shook his head, attempting to clear it. Facing the king, Lachlan could hardly believe he stood once again in His Majesty's opulent private chambers—Lachlan, a Highlander and a second son with no title, nothing but a canny wit and a sword. During the past several weeks, while he'd been at court, enjoying every moment of the drinking, feasting, hunting and other, more carnal, pursuits, he had not been caught in such a compromising situation. And now His Majesty wished to leg-shackle him to a prickly lass? It made no sense. Clearly, Lachlan had overstayed his welcome and should've already departed for his clan's Kintalon Castle in the Highlands.

"Well, then," King James said. "Has there ever been a bride unafraid of the holy state of matrimony?" He grinned. "A toast!" He motioned to his courtiers and servants, who scrambled about for drinks.

Future bride? Lachlan shook his head. Nay, he could never marry. He loved women too much to settle with only one.

"Your Majesty, pray pardon… what are you saying? You wish me to marry Lady Angelique?"

"Yes, yes. I understand you two already know each other, in a sense." James winked.

"Upon my honor, I did not touch her. She happened upon me in the room where I was napping." Had she already been in there when he and Eleanor had arrived, or had she slipped in later? And who had she been hiding from?

"Very well." The king glared at Dryden. "He did not touch her."

Lachlan accepted a crystal glass of the king's prized Greek wine.

Marriage? God's teeth! 'Twill be a disaster.

"So, what say you, lad?"

Damnation, he should say naught. He should keep his tongue trapped firmly betwixt his teeth, but given the dozens of aristocratic gazes burning into him, including the king's, he could not play a mute this late in the day. Marriage? He could not entirely grasp the concept, except that it might be torture. But he could not offend the king by refusing. Besides, he had mentioned an earldom, had he not?

"I…I don't rightly ken what to say, Your Majesty, except I thank you. I'm overcome by your generosity." Lachlan bowed. *Saints! What did I utter?* He was afraid he'd just agreed to get married.

"I'm glad you are pleased." King James raised his glass and the other men followed suit. "To the next Earl of Draughon and chief of Clan Drummagan."

Lachlan took a sip of wine, though in truth he did not want it. He must think clearly.

"Lady Angelique is much in need of a husband," the king said. "Her father, a good friend of mine, died without having a son, therefore Angelique is his heir. He wished that she marry a good Scotsman to guide her and help her run the estate. She will agree of course and, after the marriage, give you Draughon Castle, the earldom and all the lands she possesses. I will confirm it by charter. The men of the clan are headstrong and need an even stronger man to lead them. You, lad, are strong in mind and in body."

"I thank you, Majesty." Something twisted in Lachlan's gut. Though he recalled no past dealings or feuds between his own clan and the Drummagans—what if they refused to accept him?

"A distant male cousin of the fifth degree could be next in line but her father, John Drummagan, did not wish him to be chief, nor does the clan. Besides, there is some question as to his lineage. The only way I would approve of him is if Angelique wishes to marry him. Doubtful, I daresay." The king drank from his glass and a bit of the wine dribbled from the corner of his mouth. A courtier quickly blotted the liquid.

Lachlan remained silent. *Me, married?* He tried to visualize that without success.

"She is a spirited lass, but I'm sure you will tame her in no time," the king continued. "The estate is near Perth. I think you will find it most pleasant."

Lachlan's older brother was an earl and a chief, but he had never thought to rise to such a level himself. "I'm at a loss for words, Majesty. I'm sure I'm undeserving of such a grand reward."

One of the courtiers coughed and another cleared his throat—titled aristocrats, all, with more wealth and power than they knew what to do with. Everything in Lachlan rebelled at the disdain he witnessed in their eyes.

"Ah, but you do," King James proclaimed. "Does he not, Steenie?"

The extravagantly dressed man beside the king nodded. "Indeed. The brave Scot saved my life." Buckingham's gaze held sincerity.

"By the by," James went on. "I ken you have a smidgen of

Stuart blood in your veins, laddie, from a hundred or so years ago. Anyone who's a descendant of kings is surely good enough to be Earl of Draughon."

Buckingham nodded again.

God's bones! Could he become more than he'd ever imagined? More than anyone had expected of him?

You will amount to naught, his father had yelled at him more than once. *You cannot make a living swiving every wench from here to Paris and back. Not to mention the drinking and gaming. Why can you not be more like Alasdair?*

Nay, he would never be as good as his brother.

"Ah, I know what worries you, lad," the king said. "The estate is not in debt and comes with a generous income. The lands thereabout are rich and produce an abundance of crops. The sheep and cattle are too numerous to count."

"What of the Drummagan clan? Will they accept me as their chief?"

"They must. Angelique is the legal heir, and her husband, by right of the marriage contract, stands beside her and leads the clan with her. I command them to accept you. Any who do not will be dealt with as traitors to the crown."

But he would have to marry the flame-haired lass who had glared at him and fled. Had there ever been a woman, whether wench or lady, he couldn't seduce into his good graces? Well, maybe one or two, but they were few and far between.

"This is such an honor, Your Highness. My most sincere thanks to you." Lachlan gave his deepest bow.

"Are you in agreement, then?"

"Aye," he said before he could talk himself out of it. "But I would like to speak with the lady first."

The king nodded. "Be prepared for her resistance. She wishes to marry Philippe Descartes but he is unacceptable—some French nobleman's bastard, and a weak lad to boot. I will never allow it."

⁂

Angelique raced to her chamber, slammed and barred the door.

Camille shot from her chair, still holding her needlework. "What is happening?" she asked in French.

Breathing hard, Angelique turned to face her companion. "King James has found me a vile husband."

Camille's blue eyes grew round. "In truth? Who?"

"A wild Scot, a Highlander who does nothing but seduce women. A debaucher worse than Girard."

"No one is worse than Girard."

"Of course. But I cannot marry this MacGrath. You must take a message to Philippe." Angelique hurried to the desk and withdrew a piece of paper, her hands shaking. She almost overset the inkhorn as she dipped in the quill.

"Take a deep breath, *mademoiselle*. You will do nothing but waste paper in your haste."

"You are right." She paused a moment, sucked in two deep breaths, then continued at a more controlled pace.

"Would this be the Highlander who wears a belted plaid about, sinfully long hair, tall strapping man?"

"*Oui*. How can you know of him already?"

Camille gave a dramatic shiver. "The ladies and servants talk. Are you sure you do not want to marry that one?"

"No! Do not tell me he has bedded you as well."

"No. Heavens, no. I wish." She smiled. "If you do not want him…"

"You can have him, believe me. Traitor!"

"It was only a jest."

Angelique put pen to paper. She almost wrote Philippe's name. No, what if someone intercepted the message and took it to the king?

My Love, she wrote. *We must run away together. Make arrangements tonight, then come to my room before dawn and I will be ready.*

Camille read over her shoulder. "Must you lie and expect the impossible?"

Angelique frowned up at her. "What?"

"You do not love him, and he is not cunning enough to sneak you out of Whitehall. If you elope, you may jeopardize your inheritance. Anger the king, and he is likely to give the estate and title to Kormad."

Angelique thought for a moment. "Yes, you are right." She wadded the paper and took out a clean sheet. "Philippe must beg the king for my hand. That's the only way."

"Why do you want to marry the milksop anyway?"

"Because—"

"The truth." Only because her companion was also her

illegitimate French cousin and best friend did she get away with such impertinence.

"Because he is a milksop," Angelique said. "He will not order me around. He will not force me to couple with him if I do not wish it. He will be the earl, but I will run my estate myself without an overbearing, demeaning swine of a man controlling every aspect of my life. I cannot abide it, Camille. I will smother and die." Her throat constricted and tears burned her eyes.

"Shh, it's all right, Ange." Camille rubbed her arm. "Do not overset yourself. Damn Girard for ruining your life."

Angelique shoved the emotion away and wrote the second note, telling Philippe to meet with the king and ask for her hand immediately if he wished to be an earl. She folded the note, dropped red melted wax on it and stamped it with an obscure seal only Philippe knew she used. One she had pilfered from her mother's last benefactor.

"Take it to him." She placed the missive in Camille's hands. "Quickly, please."

"Oui, mademoiselle."

⋄⋄⋄

A curvaceous, flaxen-haired woman scurried past Lachlan in the passage, moving at such a brisk pace he but caught a glimpse of her. What was amiss? No one chased her. "Mmph."

Lachlan continued his search for Lady Angelique's suite along the dim, wood-paneled corridor. Though visiting her chamber was inappropriate, he had to speak with her immediately. Besides, when had he ever cared what was inappropriate? His gut clenched, making him wonder if he'd made a mistake accepting the king's offer.

Damnation. Nothing was easy to find in the confusion of Whitehall Palace, and the directions he'd gotten from a servant were unclear. Believing he'd found the correct door, he knocked.

"*Qui est-ce?* Who is it?" a woman called. Her sensual French accent and husky voice awoke his carnal urges. He held a keen fondness for the French ladies.

He knocked again.

She muttered a French curse and he smiled.

Angelique yanked open the door and her gaze cut into him. "Why are you here?"

"I wish to talk to you, m'lady." He bowed.

10

"I have naught to say to you, Highlander. I have already agreed to marry someone else."

"Indeed? Are you speaking of Philippe Descartes?"

"How do you know of him?"

"His Majesty told me he found the man unacceptable as a husband for you."

Her green eyes widened. While she was distracted by his comment, he pushed his way inside her door and closed it behind him.

"*Que vous êtes bête!*" She backed away. "Leave at once, *monsieur*. We have nothing to say to each other."

Having never before been called a beast, he almost laughed. But he didn't want her to know he spoke fluent French, as well as Italian, Spanish and German. In the past, pretending ignorance had sometimes given him the advantage.

"I would ask you kindly to please speak English or Gaelic."

"I will never lower myself to speak your barbaric Erse."

Though her disdain of his native tongue pricked at him like thorns, her closed-mouth, purring accent stirred arousal within him.

"Because you don't ken the language? I shall teach you, if you wish."

She drew her lips into a firm line. Clearly, she had never known the pleasure of a good kiss, something he would enjoy tutoring her in. 'Haps she'd never experienced a kiss at all, good or bad.

Her rich voice and wise, guarded eyes were those of a woman, but her girlish face and slender, waif-like body made her appear she had not enough to eat. In contrast, her clothing of finest gold silk told him she could not be starving.

"How many years have you?" he asked.

"Twenty."

He nodded, pleased she was not as young as she appeared...if she was telling the truth. He would ask one of the courtiers on the morrow. Nevertheless, the king wanted him to marry her and he was not one to forgo grand royal gifts, even if he didn't know what the devil to do with them yet.

"*Et vous?*" she asked.

"Pray pardon?"

"And you? You must be very old."

11

He chuckled. "You don't see any gray hairs, do you? I am twenty-six."

Her brows lifted, intensifying her haughty look, but this only increased her allure. He couldn't resist a challenge.

"We have much to discuss before we are wed."

"I will not marry you. King James cannot force me."

"'Tis dangerous to defy your king."

Her militant expression and rigid stance, hands on hips, told him she might be one of the few women in the world he couldn't sweet talk into liking him. A sinking feeling settled into the pit of his stomach.

"God's bones, I don't ken how you are a reward," Lachlan muttered. "'Haps His Majesty is wanting to punish me for saving the life of Buckingham."

Angelique murmured something in French that sounded like insolent lecher, though he couldn't be sure.

"I thank you for that compliment, m'lady." He winked.

The pink from her face spread down her neck toward her bodice and small breasts. How he loved a woman's creamy curves flushed with the glow of passion.

If she could've made dirks of ice shoot from her eyes, she would've slain him on the spot. She turned away. "Leave me at once."

Her prickliness didn't fool him. 'Twas all a front. Her blush told him she found him appealing, whether she wanted to admit it or not. But maybe she was a virgin and didn't know the pleasures that awaited her in his bed. He would attempt a kiss now, but she might bite off his tongue.

"As you wish, m'lady." He bowed. "I shall see you on the morrow."

"Bonne nuit, monsieur," she said in a condescending tone before he closed the door on his way out.

As he strode down the passage, his heart raced. She excited him more than any woman in a long while. Surely he did not enjoy her sharp tongue or chilly glares. Nay, but he loved a chase. Most women were too easy to catch—he winked, he smiled, and they came.

With determination, Lachlan continued toward the king's private chambers. He sent a message by one of the ushers and five minutes later, Buckingham emerged.

"I wish to inform His Majesty that I would be honored to marry Lady Angelique," Lachlan said.

Buckingham grinned. "I shall tell His Majesty. He will be most pleased."

"I thank you." Lachlan bowed and made his way toward his own bedchamber, trying not to think of the future or what he'd committed himself to. Could be hell itself.

From the passageway, he carried a lit candle into the darkened room. A breathy female voice called out his name in a sing-song fashion and a giggle floated from the draped bed. A second of excitement ignited within him when he thought of Lady Angelique, perhaps come for a surprise visit, but it could not be her. Unless she'd come to murder him. He parted the curtains.

Eleanor lay naked upon the velvet coverlet, gazing at him with heavy darkened eyes. "I am ready for you," she breathed.

He surveyed her ivory skin, her rosy, hard nipples highlighting full breasts, the dark patch of hair at the apex of her shapely thighs, but he felt nothing. No heat of arousal curled through him as it had the first time he'd seen her.

What the devil was wrong with him? He didn't want a naked, willing woman?

"You must go. I'm not in the mood."

He let the curtain drape back into place and set the candle on the mantel.

"What?"

He poured himself some sherry and took a hefty swig. By the saints, was he changing his ways?

Nay, he was just…distracted. Preoccupied with the startling turn of events. Worried he'd stepped in a huge pile of horse dung.

Behind him, she struggled from the bed. "I heard about your reward from the king."

"Already?" He turned and watched her shove her arms into a silk smock.

"I knew before you did. She is not a virgin, you know."

Indeed? "Nor am I."

Eleanor smirked. "She's a French whore and you shall never see a moment's happiness with her. She will never please you in bed."

"From what I've heard, French whores are excellent in bed."

"You shall regret this!"

"Aye, likely I will," he muttered, but what else had he to do? Keep wandering about, looking for adventures and women? Now, he saw the futility of it. The pursuit of revelry was losing its appeal. What would his friend Rebbie say to that?

"A title and estate do not require your faithfulness," Eleanor snapped.

"Who said anything about faithfulness?"

"Then why are you throwing me out?"

Not wanting to insult her, he simply lifted a shoulder. In truth, he even surprised himself with how rapidly he'd tired of Eleanor. "As I said, I'm not in the mood."

"All the men want to marry her, but she will have none of them, save Philippe. What makes you think she'll have you?"

"She will obey the king, I suspect."

"I wouldn't place a wager upon it. You won't last long anyway. Kormad will grind you to sausage in no time."

"Who?"

"The Baron of Kormad. Sorley MacGrotie."

"Ah." A Lowland Scotsman he'd met almost a fortnight ago. He had not been impressed with the man, medium of stature with a sizable gut. He would be clumsy on the battlefield. "Is he Angelique's distant cousin, next in line to inherit?"

"Yes. And the rumor is he will let nothing stand in the way of what he wants."

⚜

After Eleanor left, Lachlan slipped from his bedchamber and along the dark corridor. He'd traded his kilt for black trews and cowl. His basket-hilted broadsword thumped against his thigh.

Sorley MacGrotie. The longer Lachlan thought of the bastard, the more his sword hand ached to grip a hilt. How badly did the Baron of Kormad want to be an earl? And what would he do to achieve his goal?

He will let nothing stand in the way of what he wants, Eleanor had said.

Mmph. He doubted the man had ever had a Highlander in his way. 'Twas the same as a rocky crag. He intended to gain the upper hand and ferret out Kormad's plans. Lachlan's instincts told him to expect a battle. This was his opportunity to finally be someone who mattered, to live up to a potential he never knew he had. And damned if anyone would snatch it away from him.

Lachlan lowered his cowl for a moment, allowing the guards to identify him at the gate. They let him pass. Outside on the dark muddy street, he listened to the sounds of the night—the fetid Thames flowing by, a dog barking—then proceeded along King Street to the nearest coaching inn, The Golden Cross, a likely haunt for Kormad. But the man was nowhere to be found.

Lachlan stepped into the third establishment along the Strand. The Black Spur was a din of English talk and laughter. Ale and beer scented the air of the low-ceilinged room, along with roasting boar and smoke from the fire.

He scanned the dozens of men seated at tables, then spotted his friend, Dirk MacLerie, near the back. Lachlan slipped over and sat in the empty chair.

Hand drifting to his sword hilt, Dirk turned dangerous pale blue eyes toward Lachlan in his cowl. "What do you want, friend?"

"'Tis me."

Dirk's auburn brows quirked. "Lachlan?"

"Shh. Has Sorley MacGrotie, Baron of Kormad, been in here tonight?"

"I don't ken the man."

"Lowland Scot, dark hair, bushy beard. Ugly bastard."

"I've seen a lot of them like that."

The door opened and a boisterous group stumbled in. Among the six men, he found the whoreson he was looking for. "'Tis him, there."

"Why are you looking for him?"

"I'll tell you later," Lachlan said in a low voice.

The buxom alewife plunked a full tankard of ale onto the scarred wooden table, some of the brown liquid sloshing over the rim. Lachlan flipped her a silver coin. She thanked him with a wink and bustled away to see to the newcomers.

Kormad and his men took a large table on the other side of the room.

"We need to move," Lachlan whispered, picking up the tankard. "To that empty table behind them. You go first. He's seen me before."

"You better have a good reason for this," Dirk muttered and stood.

Squeezing by the chairs of other patrons, Lachlan followed Dirk to the closer table and sat with his back to the men in question. "Watch my back, will you?"

"When have I not?"

For a time, Kormad and his men talked of mundane matters. Dirk gave him a hard scowl. Lachlan shook his head and sipped the lukewarm ale.

"Any progress with the king?" one of the men at the other table asked.

Lachlan raised a finger at Dirk so he would pay attention.

"Nay," Kormad said in his gruff voice.

"If we take the lass and force her to marry you, the problem is solved."

"I don't want my head lopped off because of the hateful wench."

"You must woo her," one of his men said in a low, teasing voice.

"Aye, make her swoon with your lovely poetry."

The men guffawed.

"'Tis not a laughing matter. To be earl, I must marry her," Kormad grumbled.

"Or you could kill her," another man suggested.

Lachlan clutched the tankard of ale tightly when all he wanted to do was draw his sword and do the lopping off of Kormad's head himself. *By the saints, I will protect her.* Though he did not know why he should want to protect the thorny, insulting ice queen. Something inside her seemed vulnerable and alone. She reminded him of the wee injured wildcat he had found on his clan's lands when he was a lad. When he'd tried to help, the feline had scratched him, but she was simply protecting herself the only way she knew how.

Dirk frowned, scrutinizing Lachlan's face.

"Shh," Kormad hissed.

The men's voices lowered. "We could steal her away and hie back to Scotland. You can marry her there, legal."

"And have the king string me up like a bleeding boar? Nay, indeed."

"The lass will tell the king she wishes it. I can make certain of it."

"You're too daft to make certain of anything," Kormad snapped. "The Drummagans have been friends of the Stuarts for hundreds of years. I won't jeopardize that."

"Queen Jamie doesn't seem like a friend to you," a slimy voiced man muttered.

"Who is he going to marry her off to, then?" another man asked. "That damned Frenchman bastard?"

"Nay. The clan would never accept him as chief," Kormad said.

"Chatsworth?"

"Too old. And too English."

"The clan will settle for naught but a full-blooded Scotsman," Kormad said with finality.

"You're the best candidate. I say you should meet with the king again."

"He might be thinking of that Lachlan MacGrath what saved Steenie's life," a different man said.

Dirk's frown grew fierce and his glare deadly.

Lachlan was glad his friend finally understood.

"He's a Scot, but a damned Highlander," one of the men said.

"The king detests Highlanders," Kormad growled.

"He knighted MacGrath and took him hunting at Theobalds. He likes that one."

"Might be his bonny face."

"Maybe Steenie should watch his back," slime voice said.

Loud laughter erupted. *Bastards.* Lachlan wished he could shock them all by making his presence known, but that would not serve his purpose. Pretending to be naught but a skirt-chasing gallant would lull them into thinking he was no threat.

Moments later, the group quieted. "The lass is the only thing in your path, my lord."

"Aye."

"So let's remove the obstacle. 'Accidentally' of course."

"Not yet. Let's see who the king chooses for her first."

CHAPTER TWO

Angelique knelt before the king in the throne room the next afternoon. She blinked against the burning rose water perfume she'd dropped into her eyes and stared at the blurred patterns of the lush carpet.

"You must choose a husband from among these three men," King James said.

"But, Your Majesty, pray pardon. I love Philippe Descartes. He is a good man." Lifting her gaze as far as his royally shod feet, she blotted her faux tears with a silk handkerchief. She hated to resort to such theatrics but she knew her guardian was easily swayed with tears, especially hers, ever since she was a small child. The first time her father had taken her to court in Edinburgh, she'd been terrified of all the strangers. When the king saw her crying, he gave her a priceless gold trinket. She prayed he still had a soft spot for her, because she must convince him she was genuinely in love with Phillipe. This was her only sound argument.

"Philippe is not suitable, my child. He is too young, weak, and the bastard of a Frenchman. The Earl of Draughon must be a strong man of legitimate birth, and Scottish. 'Tis what your father wanted. The clan will accept nothing less. Nor will I."

"But—but I cannot live without Philippe, Your Majesty."

"If you do not choose, then I shall choose for you," the king said in a harsh voice he'd never used with her. "Which will it be?"

Merde! Why had Philippe not requested an audience with the king today and asked for her hand?

Deep down she knew Philippe would've made no progress, because King James had already chosen MacGrath. Giving her a "choice" was but a formality. After all, the king could not be suspected of forcing a woman to marry against her will.

Angelique glanced aside at each of the swine vying to be her future husband. The first, her fifth cousin, the Baron of Kormad, was near twice her age with a bushy dark beard and a protruding stomach. Though his face was not grotesquely ugly, she detested the incensed look in his eyes. When he had talked with her once before, the animosity surrounding him had repulsed her. He treated her as if she were a mouse he wished to stomp into the earth. Marriage to him would be a descent into hell.

The second man, Lord Chatsworth, half English, half Scottish, was old enough to be her grandfather. Likely he would not live long. He might not even survive the wedding night. When his eyes met hers, he licked his cracked lips and gave her a toothless grin. She grimaced when she imagined one moment of his attentions.

The third man, the Highlander. He was not difficult to look at. In fact, once her gaze landed on him she felt compelled to keep staring, taking in each detail of his appearance. A crisp, white linen shirt beneath a dark green doublet fitted flawlessly over his wide chest. A green, blue and red tartan kilt was belted above his narrow hips and the top portion of the plaid secured over his left shoulder with a silver brooch. The basket-hilt of his sword gleamed at his side.

Mischief danced in Sir Lachlan's eyes and he smiled more than any man she'd ever encountered. Indeed, he had even, white teeth. More importantly, he had not displayed any true anger toward her, despite her resistance to marrying him. He had an easy-going manner the other two men lacked. Perhaps he would be simple to command. Once they married, he would likely grow bored with her and return to London for more adventurous pursuits, leaving her to run her estate alone. Exactly what she wanted—a marriage in name only with an absentee chief.

"*Très bien*. I choose Sir Lachlan MacGrath," she said in what she hoped was a strong voice.

The grinning scoundrel winked at her. She wanted to kick his bare shins.

"Splendid, my child," King James proclaimed.

Her future husband stepped forward, the two disappointed suitors glowering after him. Lachlan helped her stand and kissed her gloved hand. "I thank you for choosing me, m'lady. Don't worry, I shall protect you," he whispered. Leaning close, he sniffed. "You smell lovely. What is that, rose water?"

Her eyes burned. Likely they were hideously red and swollen. But she did not care whether he found her attractive or not. And what was he talking about—protect her from what, or whom? The only thing she needed protection from was his lascivious ways... unless Girard had crossed *la Manche*. No, he would never come to England, if he still lived. He had too many enemies here.

"You two shall be married four days hence," King James said. "The Archbishop of Canterbury is granting a special license."

All bowed and curtsied before the monarch as his courtiers escorted him from the room.

The Baron of Kormad approached, his eyes blacker than jet and his face flushed above his beard. "Sir Lachlan, Lady Angelique, I'm wishing you both well. We'll be neighbors and I'm sure we'll oft be seeing each other in Scotland." He bowed.

Angelique's stomach knotted at the malevolence emanating from him.

"Kormad." Lachlan extended his hand.

Staring down at Lachlan's hand, Kormad stilled for a moment, then turned and stalked away with a stiff posture.

"I'm thinking we shall see trouble from him," Lachlan whispered. "He appears to be coveting his neighbor's future wife."

"You mean his neighbor's future estate and title. He cares naught for me." *And neither will you.*

"Come, let's talk." Lachlan offered his elbow.

"If you insist."

Her fingers surveyed the well-developed muscles beneath his sleeve. She could not recall touching such a large, solid arm before—like iron. *Ma foi!* I do not find him nor his arm appealing! She loosened her grip.

Though she had to marry the goat, she did not have to like him.

They strolled through two lavish rooms and out into one of the gardens. The odor of the nearby Thames kept the air from being pleasant. Now mayhap she could leave London for the clean country air. Though she hadn't been to Scotland since she was a child, she remembered the air had always been fresh at Draughon Castle.

She brushed by the mint sprawling onto the cobblestone path, releasing its fragrance. Warm sunlight beamed down upon them, gilding strands of Lachlan's tawny hair.

His arm tensing, he glanced about in all directions.

"Is something amiss?" She released him.

He stopped. "I thought I heard something." After a moment, he turned to her. "You're in danger, *mademoiselle*. From Kormad. You must not say anything about it. And you must never be alone for a moment. He is planning something."

A chill coursed through her. "How did you learn of this? Did he say this to you?"

"I heard him talking with his men. Have you a guard you trust?"

Feeling completely alone and exposed, she shook her head. She and Camille had been protecting each other since the year before. This was no different.

"I shall speak to Buckingham about it. Once we're married, I'll guard you myself."

She appreciated the solemn look in his eyes. She would never trust him to be faithful, but perhaps she could trust him to fend off Kormad.

"*Merci*."

"Have you any inkling why your father didn't wish Kormad to succeed him?"

She felt shamed in how little she knew of her father and his wishes, but she could not be at fault since her mother was the one who'd taken her away. "I only know they did not get on well."

Lachlan nodded, scrutinizing her until a wave of discomfort warmed her face. "I wish you to know, Lady Angelique, I only have the best of intentions concerning you, the estate and the title. And I thank you again for choosing me."

Her heart sprang up with his gallant words. But, in truth, he was trying to steal his way into her affections. The intimate murmur of his voice, the way he lowered his lashes against the sunlight, his mere presence, all contrived to charm her, seduce her into believing he was the noblest of men. But she knew differently.

"King James already made his decision. I had no choice in the matter because I am a woman. You have pleased the king and so he gives me to you, along with everything that is mine. I am but an object to be owned."

Lachlan frowned. "I don't see you that way at all. You are a lovely lady who deserves only the best."

"We are to be married. There is no need to pay courtship to me with your silver-tongued compliments."

"I am not—" Irritation glinting in his eyes, he glanced away. "Never mind."

She immediately regretted her harsh words. After all, the man had offered to protect her from danger, but he was being paid handsomely for his services—a title, an estate. Still, he could be a lot worse. He could be Kormad or Chatsworth or Girard. All bastards.

"I'll never lie to you," Lachlan said. "You cannot trust me now and that is fine, but in time you'll see."

"You are a man who cannot control his baser urges. I do not want a husband who will make me a laughingstock."

He sent her a brittle stare. "What are you speaking of?"

"Lady Eleanor." The name turned her stomach.

"Aye, you caught me with her, but I was not betrothed to you then."

"And you were with Lady Catherine the night before."

He appeared a bit sheepish for a moment, glancing away. But then his dark gold gaze found her again, challenged her. "Indeed, but I hadn't met you yet, in either case. How can you hold that against me?"

"Now that we are betrothed, do you suppose you are instantly a different person?"

You will always want many women, a different one for each night perhaps. I will never be enough for you. Her eyes burned and she stared at the lacey handkerchief in her hand. What did she care? She did not want him touching her anyway.

He remained silent and stiff beside her.

"But that is the way of men, *non*? I must accept it. Accept my place and do my duty." Her throat ached. Not for the first time, she wished she'd been born male so she would have control of her own destiny.

"No matter what I say now, 'twill not make a difference," he muttered. "You won't believe me. All we can do in this situation, m'lady, is our best. We don't yet ken what tomorrow holds. There are many possibilities."

Oui, the possibilities of new lovers for him. And loneliness and embarrassment for her.

A year ago, her girlhood dream of finding true love and happiness died. Never would she dare resurrect such a dream with this deceptive man.

"In any case, I intend to protect you. You may believe that, if naught else." Lachlan switched his gaze to the doorway. She turned to see if Kormad had followed them. Instead, Philippe Descartes waited there.

"Philippe!" She rushed to him and clutched his hands in hers, instantly feeling the calming sensation he always inspired. He was her only genuine friend here, besides Camille.

Philippe was short enough that looking up into his face did not hurt her neck. His pale skin was flushed.

"*Mademoiselle* Angelique." Bowing over her hands, he kissed her gloved fingers. "I'm sorry I could not request an audience with the king again this morn," he said in French. "I feared he would have me hanged. He does not like me."

Angelique nodded, her heart softening with understanding. Philippe was her own age, still a youth really, rather than a man.

"Do not worry over it. I will have to marry the Highlander, but he is better than the other two. At least, I think he is."

Philippe glanced toward Lachlan and his eyes widened. He immediately dropped her hands and stepped back.

"What is it?"

Philippe shook his head. "I must be going. I wish you good luck. *Au revoir.*" He turned and fled into the palace.

Lachlan approached and indeed he did look fearsome, a bit like one of the young male lions King James kept in the Tower for fighting mastiffs and bears.

"What did you do?" she demanded. "Draw your sword? Show him your dagger?"

"Nay. I did naught but look at him. He is a cowardly lad, that one. He couldn't protect you from Kormad even if he tried. You should be thankful the king won't let you marry him."

"Forgive me if I disagree. And I shall always remain very fond of Philippe no matter what."

Hours later, after the evening meal at the palace, Lachlan requested three armed royal guards placed before Angelique's bedchamber door, and made sure they were on the job. Whether Angelique appreciated his protection or not, she was getting it. Her comment about how fond she was of the whey-faced Frenchie lad still irked him. But what did he care? Philippe was not the problem. Kormad was.

After dark, Lachlan left Whitehall Palace in search of friends he trusted and strode down King Street. As he approached Charing Cross, footsteps echoed behind him. Hand on the hilt of his sheathed sword, he halted and turned, his gaze searching along the shadowed buildings and the mist off the Thames.

Silence. Nothing moved. Damnation, he hated having no one to watch his back on these dark and deadly streets.

With more purpose, he continued on his way.

A form leapt from the shadows beside him.

"'Slud!" He dodged aside and drew his sword.

Two more men rushed in behind him, grabbed his arms and pulled him off balance. Determined not to lose his grip on the sword, Lachlan lowered his body and yanked at his captors. They clung to him like tenacious wolfhounds, rendering his arms useless.

"*A mhic an uilc!*" Lachlan yelled.

The first attacker punched him hard in the stomach. His breath whooshed out, leaving suffocating pain.

He kicked the man and tried to twist away from the other two, but the bastards were strong. He stomped the toes of the man on his right, freed his sword arm and lashed out.

The man recovered and both of them tackled him to the street. One struck his arm, causing him to lose his grip. The sword clattered away.

"Damnation!" He struggled against them, tried to throw them off.

"Come now, grab his arms and drag him! This is the quickest way to the river," their leader ordered in a Lowland Scots dialect.

"We need to knock him in the head first, else he'll just swim out."

"Then do it!"

"And what are you doing but playing boss?"

Still lying on the ground, Lachlan shoved a knee toward the whoreson's bent head, but he dodged aside.

"You mewling jolthead. Hold him still."

One of the men grabbed for Lachlan's hair.

Evading him, Lachlan kicked the man in the stomach and he back-flipped into the ditch. He then jammed his elbow against the other man's stomach and punched him in the face.

"Omph!"

Their leader advanced, carrying a massive stick. Lachlan sprang from the ground, snatched the stick and landed a quick blow to the man's face with his fist. His nose made a satisfying crunching sound before he staggered backwards and fell on his arse.

Ha! Now he was getting somewhere. Lachlan hauled him up by his doublet. "Who sent you? Who do you work for?"

"To hell with you!" The ruffian tried to kick Lachlan in the groin.

He stepped aside and shoved the man to the ground.

The blackguard leapt up and fled. His cohorts scrambled from the ditch, sewage and foul water dripping from their clothing, and ran after.

"Bastards!" Lachlan retrieved his sword, gleaming from the shadows, followed a short distance but lost them to the fog.

Kormad's men—he would place silver on it.

"*Iosa is Muire Mhàthair*," he muttered and proceeded to The Golden Cross Inn.

Upon entering the sizable main room lit by lanterns, Lachlan sheathed his sword and scanned the patrons eating and drinking at the many tables. His stomach ached where the ruffian had landed two punches. He straightened his hair and clothing as he made his way toward the table where Robert "Rebbie" McInnis, Earl of Rebbinglen, future Marquess of Kilverntay, sat swilling ale.

Lachlan dropped into a chair, glanced down at his burning, bloody knuckles and cursed.

"What happened to you, then?" Rebbie asked, black brows lowered.

Lachlan wrapped a handkerchief around his hand. "I was in a fight outside. Three bastards jumped me from the darkness, then attempted to drag me to the river and drown me. I sent them scurrying like wee mice."

"What was their dispute with you?"

Suddenly thirsty from the exertion, Lachlan held up two

fingers at the tippler. The barrel-chested man nodded.

"Well, I'm waiting," Rebbie said.

"I'm thinking they object to my future bride."

Rebbie coughed, almost choking on his ale. "What the devil are you speaking of?"

"You may congratulate me, my friend. You're looking at the next Earl of Draughon. I'm getting married." Though he still wasn't sure how he felt about marriage, other than confused, Lachlan knew he had to protect Angelique. This was serious business, but he had to laugh at his friend's mouth hanging agape.

"Another royal reward?" Rebbie asked.

"Aye. Seems Buckingham's life is worth more than a knighting."

"Never thought I'd see the day." Rebbie appeared as if he had a bellyache.

"What's wrong, man? 'Tis me that's getting married, not you."

"Aye, but who will I go about wenching with now? You always find the best ones."

Lachlan grinned. He did have a talent for finding beautiful, willing ladies. "You could get married, too."

"Och! Not for a long while yet. Not while my dear da still draws breath. And he's in fine health."

The tippler delivered the fresh ales and Lachlan raised his glass in toast. "'Tis time to think of settling down. We've had more than our share of fun these ten years past."

"Aye, and they're over now."

A week ago, if someone had suggested that Lachlan settle down and get married, he would've had the same reaction as Rebbie. But now, he was excited about the prospect—a new adventure of sorts, in a whole different direction. Something he had never attempted. And he felt, for the first time in ages, a sense of purpose. A need to accomplish much and succeed in this new venture.

"You must join me when I go to Perth," Lachlan said. "I need your help. And Dirk's as well."

"Dirk, aye. He isn't married yet." A ray of hope gleamed in Rebbie's dark eyes. "I cannot see you married. Are you thinking you'll be happy?"

Lachlan shrugged and stared into his ale. Would he? He wished to be, but his future bride was more wasp than butterfly.

"Probably not, but I'll be somebody."

"What are you blathering on about? 'Tis not as if you're a nobody. Your da was an earl."

"Aye, but I'm the second son, with no lands or titles. Until I marry."

"I never kenned you were greedy and would exchange your freedom for a marriage noose and some coin."

"I'm not greedy! You ken me better than that. But I'm not a wee lad anymore either. I'm thinking I need a purpose in life. Some respect."

Rebbie sputtered. "Respect?"

"Aye, my brother has much respect, a noble chief and earl, the leader of our clan. I have naught. I am a jest." Though he had never uttered those words before, they always hovered in the back of his mind.

"Who have you been listening to?"

"Everyone. I ken well what people think of me."

"So you like the wenches. 'Tis not a crime…unless you get caught by an enraged father or husband." Rebbie grinned. "Well, then…what is your future bride like?"

"A wee lass of a score years, flaming, curling, ginger colored hair. Eyes, green as the hills of Scotland in summer." She did have lovely eyes. And an adorable but too stern mouth that desperately needed his attention to soften it up a bit. He had a fantasy about kissing her, parting those lush lips and sliding his tongue between to sample her, without being bitten. Well, he'd always loved danger, so 'twas fitting.

"Och, God's bones, would you listen to yourself?" Rebbie scoffed. "You'll tire of her in a fortnight."

"'Haps." Indeed, what if he did? He would make the best of it.

"Is she smitten with you, then, like all the other lasses?"

"Nay, she's a prickly wench who thinks she's naught but French silk. She detests me. Would rather stab me than kiss me." Imagining his fire-breathing nymph wielding a weapon, Lachlan smiled. She was different, and that held his interest.

"'Tis clear. You're a bedlamite."

"She fancies herself in love with a wee French laddie named Philippe."

"You're not wantin' a happy marriage then?" Rebbie asked in a dry tone.

27

Lachlan sipped his ale. "I am a man in need of a challenge."

"You're bored so you get hitched?"

"Not bored, exactly. Just tired of wandering. Tired of being shiftless with no plan or purpose. I want something for my lads. I'm thinking she could be a good mother to them."

"Pray pardon, but a lady such as herself will not take to raising your bastards. She'll be wanting bairns of her own."

"Aye, and I'm all for it—the bairns, that is. She'll learn to accept Kean and Orin as well." Lachlan imagined his two endearing, fair-haired sons, wee versions of himself. Och, how he missed them. He was thankful to his brother for acting as guardian of them in his absence.

Rebbie shook his head. "You've gone daft as a sheep."

Lachlan leaned forward and spoke in a low voice. "The lass isn't the problem. Sorlie MacGrotie is."

"Who?"

"Baron Kormad. Her distant cousin, next in line to inherit. He is covetous of the title and lands. He sent his ruffians after me tonight, and he has plans to hurt Lady Angelique. Dirk and I heard him talking."

A maniacal glow lit Rebbie's eyes. "You need help?"

"Aye. I'd like it if you would join me at court and watch my back. Dirk has already agreed. I'm to meet him at the Black Spur shortly."

"Count me in."

After glancing about to make certain no one was watching, Lachlan drew his jewel-hilted dagger—the one his father had given him—from its scabbard within his doublet and placed it on the table. "How much will you give me for this?"

"What, you're wanting to sell it now? I'm not believing it." His friend scrutinized him.

God's blood! How he wished he had enough coin not to worry about things like this. "I would like to buy her a gift."

"How much? I shall loan you the money."

"Nay. You ken I don't borrow money," Lachlan snapped.

"You can pay it back after you're married."

"I won't buy her a ring with her money, but mine own. So, do you want to buy the dagger or not? I wager Dirk will. Or 'haps Miles."

"I'll be damned if the Sassenach will get such a valuable

Scottish weapon. I'll give you ten pounds for it." Rebbie opened his sporran and covertly withdrew some coins. "A ring, eh? Must be a fancy one."

Lachlan shrugged. Earlier that day, he'd spoken with a goldsmith at a booth in Britain's Burse who would custom-make the ring, and it should be ready on the morrow. Though 'twould be a small token, he hoped it would say to Angelique that he was trustworthy and honorable.

Watching Rebbie take possession of the dagger felt like someone ripping out his spleen. His father had given him the weapon on his deathbed, and Lachlan had sworn never to part with it. But at the moment he had little choice. He couldn't risk gambling, nor could he part with his sword.

"Don't worry, man. 'Haps I'll let you buy it back someday…if I don't get too attached to it." Rebbie sent him an evil grin. "And if you can afford my price."

"To hell with you. I will not want it back."

"Bah! You're a terrible liar."

Lachlan drained his ale tankard. "Time to meet Dirk."

⋘ ❦ ⋙

The next day, Angelique sat in the richly appointed drawing room with the other ladies who had accompanied her from the queen's court, but she was in no mood for conversation. She would rather be in bed with her head covered. Camille was the only person who understood her, but she was not entirely welcomed into these social gatherings.

How Angelique wished she could have married Philippe or another biddable man before her mother had passed away. *Maman* would not have approved of the Highlander as a husband. She would say Angelique was headed for a repeat of her parents' marriage. And she knew this to be true. Scotsmen knew not how to remain faithful—her mother had said it many times.

"'Twas in this very room where you intruded upon Sir Lachlan and me…" Eleanor whispered and took a seat beside her on the burgundy velvet settle.

Disgust rising within, Angelique glared at the other woman.

"In the throes of passion."

"I understand your meaning, Eleanor." The *putain* was worse than a cat in heat. "And where was it you crawled away to hide that night?"

29

Eleanor's smugness disappeared. "At least you have bagged yourself a man who is proficient in the bedchamber. My late husband was not."

"A pity."

"You may not care now, but you shall one day."

Angelique ignored that. 'Twas true, she didn't care now. She had experienced naught in the coupling she was fond of. It was a painful and loathsome activity.

"Was your lover in France very gifted?" Eleanor asked.

"I had no lover. Merely a faithless fiancé." Few people knew of her compromised virtue. Some believed it only a rumor and she didn't wish King James to know the truth of it. Though Girard had asked for her hand in marriage, and she had thought to marry him before his fit of violence, they were not formally betrothed because her father would not permit it. She and her mother had written to him in Scotland to ask. His answer was a resounding *nay* and a demand that she return to Scotland. She, of course, had not gone. Besides, Girard had turned out to be a bumbling, cruel oaf who'd forced himself on her in the end, and she was relieved she hadn't married him. But now she must marry the Highlander.

Eleanor chuckled. "And soon you shall have a faithless husband."

Indeed. Nausea took Angelique's appetite and she put down her puff pastry.

"Lachlan told me two nights ago in his bedchamber he knew his faithfulness was not required. You may have to share him, but believe me, he's worth it." Eleanor sighed.

The ruttish varlet. "I am fortunate, no?" Angelique wanted to toss her wine onto Eleanor's head and watch it ruin her perfect dark curls.

"Indeed, you are most fortunate. His broadsword is long and stiff and—"

"Enough." Angelique knew exactly what the other woman spoke of.

Eleanor giggled.

"We all know you have sampled most every male member at court," Angelique said.

Eleanor smirked, dropping her gaze to Angelique's chest. "Well, Sir Lachlan is rather fond of large breasts, so I don't imagine he will be overjoyed with you."

Angelique stiffened and forced herself not to draw her wrap closer about her body and hide. "I do not care what sort of breasts he fancies." *He will not be touching mine.* She wondered if she could lure the bitch into an alcove and squash her nose like a Scottish bannock. Instead, she sipped her wine in a very collected manner.

"Perhaps I shall pay him a visit one day to alleviate his frustrations," Eleanor said.

"You will stay away from my home," Angelique said with smooth calmness. "If you do not, you shall regret it."

"Is that a threat?" Eleanor glanced toward the doorway. "Speak of the virile and handsome devil."

Angelique almost dropped her Venetian glass before she turned to face Lachlan, striding across the Turkish carpets, three large, fearsome men trailing behind him.

Eleanor rose and gave a deep curtsey. "Sir Lachlan," she purred.

Angelique wished to send her sprawling across the floor.

"Lady Eleanor." He bowed, proceeded to Angelique's side and lifted her hand to kiss the back. "M'lady," he murmured in an intimate tone. She avoided his gaze for she was suddenly most irritated at him and Eleanor. Lachlan turned to his friends. "This is my lovely future bride, Lady Angelique Drummagan, the countess of Draughon. M'lady, I would like you to meet my friends. Robert MacInnis, Earl of Rebbinglen."

The attractive dark-haired man stepped forward, took her hand and kissed it. "A pleasure most sweet, countess."

"Dirk MacLerie," Lachlan said.

"M'lady." The auburn-haired man, tall as Lachlan, bowed briefly but remained in place, his steady blue eyes assessing her.

"Miles Seabourne, the only Sassenach unconventional enough for me to trust."

The man laughed and bowed. "My lady, 'tis an honor."

Angelique rose and curtsied. "*Enchantée, messieurs.*"

"Did I not tell you she is beautiful?" Lachlan asked. His smile and the pride in his eyes made her heart flutter. She could almost believe he liked her. How she wished…

"Aye, lovely." The men bowed and expressed further delight upon meeting her.

"*Merci.*" Angelique's face flushed hotter than it had in a long while. She was unaccustomed to having so many handsome men's regard at one time. The bit of happiness welling within her chased away her doldrums.

To the side, Eleanor cleared her throat, drawing everyone's attention.

"And this is Lady Eleanor." Lachlan was not often embarrassed by his past trysts, but in this case, Eleanor made him highly uncomfortable. He wished she would leave off her blatant pursuit of him.

While the other men greeted her, Lachlan turned to Angelique. "Could we step into the gardens again?"

"*Oui.*"

He escorted her out, trying to decipher the expression in her eyes. *Damnable Frenchie.* If she'd been an untutored Highland lass he could've read her easily, but Angelique was a mystery he yearned to uncover. With her first glance at him when he'd stepped into the room, her expression had been pleased and surprised, then she'd schooled her brows into that disdainful arch that told him he was lower than a worm. At least she didn't mean it. She was still jealous of Eleanor—that had to be the problem.

Dirk followed at a distance, hanging back and surveying the surroundings. He was the best guard in the kingdom, and Lachlan was fortunate to call him a friend.

"How pleasant you have brought your Highland friends with you today." A bit of her sarcasm bled through but he chose to ignore it.

"Aye. Friends are important."

"I would not know," she said in a bitter tone, then pressed her lips together and turned away.

"You have no friends?"

She shrugged.

"None?"

"My companion, Camille. Philippe. I had several friends in France, but not so many here."

She had to bring up the French lad again, didn't she? He would ignore that as well. "'Tis a shame. I wager you will find many friends in Scotland."

"It matters not."

He took in her sour expression and what lay beneath it. "You're not a happy woman, Angelique."

She directed a cutting glare at him.

"Why not?" he asked.

"I do not wish to discuss it."

"I ken marrying me is a chore, but surely you prefer me to Chatsworth or Kormad. If you didn't, why did you choose me?"

"The lesser of three evils."

"Ah. You think me evil, then?"

"*Non*, merely wicked."

Lachlan grinned, imagining all the wicked things he'd love to do to her, starting with slow exploring kisses. He'd then unlace her and strip every piece of clothing from her sweet little body. He'd make her ache and moan and whisper his name. Finally, he would give her what she sought, sliding into her wet, hot passage over and over until they both found paradise. His wickedness was to her benefit; he had only to make her see that.

"And are you without fault, then?" he asked.

"*Naturellement*, I have faults but none so noticeable as yours."

"Of course not." Her main fault may not have been obvious to her but it was clear to him—something had made her bitter. How in the devil was he going to sweeten her up?

"This will be a marriage in name only," she said.

"Is that so?"

"*Oui.*"

Like hell. When she allowed him to seduce her, he would make sure she enjoyed the bedding more than anything she had thus far experienced.

Lachlan shrugged. "Whatever you desire."

"I do not desire anything beyond saying I have a 'husband.'"

"I'm not arguing, my angel." He prided himself on his diplomacy skills.

She clenched her jaw. "I wish to leave immediately after the ceremony for my estate."

"As do I. I've had enough of London. 'Tis a foul stink-pot. And I'm missing Scotland."

She remained silent. How could he convince her to talk civilly? He wanted to know her better, wanted her to trust him a wee bit.

"When were you last in Scotland?" he asked.

"Eleven years ago."

"Do you miss it?"

"*Non*. I miss France. And my mother." She strode toward the shade of an arbor covered with climbing roses.

He followed. "Your mother?"

"She passed away last year."

"I'm sorry to hear it, truly."

. Inside the arbor, she sat on a bench and he joined her.

"My mother died when I was a wee lad," Lachlan said. "I hardly remember her at all. And my father died five years past. 'Twas hard to get through. I still miss him sorely."

Angelique gave him an assessing look. He preferred it to her glares.

"I had not seen my father since my mother left him and took me to France," she said.

"When did he pass?"

"Two months ago."

He nodded. "Do you wish you had seen him one last time?"

She lifted a slim shoulder and stared at her entwined fingers. "I did not know him, really. He sent for me several times, but I did not want to return to Scotland."

"Why not?"

"He wished to find me a Scottish husband." She flicked a glare at him.

"Ah. So, you don't have any brothers or sisters?"

"*Non.* You?"

"I have one brother who is chief of the MacGrath clan in the Highlands. He's an earl as well. We're very close. You would like Alasdair. He is the most honorable of men."

She shot him a challenging look. "How can he be so different from you?"

"Och, Angelique." Lachlan harbored the small hope she was teasing him in her own waspish way. "You are too much like this lovely rose." He fingered the petals of a late season pink blossom, sniffed the lush scent. "Beautiful, fragile, but your thorns drive deep."

This time he caught a glimpse of vulnerability lurking in the depths of her green-gray eyes. She needed someone to protect her, someone to teach her how to laugh again. Someone she could whisper her hopes and dreams to. Aye, he wished to hear her whispers in his ear at night, and feel her hot breaths upon his skin.

"Do not try to seduce me," she muttered. "You will only be disappointed."

34

"I'm not trying to seduce you." Though this arbor would be a pleasant, secluded place for a tryst, the seduction would come later.

"*Très bien*. Save it for your paramours."

God's teeth. He had never known a woman such as her. Jealousy was eating her up. That had to mean something. Mayhap she wanted him all to herself. He grinned and glanced away.

"What is it?"

"Naught."

She stood. "I wish to return to my room."

"Before you go... I want to give you something." A fit of nerves seized him, a feeling such as he'd never before experienced with a woman.

"*Oui*. What?"

What the devil was wrong with him? *Just give it to her.* He knelt on one knee and extended his empty hand.

Her eyes widened and he thought she might bolt. After a moment, she placed her hand in his.

"I ken I didn't propose to you and likely 'twould seem silly to do so now." He pulled the golden ring from inside his doublet. "But I wish to give you this betrothal ring. I had it specially made for you with this emerald because it reminds me of your eyes." He slid it into place on her finger, and he was happy to see it fit perfectly.

She lifted her hand, examining the ring. "It is lovely," she whispered. Her gaze softened a wee bit. "*Merci*. I thank you, sir." She curtsied.

"You're welcome." Smiling, he rose and extended his elbow. "'Twill be my pleasure to escort you to your room now."

"I wish to go alone," Angelique said firmly to combat the sensual way Lachlan had said *pleasure*.

The ring was a sweet token, but he could not win her heart with one piece of jewelry. The gold near burned her finger, warmed as it was from his body heat. And the feeling behind the gift clutched at her heart—or rather, the feeling she wished was behind it.

"Of course." His full lips still held a hint of smugness.

He knew he would get her into bed as his wife. At least, he thought he would. No one said she had to go willingly to the lion. She would lie like a dead fish in his bed and he would soon leave her alone.

She smiled.

"Glad I am to see you smiling."

Not for long.

జరి జరా

"Damn that MacGrath!" Sorley MacGrotie, Baron of Kormad, paced the small room at the Red Bull Inn.

"Damn the king," Arnie said in the same tone.

"Damn Angelique," Rufus said.

"Shut up, you fools! I won't let him steal the estate and title away from little Timmy." Kormad wanted to get this mess cleared up so he could return to his nephew in Scotland. His sister's son would inherit what was rightfully his, despite what Timmy's bastard of a father, John Drummagan, had wanted, and Kormad would make certain of it. Drummagan would pay, from beyond the grave, for shunning sweet Lilas.

Angelique was not the rightful heir, and MacGrath sure as the devil should not be earl.

"We tried to throw him in the river," Arnie whined. "He's big."

"And strong. A highly trained warrior," Rufus said. "He has three men with him now, two Highlanders."

"I don't give a damn where they hail from," Kormad said. "Highlanders, Lowlanders, Sassenachs, I will destroy any man who follows MacGrath. Tell Pike to come in here as the two of you leave."

The dolts hung their heads and shuffled out. He didn't know how he suffered their stupidity.

Pike was his most resourceful man, not to mention ruthless.

Minutes later, he entered, his bald head gleaming in the candlelight. "Aye, my lord."

"Desperate measures are called for with this MacGrath."

Pike gave an evil half smile; his gray eyes glinted like dirty ice. "What did you have in mind? Let me torture him."

"As much as that would please me...I just need Lachlan MacGrath dead. In an 'accident.' Angelique, too."

"Indeed?" Pike looked ravenous of a sudden. "The lady, too?"

"Aye, the bitch will never marry me. Don't bungle this. The king mustn't suspect foul play."

"Of course not, my lord. 'Tis my specialty."

"I will pay you well if you succeed."

36

"I ken not how to fail." Pike grinned.

"Accident, I tell you. 'Haps they could fall from a high window, a rooftop, a bridge."

Pike nodded with enthusiasm. "Can I have the woman first?"

"I don't care. Just leave no evidence of foul play, no marks upon her save the ones from her fall."

Pike's head bobbled up and down again before he left. The man belonged in Bedlam.

CHAPTER THREE

Angelique awoke in the night, thinking she'd heard a thump. Her eyes searched the darkness of the bedchamber. She snatched her dagger from beneath her pillow and slid to the floor behind the bed. The faint moonlight glimmering through the window did little to illuminate the room. Only embers glowed in the hearth. She caught the whiff of a masculine scent. *An intruder!*

A floorboard squeaked and a large dark silhouette moved forward. *Parblue!* Immobile, she waited for the moment when she could best strike.

When the intruder bent over her bed, she lunged toward him, stabbing her blade at his neck. Before she met her mark, he jerked back, grabbed her forearms and dragged her against him. She lost the grip on her dagger. *Heaven help me.*

"M'lady?"

She screamed, trying to wake Camille, sleeping on a cot in the corner. A hand clamped over her mouth.

"Release me!" Her demand came out muffled.

"Shh. 'Tis me, Lachlan. You must come with me." He uncovered her mouth.

She went limp with a bit of relief. The heat of his strong hands and solid body burned through her. Now she recognized the pleasant but disturbing male scent of him. "Why?"

"Someone is trying to kill us. We must go into hiding," he said, low and fierce in her ear, his breath fanning her hair and tickling her skin.

"You have lost your senses. No one is trying to kill me." Were they?

"Indeed, Kormad is making plans."

Kormad. Mon Dieu. "I must have my clothes, my trunks."

"We have no time. Bring one change of clothes. I'll have the others shipped to Draughon."

"Camille must come with me. I go nowhere without her." Angelique wrested away from Lachlan, hurried to the corner and shook her cousin out of a deep sleep. "*Parbleu!* Camille, wake up."

"Whaa?" She stirred a bit.

"She is a heavy sleeper."

Lachlan went to the door. "Dirk, we need your help. Can you carry Lady Angelique's companion?"

The fearsome man appeared at the threshold, the lantern in his hand illuminating his long red hair and exaggerating his frown. "Can she not walk?"

Unable to wait for Camille to wake, and with no maids about, Angelique quickly threw smocks, stays and a change of clothes into a sack for herself and the same for Camille.

"I must dress," Angelique said.

"No time."

She yanked a blanket off the bed to wrap around herself seconds before Lachlan dragged her from the room.

After meeting Dirk cradling the sleeping Camille, and Rebbinglen carrying a lantern and a sword, they slipped through a narrow doorway she'd never seen before, and entered a tight dark passage. The dank air and close space made her feel she would suffocate. Apparently this was one of the secret passages she'd heard about that riddled Whitehall.

They reached an exterior door—near the stables if the stench was any indication. Wind twisted the trees and bushes. The faint glow of the lantern revealed the muddy ground. Angelique hung back on the threshold. "I am barefoot."

"Come." Lachlan scooped Angelique into his arms abruptly, making her head spin, and rushed her outside. *Ma foi!* She did not want to notice the warmth of his breath against her hair or the hardness and strength of his body. Before she had time to decide whether or not she liked his touch, he pushed her inside a coach with her cousin and slammed the door. The team and coach took off and raced through the gate, then along King Street. Horses' hooves clomped all around them—guards, she hoped.

"Camille, wake up, damn you." Angelique shook her on the opposite seat. "You are one worthless companion."

She roused a bit. "Huh? Are we moving? Where are we?" she asked in a groggy voice.

"In a coach, heading for God knows where. Lachlan says our lives are in danger."

"Is it Kormad?" Camille sat up.

"Lachlan says yes."

"You do not think it is Girard?"

"No, I hope he is dead of a fever." Angelique slid back on the leather seat. The coach careened around a corner, and she grabbed for a handhold.

"But we cannot be certain."

"We must not speak of it." Angelique's stomach knotted with the very thought.

"Did you get...the item?"

"Of course. You know I would not leave it."

After taking another corner too quickly, the coach drew to an abrupt halt and the door opened. Lachlan now held a torch aloft. "Come, both of you. Hold this." He handed the torch to Rebbinglen.

"Where are we going?" Angelique asked.

"No time for questions now." He motioned her forward.

Again, he lifted Angelique into his arms and carried her across an alley as if she weighed no more than an infant. Amid the chaos, he seemed an island of strength and protection. She was finding, of a sudden, that she liked this feeling. She had not experienced true safety for a long time. And besides, he smelled appealing, like clean male blended with leather. In the torchlight, their gazes mingled for a moment. He was not the seductive charmer now. No twinkle of humor danced in his eyes, no smirk upon his lips. He'd transformed into a formidable warrior with a firm mouth and dark, indomitable eyes—a side of him she'd never fully seen.

They slipped through a narrow doorway, Dirk carrying Camille behind them.

"What is this place?" The scents of tallow and musty books irritated her nose.

The passage opened up and they moved through a large dim

church filled with empty pews. Only a couple of candles lit the plain interior. Five of King James's retainers wearing royal livery waited near the pulpit along with a dour Protestant minister.

"What is happening?" Angelique asked.

"We are to be married, as you ken." Lachlan set her on her feet at the front of the church.

She pulled him aside. "Have you lost your mind? We cannot marry now. Not like this," she whispered loudly.

"Aye, 'tis necessary to marry in secret. Someone wishes to kill us. They are wanting your estate through any means, fair or foul." His harsh expression told her of the seriousness of the matter. "King James bid us to go ahead and marry. Now. We have the special license."

"But I must wear my wedding gown and I did not bring it. I will not marry in my shift and a blanket. Barefoot."

"No time." Lachlan dragged her before the minister. "Please begin." He placed his hand over hers, tucked against his elbow.

The minister began in a dry monotone.

Parbleu! Angelique felt paralyzed for a moment, her mind racing. What to do? She glanced aside and found Camille standing barefoot, dressed much as she was. She gave an almost imperceptible nod and faint smile, her gaze steady. She approved? *Merde!*

How preposterous Angelique should get married in such dishabille. Her hair was a bedraggled disaster, tousled and hanging to her waist. She was a countess, not a prostitute. Since she had been a small child she had dreamed of the day she would wear her mother's enchanting French wedding gown, say her vows and kiss her own charming prince.

Today was not that day. That day would never come. She glanced up at Lachlan, and sensed some understanding in his eyes, a silent communication she could not fully grasp because she didn't know him. Lowering her gaze, she thought of the emerald ring on her finger and how he'd given it to her on bended knee. A romantic gesture, but had he meant it in the way she hoped?

Mère de Dieu, do not let this be a mistake. Do not let him slip inside my heart and destroy it. I cannot dare trust him.

Lachlan nudged her. "Say 'I will,'" he whispered without moving his lips.

"I will," she said in a strong voice. She could have been

agreeing to anything. The minister droned on. In shock, wishing this over with, she let her attention slide away to other things, the creaking of the old building, Lachlan's warm, slightly roughened fingers on hers as he pushed another ring onto her finger, a shiny gold band.

"With this ring, I thee wed. This gold and silver, I thee give. With my body, I thee worship." Lachlan's smooth baritone voice reciting those vows stripped away the fog. Her attention riveted upon him, and she knew she would remember this moment forever.

She repeated her own vows rather stiffly, in a halting voice. Only Lachlan's steady hands kept her upright. She wanted to do nothing but burst into tears, though she didn't know why. The way she was dressed—or rather undressed—like a whore for her wedding, or the satisfied, hopeful expression in his eyes, such a contrast to her own misery.

Naturally, he should be pleased. He would be an earl and worth a goodly sum. Her possessions became his. He owned her now.

Sliding his fingers into her unbound hair, Lachlan lowered his head toward her and panic tightened her throat. He touched his lips to hers, the first contact startling, but warm and compelling. His full lips sipped at hers gently, drew away a breath and came back for a firmer, more possessive kiss. His beard stubble rasped her chin and the tip of his tongue tasted her lips, between. Such an unexpected and erotic action. She could not even draw breath.

Whistles and yelps from his friends echoed into the rafters. The minister cleared his throat.

I must shove him away. But no, she couldn't. Not because he was her husband, but because the damnable seducer had mesmerized her.

෧෧෧

"With my body, I thee worship," Angelique whispered next to the velvet draperies of the room they'd locked her in alone at the Earl of Knightly's residence.

Lachlan's eyes, as he'd said those words, had gleamed gold and sincere. He knew her not. How could he look at her as if she were the only woman in the world? When but days ago he had been fornicating with two different women in the space of two nights.

He was a talented liar. So good at it, so good at everything...

especially kissing. The moment they'd sealed their vows had been the most shockingly arousing of her life—in a church, no less. The kiss couldn't have lasted more than five seconds, but had instigated such conflictive feelings within her.

The bedchamber door opened and closed back with a soft thud. Her new husband sauntered toward her in the dark English clothing he'd worn for the wedding. It lent him a dashing grace with his light hair pulled into a queue. A mask was all he required to become the epitome of a roguish highwayman. A pistol grip and the polished steel basket hilt of his sword gleamed at his waist.

What did one say to a new husband? Especially when she didn't trust him...nor herself.

"You did not wear your belted plaid," she said to fill the void.

He halted two yards away. "Nay. Draws too much attention here in London, and 'tis best to wear black for secret movements at night. I'm hoping my father was not here in spirit to witness it. I wouldn't have any of the MacGrath clan ken I wore English clothes to mine own wedding."

"They are better than a shift and a blanket."

"I'm sorry for that, but it couldn't be helped. We'll have another ceremony at Draughon Castle, afore your clan—our clan—if you wish. You can wear your wedding gown then."

His words disoriented her. "In truth?"

"Aye. Would you not like that?" His gaze remained steady and sincere upon her.

"*Oui*. But...why do you care?"

"Why should I not care?"

She shook her head. "You are a man."

"Aye. And?" Waiting, he stared at her with lifted brows.

"Men have no patience for...never mind."

"I have much patience. I'm not a demonic goat as you assume." With that he removed his sword belt and started disrobing, throwing each article of the rich clothing into a heap on a chair. First his doublet, then waistcoat and trews. He was certainly acting like a goat with his lack of modesty.

She turned her gaze to the window before he removed the long shirt. *Parbleu*, she could not look at him unclothed. Could she?

She cleared her throat. "Where is your Highland clothing?"

"I don't ken. In one of these trunks, I'm thinking."

Her gaze darted to his nakedness, then away. Sweet heavens.

He possessed defined muscles as if he were carved in warm, burnished marble, like the statues she'd seen in Italy. A wickedly improved version of Michelangelo's David with a pagan's long golden mane. A feverish heat consumed her.

She forced air into her constricted lungs. "Need I remind you this is a marriage in name only?" Was she proclaiming that to him or herself?

"The king wants the marriage consummated to make it legal and binding."

The king? Plague take the king. She had done what he commanded. But her body was her own, to give to whom she chose, when she chose.

"Tonight," he added.

She stared at a blue vase of white lilies on the dresser, surprised it did not shatter beneath her glare. "I do not care what the king wants."

"Are you wanting to be the one to tell him that?" A tinge of amusement crept into Lachlan's voice.

"*Non.*"

"Well, then." Lachlan waited. "He wishes proof given to his men within the hour."

"Proof?" Her gaze darted to him again. He still had not donned clothing, damn him. She gave him her back.

"Aye. Your virgin's blood on the sheet."

"The king is naught but a Scottish barbarian!"

Lachlan snickered. "Indeed. 'Haps you would like to tell him that as well."

"I have no virgin's blood. I am not a virgin." There, she hoped that shocked him speechless.

"I'd heard," he said in a mild, almost pleasant tone. The bastard.

"From whom?"

"It matters not." He strode toward the other side of the room and flipped open his trunk. "But I didn't ken the king would want a bloody sheet until a short time ago. I'm not saying I agree with it, but he's the king. To oppose him is not wise. Besides, he but wants to assure the marriage is legal and your estate is secure."

Did Lachlan not care she wasn't a virgin? Most men— husbands—would be furious. She peeped at him from the corner of her eyes. His back was toward her, and she could not help but stare at his wide, muscular shoulders, arms thick from swinging a sword, his narrow waist and compact derriere. *Sacrebleu!* All men were not built like him. The sight of his nude body usurped her other thoughts, even her anger.

"Aha." He withdrew his plaid, a linen shirt and various other articles of clothing along with a flask. He threw his clothes on the foot of the bed and unsheathed a small knife.

She backed up a step. "What are you…?"

He flung back the covers to expose the white linen sheet. He stared at her then down at his own body. "Which part of my body do I wish to mutilate?"

None of it! Was he a lunatic? Though he already had several pale scars on his chest, arms and leg, she didn't want to see a fresh wound.

"God's bones. The things I'll do for a hellish woman." He opened the pewter flask, drank a long swallow, and then poured some of the liquid upon the knife blade. He set the flask on the bedside table and climbed onto the huge bed to sit upon his knees.

"My first battle wound for you, sweet wife." With a flick of his wrist, he placed a short cut on his abdomen several inches above his waist.

"*Ma foi!*" She covered her mouth and gaped at him. What in Heaven's name possessed him?

His blood dripped onto the pristine sheet for a few seconds. He smeared it in. "There's your virgin's blood, lass. And don't be telling anyone how it got there." Glaring at her, he yanked at the top sheet and pressed it against his cut. "Damn, who kenned I was such a free-bleeder?"

She rushed forward. "You have cut yourself too deeply. Lie down."

He obeyed. "'Tis but a scratch. But I am oft too enthusiastic about things. Here, pour some of this on it." He handed her the flask from the table.

"What is that?"

"*Uisge beatha.* Water of life. The best, made in the Highlands of course. Take a sip."

The strong whisky burned her nose. "*Non.*" She poured a dribble on his wound.

He jerked, breath hissing through his teeth.

She pressed hard against the sheet over his cut. The material draped down, covering his man parts, thank heavens, or she would've been too nervous to remain this close to him. He was her husband, *oui*, but something about him defied her to touch him, like a hot kettle. He would sear her in the same manner as that kiss at their debacle of a wedding.

"Are you in pain?"

"Nay. 'Tis fine now, I'm thinking." He lifted the edge of the sheet.

"I shall make you a wrap for it, else you will bleed on your clothing and our ruse will be for naught." She ripped the bottom edge off the sheet. "Stand, *s'il vous plaît*."

Again he obeyed her, rising without the sheet to cover him. "You enjoy ordering me about, aye?"

She tried not to let her gaze drift below his waist as she wrapped the strip of cloth around his trim, muscled abdomen, but his male member was impossible to ignore, especially when it appeared larger each time she happened to glimpse it. She thought her imagination was playing tricks on her, but then it started jutting out toward her.

She moved to his side to avoid contact.

His lips slowly lifted into a smirk. "You have a lovely blush, Frenchie."

"I am not blushing." But contrary to her words, her face heated furiously.

"Och! Pray pardon, but you look very virginal. Are you sure you're not one?"

"Of course."

"So, you have seen a man naked afore?"

She thought he must be teasing her, but his voice had hardened a bit. She concentrated on her work, keeping the bandage tight around his ribs.

"Angelique?"

Damn him, why could he not leave her be? "No, not completely. Do not most people…couple in the dark?"

His grin was pure mischief. "If they're Puritans."

"It is not only the Puritans."

"Catholics, too, huh? Ah, well. I'm glad then you're not too familiar with men's bodies."

She tied a knot in the bandage beneath his arm. Her task complete, she stepped away to the window, refusing to look again at his nicely formed body and growing, erect tarse. She had, in truth, never seen one before and found she was more curious than she wished. Was he normal sized? Surely, he was large enough to cause great pain during coupling. But if that were the case, why did women clamor to occupy his bed? Her body felt as if she'd been standing inches from a roaring fireplace. Sweat chilled her skin.

"I thank you," he said.

"*C'est rien*. I thank you for your…blood sacrifice."

He chuckled and she glanced back at him. He held the plaid before him, but his eyes met hers, the expression wicked, perceptive. Dropping his plaid, he stepped forward, and she stared out the window again.

Non. Go away. Do not touch me.

"Angelique." When he traced a fingertip down the sensitive skin of her neck, she stifled a shiver. He placed his large hands at her waist, the strength of them possessive. With seeming affection, he kissed her temple, her ear, feather-light, his warm breath teasing her. He trailed his lips down to nibble at her neck and the bend of her shoulder. His beard stubble lightly rasped her sensitive skin, causing both slight pain and alluring tingles to dart down her arms and to her breasts.

He pushed his hand around to her stomach and drew her back. The heat of his skin near burned her through the thin silk smock and caused a liquid swirling sensation low in her belly beneath his hand. *Sacrebleu!* What was he doing to her?

His body was a solid wall at her back. She had not yet put on her stays and farthingale and his hard shaft prodded her derriere. Her body's primitive instincts urged her to arch her back and wantonly grind her hips against him. *Non!* She forced herself not to respond.

But she could not get the image of that part of his body out of her head.

His other hand splayed on the upper part of her chest, his fingertips stroking her throat even as he teased and seduced the skin of her neck, her jaw line with his lips. She would only need to turn her head a bit to experience another kiss like the one in the chapel.

"Allow me to give you pleasure, Angelique," he whispered.

Her traitorous body sang with tingles and strange yearnings. Her lungs locked down and she gasped for breath. He was naught but the god of lust and fornication casting his spell upon her.

"Saints, you're lovely. Your skin tastes like honey."

What if he forced her?

"*Non.*" She pulled away. "I do not want to hear the practiced lies you tell your paramours."

"I was telling you true, lass." His deep voice was softer than it had a right to be, a bit rough and intimate. He waited quietly. "You're beautiful. As delectable as a puff pastry I wish to taste every inch of."

She pressed her eyes tightly closed, willing the images away—images of his mouth on her, all over—willing the disturbing arousal to drain from her body and leave her cold. But it was stubborn. And dear heaven, his voice was as persuasive as his touch.

"We are wed," he said. "There is no shame."

She forced air into her lungs. "I do not care. You will not touch me." *You will not hurt me. You will not take away my control.* A tear slipped from beneath her lashes. With her back to him he would not see it, thank the saints.

He released a tired breath and stepped away.

"Mayhap one of your paramours will give you a wedding night you will enjoy."

He muttered blunt words in a language she didn't understand, Erse, without doubt. Good, she had driven him away. Excellent indeed, even though her body was frustrated and restless. She fought down her own irrational desires.

A loud knock sounded at the door. She jumped and quickly swiped the damnable tears away.

He yanked on his long-tailed shirt and opened the door. After murmuring a few words she couldn't understand, he handed the rolled up, bloody sheet to one of the king's men and locked the door back.

"We leave on one of the king's smaller galleons for Perth in a half hour." Lachlan finished dressing. He spent so much time glaring at Angelique's rigid back that he did a shoddy job pleating his kilt. The damned cut on his abdomen stung like a bee possessed of a kelpie.

Devil take having a wife. He should've known this would happen. Luscious, alluring, hell-hated wench.

God's teeth, he yearned for her. Her skin was like finest ivory silk sheened with honey dust. And her mouth, when he'd kissed her in the chapel, had tasted like—he didn't know what. But he hadn't been able to resist dipping his tongue inside for a fuller taste. He wished to suckle her tongue like a sweet comfit even as he slid himself deep inside her and near drowned in her wet pleasure. He wished to take her hard and fast, while she moaned—nay—screamed his name and begged for more.

His tarse further hardened at the image.

"*Iosa is Muire Mhàthair!*" He should go out and find some willing lady to swive, just as his loving wife had suggested. 'Haps he could even locate Eleanor. But that was exactly what Angelique wanted. He would not prove her right if he had to become a beef-witted monk.

He slammed the bedchamber door on the way out and hastened down the wide staircase. Plush carpets underfoot and the gleam of gilt from the shadows told him this was an elegant home, far different from the old, but beloved Highland castle he'd grown up in. He joined his friends and the king's retainers in the library.

They dropped silent and turned curious eyes toward him when he entered. This was nothing new; he was used to being stared at for one reason or another. He proceeded to a table and poured himself a generous helping of sherry.

Rebbie approached hesitantly. What the hell was wrong with everyone? Was his scowl that fearsome?

"Should we send for a physician?" his friend asked in a low tone.

"What for?" Hoping they didn't know he'd cut himself, he glanced down at his shirt. No blood seeping through as of yet.

"Your wife," Rebbie whispered.

"Why? She was fit as a shrew-fed badger last time I saw her."

Rebbie clamped his lips between his teeth for a moment, fighting hard to keep from laughing.

"What the devil is wrong with you?"

"We feared you'd killed Lady Angelique when you bedded her."

"Oh, that. Nay. She's a strong lass, half Scottish, you ken."

He wouldn't have to keep up the pretense for long. In short order, he'd have her aching for his attentions and clamoring for a goodly piece of paradise betwixt his sheets.

※

The coach lumbered along the rough street, through holes and ruts that jarred the teeth. Angelique sat stiffly, fully clothed this time and tried to avoid Camille's direct gaze.

"What did he do to you?" Camille whispered in French after a long while.

"Nothing."

"But all that blood. The men were talking."

"I will tell you later but it is nothing to worry about." Angelique tried to sort through her jumbled feelings about her scoundrel of a husband. Though she was loath to admit it, Lachlan had been the epitome of a hero when he'd cut himself. Not only did he not force himself on her, but he'd covered for her lack of virginity to appease the king. But afterward, the way he'd touched her and the thrilling yet frightening sensations he'd wrought in her body...that was the perplexing part.

"Did you couple with him?" Camille asked. "Did he force you?"

"*Non.* But you must tell no one."

Her cousin remained silent a long while. "You cannot deny your husband forever."

Angelique knew that, but she would keep him at bay as long as possible. They would need an heir of course, and she would do her duty. But she dreaded the task.

Some part of her feared if she let him tear down her wall, she could not re-erect it. If she let him in, he would take advantage of her in every way, walking over her and asserting his control over all aspects of her life, her estate, her clan. She feared he would force his way into her bed and into her body. Worse, she feared he'd use another tactic, a manipulative one, forcing his way into her heart. And then expect her to accept his whoring.

He wasn't like Girard, the oafish swine. Already, Lachlan's kiss...she could think of little else, except his nude body which he'd proudly displayed, hoping to arouse her, she was certain. He knew of naught but seduction. The man was deluded and full of himself.

"He will seek out the favors of other women," Camille said.

"*Oui*, he will anyway, sooner or later, whether I lie with him or not. Men like him tire of one woman easily."

"Hmm. Maybe you will also find a brawny Scottish lover once we reach Draughon," Camille purred.

"I do not want one," Angelique snapped.

"Very well, but I do."

Angelique wished she could be so blasé about the coupling. And she knew her cousin was but trying to erase some of her fears about it.

An influx of galloping and neighing horses surrounded their coach. The conveyance sped up. Pistol shots rang out.

"Mère de Dieu!" Heart lodged in her throat, Angelique held on. Had Kormad caught them?

"Halt!" a male voice outside yelled.

More shots popped; burning gunpowder filled the air. Shouts in English and Gaelic echoed off the buildings. The coach slowed to a stop.

"Merde! This cannot be good." Camille blew out the lamp and bolted onto the bench seat with her. They flattened themselves against the back, away from the windows.

"Kormad will kill us if we do not do something," Angelique said.

More pistol shots exploded and swords clashed. What if he'd already killed Lachlan. No, she could not bear to think of it.

"Ready yourself." Angelique removed the dagger from her pocket. This would not be the first time she and Camille had fought for their lives.

"I will shoot their stones off," Camille whispered, drawing a small pistol from her pocket.

"I did not know you had that." Angelique wished she hadn't left her own pistol in her trunk, now on top of the coach. "Is it loaded?"

"Oui. Why would I have it otherwise?"

Angelique peered out the window, saw no one, and stretched her neck further. She recognized the poor man lying on the ground as their driver. Another man crawled from beneath the coach and sidled toward the front.

Angelique ducked back inside. "They've killed our driver and now someone is trying to make off with this coach. We must get out and hide."

Camille nodded and opened the opposite door. They both slid out into the muddy darkness. Clutching Camille's hand in hers and dragging her along, Angelique crossed behind the coach and searched for a safe place to hide. The shadows of the buildings were pitch black.

"Get back inside!" yelled a man sitting atop a large horse.

She didn't know whether he was one of Lachlan's men or one of Kormad's.

"Damnation," the man muttered and glanced away. "Mac-Grath!"

The stolen coach started rolling away. Another horse galloped by. The rider leaned down and snatched Camille off her feet. She screamed and dropped her pistol.

CHAPTER FOUR

Angelique snapped up Camille's pistol, aimed at the fleeing abductor's back and pulled the trigger. A shot exploded from the small weapon, jarring both her arms, the scent of gunpowder burning her nose. The man cried out and dropped Camille from the horse. She toppled to the ground.

"*Sacrebleu!*" Ignoring her stinging hand, Angelique rushed forward and knelt by her cousin, touched her face. "Camille?"

Horseshoes clattered on cobblestones, but she could not take her eyes off Camille's still face.

"God's bones! Why did you not stay in the coach?" Lachlan demanded with thickening burr. He dismounted and crouched beside her with a torch. The heat from it near scorched her skin.

Camille's blood painted the cobblestones red. *Mère de Dieu, have I caused her to die?* Angelique crossed herself, vile nausea coiling in her stomach. "They killed the driver!" she told Lachlan. "Another man was going to steal our coach. I saw him."

"And now he's dead, too. We wouldn't have let them take you." His voice was rough, almost a growl.

"You were outnumbered."

"Nay, we were not. We had the situation under control."

She pressed her eyes closed, forcing the burning tears out. "I did not know. Pray, forgive me, Camille." Bending, Angelique placed her ear before Camille's mouth and nose. Breaths puffed out, warming her ear.

"She lives! Thanks be to God. Help me with her."

53

Lachlan handed the torch to his English friend, Miles, then gently slipped his arms beneath Camille and lifted her. Angelique followed him to the coach and helped him position her cousin comfortably on the seat.

"*Merci.*"

"Do not leave the coach again until I tell you to!" Lachlan slammed the door.

She wanted to fling a sharp retort at him, but she deserved a much worse scolding for hurting Camille. The coach lurched forward, knocking Angelique to the floor. Damnable driver.

"Camille?" She patted her cousin's face, wishing she had cold water to bathe it in. Camille was the person she cared about most in the world, like a sister, and she'd endangered her life. "I pray you will forgive me. Please wake up."

Shots rang out again.

Merde! She ducked low over her cousin.

An onslaught of clomping horses' hooves approached from an alley and the coach sped up, jostling along rutted streets. The new driver shouted commands at the team and snapped a whip in the air. When the pistol shots echoed further away, she peered out. The king's guards were thick around them.

"*Grâce à Dieu,*" she said when the coach ground to a halt. The salt scent of the ocean, the clanging of a bell, and the water slapping the hulls of the creaking ships told her they'd reached the wharf.

Lachlan wrested open the door. "Come. We must hurry."

৯৫ ৯৫৹

A half hour later, Camille, still unconscious, lay in the captain's cabin on the lower berth. A small hanging lantern provided illumination. Angelique fingered her Rosary beads and paced, praying her cousin would awaken. She had bathed her face in water over and over but it proved of no benefit.

"*O Marie, s'il vous plaît—*" A sharp knock sounded at the door. She jumped. "*Qui est-ce?*"

"Lachlan."

She opened the narrow door.

"The ship's barber surgeon went ashore earlier and cannot be found. I sent for a physician but he hasn't yet arrived. The captain says we must leave forthwith because of the tide." Lachlan glanced at Camille. "Och! She has awakened?"

54

Angelique spun around and rushed to her. "Camille, are you well? Thanks be to God."

She placed a hand on her head and groaned. "*Qu'est-ce qui s'est passé?*"

"You fell off a horse."

"I remember now. Did you shoot the bastard who grabbed me?"

"*Oui.* Do you want us to wait for the physician?"

"No, I hate them. I am well."

"If you're sure, we shall set sail," Lachlan said. "'Tis not safe for us to stay here."

"*Oui. Allez-y.* Go."

᭯᭯᭯᭯

Kormad glared at his men who stared at the worn floor planks within his room at the inn. Six imbecilic failures, they were. The damned MacGrath bastard had stolen away Angelique and married her. Worst of all, he'd become chief, earl and now held Draughon Castle and lands.

"'Tis mine by birthright!" Kormad slammed his fist against the table. The candle flickered wildly.

"Y–you mean Timmy's, m-my lord," Arnie said.

"Aye! And mine until he comes of age. I have waited to take my place at Draughon the whole of my life." At least he had yearned for and coveted the rich estate the whole of his life. It was so close he could almost touch it. "I will not let some whoring, kilt-wearing MacGrath snatch it from me! He is all that stands in my way."

"She chose him," Rufus said.

"I know that, you whoreson! And she'll regret that decision. I intend to make sure of it."

If she would not choose Kormad, he would not suffer her to live. She was naught but a pebble in his path and he would kick her out of his way. The bigger obstacle was King James himself and this damnable Highlander he chose for Angelique.

"What are you going to do?" Arnie asked.

"Go back to Burnglen and rally support amongst the Drummagans and the neighboring clans."

A fist wrapped at the door.

"Come!"

One of his men, MacFie, burst through the door, breathing

hard. "I came as quickly as I could, my lord. I had to hide for hours, but Pike got on board their ship."

"You jest." A thrill passed through Kormad.

"Nay. 'Tis true."

"Pike. Now there's a man what knows how to get things done!" Kormad laughed and let loose a hoop of victory. "Where is the ship headed?"

"Direct to Perth. Pike said he would meet you there at the Ram's Head Inn three days hence. Likely MacGrath and the lady will be dead by then."

"Aye!" A sudden bloodlust came over Kormad. Too bad he couldn't spend it on MacGrath and his bitch. But Pike would make short work of them. "Secure us passage on a merchant ship to Perth. A swift one!"

ഏ ഏ

"There you are," Rebbie called.

The wind whipping his hair, Lachlan turned from surveying the turbulent sea and the waves crashing onto the distant rocky shore as they made their way up the English coast. Rebbie approached along the rocking deck, his hair stark black against the orange dawn light.

"Aye." The nausea tormenting Lachlan had naught to do with the horrid breakfast he'd eaten nor the choppy water and rolling of the king's small galleon.

"Is aught the matter?" Rebbie eyed him with concern—or nosiness—he couldn't be sure which.

"Nay." He had but wanted a few moments alone to think; the few crewmen on deck were easy to ignore. And the chill air helped clear his head.

"You're pale as January snow—nay—you're looking a wee bit green. Seasickness?"

"The sea is rough this morn." Lachlan took hold of the wet rail to steady himself, hoping Rebbie would cease his questioning.

"Indeed. How are the ladies?"

"Camille improves, but Angelique has seasickness."

"She will be well once we reach Perth."

Lachlan nodded.

"'Haps you should be abed yourself. I believe you are more ill than you will admit."

"Nay." Lachlan sucked in a deep breath of salt air and tried to slow his racing heartbeat. He wanted no one to ken how he felt at the moment. A frightening realization had snuck up on him in the wee hours of the night and gored his vitals.

"Too much drink last night?" Rebbie asked.

"Nay."

"What then? I'm not good at guessing games."

"Devil take it," Lachlan muttered. Rebbie would never leave off when he sensed something amiss. "'Tis only that...I'm married," Lachlan said far more calmly than he felt. The blood drained from his head, like a physical weakness washing over him. Saints! He was not weak! He had fought in and survived clan battles and skirmishes. He had traveled across Europe, rubbed elbows with the nobility, and won the favor of his king. How could a vow uttered to one wee thorny lass snatch his equilibrium?

"You're only now figuring that out?"

Lachlan should've said naught. Rebbie would never give him peace now.

"Of course not! But it didn't seem so real yesterday, no different from any other adventure we've been embroiled in. When I woke up this morn, my first thought was 'what the hell have I done?' I even had to take her clan name in order to be chief. I'm a Drummagan now, more fully than a MacGrath."

A wave hit the hull and a cold mist sprayed onto them.

"So, you regret it?"

"Nay. I don't ken how I feel about it. I only know 'tis something I cannot walk away from. 'Tis permanent."

"Like prison. I tried to tell you, but you wouldn't listen."

He would not liken it to prison. More, he was simply afraid he'd fail and not be very good at being a chief, earl or husband. Or that he wouldn't enjoy marriage.

"'Tis only a bit overwhelming at the moment is all. I'm sure 'twill pass. I am responsible for someone besides myself now. Not only a wife, but a whole clan. 'Tis something new to me." He pressed a fist against his aching stomach. "A wife, God's bones. What the devil will I do with a wife?"

"I wager you'll think of something." Rebbie grinned.

♦☙♦♦

"My lady." A knock sounded at the cabin door. "I have food so you may break your fast."

Lying on the top berth, Angelique groaned, nausea roiling

inside her so intensely she couldn't lift her head. With the swaying of the ship, everything spun around. She had already vomited several times and had nothing left in her stomach.

"*Non.* I do not want it," she called, hoping the crewman heard her through the door.

"My lady, you must be hungry."

"*Non!*" *Damn you, go away.*

The normal wood-against-wood creaking of the ship filled the silence. Thank the heavens he'd left. She drifted to sleep. What seemed only minutes later, something thundered against the door. She sat bolt upright, a pain shot through her head and her stomach rebelled at the sudden movement.

"My lady," a male voice called outside the door. "'Tis your husband. He's injured and bleedin' severely."

Cold prickles showered over her. "What? Lachlan?"

"Aye, he asks for you."

Mère de Dieu, protect him. She slid from the top berth, down in front of Camille.

"*Qu'est que c'est?*" she asked.

"Lachlan is injured." In her mind, Angelique only saw his smiling eyes. She missed his warm protectiveness. Holding to the table, then the chair, she made her way to the door.

She unlocked the portal and opened it. A brawny bald man waited outside. His gray eyes bore a hole through her and his expression was odd…leering for a moment, then blank. Had he never seen a woman before?

"Where is Lachlan?" she asked.

"In the galley. We were eating midday meal when a fight broke out and he was cut on the arm. He's lost a lot of blood."

"*Sacrebleu.* He's a free-bleeder. Take me to him."

She clasped the smelly man's elbow and allowed him to escort her from the stern and along the deck. The strong, chill wind pierced her clothing with icy needles. She wanted to run, but her skirts clung fast to her legs, hampering her movements. Shivering, she realized she had forgotten her cloak. Surely they would be below deck in a moment and away from the wind.

She had to see Lachlan. Why did she care? *I do not know; I just do.* He'd protected her and now she must do the same for him. "I hope he does not lose too much blood."

The man grunted and quickened his pace.

The ship tossed and she near lost her footing on the wet decking. Her stomach ached, a new bout of nausea rising.

No, go away. I cannot be sick now! She pressed a hand to her throat. The gag doubled her over and she could not stop it. Retching, she fell to her knees.

"Come!" The man jerked at her arm, dragging her up. "We got to hurry."

A pain shot through her shoulder. What the devil was he doing?

"*Non.*" He yanked her into his arms and tossed her over his shoulder, panic clawing through her. *"Mère de Dieu!"* She screamed.

Running footsteps approached. "You, there! Unhand her!"

"Whoreson bastard!" someone else shouted. More running.

Upside down, she could see little. The blackguard's shoulder drove into her aching stomach. Someone else grabbed her upper body and a tug of war ensued. She kicked. The bald man released her and fled.

"Catch him!" Was that Lachlan's voice? It sounded too harsh. "Angelique?" Someone lifted her high into his arms. "What the devil happened?"

"Lachlan?" Head spinning, she looked into his eyes.

"Aye."

"Are you bleeding? How is your arm?"

"What? Nay, I'm not bleeding. Is that what he told you?"

"*Oui.* That you had lost a lot of blood. And you wished to see me. You are a free-bleeder."

"Och. I'm not injured." Lachlan turned with her and everything whirled around. She slammed her eyes shut against the illness. "Is he one of your crew, Captain?" Lachlan asked.

"No. Never seen him afore," a deep, rough voice said.

Yelling and curses sounded from several yards away. She opened her eyes a crack. Rebbie, Dirk and members of the crew fought the bald man and tried to restrain him.

"Who is he?" Angelique asked, shivering, trying to snuggle closer to Lachlan's body heat.

"I wager he's Kormad's man. How did he get on board?"

"I know not, my laird," the captain said.

The blackguard broke away from the other men and jumped overboard.

"God's teeth, he's getting away! Shoot him!" Lachlan yelled.

Rebbie and two other men fired pistols into the water.

"We're too far out for him to reach shore, even if he can swim," the captain said.

"I'm not taking any chances. Keep firing!" Lachlan told the men, then carried Angelique toward the captain's cabin. "What happened to the two guards I stationed by her door?" he called back.

The captain cursed and trotted away, shouting orders.

"I bet the bastard killed them or knocked them out. You must be half frozen, Angelique." Once inside the cabin, Lachlan closed the door.

She nodded, still appreciating the warmth of his skin.

"What happened to her?" Camille came forward.

"Some knave tried to throw her overboard. Kormad's man, no doubt."

"*Sacrebleu!* Put her here." She motioned to the lower berth.

"What are you doing up, Camille?" Angelique asked. "How is your head?"

"I have pain but it improves."

"And how are you feeling?" Lachlan lay Angelique on the berth, covered her with a thick blanket, then knelt by her side.

"Terrible. So sick." She pressed a fist against her stomach, praying the nausea would diminish.

He smoothed her hair back and stroked the side of his thumb along her cheek, his gaze intense and concerned. "Did he hurt you, lass?"

"Only my shoulder a little. I shall be fine."

Frowning, he gently massaged her tender shoulder with strong, warm fingers. "That bastard. He got his just due. I'm going to see if he resurfaced." He kissed her forehead and stood. She closed her eyes and savored the lingering tingle from the kiss that did much to assuage her discomfort.

"When I leave, lock the door and don't open it for anyone save me, Rebbie or Dirk. More of his men could've slipped aboard."

Camille nodded, obeyed his orders and returned to the berth. "*Pour l'amour de Dieu*, Kormad is persistent is he not?"

"*Oui*," Angelique said. "The beast wanted to drown me, I'm sure of it. I fear Kormad will not give up until I am dead."

Angelique had never been so thankful in her life to set foot on solid ground in Perth. She had crossed *le Manche* twice before in her life and always became ill. Even more, she was thankful to be far away from that bald brute who'd tried to kill her. The men on deck had spotted him swimming for shore, but couldn't tell if he'd made it.

She prayed he wouldn't come after her again.

Now she and Camille rode in a coach that lumbered north from Perth toward her childhood home. She pushed the curtain back and took in the familiar Scottish Lowlands outside the window. The rolling green and brown fields and the tree covered hills brought back memories of long ago. She drew in a deep breath of the cool, fresh air but could find no comfort in it. What if her clan didn't like or accept her? What if she was more French than Scottish now and could not make a connection to them? What if Lachlan found a buxom serving wench to warm his bed?

He and his friends rode before the coach, and others along with the king's retainers followed on the narrow, winding road.

Camille cradled her injured arm—the one she'd landed on when she fell from the horse. Her eyes were swollen and the skin around them blackish-blue. Thankfully she had washed all the blood from her hair and it now shone fair blond.

"I still feel terrible that you fell," Angelique said.

"We did what we had to do, as always. Do not regret it. I thank you for saving my life."

"But I put your life in danger to begin with by having you leave the coach."

"Do not worry, Ange. I saved your life one time, and now you have saved mine."

Angelique pressed her eyes closed, hating that memory. Hating to even think of Girard. She would've prayed he was dead if such a prayer did not seem like sacrilege.

She shoved the thought from her mind. "We are a pair, no?"

Camille smiled. "And now we go on our grandest adventure yet, with several handsome Scotsmen."

Angelique snorted. Indeed her husband was handsome, but she was not certain that was a good thing. Women everywhere, from all classes, either stared at him outright or slipped him covert glances and smiles. To his credit, he pretended not to notice.

A huge boulder beside the narrow lane caught her eye. She

remembered her father lifting her onto it when she was a small girl.

"We are near Draughon." Her pulse rate increasing, she gazed out. Through the trees, the wide River Tay glistened, reflecting afternoon sunlight. All seemed familiar to her, but like something from another life.

The coach drew to a halt, and she craned her neck out the window. The tall black iron gates stood before them, and beyond, the great stone medieval castle, Draughon. A large group of unfamiliar armed men swarmed in front of the gates. A shiver passed through her.

∞ର ଚ∞

"Halt!" yelled a short, armored guard.

This one wee man didn't concern Lachlan, but the additional men did. They carried all manner of swords, axes, pikes, and pistols forming a line before the gates.

"Who are you?" the guard demanded.

"Lachlan MacGrath…Drummagan, the new chief of Clan Drummagan and Earl of Draughon."

"Ba ha ha," the guard bellowed in a mock laugh. "'Tis a funny jest."

Lachlan tensed at the derision. A sickening feeling tightened his stomach. In truth, he felt like a fraud. Him an earl? A chief? But no one had to know of his doubt. He could bluff until dawn.

One of the king's retainers strode forward and unrolled a legal document containing the king's seal. "The countess of Draughon, Lady Angelique Drummagan, is in the coach and we are sent by His Majesty, King James. This man tells you true. He is the new Earl of Draughon and your chief."

The force of armed, leather-clad men increased to two or three dozen behind the main guard.

"No one such as yourself will be entering this gate afore Laird Kormad returns," the guard growled.

Did Scots always have to be such a rebellious lot? At times like this he wished to throttle his own countrymen. "Kormad?" Lachlan asked. Damn the whoreson.

"Sorley MacGrotie, Baron of Kormad, rightful heir to the earldom."

"I ken who he is, but about the earldom, you are wrong. I am Earl of Draughon. 'Tis official."

"In the name of King James, lay down your weapons, open

62

this gate and stand aside!" ordered the king's retainer.

"I think…" The guard pretended to consider. "Nay! I'm a Drummagan and I won't be havin' a damned MacGrath Highlander as my chief. King James detests you lawless wild Scots so he wouldn't send one to lead us."

"We are on the edge of the Highlands here. 'Tis not as if we live in different countries. We're both Scotsman," Lachlan said, acting his most calm and civil.

"You're naught but a barbarian. I can tell by the look of you." The guard eyed Lachlan's plaid, thrown over his shoulder. At least he wore trews instead of a kilt this day. Better for riding a horse.

"I was educated in Edinburgh, just as your former chief, John Drummagan, was. My brother is a Scottish earl and a chief as well. I have noble blood flowing through my veins."

"But you don't have Drummagan blood."

"My wife is Drummagan through and through."

"Pah!" The man spat on the ground. "She's a Frenchie."

"We shall have a contest, you and me. Whoever is the victor will claim the castle, aye?" Lachlan said.

The retainers eyed him as if he were a lunatic. Rebbie grinned and Dirk frowned.

Lachlan dismounted and strode forward. "What say you?" He towered over the guard and glared down at him.

"Um, what sort of contest?"

"One on one, man to man sword fight." Lachlan drew his basket-hilted sword, stepped back and held it at the ready.

The guard hesitated.

"Come, wee man. I wish to get this over with. We have been traveling a long while and we wish a bite to eat. My wife is ill and requires a bed to rest upon."

"What is causing the delay?" demanded a female voice with a French accent behind him. He glanced back to find Angelique striding forward, her eyes blazing wrath and her blue silk skirts swishing.

She held a small pistol in her hand.

"God's blood," Lachlan muttered.

"My lady! You must not." Two of the king's men chased her.

"Watch my back," Lachlan told Dirk and Rebbie as he started toward her. What a wee angel of vengeance she was. He sheathed his sword, plucked the pistol from her hand and escorted her back to the coach. They halted by the door.

"Listen to me, Angelique," he whispered in her ear. "You will stay within the safety of the coach until I settle this." Her floral female scent startled his senses and stirred his body with lust at a very bad moment.

"But—"

"I am the laird here and I will protect you, the lady. Not the other way around." He kept his tone firm but gentle.

"But this is my home. I grew up here and they cannot keep me out!"

"Nor can they keep me out. I alone must show them who is leader. You must trust me on this. I will send a message to Kormad he cannot ignore."

She grasped his sleeve and appeared as if she might argue further, but her mouth became a firm line. "Have a care," she said and released him.

"Always." He winked, leaned quickly forward and gave her a peck on the lips. Her jaw dropped.

Smiling, he opened the door and motioned her inside. She obeyed but held out her hand for the pistol, giving him a stern look.

"Put it away before you kill yourself with it," he whispered, relinquishing the wee weapon. "Don't allow her out," he told the royal guard. Lachlan wanted to continue smiling because she worried about his safety but he forced it away. That kiss had been too brief and he was in need of more.

He again faced the "leader" of this ragtag group of rebels, praying the whole of the Drummagan clan did not side with them and Kormad.

⋅ॐ ॐ⋅

Angelique peered out the coach window, Camille beside her, watching Lachlan and his swaggering, confident stride. He had kissed her, damn him, and distracted her, seized control. Now what if he got hurt in this ridiculous sword fight?

"We could've settled this peacefully if he'd listened to me."

"You were brandishing a weapon just as he is," Camille said.

"*Oui*. But I was not going to use it." Well, only if she had to.

"A man always prefers to show force alone. And look how well he does it."

Angelique snorted. But yes, he did do it well. She admired the

64

commanding way he brandished a sword. "Are you observing my husband?"

"No more than anyone else." Her friend gave her an innocent look. "Are you jealous?"

"*Non*. But make sure you do not become his mistress or I will have to disown you and find a new companion."

"Do not worry, Ange. I much prefer his friend."

"Which one?"

"Look." Camille pointed.

Lachlan moved with skill and grace as he engaged the shorter man in swordplay. They parried and thrust. A hint of a wicked grin played upon Lachlan's mouth. To him this was but a game. Did he not realize his life was in danger?

What do I care?

But she did care, for whatever reason. He had protected her and helped her escape Kormad and his men. As well, she had grown used to his smiling eyes and tall, muscular body...which she had seen every bare inch of. And taken note of every scar and bulge of muscle.

Metal clanged and flashed in the bright sunlight while Angelique held her breath. Swordplay was much like a violent dance of death, beautiful and dark. She had not hated it so much until this moment.

The men of both sides shouted encouragements.

A sword flew up into the air and tumbled to the ground. "*Sacrebleu,*" she whispered before Lachlan turned and she saw he still held his sword. "*Grâce à Dieu*. He has done it."

"Did you have any doubt?" Camille asked.

Angelique shrugged and kept her eyes on the action.

Kormad's man, now unarmed, backed away, tripped over a rock and sprawled to his back. Standing over him, Lachlan pressed the tip of the sword against the man's throat. "What are you called?"

"Edward."

"Well, Edward, I shall spare your life if you deliver a message for me."

"A m...mes...message, m'laird?"

In Angelique's estimation, Lachlan looked a bit too pleased with himself.

"Aye. Tell Kormad if he wants this castle, to come get it

himself, if he is brave enough. It belongs to Lady Angelique and me." He nicked the man's cheek. Blood trickled from the small wound.

He included me first. Pride swelled within Angelique, and a warm spot inside her chest softened for Lachlan.

Stepping back, he sheathed his sword. "Get up. Gather your men and go."

The prone man lurched to his feet and stumbled away. Four men rushed past, following him.

"Does anyone else wish to challenge me or leave with your friends?" Lachlan asked.

No one moved.

"Anyone else loyal to Kormad?"

Angelique noticed a tall, skinny man off to the side, clothed in dark brown leather, holding a sword behind his back. His face was hard as he watched Lachlan, like a terrier intent upon his prey.

"Who is the steward here?" Lachlan paced before the remaining clansmen, looking into the face of each one. When he turned his back, the thin, suspicious man charged forward, his sword aimed directly at Lachlan's back.

CHAPTER FIVE

Murder in his eyes and his mouth pulled into a grimace, the stranger charged Lachlan's back with the broadsword.

"*Mère de Dieu.*" Angelique lifted her pistol. Holding it steady with both hands, she aimed at her target and fired. The pistol popped and the recoil jarred her teeth.

Crying out, the traitor flipped to the ground and slid a few inches. His sword clattered away.

Lachlan ducked, his gaze darting to the groaning man she'd downed, then to her. "What the devil?"

Where did I get such reflexes? She coughed against the thick smoke, stared at the pistol and lowered it with shaking hands spotted with black powder.

"You have done it again, Ange!" Camille said. "Maybe someone would hire you as a mercenary."

"Do not jest with me so."

Now was the time to assert her power, before Lachlan and the clan. He would not lead alone. Carrying the pistol, she climbed down from the coach and strode forward, trying to conceal how her knees shook.

Lachlan stood over the traitor. "Lock him up," he told two of the Drummagan men. "Have someone see to his injury." Blood soaked the man's right sleeve. Lachlan turned to one of the king's retainers. "If you would, see they do what they're supposed to."

Two brawny Drummagans carried the man away and two retainers followed. Lachlan shifted his attention to Angelique, his expression showing mild amazement—or was it amusement? *Oui.* Again, he had the smiling eyes which taunted and teased, but now she glimpsed a bit of pride there as well. Perhaps he had underestimated her before, but now he saw what she was capable of.

Get accustomed to it, she wanted to say to him but faced her clan instead. "Do you know who I am? Lady Angelique Drummagan, countess of Draughon in my own right. The rightful heir and daughter of John Drummagan. Lachlan is my husband, the earl and chief. We are laird and lady here. This is our home. You will put away your weapons and let us pass."

Lachlan sidled in close beside her, his sword again drawn, and put his arm around her shoulders. She savored the way he always wanted to protect her, but she'd shown him she was strong enough to protect him as well. And she wished he'd remove his arm before he felt her tremble.

The worried gazes of the male clan members shifted from her to Lachlan and back again. She looked into the eyes of each one, some of them vaguely familiar, from her childhood, and others foreign to her. They must trust and respect her and Lachlan. For this to happen, they must see no sign of weakness or fear.

"You have the look of your father, lass," the man directly in front of her murmured, then dropped his gaze and went down on one knee. "M'lady. Pray pardon."

His was one of the familiar faces. What was his name? Byron? Bryce. No, Bryson. "Are you Bryson?" she asked.

"Aye, m'lady." He grinned, a light of awe entering his brown eyes. "I was sword-bearer for your father."

"I remember you." She glared at the armed men behind him, meeting the wild, pale eyes of another man she recalled. His thick beard had gone white. "Heckie," she said. "You were Father's bard."

He winked. "Indeed, m'lady. And I can recite the clan's history back to the time of Noah."

His ridiculous comment caught her off guard and she smiled.

"You've grown into a lovely young lady, lass. Glad I am you've returned to us so another chapter of the Drummagan story can unfold." He laid down his sword and knelt.

One by one, the rest of the men put their weapons upon the ground and knelt.

"We are grateful for your loyalty." She curtsied, feeling a bit of awe herself.

"Indeed, good men," Lachlan said with a bow. "Now if you would please, open the gates."

One of the men lurched up and fumbled with the lock.

When the black iron gate swung back, she strode forward, her legs a bit stronger now. Lachlan walked beside her, the retainers and his friends following.

"We shall all assemble in the great hall at supper," she called, almost stepping in a pile of horse dung, one of many littering the bailey. "Clean this place forthwith! It is no better than a pigsty." She held a fondness for her clan, but they would not shirk their duties or view her as weak. She had observed her father giving orders often enough.

Once she and Lachlan climbed the stone steps and entered the great hall, she saw that it was much cleaner than the outside and looked just as it had during her childhood. She inhaled the sweet scent of fresh rushes and pungent herbs scattered about the floor.

When she was a child, Heckie and other clan members had told the stories depicted on the large, colorful tapestries that decorated the stone walls. A barrage of nostalgic memories flitted through her mind, most bittersweet. She truly had loved this place. And missed it more than she realized.

Her father's ornate oak chair sat at the elevated high table. How she wished she could see him proudly sitting there one last time, his russet hair gleaming in the firelight. She could not imagine this place without him. He belonged here much more fully than she did.

He had sometimes remarked in anger he wished she'd been a boy. But at other times, he looked at her with kindness and stroked roughened but gentle fingers over her cheek. Often, when he returned from trips, he brought her a baby doll or some other trinket.

"Angelique," Lachlan whispered in her ear.

Realizing the whole of the household was assembled before them, Angelique blinked back the burning in her eyes and tried to wipe the past from her mind. Several of the female servants and clanswomen curtsied or bent their heads in respect.

"A good day to you. I thank you for your service. The castle looks splendid." Was that the right thing to say? She glanced up at Lachlan as if he would know.

"Indeed." He tucked her hand around his elbow. "'Tis a lovely home."

"I am Angelique Drummagan. Some of you may remember me from when I was a child. My mother took me to France when I was nine but I always missed this place. This is my husband, Laird Lachlan MacGrath Drummagan, your new chief and the earl."

The women curtsied again.

He bowed. "'Tis my great pleasure to meet all of you."

The women, especially the younger ones, did what all women did around Lachlan—stared as if mesmerized. She wanted to snap her fingers to break their collective trance. Ninnies.

"We have traveled from London and would like to rest a bit before evening meal. Please see that the guests in our party and the king's retainers are well cared for," Angelique said, her tone a bit more irritated than she'd meant. Clearly if Lachlan wanted a paramour—or several—to warm his bed, he'd have no trouble finding such among this lot.

The servants curtsied and disbursed, murmuring amongst themselves. A giggle or two reached her ears.

A round, gray-haired woman rushed forward with a wide grin. "Welcome home, m'lady! You may not remember me but I was your nanny when you were a wee bairn. I'm so pleased you've come home again, and with such a strapping and handsome lad for a husband."

"Thank you, Mistress Mayme. *Oui*, I remember you. We used to play games together. And you told me many stories. I have not forgotten them."

"Bless you, child." The older woman patted her arm. "I will show you and the laird to your chambers so you may rest. We've kept them clean and maintained these last months because we expected your return, though we didn't ken when. I'm so glad Kormad wasn't allowed to take over." She kept up the chatter the entire time they climbed the narrow spiral stone stairwell and entered the master's chambers, Lachlan following.

"As you recall, this was your mother's suite," Mistress Mayme said. "And the laird's suite is just beyond, with a door connecting the sitting rooms. I hope you will find it to your liking, m'laird."

"I'm sure 'twill be excellent."

"I had best get busy and see that the evening meal is prepared properly. Let us know if you have need of anything." She hastened away.

Angelique entered the sitting room that used to be her mother's. Was that her mother's perfume lingering in the air? A blend of lavender, violet and ambergris. Angelique half expected her to be sitting in her favorite chair by the window. She moved forward, as if through a dream of the distant past. The chair was empty, of course, but the view the same, sheep grazing on the rolling hills. Beige stalks of grain waiting to be harvested in the fields. And in the distance, the sparkling River Tay; her mother had loved looking at it.

"I thank you for saving my life," Lachlan said behind her.

Angelique jumped, her blurry gaze darting to where he stood just inside the doorway.

He moved forward. "Is something wrong?"

She dabbed at her misty eyes and tried to put the past behind her, but not before Lachlan touched her face. "Why are you crying?"

"I am not." Chills showered over her from his warm hand. His concern, his every touch felt like affection. But it was manipulation, she knew. She would not allow him to draw her under his charmed spell. A man such as Lachlan inside her soul would cut her to bits and leave her bleeding. Heavens. Each day she found him more appealing. And each day she told herself he could not be trustworthy or faithful...but those things, she wanted above all.

She paced away from him, shoving her fragile, daft emotions behind the cold protective wall, then turned. "Shooting the traitor...it was the least I could do for mine own husband, a man who trusts too easily."

Lachlan stiffened. "I would've stopped him if you hadn't."

"Indeed? Before or after he stabbed you in the back?" This was what she needed to forget her nostalgia—a good dose of reality.

"I'm not daft. I ken what you're doing." Amusement returned to his eyes. "Unsheathing your claws, wee hellcat. The rose is becoming thorny again, hmm? And considering what you did out there, I'm thinking you're a bit too cocky for a lady."

Her face burned. She hated his damnable perceptiveness. Why

could he not simply keep his distance? The distance she required for her own sanity.

"*Non*, you are the cocky one, sir. Very confident and trusting of strangers. I wonder if you are up to the task of leading this clan."

"Oh, believe me, I am." His grin disappeared and his jaw hardened. "And I shall be proving it to you."

She had to turn her eyes away from the determination lighting his. He would not fail without a massive fight to the death. But boredom might claim him first. He wouldn't be able to pursue his favorite pastime here. No elegant skirts to be lifted, only the serving maids'. But she was sure he would keep them busy.

"You will quickly grow bored here, I fear." *I hope.* Did she hope or not? What would it be like to lead her clan alone? To not be able to look upon his arrogant face each day? A face that—with its square jaw, sensual lips and intelligent golden eyes—threatened to cast a spell on her.

"I've never been bored, and I won't be here."

"You have never been married before, either. Have you?"

"Nay, but I have a feeling our marriage will never be dull." He winked.

She hated being an object of his twisted amusement. He didn't take her seriously. She must remedy that. "Mayhap I will be the one who is bored."

His grin appeared, broadened. "That, I consider a challenge, *madame*. I would never allow such a thing."

"Everything is not under your command or control." She forced the words out.

Lachlan moved forward, closer to her but she stood firm, her heartbeat accelerating. *I do not find him appealing. Not his big, strong body nor his clean male scent. Not the seduction gleaming in his eyes, nor the smile on his sensual lips.* Though she tried to convince herself these things were true, her instinctive side would not listen.

"There are different kinds of control. My own is very subtle." He bent to her ear and lowered his voice. "And I wager you will like it." His breath and lips brushed her ear; tingles raced down her chest. Her nipples hardened against her corset and she silently cursed them...but they craved his touch, his roughened but gentle fingertips squeezing them. His subtle control, his hot breath and wet tongue upon them.

Ma foi! She swallowed hard and tried to extract herself from beneath his seduction by turning away. She licked her lips and noticed they had become overly sensitized, as if craving... *no, do not think it.*

Several paces away from him, she gauged his reaction. He watched her from the corner of his eye, his gaze astute and delving.

She couldn't allow him to perceive even one small speck of her feelings, nor her uncontrollable and instinctive yearnings.

Clearing his throat, he strode away from her. "I'll be in the great hall...or 'haps outside, meeting some of the clansmen. I shall see you at supper." He bowed and exited.

Meeting the clansmen? He was trying to get ahead of her already, exerting his male power.

She ran to the door only to come upon two footmen carrying her trunk, several more servants and Camille waiting there.

Parbleu. She must see to them before she followed Lachlan.

৵৶৹৶

During supper, Angelique sat beside Lachlan at the great hall's high table. She squirmed, wishing this meal finished. His friends, the king's retainers, the steward and his wife, along with Camille sat with them. The rest of the clan ate at lower tables, a loud drone of conversation echoing toward the lofty ceiling. Angelique couldn't recall half the names of the people who'd been introduced to her this evening. Some of them, she remembered from her childhood. With others, her mind drew a blank a moment after they'd given their names. What was distracting her?

She picked at her fish. She'd had no appetite since her illness on board the ship.

The way the clan—both men and women—watched her, flicking covert glances her way when they thought she wasn't looking, disturbed her. Were they suspicious of her? One woman in particular—the steward's wife—glared at her. What was amiss?

She wanted to edge closer to Lachlan's protective presence, though she forced herself not to. He was more pleasant to focus on than her clan, and nothing about him escaped her notice. He had cleaned himself up and changed clothes since she'd last seen him that afternoon. His voice rumbled in conversation with the steward, Fingall Drummagan, on his other side.

Rebbie sat by her on one side and Camille next to him. She only caught a few sentences of Lachlan's discussion as Fingall filled him in on the food and drink he was so proud of, where it came

73

from and its cost. Rebbie seemed intent on distracting her with frivolous conversation she had no interest in, though Camille ate it up. Angelique wished to learn every detail of how the estate was run.

"The late Laird Drummagan, God rest him, preferred Gascoigne wine from Bordeaux. He considered it the finest of its sort and always imported large amounts so he'd never be without, you see." Fingall downed a long swallow. "Though he always insisted on ale served at midday meal. Our own ale, made right here on the estate. 'Tis the finest in Scotland."

Lachlan nodded, his neutral gaze shifting to Angelique. Was he angry about the way she'd challenged him earlier? She didn't know what had possessed her; she simply had to keep him at a distance. And sitting by him was not helping.

"We're glad you've come home, m'lady, m'laird." Fingall toasted them.

"I thank you," Angelique said.

"Mmph," said the woman sitting across from Fingall, his wife, Bernice. "'Twould've been better if the lady hadn't shot my brother."

Parbleu! The sister of the traitor?

"Close your mouth, Bernice," Fingall said in a low growl then gave Lachlan and her a placating grin. "I apologize for my wife. She often speaks when she should not."

"Your brother should not have tried to kill the new laird," Angelique snapped, sending the woman her most intimidating glare. "I will not abide such violence, treachery and insolence."

"Indeed," Lachlan said, his approving gaze locked on Angelique, then he winked.

Heavens, could he take nothing seriously? He could've died out there.

"My brother was not trying to kill him." The woman's tone was grumpy and defensive.

"Bernice!" her husband warned. "Shut your mouth."

She glared a hole through him. "She better hope he lives," Bernice muttered.

"Go!" Fingall pointed toward the stairs that led down to the kitchens. "I will deal with you later."

Once she stalked away, Fingall again apologized several times for his wife's poor manners and traitorous talk. "You don't have to worry about her, m'laird. I have her well in hand."

"I'm glad," Lachlan said.

Angelique hoped the man she'd shot would live, in truth. But she did what she felt right at the time, acted on impulse to protect Lachlan. But she feared Bernice would cause trouble. She might even try to poison their food. If the two lived in the castle she would have to see about securing them a cottage in the nearby village. And Bernice would be relieved of her duties here.

Moments later, a fiddler struck up a tune. Perfect time to make good her escape. Angelique excused herself. Lachlan's perceptive gaze trailed after her toward the stairs and she prayed he would not follow.

      ◌෴

Sleep eluded Angelique for the next hour, no matter that exhaustion weighed her limbs and scratched at her eyes. She pounded her fluffy pillow covered in a clean, lavender scented linen case. The raucous music filtering up from the great hall—mostly bawdy Scottish jigs—ground on her frayed nerves.

She had too much on her mind, but at least part of her clan made her feel welcome. Mistress Mayme had assigned a trained lady's maid, Inga, to Angelique as well as a chambermaid. Inga had helped her undress and take down her hair while the chambermaid had built a cozy fire, then they'd left. Angelique stared into the flames, trying to sort through the mayhem her life had become.

A soft knock sounded at the door. Angelique jerked upright. What if Bernice had come to exact revenge for her brother? No, maybe Camille, finally tired of the celebration, stopped by to wish her a *bonne nuit*.

Angelique rose, pulled on a dressing gown over her smock and approached the door. "Who is it?" she called, trying to adopt the habit of speaking the Scots variant of English instead of French in hopes her clan would accept her more quickly.

"'Tis me, Angelique," Lachlan said.

His baritone voice pronouncing her name in that Highland accent spread a pleasant shiver through her. But he could be here for the "wedding night" bedding. She froze. *Sacrebleu*. Why hadn't she barred the door?

Too late; it opened. Her pulse-rate spiked and she backed up a step. Lachlan entered with a basket and closed the door. "I missed you at the *céilidh*."

"I was too tired to stay for the music and dancing." She clenched her hands, trying to hide her unease. "What is in the basket?"

"I couldn't help but notice you ate hardly anything at supper. And who could blame you what with the way Bernice went on? So I brought you some bread, cheese and wine."

"I am not hungry," she blurted before his generous concern could breach her defenses.

"You must be. You ate only two or three bites. I wouldn't be accused of starving my wife." He broke a small, soft chunk of bread and held it before her lips. It smelled heavenly and she noticed her appetite had returned. She opened her mouth and he pushed the bread inside.

"Good, hmm?" He took a bite for himself, sauntered toward the fireplace and dropped onto the settle. "Come. Sit."

What was he scheming? She did not wish to become cozy with her husband. But he did not seem threatening at the moment. When she sank into the plush cushion beside him, he broke a bit of the hard yellow cheese and offered it to her in the same way. The fire warmed her legs in the inviting dimness. While they chewed, the silence stretched but it was not an unpleasant moment.

"Bernice won't be working in the castle anymore," he said.

"Did you speak with Fingall about it?" Perhaps she should have done that, but she had only wanted to escape the animosity and everyone's scrutiny. She had to show more strength tomorrow.

"Aye. They don't reside at the castle anyway. They have their own home on the outskirts of the village. His good income is enough to provide them what they need."

"*Grâce à Dieu.* Bernice is a menace. And her brother did try to kill you. *C'est qu'il est goujat!* Did Fingall take offense at me?"

"Nay. He continued to apologize and wished to make it up to us."

"I pray she is the only disloyal one left."

"As do I. All the Drummagan clansmen I've met have sworn their allegiance," Lachlan said. "Tomorrow, Dirk, Rebbie and I will begin training them more rigorously. In the event Kormad attacks, we shall be ready."

The thought of an attack or battle produced an icy sensation in the pit of her stomach. "Do you think he will?"

"I cannot rightly say. But he won't give up easily." Lachlan offered her another piece of bread. When she tried to take it into her hand, he shook his head and pressed it to her lips. She ate, watching him carefully. His tiger's eye gaze gleamed in the firelight as did the trace of dull gold stubble on his jaw.

"When would you like to have the second wedding and the feast?" he asked.

She swallowed, surprised at this change in subject. "After my wedding gown arrives from London."

"A week and a half, then? If your gown doesn't arrive within a week, I shall send someone to London to fetch it." He gave her a bite of cheese, his finger carelessly grazing her lip, then popped a bite into his own mouth. "The women of this clan make good cheese, aye?"

She nodded; indeed it was better than most of the French cheeses. But she feared what made this cheese so tasty was that he was feeding it to her. Never had a man done this before.

He uncorked the half bottle of wine and offered it to her. "'Tis Brabant."

She was not accustomed to drinking from a bottle but it seemed like a fun thing to do. She turned it up. After two sips of the wine sweetened with honey and spiced with cloves, she passed it back to him. He drank a long swallow, then licked his lips.

The primal side of her craved another sip so she could place her lips where his had been. What an insane thought. She recalled the way, at their wedding, he had kissed her possessively, his tongue darting into her mouth in a startling and disturbing manner. The memory sent heat searing through her.

"Would you like to work with the other women on planning the wedding and feast?" he asked.

She swallowed hard, shoving the memory away and suppressing her reaction. "*Oui.*"

"Arrange it as you desire."

Desire? She scrutinized his neutral expression, then nodded.

He stood, stretched and yawned. "'Tis late." He headed toward the door. "I'll leave this in case you get thirsty." He sat the corked bottle of wine on a table.

"*Merci.*"

He bowed. "Good night."

"*Bonsoir.* Where are you going?" she blurted, then hated herself for it.

77

Pausing, he hid a grin, unsuccessfully. Wickedness entered his eyes. "I could stay, if you wish?"

"No. I was just...never mind."

His heated gaze lingered upon her for a moment longer, then shifted. "I might have a wee dram of whisky, if that meets with your approval."

"*Oui.* Enjoy."

"Sleep well." He bowed again.

The door snapped closed. She could not believe he'd truly walked out without trying to kiss her.

Whisky? He had evaded her question nimbly by not telling her where he would drink the whisky. Was it an excuse? Had he already found a paramour here at Draughon?

Hmph!

She had not saved his miserable life only to have him embarrass her the first night here. After putting on her slippers, she crept to her sitting room and listened at the door that joined his. No sound. She strode through his sitting room and paused at his bedchamber door.

No giggles or moans. He'd had no time to bring a woman back here.

She tapped softly, then harder. *Silence.* Holding the candle aloft, she eased the door open and entered the empty room. Sidestepping his trunk in the middle of the floor, she moved toward the bed. A servant had turned down the covers, neat and tidy. She plucked his whisky flask from the bedside table and shook, the liquid inside sloshing. If he had only wanted a nightcap, why would he not drink it here? Where had he gone?

To a woman's bed elsewhere in the castle?

What was he up to? Maybe she could find him without his knowledge. At the cold fireplace, she removed the rock at the bottom, where the hearth connected to the wall. She pressed the metal lever with her foot. A screeching clang sounded behind the tapestry. Cringing at the noise, she glanced back at the door, then picked up the fire poker.

Careful to keep the candle flame away from the fabric, she burrowed behind the tapestry and pushed open the hidden door to reveal a narrow spiral stair. Spider webs crisscrossed before her. She used the poker to clear them away, then descended into the musty darkness. Debris and rubble crunched underfoot, poking up into the bottom of her leather slippers. Likely no human had ventured here in over a decade.

As a child, she had played in these hidden passageways and learned the dangerous but fascinating art of eavesdropping. No one would ever tell her what was going on, but she always learned the secrets anyway.

She certainly remembered the vicious arguments between her parents about her father's infidelity and mistresses. Her mother had loved him and that's why it had hurt her so much. And now, what if Angelique slid into the same predicament? No, she would never love Lachlan. She couldn't. To do so would be self-destruction of the worst sort.

At the bottom of the stairwell, the stone floor leveled out and the narrow corridor stretched behind two rooms, a guest bedchamber and the library. Further along, it ran behind the upper portion of the high-ceilinged great hall where small apertures allowed full views of the occupants, unnoticeable from floor level. If Lachlan was down there, she would see him. In the old days, the slits had allowed guards to keep an eye on guests and even to shoot arrows if necessary.

No sound came from the guest chamber, and through the crack, she saw that the room was dark. Male voices carried from the library. Pausing behind that room, she set the candle on the floor and peered through the crack.

Lachlan, Dirk, Rebbie and Miles sat at a table, playing cards and drinking amber-colored whisky from small crystal glasses. So, he hadn't lied. Thank the heavens. For a time, she relaxed and simply listened to the rich sound of his voice. How pleasant and persuasive it could be, and that Scottish burr made it even more so. They discussed the clan and things that had happened during the day. A short time later, Dirk and Miles left, headed to their guest quarters.

Rebbie shuffled the cards while Lachlan stirred at coals in the hearth.

"Why are you not with your wee wifey? Surely, you would like to show your gratitude to her for saving your life today." Rebbie snickered.

"I don't find that funny. 'Tis a wonder I'm not a laughingstock after what she pulled."

"Better than being dead."

79

"I would've put a stop to him soon enough."

She couldn't believe he was so ungrateful for her help; his arrogant pride spoke for him.

"From what I can tell, the men of the clan respect you," Rebbie said.

"They don't trust me."

"'Tis your first day here. Once they get to know you, I'm sure they will be so loyal as to give their lives in your stead."

"I hope they will allow me to lead them. I intend to protect them as well. I only hope Angelique doesn't undermine my authority. 'Tis her clan by birth, I ken, but I am chief."

"I'm sure you know well how to keep her reined in."

"'Tis easier said than done. But indeed, I have her under control for now. I'm starting to understand her a bit more. She loves to pick a fight more than anything. But I don't yet ken whether this fight is with me or herself."

Angelique clenched her teeth so tightly she feared they would break. *That lout! Balourd! Goujat!*

"Hmm," Rebbie mused. "Why would she fight herself?"

"Though she doesn't want to, she likes me more than she will admit." Lachlan's voice held an amused tone. "And I've made sure she'll be busy planning the second wedding ceremony and the feast for the next week and a half, while I attend to important clan business."

The bastard! Her hands fisted, her nails biting into her palms. Angelique wished she could crawl through the crack so she could throttle him now. She could scarce concentrate on the rest of the damnable conversation for the blood roaring in her ears.

"Your wedding is not important?" Rebbie asked.

"Aye, but we're already married. This wedding will be a formality, for Angelique and the clan."

"She doesn't ken what an indulgent husband she has," Rebbie said in a dry tone.

"Aye." Lachlan turned from the hearth. "'Tis late and I'm off to find my bed."

"Not your wife's bed?" Rebbie opened the door.

Lachlan picked up the candelabra and followed. "The doors of our sitting rooms connect so…" Lachlan's voice trailed off into a mumble as they left the room.

Damn him! *The beast.* He thought he was controlling her?

Angelique picked up the candle and rushed up the narrow stairwell. She stubbed her toe on one of the stone steps. The pain near blinded her. "*Mère de Dieu*," she gasped. Was it broken? The thin leather slipper offered no protection. The poker fell from her hand with a loud clang among the debris on the steps. Holding tight to the candle, she continued up the stairs, limping.

At the top, the door was still ajar. She passed through and closed it. Fighting her way from beneath the heavy tapestry, she rushed forward to replace the rock over the latch at the base of the hearth. She set the candle down and it toppled to the floor, extinguishing the light.

"*Parbleu*," she whispered and ran for the door through the pitch blackness. Her leg slammed into something large and solid. She fell, cursing and rubbing her shin. Lachlan's damned trunk.

A distant door opened, Lachlan's sitting room door. *Merde! I must hide.*

CHAPTER SIX

Angelique crawled across the floorboards and a carpet but could see nothing. She found the bed and slid beneath, praying no spiders lived there.

The bedchamber door opened and candlelight flowed into the room. Lachlan hummed a bawdy Scottish song, then whistled part of it. She watched his booted feet as he crossed to the hearth. A clunk sounded as he set his lit candle on the mantel. He stopped whistling, bent down and picked up the extinguished candle she'd dropped. *Sacrebleu.*

Silence followed. His feet turned slowly. Metal hissed against leather. She could scarce breathe. She didn't want to reveal herself, nor did she want him to take his sword or dagger to her, thinking she was a thief.

The light from his candle descended as he set it on the floor. He knelt, then peered beneath the bed. He squinted. "Angelique? Is that you?"

"*Merde,*" she muttered and scooted from her hiding place.

"What the devil are you doing beneath my bed? I'd much rather find you *in* it."

Face burning, she rose and hobbled toward the exit, her shin and toe throbbing. He was faster, running to stand before the door. "Are you limping?"

"I slammed my shin against your damnable trunk." She tried to reach the door latch, but he blocked it. "I am tired and I wish to go to bed," she snapped. Control her, would he? A string of foul

82

names formed in her mind.

"Let me see." He sheathed his sword, then swept a hand toward the chair near his bed. "Have a seat over there so I can see to your injury."

"*Non.* It is nothing, I assure you." *Balourd!* How dare he think to "keep her busy" with their wedding while he did "important" things?

He tilted his head and observed her with a charming, seductive expression. It only made her want to throttle him.

"You're angry with me," he said.

"*Non.* Why should I be?" *Nullard!*

"Why, indeed?" His grin lingered, as did his perceptive gaze. "So...you were paying me a wee visit."

"I only wished to look around this room to see if anything of my father's remained." Good lie, she congratulated herself.

"Aye, lots of his things are here. What would you like to see?"

"*Très bien.* I will look at them tomorrow. *Excusez moi, s'il vous plaît.* I must bid you good night."

"Angelique, tell me true. Why were you in here? I won't be angry."

No, but she was angry as Hades. She yearned to confront him about the arrogant and callous things he'd said to Rebbie without him knowing she'd eavesdropped, but that was impossible. She didn't want him to suspect the presence of hidden passages so she could further spy on him in the future. She must get to the bottom of his deception and manipulation.

Besides that, one of the reasons she'd married him was because she thought he would be easy to control. And he thought he was controlling her? *Merde!* She would show him!

"Angelique?" His voice this time came out low and intimate, stirring. And though she was ready to clout him, her thoughts scattered.

She tried to think of a lie quickly, but her mind went blank. "I but wondered where you were."

"You wanted to see me?"

"I wondered if..." She closed her eyes, wishing she had said anything else.

"What?"

"If you had a...companion with you."

"Companion? You mean a woman?" He spread his arms

toward the room. "As you can see, nay, I don't." His voice dropped an octave to deep and seductive. "You have me all to yourself."

A pleasant, thirsty heat spread over her face and body. She hated him because he easily broke past her defenses despite her best efforts to remain cold and unaffected. "I wish to go to my room now."

"If you want to pass through this door, you must pay the penalty."

"How much?" she blurted, then realized he couldn't have meant coin.

"Hmm. Let me see." He lifted a brow. "Three."

"Three what?"

"Three kisses, *madame*," he murmured.

She backed up a step, then two, desperate to escape his magnetism.

"'Twill be painless, I vow."

She wasn't worried about the kiss being painful, but anything that might follow, the coupling, the control he would gain over her. Which she could not allow. Besides that, she still wanted to strangle him.

"You look like a trapped hart, love. I would never hurt you. Why can you not trust at least one small thing I do?"

Love? Trust? After what he'd told Rebbie in the library? Trying to manipulate her.

Lachlan leaned a shoulder casually against the door and observed her too closely. "Why do you fear me?"

"I do not fear you. I'm sleepy," she said through clenched teeth.

"You don't appear sleepy. Instead you're angry, but you weren't earlier, when I came to your room. 'Haps you didn't wish me to leave," he said in an enticing tone. "You wanted me to sleep in your bed."

Her mouth dropped open, but no words would emerge. The image of him sleeping in her bed was too overwhelming.

"Aye. That's the reason." A mischievous glint sparked in his eyes.

"You are wrong, *monsieur!*"

"Well then, explain your mood change."

She wanted to punch him.

"Ah. Mayhap you suspected I had gone off to meet another

woman. Which tells me…you are jealous."

"I am not jealous," she ground out.

"In any case, you cannot leave this room until you pay the penalty. And if you have a weapon, put it down."

"I have no weapon."

"'Twill be the first time, then. You were not going to murder me and this imaginary woman you thought was in my bed?"

"*Non.*"

His gaze trailed down over her. "'Haps I should search you to be sure. A man can never be too careful, especially when his wife has a fondness for daggers and pistols."

She took another step away from him and found her back against a wall. Surely he would not do as he suggested.

He cocked his head and watched her. "Come. I won't search you." He held out his hand. "I shall tell you a secret."

She shook her head, her pulse running away, as she wished to do. Heavens, she did not want to touch him. That would too easily distract her and give her those disturbing and frightening carnal urges again. He was so alluring, his deep voice rumbling gently over the words.

He moved in front of her and she committed the error of letting him trap her against the stone wall.

His seductive eyes darkened in the dimness and his lashes lowered. His tall body and the entrancing scent of masculinity enveloped her. She wondered if his tawny hair felt as silky as it looked.

He brushed his warm lips over her forehead, then kissed her there, an affectionate gesture such as she had not received in many years. She could not resist the persuasion of his fingers beneath her chin and did what they compelled her to do, lift her chin. He breathed hot against her mouth. Touched the corner with his. The shape and fullness of his lips aroused her, robbed her mind of rational thought. Her nipples tingled. He pressed his mouth fully to hers, tilted his head and flicked his tongue against her upper lip. A bolt of something dangerously sensuous shot through her. She opened, from shock or from obeying him, she didn't know. He stroked one finger along her cheek and slid his tongue briefly into her mouth. Excitement flowed through her like a searing river of sensation.

"Mmm. The secret is—" He kissed her again, his tongue

sweeping into her mouth, wet and erotic, and toying with hers, then leaving before she was ready. "—you're the only one I want."

Her heart gave a lurch. Some deep, hidden part of her wished his words to be true, craved them to be true as one craves air. For one radiant moment, she imagined they were. While she wasn't paying attention, her hands had buried themselves in the warm silk of his hair and her fingertips grazed his neck. He felt wondrous, his hard chest flattening her breasts.

His talented lips nipped and ate at hers. His tongue ignited a hunger she had never imagined. *Sorcerer.*

His hands skimmed down her sides to her derriere. Only her thin silk smock and wrap separated their skin, and the heat of his hands burned through. He tugged her against his body. The granite hardness of his male member pressed against her stomach, startling her out of the sensual daze. *He will force me! He will hurt me.*

A shock wave jolted her. She tore herself away and dashed out the door.

⋅১ﬞ ৯৯৹

Damnation! Lachlan almost had Angelique calmed and aroused. But he'd gone too fast. What the devil had scared her? Not the kisses; she liked kisses. Mmm, she'd tasted like heaven, sweeter than a honey-drizzled tart he wanted to sink his teeth into.

He pressed a hand against his erection to ease his frustration. Maybe that was it. Maybe his aroused shaft frightened her. Though she had seen it in London. He didn't know what would be frightening about that part of his body. Women had told him his tarse was of a large size, compared to most men, but they always seemed to like and appreciate that. But maybe the size did scare Angelique, if she hadn't much experience. She might not be a virgin, but he would wager, she was almost so.

She'd been in his room to see if a woman was in here. What a jealous lass she was. She didn't wish to occupy his bed nor would she allow another woman to occupy it. She wanted him to become a monk in truth.

Not since he'd been a lad of fourteen had he needed to relieve his frustrations himself. Women had spoiled him. He wanted sex and he wanted it a lot. But now, none. Cut off from one of his favorite activities because of his wife. A wife he had erotic dreams about. And waking fantasies of soothing the hellcat, making her purr in his ear and sink her claws into his back to hold him in place

86

on top of her. Between her legs.

Cursing at the intense need plowing through him, he paced. 'Twas easy to see she wanted him, from the languid, curious look in her eyes to the way she'd held onto him and accepted his kisses moments ago.

A fantasy formed in his mind... she would straddle his thighs and impale herself upon him. Sliding up and down... so wet. *Mmmm.* How he would love for her to ride him fast and hard as if possessed by some erotic demon. He would give her so much pleasure, if only she would allow him.

Tomorrow. Indeed, he would seduce her tomorrow.

ംരെ ളെം

Three days after Kormad and his men had left London, they sat in the drab common room at The Ram's Head Inn in Perth. The bones and remains of their meal littered the table before them.

"Where the hell is Pike?" Kormad muttered. "He said he would meet us here this day. The ship's already come in and he should've been here by now." He hoped Pike had thrown MacGrath and Angelique overboard into the deep, chill waters of the North Sea.

Kormad's men, sitting around the table, shook their heads and shrugged. He had just bought them a fine meal, and this was what he got for it?

"Well, go look for him, you louts! Search the other inns and taverns."

"Aye, sir." All his men sprang up and headed toward the door.

"MacFie, you stay!"

The most intelligent of his men returned to the table.

"I've got another job for you," he said in a low voice. "Snoop around and see if there is any news about a laird and lady dying or drowning on their way here. You ken how to do it without raising suspicion."

"Aye, m'laird." MacFie hurried away.

Kormad grunted and downed another swallow of warm, stout ale. He had a few loyal men he'd sent to guard Draughon a month ago, and he hoped they still held their posts. They did if MacGrath and his lady-whore were no longer in the land of the living.

An hour later, MacFie returned. "Word is the Earl of Draughon and his lady arrived yesterday in sound health."

"Damn!" Kormad smashed a fist onto the table, rattling

87

everything upon it. Could no one get anything right? Not even Pike? What was the world coming to when you couldn't even hire a good mercenary?

Kormad cursed, fumed, and paced for another hour, fantasizing about killing MacGrath and Angelique in a dozen different ways, without implicating himself, of course. Aye, he could get inventive. Draughon would be his—and Timmy's—soon. Very soon.

Arnie and Rufus struggled through the doorway with the brawny, limping Pike supported between them. His filthy trews and doublet were ripped and his leg bloody. Even his bald head was covered in blood and dirt.

Kormad charged forward. "What the hell happened to you?"

His face black and blue, Pike raised unfocused, bloodshot eyes. He smelled strongly of whisky and fishy seawater. "MacGrath's men ganged up on me. Had to... jump ship. Almost drowned. Fishermen... hauled me out, then... robbed me and beat me up."

"Bastards! Did you do the job?" Kormad growled.

"Nay." He clenched his teeth, body quaking. "But I'm ready to take my revenge on MacGrath for all my pain and sufferin'."

"Aye, there's the spirit!" Kormad grinned. Why couldn't he have ten men like Pike? "Well, what are you whoresons waiting for? Help Pike into a coach. We go to Burnglen." The healer there would patch him up, then Kormad and his men would charge into Draughon when least expected.

༺ ❀ ༻

The next evening, Lachlan sank into the wooden tub of hot water in his bedchamber before the fireplace. Light from the dancing flames glowed upon the stone walls. The deep scratch on his arm stung and his muscles ached from the full day of punishing training he'd given his body.

His friends and the Drummagan clansmen hadn't fared much better. They didn't have to know he was working out a monumental sexual frustration, something he had never before experienced. He feared the Drummagan men might hate him for the demands he made on them, but the contrary appeared to be true; their expressions showed more respect, trust and admiration after the hours of bruising exercises.

His muscles relaxed in the heat and his mind drifted to

Angelique. He hadn't seen the wee hellion all day. She hadn't joined him for breakfast, nor midday meal, sending a servant with some excuse about being too busy with planning the wedding and feast.

He was glad she occupied herself with household duties, but he missed seeing her. Thinking how Angelique had sought him out in this room the night before, suspecting him of seducing another woman, he smiled. She was a possessive little hedgehog. Which meant she liked him and wanted him on some level. Perhaps a level she couldn't face yet, but it was a start.

Why couldn't she have crawled into bed with him last night? 'Twas but a fantasy. Never had he experienced such a hard time seducing a woman.

A knock sounded at the door.

He lifted his head. "Who is it?"

"Bryson, m'laird."

"Come." Since Bryson had been the former chief's sword-bearer, Lachlan had given him the same position. It was hereditary, after all, and the man seemed skilled.

"Sorry to disturb you, chief." Bryson, dark-haired and stocky with muscle, stopped before the door and executed a brief bow.

"I asked you to. What of Kormad?"

"He is home. Arrived by coach this eve. You mentioned a tall, bald man."

"Aye?"

"They carried a man like that on a litter into Burnglen Castle. He appeared to be awake but in pain."

So the bastard had survived jumping into the North Sea. Astonishing, given that few people knew how to swim. Someone that tough and hardened, he'd have to watch out for. "What did Kormad and his men do after that?"

"He sent two men to spy on us from a hilltop, but they didn't set foot on Drummagan land. Everything else was as normal. Same amount of guards at their usual posts."

"Good. I thank you, Bryson. You're a good man."

"M'laird." He bowed and left.

Lachlan laid his head back against the tub again, thinking how proud and happy he was to be given the privilege of leading these Drummagan men. They were sturdy, strong and intelligent. Proficient fighters already. Their skills but needed a bit of honing.

He was grateful to his father and his older brother, Alasdair, for showing him how to lead men and train them. What would Alasdair think of him now that he was an earl and chief? He would send him a missive and relay the news.

The door burst open without warning. Lachlan's hand shot down to his sword behind the tub. Angelique stepped into the room.

Releasing a breath, he relaxed back with a grin. "What a pleasing surprise, my angel."

Her expression stern, she strode forward, then halted abruptly in the center of the room, her gaze darting down his chest and back up. "My maid said you were cut today during practice. Why must I hear about your injuries through gossip? Why do you not tell me when you are hurt?" she demanded. "You are a free-bleeder!"

He almost chuckled. "Naught to fash your bonny head over. 'Twas but a scratch. I am well."

"Let me see."

"You must come closer, then." Why did he feel a bit wicked saying those words to his own wife?

She inched forward.

"Right here." He pointed at his forearm, resting on the tub's edge.

She rushed to him and knelt. Surprising him, she lightly stroked a finger over his forearm alongside the injury. "Scratch? Mère de Dieu. You call that a scratch?"

"Aye. 'Tis not bleeding now, and did not require stitching."

"What were you doing?" Angelique's vibrant green eyes sparkled in the firelight, bewitching. Her intense concern for him made his heart ache and yearn... for what, he didn't know. He only knew she cared about his health, and deep down that meant she cared about him. Why wouldn't she let him touch her? Kiss her? Make love to her?

"Training the men, as I mentioned last night," he said.

"Sword fighting?"

"Aye. Practice."

She pushed to her feet and her gaze drifted down his body beneath the water. She slammed her eyes closed, turned her back and paced to the other side of the room. He couldn't help that he got an erection every time she was near. How he would love to drag her into this tub and get her all wet. But likely that would turn her into a clawing hellcat again. He must be far more subtle.

"I thank you for your concern. What did you do today?" he asked.

"Met with Mistress Mayme and planned a menu for the wedding feast. Made a long list of supplies we need."

"I can hardly wait to see what delights you have in store."

She flicked a glare at him. He bit his lip to keep from grinning. What fun to tease her!

Again her gaze lingered a bit too long on his chest. That was definitely a spark of interest. He pretended to ignore her, took the soap and stroked it over his chest and neck. Lifted an arm and washed underneath.

She appeared spellbound by his actions for several moments before she snapped to attention. "I bid you a good night, *monsieur*."

"I wish you wouldn't call me *monsieur*." Too cold and distant.

"*Très bien*. My laird."

"Lachlan," he corrected.

A moment of silence stretched out in which she stared at the floor. "Lachlan," she murmured.

Had she ever said his name before? The sound of it in her husky voice and beguiling accent made his blood heat like mad. His shaft hardened more fully, tingling, and he wished she'd take another peek at it. Stroke it. He hungered for her soft, smooth hands on him.

"Would you care to join me?" he asked.

She stiffened and took a step toward the door. "*Non.* I have already bathed. I must go."

"Would you like to sleep in here? I'd like it if you would." *Nay, I would love it.* Saints, what he would do to her. Kissing, licking, caressing. The slowest, most tantalizing seduction he had ever indulged in... if he could keep himself under control. Aye, he could. For her, he would go to great lengths to ensure her enjoyment. Great lengths. He almost smiled.

"*Non.* I am not ready," she said in a quiet voice.

"'Tis understandable to be nervous," he said mildly. Hell, he was growing a smidgen nervous himself. And eager. He rubbed the soap down his abdomen as if they were discussing naught more significant than what to have for supper.

"I do not care for... the coupling," she said.

"What happened?" he asked. *And who was the whoreson who turned you against the most pleasurable experience on earth? Some bumbling, selfish imbecile, no doubt.* Over the years he'd changed more than one woman's opinion of sex, usually after their much older or unskilled husbands had died. 'Twas a crime they'd never satisfied their wives nor given them a jot of pleasure.

Angelique exhibited that trapped hart look again. "Nothing. I simply detest it."

"I shall remedy that as well, for never have I been with a woman who didn't enjoy it."

Her glare speared him with pure hatred. She turned and strode from the chamber, slamming the door.

"God's blood! I'm daft," he muttered to the quietness of the room. Could he never learn to guard his tongue?

He quickly finished his bath and dried off. He wrapped the damp piece of linen around his hips, stalked across the sitting rooms to her chamber door and knocked.

Silence.

"Angelique?" He knocked again.

"*Va-t-en!*"

"I'm sorry for what I said, and I won't be leaving." He lifted the latch and opened the door. Why had she not barred it if she truly wanted him to stay out?

She stood by the fireplace, glaring icicles at him. "You may not enter my bedchamber unless I give you permission."

"I am your husband and I will enter whenever I wish." He closed the door behind him.

"*C'est que tu es goujat!*"

She thought him a lout, huh? "I take it that was not a compliment. We are wed. Get used to it, Angelique."

"Need I remind you it is a marriage in name only? You agreed to this."

"Nay, I did not."

"You did! Does your word mean naught?"

"Don't question my honor. What I said was, 'whatever you desire.' And what you 'desire' has not been established yet."

Her eyes narrowed further, her expression militant. "I have made my desires quiet clear, *monsieur*. We will not share a bed."

"And how do you propose to have an heir for this illustrious estate? Immaculate conception?"

"Do not mock me."

"'Tis an honest question."

With big eyes, she watched him. "Do you intend to force me?"

He drew back, feeling as if he'd been slapped. "Nay! How can you ask such a thing? I would never force you, or anyone."

She turned away, facing the small fire in the hearth.

"Angelique. I wish you wouldn't fear me so much. I would never hurt you, or make you do aught against your will. I but wish to show you how it can be between a man and a woman. Believe it or not, the bedding can be quite fun, pleasurable and astonishing."

"For you, I'm sure it is."

"And for you. I would ignore my own needs and fulfill yours first."

"I do not have those kinds of *needs*." Her gaze was cutting.

"Aye, you do. You just don't ken it yet. Either that or you're lying about it."

"*Non,* believe what I say."

"I'm thinking you protest too much. I've seen the way you look at me. You enjoyed the kisses." And so had he. In fact, he craved another now. He would cover her sweet, delectable body in kisses if but given the chance.

Her face reddened but her mouth appeared sealed tight.

"I'm also thinking no man has ever pleasured you." Deep down, he was glad for that because he wanted to be the only one to teach her about pleasure. And he wanted her addicted to the carnal delights he would dole out.

"I told you, I am not a virgin."

"That makes no difference. 'Haps you have been with a man but you didn't enjoy it. A woman deserves as much pleasure as a man." And for her, he'd endeavor to give her twice as much.

"I am not interested," she said in a small voice. But, like a light caress, her curious gaze slid down his chest, over the thin material draping his hips and becoming tented at his groin.

Not interested? What a terrible liar she was. "One kiss," he said.

"What?" The ambivalence—fear and desire—in her eyes made him ache to the depths of his soul. How could she think he'd hurt her?

"One kiss is all I ask of you this night."

"I do not wish it."

"You enjoyed the one last night. I didn't think you feared

anything."

"I do not fear you." Her tone was almost like a wee wildcat's growl. So fragile, yet so fierce.

"Aye, I'm thinking that's why you chose me over those other two men." He needed to remind her it was her decision to marry him. And remind her of the bastards she could be married to at this very moment instead. Neither man would be so lenient as Lachlan.

"I did not wish to marry a man old enough to be my grandfather."

"Understandable. And Kormad?"

"Him I detest beyond anything."

Lachlan nodded. "What of Philippe? Did he give you pleasure?"

She remained silent, staring into the fire.

"I didn't think he had."

"He did."

Och! Another lie. "Indeed? Then I deserve a chance to wipe him from your memory."

"You cannot. I shall never forget Philippe."

What the hell did she see in the cowardly laddie? Likely, that was another lie to keep Lachlan at bay. "A kiss, Angelique. 'Tis all I'm asking. If you'd married Chatsworth or Kormad, either of them would've already forced you into bed. But I wouldn't do that. I ask you to come of your own free will."

The fire crackled in the long silence.

Stomach aching, Angelique clenched her sweaty hands, unable to forget the pain and humiliation she'd suffered at Girard's hands... and body. The way he forced his erect member inside her, like a battering ram, making her flesh bleed, even as he slapped her and hit her. Tears stung her eyes. She turned away from Lachlan, hoping he would not see.

Lachlan was not Girard, not a rapist, nor was he angry. Everything about him was different from Girard, but he was still a man who wished to take her body, control her life. Sex was a dangerous instrument, whether done violently or gently, it was meant to bring her under his command. Bend her to his will. And clearly, he intended to be in charge, marching into her chamber whenever he pleased.

For one brief moment, she allowed herself the truth. Lachlan appealed to her in a most frightening way. His charm drew her in, against her will. It wasn't only his masculine physical appeal and the raw male beauty of his defined muscles, but the heated look in his eyes, the spellbinding sound of his deep, rich voice. She could not control the rhythm of her own breathing when he was near, observing her closely.

What if she coupled with Lachlan and all the pain and terror of Girard came rushing back to her, in her mind. As if it were happening again now. What would she do? The memory might be too real, too much to endure.

"One wee peck on the cheek," Lachlan said, his tone light, such a contrast to her inner turmoil.

"Very well." *Get it over with and go!* She could abide this pressure no longer.

Slowly, he approached her, each step closer quickening her heart rate.

She glanced into his dark gold eyes and turned her cheek to him. *Please, let him be quick.*

Drawing near, he pressed his nose to her hair and inhaled. The release of his warm breath caressed her temple and her ear. She shivered at the tickle and waited.

His breath, softer this time, touched her cheek. She had never felt anything so bewitching. And he smelled appealingly male. What fragrance of soap did he use?

He brushed smooth lips over her cheek, but his rough masculine stubble called to everything in her that was feminine. Immobilizing tingles spread down her neck, across her chest, peaking her nipples. He exhaled against her—hot, sensual, subtle—without touching her.

Disturbing carnal sensations raced over her and her eyes drifted closed. "Go away," she whispered.

"That is what you desire, in truth?" he murmured against her ear, but continued with the seduction. He drew her earlobe into his mouth. The erotic overload drove a shaft of terror through her and she shoved at his chest.

He grasped her wrists and pushed them above her head. Trapped.

Panic seized her. *"Arrêtez! Bâtard!"* She tried to yank herself from his firm grip.

He paused, restraining her against the wall and staring into her eyes at short distance. *"Oui. Je suis un bête. Non? Goujat?"* he asked.

"A stupid beast, a lout, a bastard?"

Iciness drifted down through her. *"Vous ne parlez pas la Francaise."*

"Oui, madame, I do speak French. I was in France for more than a year."

"You lied."

"Non." The anger in his expression gave her chills.

"You pretended ignorance."

"I have been called a canny lad. I ken what you have called me when you thought I couldn't understand. How would you like it if I said things about you in Gaelic?"

He did talk about her to his friends, but in English and behind her back. Damn him.

"I wouldn't call you degrading names in Gaelic, neither to your face nor behind your back. I am not as much a bastard as you think."

"Pardonnez-moi." She lowered her gaze, submitting, praying he would release her and not force her. She might go insane and try to kill him if he did.

"I forgive you." His lips quirked and a long moment later, he brushed them against the corner of her mouth—persuasive, determined, fervent. He nipped at her lips, flicked his tongue against the seam. Unwanted arousal shot through her like a bolt of lightning. Such power and control he wielded with his practiced seduction. He used his magic on her as he had many other women.

Her throat closed off. Gasping, she turned her head away and tried to twist from his hold. "Release me!"

"Not until you kiss me properly as a wife should kiss her husband."

"Bastard!"

"I was born well within wedlock. As our bairns will be."

She shook her head. "Do not touch me. You have been with hundreds of women. I do not want a disease." There, good reason. And *Mère de Dieu,* what if it were true? She had not considered it until this moment.

Eyes narrowed, he stepped back, releasing her at last. "I have no disease, *madame,*" he said firmly.

"How do you know?" She inched away from him.

"I have no symptoms of any sort. I am always most careful. I have never bedded whores or barmaids."

"Ladies have been known to carry diseases."

"Aye, but word gets around."

"Or maybe debauching virgins is your specialty."

He shrugged. "If they asked nicely. But that is all in the past. My body is yours alone now."

Ha. Did he honestly think she believed that? "Prove you do not have a disease. Have a physician come."

He glowered. "You jest."

"*Non.* I mean it. I wish a physician to inspect your... member and see that it is healthy."

CHAPTER SEVEN

Lachlan laughed, but this shifted to a perplexed scowl. "I assure you, m'lady, my 'member' is healthy."

"I do not know that," Angelique said. A libertine such as him had been with too many women to count. She was glad she had thought of this before it was too late.

"If I am examined and found healthy, I am welcome in your bed, aye? Every night."

Parbleu. She had not considered what would happen afterward. "I shall think about it."

"No thinking. I want your word." His eyes had become those of a hardened warrior again. "A signed contract."

"Have you lost your mind?"

"Nay. 'Tis only fair. I meet your demands; you meet mine. And to sweeten the deal, I will allow you to accompany me as I meet with some of the clan chiefs we have alliances with in the surrounding area, and their wives, within the next few days."

She stiffened. How dare he? "I will go whether you 'allow' it or not. I am the countess."

"Nay. Our marriage vows said you must obey me. I always must do what is best for the clan. And for your safety."

What a ridiculous excuse. "I think your seduction skills are slipping, *monsieur.* You are having a problem seducing your own wife and have to resort to contracts, deals and blackmail."

"I haven't yet begun to try seducing you. But if that's what you wish..." He shrugged. "I thought you valued honesty above all.

Seduction doesn't always involve honesty and forthrightness. Seduction is a game, manipulation, pleasure for both players. Is that what you desire?"

"*Non.*"

"What do you want then?" In the firelight, his golden gaze was too perceptive, prying into her very soul. "What are your deepest desires, Angelique?"

She would never tell him her deepest desires. If she had any, they were hidden, buried beneath the rubble of her heart where Girard had shattered it. She had not the will nor strength to go a second round, to entrust her dreams to another seducer. No, in truth, her dreams were dead.

"I want nothing of you." Though she tried, her voice would not raise above a whisper.

"Forgive me if I don't believe you. You want something or you never would've picked me."

"I had no choice."

"Aye, you did. If you'd chosen Chatsworth, you probably would've been a widow soon."

She shook her head. "I could not abide him, even one night."

"Can you abide me one night?"

"I do not know. Mayhap."

"One night then." At her desk he took out a piece of paper, dipped a quill into the inkpot and started writing.

"What are you doing?"

"Drawing up a contract. If I get my 'member' approved as healthy by a physician, then you must give me a whole night in your bed. Or you can come to mine. And not for sleeping. Is my meaning clear, or do I need to spell it out?"

"If this is part of your seduction, it is sorely lacking."

"Do you want seduction or honesty?"

"Both," she blurted. *Merde!* She covered her mouth.

"Ah." His eyes sparkled with mischief. "Well then, the lady has made her desires known. Duly noted."

"I spoke in haste. I did not mean it."

"No need to explain." He continued writing and the realization struck her that he must indeed be well-educated if he could scribe with such speed. "I only need your signature here." He presented her with the paper and pointed to the bottom.

She read his scratchy script. *I, Angelique, wife of Lachlan, agree to one full night, from nine in the evening until nine in the morning in the same bed with Lachlan for purposes of sexual pleasure, under any name, coupling, swiving, procreation, if he brings documentation of his sexual health and absence of any diseases, signed by a physician. And if I spend the night with him as described above, I may accompany him to visit neighboring clan chiefs and their wives.* He had signed as a witness.

"Damn you," she muttered, strode to the desk and signed. *"Là. C'est fini."* She shoved the paper toward him and threw the quill onto the desk.

He smiled like a fox with a hen in its jaws. *"Merci, belle ange."* Blowing the paper to dry the ink, he approached the door.

"I want a signed and sealed testimony from the physician, the one in the nearby village."

Lachlan bowed. "Anything else, my queen?"

"Hmph."

⋄৩৩⋄

"What the hell is going on at Draughon?" Kormad stood before the fireplace in the drafty, dark great hall of Burnglen.

MacFie, who'd just returned from scouting, strode across the worn out rushes. "I didn't see the men you left there, m'laird."

"Damnation!" Those had been some of his bravest, most canny men. He had few left. Pike was out of his head with fever. Several of the others were witless, good for no more than mucking out stalls. What he needed were the Drummagan men as his own. And if he were their chief it would be so. "Did my men flee the castle like rabbits? Are they dead? In Draughon's dungeon?"

"I don't ken, sir."

"Send out Murray and Rusty to look for them. Keep three men posted to watch Draughon at all times. If they get a chance to kill MacGrath or the wench tell them to do it!"

"Aye, m'laird."

Something thumped off to the side. Kormad turned to find his wee, fair-haired nephew partially hidden behind a chair, wide curious eyes locked on him.

"Timmy." Kormad crossed the room, sat down in the chair and held out his hand. The lad rose and crept to him. He looked so much like Kormad's sister, each glimpse of those innocent blue eyes was like a kick in the gut. "Don't fret, Timmy. I'll put everything to rights. You will inherit the title and lands your father denied you. You will one day be Earl of Draughon and chief of

Clan Drummagan." *But I will be first, so that I can secure it for you.*
And the Drummagan wench would pay for her father's sins.

ঙ্গু ও্র

Early the next morn, Lachlan passed Dirk, Rebbie and several
clansmen breaking their fast in the great hall. Too late, he realized
he should've made good his escape through the servants' back
entrance so as to not rouse curiosity.

"A good morn to you," Lachlan called when they spotted him,
then headed toward the exit.

"Where are you off to with such haste?" Rebbie called, his
voice echoing off the high ceiling.

Lachlan paused. They awaited his response, all their eyes upon
him.

He refused to let them know he was going to the physician or
what rubbish Angelique demanded of him, blast her hide. He was a
supreme, shining example of an indulgent husband, and she should
be thankful for him and his leniency.

He gave a tight grin. "I shall be back in a trice."

Rebbie rose and followed him to the door, curious eyes
locked upon him.

"'Tis naught but an errand for my lady wife," Lachlan said in a
low voice. Hell, if Rebbie got wind of this, Lachlan would never
live it down.

"What sort of errand?"

"Naught to worry about. Continue with your meal."

Rebbie shrugged and returned to the table. Lachlan hurried to
the stables and saddled a horse, while the stable lads scurried about
bringing him what he required. He hoisted himself into the saddle,
kicked the horse into a gallop and rode away from the castle.

Twenty minutes later, after cursing Angelique the whole way,
he dismounted before the physician's cottage in the nearby village.
'Twould be easier to get this over with here than have Doctor Ellis
come to the castle where everyone would want to know the
purpose of his visit. A light rain misted his hair and he glanced up
at the low-hanging gray clouds. Aye, 'twas good to be in Scotland
again.

Fast hoof-beats approached on the castle road and he curled a
hand around his sword hilt.

Dirk and Rebbie raced around the curve toward him.

Damnation!

They drew up even with him, their mounts snorting and kicking up clumps of black mud. "What the devil are you doing riding out alone?" Dirk asked. "Kormad would like naught better than to ambush you."

"I am always on guard against such. And I don't fear him." Lachlan had two pistols and a sword on his belt.

"What are you doing here, at the physician? Are you ill?" Rebbie asked.

"Nay. Never mind. Just don't tell anyone I came here."

"Only if you tell us the truth."

"Damn you," Lachlan muttered, turning away.

Rebbie laughed. "Come on then, out with it. Are you needing a potion to enhance your virility?"

Dirk snickered.

"After the thorough bedding you gave her in London, I would've never guessed." Rebbie was determined to grind salt into his wound.

"Nay, I have no need of a potion," Lachlan growled. He released a long breath. "Angelique kens of my reputation with the ladies so she wishes assurance I don't have... a disease."

Dirk and Rebbie guffawed and almost toppled to the ground. Their horses stamped and danced about.

"'Tis not funny. Now, don't be telling anyone or I'll no longer associate with the two of you bastards." Lachlan knocked on the door.

⋙⟐⟐⟐⋘

A half hour later, Lachlan closed the same door behind him on the way out, feeling more violated than he had in his life. He cringed. Doctor Ellis had examined his member beneath a magnifier. And checked every other part of his body while he was at it. The man had inspected the hair on Lachlan's head for thickness and sniffed his breath. With some of the prodding and squeezing he did, if the man hadn't been a professional, Lachlan would've cut off his fingers.

Lachlan stuffed the damnable signed and sealed document into his doublet, glad to see the rain had stopped.

"And are you carrying the French pox, then?" Rebbie asked, standing by his horse.

"Nay. Officially healthy." As he knew he was. Angelique would have to pay the piper now and spend the night in Lachlan's

102

bed. He couldn't wait.

Rebbie hoisted himself into the saddle. "How much did you have to bribe him with?"

"To hell with you!"

Rebbie laughed.

"You haven't had a wedding night yet, have you?" Dirk's tone was understated but his question pointed.

As if that was any of his business! Lachlan scowled.

"What of the bloody sheet?" Rebbie asked.

"'Twas mine own blood. I cut myself. But don't be telling anyone. The king wanted the marriage consummated but Angelique wasn't in the mood."

"He beds all the ladies in London but cannot bed his own wife," Dirk said with exaggerated amazement.

"You're daft. I didn't bed all the ladies in London." Lachlan mounted. "And 'twill not be long afore mine own wife drags me to her bed and refuses to let me leave."

"Would anyone care to place a wager on that?" Rebbie rubbed his hands together eagerly.

"Aye," Dirk said.

"Don't you dare even think about it." Lachlan nudged his horse into a trot and they raced up the road toward Draughon, passing beneath the trees. He couldn't wait to see Angelique's face when he showed her this document. Nor could he wait to have her naked betwixt his sheets.

Something whizzed past Lachlan's head. "What the hell? Arrows!"

Dirk yelled curses.

Lachlan kicked his mount into a gallop and ducked low, scanning the bushes off to the left but seeing nothing. Cowardly bastards! An arrow struck his saddle. Where was his targe when he needed it?

The hooves of Dirk's and Rebbie's horses thundered behind him. Lachlan glanced back. Rebbie fired a pistol toward the bushes. An arrow protruded from Dirk's shoulder, a fearsome scowl on his face.

Damn Kormad and his men! If he wanted war, he would have it.

⚜ ⚜

An hour later, Lachlan himself had removed the arrow from

103

Dirk's left shoulder and helped hold him down while the blacksmith cauterized the flesh wound. No easy task; Dirk was strong and mad as two scalded oxen.

"You're fortunate 'twas not your sword arm." Lachlan handed him a bottle of peat-colored whisky.

"Aye, cause then you'd kick me out on my arse." He drank a hefty swallow of the water of life.

"Indeed." Lachlan grinned and strode from the room. Dirk was one of his best and oldest friends and he prayed he didn't suffer fever from this wound. While he rested, Lachlan would deliver the signed document to a certain lady.

Angelique waited outside the guest chamber door, her eyes wide and worried, her skin pale. "How is he?"

"He'll be well in a few days. Come. I wish to speak with you." He motioned her toward the spiral stair and waited for her to precede him up.

In the corridor, he opened his sitting room door and motioned her inside. Looking wary, she passed him and entered, her silken skirts brushing his legs.

After closing the door, he gave a formal bow and presented the paper to her. 'Twas unfortunate he didn't have a gleaming silver tray to place it upon. "'Tis what you requested, m'lady."

With a tight expression, she broke the red wax seal and read the document... very slowly. Nay, she was reading it twice.

"As you can see, my 'member' and every other part of me is healthy."

"One moment." She passed into her sitting room and opened a box on the table. He followed. She withdrew another document and compared the physician's signatures.

Damn her. She did not even believe him. When would she begin to trust him?

"Now you're thinking I forged Doctor Ellis's signature? I am not a liar, Angelique. If I said I went to the physician, I did. He examined me head to toe. You can ask Rebbie and Dirk if you need further witnesses."

Angelique's cool green eyes assessed him.

"Shall we meet in your chamber or mine tonight?" he asked.

"Neither."

His temperature blazed. Rage clawed its way up his chest, near choking him. He'd known she'd somehow try to get out of it despite giving her word and signing a contract. He was known to have a very balanced temperament but she destroyed his patience. "Your word means naught then!"

"Your contract does not say *when* I am to spend the night with you. And I will, but after the second ceremony. I am glad you are healthy in every way, but I am not yet ready to... do this. We should get to know each other better first."

Remain calm, he told himself over and over. "The night of the ceremony you will be in my bed. And every damned night thereafter."

Deep breath.

She did not respond, merely stared at his doublet. If she feared him, his anger certainly wouldn't help matters. Why couldn't she be reasonable?

"Angelique, I risked my life to get you that ridiculous signed document. I ken you wish Kormad's arrow had gone through my heart instead of Dirk's shoulder. What would you do then? Do you think you can lead these men and this clan by yourself? Do you think they can protect you from Kormad with me out of the way? Nay. You would either be married to him or dead yourself. That's how ruthless he is."

Tears glistened in her eyes. "I am glad... you were not hurt," she said in a tight whisper. She turned and fled the room, disappearing into her chamber.

Entering his own sitting room, he slammed the door, picked up an iron candelabra and flung it against the stone wall. The loud clang reverberated. *"Iosa is Muire Mhàthair!"* Damn the ice in her heart. He dropped into the chair behind the desk. Several more days until their second wedding ceremony.

He had never worked this hard to get a woman into bed, and this his own wife—something he had never wanted to begin with. He knew marriage would be a disaster for him.

She hated him. That was it. She did not want him, and was completely immune to his charms. Witch!

Still, he yearned for her. Each time she made the challenge more difficult, he got even harder for her.

Slamming the door on his way out, he strode downstairs. Not only had his wife declared war on him, so had his neighbor. Now he had to meet with the other clans in the surrounding area to make sure Drummagan alliances were strong. If Kormad wanted a feud, he'd get one.

꧁ ꧂

Two days later, Angelique's additional trunks arrived from London, including her trousseau and wedding gown. In her chamber, she took out the pale blue French lace and silk confection and spread it upon the bed. "Exquisite," she breathed, then gathered it to her with reverence and pressed her nose to the folds. Her mother's perfume lingered upon it.

I miss you, Maman.

Her mother had given her the gown in France five years ago. Angelique remembered clearly the sound of her mother's rich voice, as if she now spoke in her ear. "I was so in love with your father when I wore this to marry him," she'd said. "We met at King James' court, at Holyrood Palace. Everything was so elegant. I was a young girl, not much older than you are now, filled with hopes and dreams." Her mother's wistful smile had turned bittersweet. "My dreams were shattered but that does not mean yours have to be, Angelique. Each woman must find her own happiness in her own way. I soon learned your father did not love me in the way I loved him. That is why you must choose your husband very carefully. Do not fall in love with him until you know he loves you. Do not marry a Scotsman because they are barbarians and know nothing of feelings."

"How do you know all Scotsmen are like Father?" Angelique had asked.

"I knew several when we lived in Scotland and, in my experience, they are all alike. They love the excitement of war and fighting above all. They only wish to exert their power over others, especially women. And they desire a different woman each night. They care not whether the woman is a lady or a common servant. They will take them all."

Angelique believed her mother. How could she not? Her mother's ideas were all she knew. Thus far Angelique had noted that most men fell into the barbaric, power-hungry, lust-obsessed category, not just Scotsmen. Women's feelings meant nothing to them.

"Why could you not be here, *Maman*?" Angelique whispered to the empty room. Wearing the precious diamond pendant *Maman* had given her, hidden beneath the gown, would make her feel her mother was close in spirit on her wedding day.

106

A knock sounded at the door. Angelique spread the gown upon her bed, wiped her eyes and swung the door open.

Camille rushed in, her cheeks flushed and her breathing elevated. "Lachlan and his men have returned. You wanted me to inform you."

"*Merci.* Where has he been?"

"Visiting a neighboring family—er clan, I mean."

Annoyance flashed through Angelique. "He visited another clan? Without me? He promised to take me. And even if he hadn't promised, it is my right to go."

She well knew he was doing this because she'd refused to allow him into her bed and she would tell him what she thought of that. If not for her, he would own naught but the clothes on his back. He owed everything to her. And he would treat her with more respect!

The door to the chamber burst open and Lachlan barged in, his long, tawny hair loose and windblown, a light of excitement in his gold-brown eyes. He smelled like the fresh outdoors. "M'lady." He bowed deeply and presented her with a bouquet of wildflowers.

"My laird, *merci.*" The mingling scents of daisies, roses and green sap distracted her for a moment, as did his unexpected romantic gift. No man had given her flowers in long time. But maybe that was his intention… to distract her.

"So, the wedding gown has arrived at last." He swept a dramatic hand toward her bed.

"Where have you been?" Angelique asked, returning to the heart of the matter. "Visiting neighboring clans?"

His gaze held a bit of spite when it landed upon her. "Pray pardon, Camille. I need to have a word with *my wife.*"

Angelique did not care for the derisive way he'd said that.

Camille scuttled out the door and closed it behind her. Silence reigned for several moments. The tension was so pervasive Angelique could hardly breathe.

"Well?" she demanded. "Where?"

"Ask nicely and I'll tell you." He bestowed a mock grin.

"Where have you been, my laird?" she asked with the utmost sweetness. She held the bruised flower stems in a stranglehold, wishing to throw them at him.

"Better, but still needs a bit of work. I was visiting with the chiefs of Clan Robertson and Clan Buchanan. They will attend our wedding."

"I have every right to visit neighboring clans with you," she snapped.

"And I have every right to have my wife in my bed at night. We don't always get what we have a right to. Do we, *madame*?"

"If not for me, you would have naught but the sword at your side and your damned plaid."

He surveyed her with a deadly gaze. "And if not for me, Kormad would've already murdered you."

"Hmph. You are a well-paid bodyguard, *monsieur*."

"Or 'haps I am but an expensive stud whose services you cannot handle."

Did he always have to bring sex into everything? Stubborn heartless barbarian. "We lead this clan together. I am the countess!" She flung the bouquet at him. It bounced off his chest, blooms scattering.

He but acknowledged her attack with a blink and a clenching jaw. "And I am the earl. As well as the chief."

"Thanks to me."

"And thanks to King James. As well as my own cunning which garnered the king's favor." One corner of Lachlan's lips quirked up. "I'm glad we both remember how this debacle came about," he said in a dry tone.

He was right of course. Despite being a countess in her own right, she was naught but a woman stripped of any real power. And yet, she refused to give up anything to him. He was merely helping her lead the clan. "I wish to be informed about the clan's affairs."

"I'll inform you. What would you like to know?" he asked with sugary politeness.

"Do not mock me. It is my right to stand beside you and help make decisions that affect the clan and estate. Those men think you alone lead them."

His expression turned serious. "If you undermine my authority, you will only be causing more conflict. Do you wish peace or strife? Have you any inkling how vicious Scots are when a conflict arises? A simple disagreement can turn into a massacre. I don't wish any bloodshed."

"I don't want bloodshed either, but I want to go with you to visit the next clan."

"There is no need. I sent a messenger to invite two other clans to the wedding and the feast. You can meet them then."

"*Très bien*, but I have a right to know what's going on. The disputes, the judgments and agreements. My father would wish it if he were here."

"I'll tell you in private if that's all you wish. But I won't allow you to order me about before my men."

"*Your* men?"

"Aye, the Drummagans are my men now. When you chose me and married me before the king's men and God, you gave me that right." He turned and slammed the door on the way out.

⚜ ❦ ⚜

"M'laird?" The male servant's whiney voice and the scratch on the library door grated on Lachlan's nerves.

"I'm working! I need quiet," Lachlan yelled.

"Aye, m'laird." Footsteps retreated.

Lachlan took another long swallow of sherry. In the candle-light, he squinted at the lines of numbers on the book in front of him. God's blood! He was losing his mind. The laughter in the great hall made him want to take a cannon to it. 'Twas not like him. He used to enjoy revelry. Never had he been in such a despicable mood.

The king's retainers, along with his English friend, Miles, had departed that morning, leaving Lachlan in complete control of the estate and the clan.

Ha! "Control," he muttered. Indeed, he was in command of the men, the clan members, the security of the castle—that was easy—but controlling Angelique and bending her to his wishes was like trying to cuddle a fiendish wildcat.

Then, Rebbie and Dirk had convinced him they all needed a day off because they'd trained hard for a week and the men were too sore to move. Never mind they'd had a reprieve when they'd visited the two other clans. Soft as lasses, they were.

If he couldn't train or travel, then by the saints, he would drink. Anything to take his mind off Angelique, daughter of the devil. He wanted to throttle her! But at the same time, he knew if he got his hands on her pretty, delicate neck he'd be too busy appreciating her smooth, silken skin and end up running his lips over it instead, and down toward the bodice of her dress. Trailing kisses. Biting. Her female scent would fill his nose and he would become intoxicated with it.

109

"Saints!" What would her breasts smell like? Taste like? Lower, between her legs, she would be luscious as a plum tart. Sweet, tangy. He wanted to dine on her whole body, licking, nibbling. His erection growing beneath his kilt, he moaned and poured another finger of sherry.

He hoped she wondered if he had been with another woman the past couple of nights he hadn't spent in his chamber. He hoped like hell she was so jealous she couldn't sleep. Trouble was, it wouldn't matter if ten women were in the room with him at the moment. He wouldn't want any of them... unless one was Angelique.

Lack of sex had turned him into a lunatic and he'd become obsessed with his maddening wife. Once he had her, he'd probably tire of her. At least, he feared he would. But since she was the only woman he'd ever wanted who was able to resist him this long, he knew not what to expect. Without doubt, he was losing his grasp on reality in this pursuit. He didn't even *want* to want her. Blast her! He wished she wasn't so feminine, beautiful and appealing. He wished he could give her nary a thought.

Rebbie and Dirk couldn't understand. No one could, except maybe his brother, Alasdair, but he was too far away to visit, deeper in the Highlands. Of course, Alasdair would probably rub his nose in it and tell him this whole hellish situation was no more than he deserved.

Lachlan let his head drop to the desk. What could he do about Angelique? How could he earn her trust? What would he do if she refused him on their wedding night? He almost dreaded it more than he looked forward to it because he knew what would happen. Another argument. Another fight. And he would go mad. He would fail at being a chief, an earl, and a husband, just as he feared he would.

♦

Angelique dressed in a fine green gown and descended toward the great hall for supper, her two guards behind her. She felt like a prisoner in her own home. They had taken to following her while Lachlan was visiting with the other clans. When she'd ordered them to leave off, they'd said the laird's orders superseded hers. She didn't know whether to curse Lachlan or appreciate his concern for her safety.

In the great hall, she approached high table but no one was

seated.

"Where is the laird?" she asked Fingall.

The steward bowed. "Working in the library, m'lady. He didn't wish to be disturbed."

"What is he working on?" she muttered, striding down the corridor. "Wait here. I wish to speak to the laird alone," she told her guards. Opening the library door, she found Lachlan with his head laid on the desk, his face toward her. Softly, she shut the door and tiptoed closer.

Breathing deep and even, he didn't move. With his eyes closed and his expression relaxed, he looked like a precocious little boy... except for his manly square jaw, beard stubble and those sensual lips. At the moment, he was not trying to seduce her with his calculated, too-knowing eyes. Nor was he angry. She would not mind sitting and staring at him like this for a while. He was indeed pleasing to the eye.

A half empty bottle of sherry sat by his elbow, along with a glass containing a sip.

"Bien entendu," she muttered. Of course, that explained it.

Lachlan jerked awake and sat up. Blinking rapidly, he shook his head as if trying to clear it.

"You are, as they say, cupshoten," she said, enjoying his befuddled expression, a rare sight.

"Nay. 'Twould take more than a wee dram of sherry."

Black ink numbers dotted the side of his face. She snickered, then covered her mouth.

His expression turned most serious. "What?"

She withdrew a clean linen handkerchief from her pocket and dipped it into the sherry. "You have ink on your face."

He glanced down at the books. "Hell, I smeared it."

"Here, let me wipe the ink away." She pressed a palm against one side of his face, his beard stubble prickling her skin, his breath warming her wrist, and wiped at the smudged ink numbers. Her hands tingled from touching him; sensations raced up her arms.

Lachlan gazed at her with sleepy seductive eyes that held a hint of petulance. In that moment, she figured him out. He was naught but a spoiled, overgrown lad used to getting whatever he wanted from the ladies. But not from her, and he didn't know how to handle that. Biting her lip, she suppressed a grin.

"It is time for supper." She dabbed one last ink spot. "There now, all gone."

"I thank you." The unhappy look in his eyes clutched at her heart. He seemed... not himself at all. Not arrogant.

"C'est rien."

"Damnable books." He slammed the ledger closed, rose and paced toward the window.

"What is wrong?"

He stared out the window into the twilight a long moment. "Naught."

"Stubborn," she murmured.

"That's the pot calling the kettle black."

His bitter words made her want to scowl, but she didn't. She knew he was right. Her mother had called her stubborn on more than one occasion. And Lord knew she'd been stubborn with him. But she had no choice.

"So, where have you been these last two nights?" she asked.

He shrugged. "Here and there."

She had peeked into his room each night two or three times. Once, she found him asleep in the early morning hours. Other times she wondered if he had done as she expected and found a paramour. Camille had warned her countless times he would find someone else to slake his lusts, and urged her to go to him. Even though she knew Camille was right, she could not make herself crawl into his bed. Every time she considered it, she froze up, recalling the pain.

She pushed the fear away and focused on something she could control. "Is something wrong with the estate books?"

He released a long breath and turned to her. "I'm good with languages, not numbers."

"Languages?"

"Aye, I can speak and read six languages. Pick them up easily in a short time. But the estate accounts... I simply want to cast them into the fire."

"I am good with numbers," she said, proud of her education and abilities.

"You are?"

She nodded. "My cousin taught me in France."

"Then 'haps you can help me look these over. I'm not sure I trust Fingall, or the treasurer, or a few of the other servants. Anyone who's dealt with the funds."

"I will help you on the morrow. Supper is being served and they are waiting for us."

He exhaled as if tired. "Are you certain you wiped all the ink off my face? If Rebbie sees that, he'll have something else to needle me about."

She suppressed a grin, but feared he noticed it anyway when his gaze sharpened on her. "*Oui*, it is clean," she said. At times like this she could actually see herself enjoying being in Lachlan's company. Not because he was in a surly mood, but because he was showing her he could be real and humble... and a bit unsure of himself—the way she felt all the time. "What is Rebbie needling you about?"

"What do you think?" He gave her an accusatory look.

"Oh." Her face heated. "Well, that is none of his concern."

"Do you think he cares? He's the nosiest man on God's earth."

"He is not married so he cannot possibly understand."

Lachlan snorted. "I doubt every married couple is like us."

"Probably not."

"Likely, we are bizarre beyond measure."

She glared at him. Did he have to exaggerate everything?

"What?" he asked. "I tell you true."

A crash sounded in the far corner of the room... from the crack between the stones. Someone lurked in the hidden passage behind the room.

CHAPTER EIGHT

Angelique dashed toward the break between the stones, the same one where she'd eavesdropped on Lachlan and Rebbie several nights ago. "Who is there?" She peered into the crack. No candlelight escaped.

Silence. Sickening shivers covered her.

"What the hell is going on?" Lachlan stood at her elbow.

"Someone was listening to us."

"How?"

"See the crack between the stones? It is wide enough to see and hear through. There is a hidden passage behind this room."

"God's blood! Why did you not tell me?" He turned a dark scowl on her.

"I... I'd forgotten." She had wanted to keep the passage a secret so she could eavesdrop on Lachlan again, but if a traitor was using it, that would no longer be safe.

"How does one enter the passage?"

"I shall show you when we have more time." She headed toward the exit and he followed.

"Aye. You must show me all the hidden passages and entrances to them. 'Tis vital to the safety of the clan. And our home."

"Who do you think was listening?" she whispered.

"'Haps Fingall, the treasurer, or any of their cohorts. I hate to say it, but we cannot trust our own clan."

৵৹ঌ ঌৡ৹

114

After supper when the fiddler struck up a lively jig and most of the clan was busy watching the lasses dance, Lachlan escorted Angelique to her sitting room. He had to find out more about this secret passage and who had been spying on them. Their four personal bodyguards followed but waited outside in the corridor.

"Is it safe to talk in this room without anyone eavesdropping?" he whispered in her ear.

"Oui." She drew back and appeared to stifle a shiver. Her eyes were darker green when they met his. "I'll show you the easiest way to enter the secret passageway."

Carrying a candle, he followed her to his bedchamber. "You jest. My room?"

"Indeed. 'Tis the laird's bedchamber, after all." She barred the door from inside. "My great-grandfather had the newer section of the castle designed this way so he could keep an eye on his guests." She moved a stone from the base of the hearth, then pressed a lever. Metal clanged behind the tapestry.

He had not even thought to lift the tapestry to see what was behind it.

"Have a care with the candle." She burrowed behind the heavy tapestry. After lighting another candle on his mantel, he followed, holding the material out like a tent.

He had his sword sheathed at his side, as well as a small dirk, in the event they ran into the clan traitors.

She pushed open the door.

"Allow me to lead since I have the candle." He ducked his head and took a step down onto the steep stone stairs, barely wide enough for a man his size to squeeze through. Debris crunched beneath his boots. He enjoyed the feel of Angelique's hand lying lightly on his shoulder for support as she crept behind him downward into the depths of darkness. But that was the only appealing thing about the situation. Hell, he did not like this eerie place. He carefully unsheathed his sword and held it at the ready.

"Could someone sneak up this way and murder me in my sleep?" he whispered, imagining a horrid scenario.

"No." Angelique said quietly, close to his ear. Her warm breath fanning his hair sent a curl of arousal through him. "No one can open the door from this side... at least not without making a lot of noise. Which would wake you, no? We left it open and that is the only reason we can go back through. Only one of the passage doors opens from this side and it is in the armory."

"Ah. 'Tis a good thing then." On the next tread, his foot landed on something. He sidestepped it and lowered the candle. "What the devil is this? A fire poker?" He pushed at it with his toe to see it better. "Is that mine? I noticed it was missing and had one of the servants bring me another."

"I do not... know." Angelique whispered, sounding a bit unnerved.

"Careful you don't step on it." They reached the bottom of the stairs and the passage stretched ahead, how far he couldn't tell. Pitch blackness surrounded them beyond the candle's glow.

"The castle's finest guest bedchamber is on the other side of this wall," she whispered. "And here is the fissure to look through."

"Your ancestors spied on their guests in bed?"

"I suppose so. Several Stuart kings and queens have slept in that room, even our own King James many years ago. Dukes, an assortment of earls and other nobility have also stayed here. Did your clan have nothing like this to spy on guests?"

"Nay." 'Haps his clan was too trusting.

"Go a few yards more and you will be behind the library."

Lachlan moved forward. "Aha. Look at that." He had intentionally left a candle burning on the library mantel, and indeed near the whole room was visible through the horizontal opening.

"Further along and up more steps are the spy holes to the great hall. Hear the faint music?"

"Aye. But where are the other entrances to this passage?" he asked.

"As I mentioned, one is in the armory—an exit doorway concealed behind a weapons display. Another entry is in the treasury room, hidden behind a tapestry. This passage also leads to tunnels that run beneath the estate."

"Where do they come out?"

"I do not know. When I was a child, they had locked iron gates across them, and beyond was dark. Perhaps the exit is concealed from the outside and would only be used in dire circumstances for the chief and his family's escape. Almost no one had access to this passage back then, or even knew about it."

"Well, someone does now. We need to find out which entrance this person uses and try to catch him entering or leaving. If he listened to our earlier conversation, he knows I suspect someone of tampering with the books."

"Oui."

"Let's go back now. I'll investigate more on my own or with a man I know I can trust. I don't wish to endanger you further."

"I am not endangered." She sounded insulted. "I explored these often as a child."

"You're a brave lass. But there's a traitor about now." The passage was too narrow for him to maneuver around her. "You must lead on the way back. Take the candle." She moved along quickly and climbed the stairs. He took two steps up and accidentally bumped into her derriere. She gasped and dropped the candle. The flame sputtered out and cast them in absolute blackness.

"Merde!"

He laid a hand on her shoulder and caressed her neck. "Shh. Don't fash yourself. Stay calm."

"It is dark as a dungeon," she said in French, her breathing escalating.

"I can see that. Now, slowly take one step up at a time and we shall make it out."

"Très bien." She did just that, as did he, his palm flat against the rough stone wall for support.

A sound of metal against stone clanged behind them. They froze. He turned sideways, staring back, but saw naught, not even a glimmer of light. Silence followed. If he'd been alone, he would've crept through the darkness to see who was there, but he wouldn't jeopardize Angelique.

"What was that?" she said in a near inaudible whisper.

He faced forward again, his mouth and nose bumping into what felt like her cheek. She released a breath but did not draw away. That soft, smooth skin and the sweet woman scent of her made him forget where he was. He brushed his lips over her again, inhaling.

Her lashes fluttered, tickling his nose. "Oh." The sound was no more than a breath from her.

His next contact was lips against lips; she'd turned to face him more. Arousal blasted through him like a trumpet. In an attempt to draw her closer, he almost dropped his sword but managed to hold onto it and slide his other hand around her lower back. And, saints, when her arms encircled his neck, he thought he would die with happiness and lust. She wanted him.

Without a protest from her, he ate at her mouth, nibbled her lips and slipped his tongue between. Her unique flavor drove him mad and he wanted to drown in her. She shyly touched her tongue to his, giving him a pleasurable rise beneath his plaid. *Iosa is Muire Mhàthair!* He could take her right here.

Footsteps registered in the back of his mind. A shock of alarm smothering his desire, he turned his head abruptly, breaking the kiss. "Listen," he whispered. Faint footsteps receded into the distance, then a door closed.

More silence.

Who the hell was that?

Angelique continued up the steps and he followed, one thing on his mind... nay, three. Another kiss. Undressing her. Dragging her into his bed.

Once they passed through the door, he closed it and pushed from beneath the tapestry. He squinted against the brightness of the candle remaining on his mantel. Angelique replaced the stone in the hearth, and he sheathed his sword.

Despite the danger, his first instinct was to seduce Angelique; she was in his bedchamber, after all. But on second thought, 'haps this was not the best course of action. Every time he'd tried that, she'd become angry and launched into an argument. A slower approach might lead to success. She would let down her guard. Aye, he had to convince her to like him first—and not fear him— then she would want him in her bed every night. He would teach her to love sensuality and sex, at her own pace. She had said she wanted honesty and seduction. He could give her that.

"How will we discover who was down there?" she asked.

"I don't know yet. Leave it to me." Damned if his need for her wasn't overriding his common sense. He could scarcely think at the moment. Celibacy did that to him.

"Why are you looking at me like that?" Her gaze communicated warning. His lust must be showing. After a kiss like that, how could she blame him?

He inhaled deeply and tried to change his expression. "Like what?"

After a suspicious glance, she removed the bar from the door. *"Bonsoir, monsieur."*

"Lachlan," he corrected.

"Lachlan." Her accent caressed his name in a most arousing way. He considered changing his mind about delaying the seduction, but then she was gone, flitting out the door and closing it behind her.

He cursed.

Though frustrated, he thought his new plan might be ingenious. For once he was using his head instead of his... He stared down at his erection, straining to tent the plaid behind his sporran. "Just be patient, lad. Not much longer."

Besides, he should be focused on discovering the identity of the traitor in the passage.

୬ଓଓ ଓଡ଼୬

The next day, Lachlan again trained with the men all morning but he could think of naught but meeting Angelique in the remodeled solar to go over the books. He had gone daft in truth, calf-eyed, like his brother had been over an Englishwoman the last time he'd seen him. Even the arrival of the Clan Buchanan chief, his family, and entourage could not sway Lachlan's thoughts. He caught himself staring at his beautiful... nay, irritating wife during midday meal, and missed part of the conversation going on around him.

Once the Buchanans were settled into guest quarters for a bit of rest after their travels, Lachlan headed to the solar.

Angelique stood at the edge of the large window, staring out and waiting for him. He wanted to smile but didn't for fear she would become annoyed again. For some reason, she seemed to smile more when he was in a dark mood. Clearly she didn't wish him happy.

"Here you are, Angelique."

She turned. "The sky is lovely today. So blue, and the clouds look like great piles of clean, white wool."

"Aye." He carried two straight chairs and placed them before the desk at the window. Afternoon light flowed in. "But you are lovelier."

Pink colored her cheeks and her gaze skipped away. *"Merci."* She took her seat and he sat down close beside her.

"You're certain no one can spy on us here?" He drew in a breath of her subtle rose scent, wishing he could bury his nose in her hair.

"No. Before the wing containing our suites was constructed,

this was the chief's bedchamber. He had no reason to spy on himself."

"Ah. That makes perfect sense." Of course, he knew what early solars were used for because Kintalon, his clan's castle deep in the Highlands, had a similar structure.

"But my father did have this large window added so he could look down on the grounds and enjoy this view."

"'Tis very nice." Within the bailey walls, several of the servants went about their daily chores below them. Above the green trees, brownish, heather-covered mountains rose in the distance, to the north. That way lay MacGrath holdings and his home, which he had not seen in several months. But... nay, now his home was here, with Angelique. Each day he was growing to love this place more. The landscape here was lusher and the weather warmer than in the more northerly Highlands. The Drummagans had accepted him as their chief, and Angelique was slowly warming to him. Very slowly. Still, he was making progress.

His bare leg below his kilt nudged hers through the material of her skirts. Sparks of sexual awareness ignited within him. He yearned to feel her smooth bare leg sliding against his. Nay, wrapped around his waist... while he stood, pinning her against the wall. Saints! What an image. He had only to be in the same room with her to get hard, but with fantasies like that, his frustration mounted. His tarse thought he had lost all seduction ability.

Angelique drew her leg away. Hmm, maybe she'd felt that spark, too. He opened the account books and turned to the appropriate page.

"Oh, what a beautiful horse!"

Lachlan followed Angelique's gaze out the window to the far left, over a wall. One of the groomsmen led a saddled white horse across the courtyard to the stables.

"You have a fondness for white horses?"

"*Oui*, I had one in France—Blanche—but had to leave her behind. She was very affectionate and fleet of foot."

As she focused on the horse, Angelique's tender, longing expression arrested Lachlan, for he had never seen that look in her eyes before. In that moment, he knew he would strive to give her anything she wanted.

"I have never ridden a white horse. Too visible at night," he murmured so she wouldn't suspect his intentions. He would find the owner and see if he could buy the horse, or one like it, for Angelique. Though she'd laughed at his expense last night, when he'd had ink on his face, seeing her smile and giggle had been worth it. Her face alight with amusement and happiness did bizarre things to him inside... things he did not understand or want to examine. A horse would be the perfect wedding gift for her; it would make her happy.

"As to the books," he said. "I tried to repair this where I smudged it. You see?"

The horse now disappeared from sight within the stables, she lowered her gaze to the ledger. "It is clear enough."

He explained what each row represented in the way of estate income and expenses.

"That is a lot of expensive Italian Vernage." She pointed to the figure.

"Aye, bought only three months ago and I have yet to see drop of it."

"Perhaps that wine has not yet arrived."

"It has been checked off on the inventory." He flipped through his stack of papers for the correct one. "Here." He showed her the document.

"Maybe the servants, clansmen or even Kormad's men drank it before we arrived."

"Aye. Or 'haps no one drank it because it never existed."

They analyzed the books for more than an hour and she took notes of problems they ran into. Not only were things listed as paid for which he had not found on the estate, but many of the additions were wrong.

"Surely Fingall cannot be worse at numbers and calculations than I am," Lachlan said. "Should be his specialty."

"Indeed."

He sighed. "I hate to release him from his duties. 'Tis a hereditary position. He told me the males of his line have held *Am Fear Sporain* for over two hundred years within the Drummagan clan."

"But he is robbing us blind," she said. "And I do not think it is simply that he is unskilled at calculations."

Lachlan nodded. "We shall question him."

"Both of us?"

"Aye."

Angelique's gaze warmed and softened upon him, as if she might actually like him for this one moment in time. The look he'd so yearned to see on her face. Arousal flowed through him like warm honey. But any move he made might drive her away or make her revert back to her old animosity. Though she hadn't last night on the dark stair.

Watching him, she lifted a hand and tucked a lock of his hair behind his ear. The simple gesture riveted him and became more sensual than it should've been. He caught her hand and briefly kissed her wrist as her hand slipped through his.

Her eyes grew round for a few seconds before she averted her gaze. He made no other movements. God, he loved her touch. His skin still tingled from the stroke of her silken fingertips. And the fragrance from her wrist—roses and woman—remained in his senses, intoxicating him.

He imagined her crawling onto his lap, kissing him deeply and yanking their clothing aside. Near attacking him. Aye, right here in the solar, he wanted to take her, gently pushing into her, inch by torturous inch. She would be small and tight. Drenched, whimpering and moaning for him. But he would go slow and make her wait. Make her beg for more, faster, deeper.

She faced him again. He did not know what she saw in his eyes, but her breath hitched and her eyes darkened. *Do not look away*, he wanted to tell her.

He leaned forward and pressed his lips to hers. It was almost a chaste kiss, so simple and innocent. So different from the desire rampaging through him. She closed her eyes. Hesitantly, her lips moved beneath his. He cradled her face in his hand, stroked her brow.

The tip of her tongue briefly touched his upper lip. A renewed surge of arousal shot through him. Wanting to devour her, he quelled his instinctive response which might have frightened her away. He was rewarded with another brush of her tongue. Damn, did this Frenchie know how to kiss. Her tentative movements were the most arousing he had ever experienced.

He responded in kind, but more briefly than she had. She seemed to hold her breath. Again he flicked his tongue at the underside of her upper lip, then away.

She gasped and buried her fingers in his plaid and his hair, drawing him closer. *Aye, lass, take what you need.* With more subtle movements, he teased her with his tongue. She accepted each kiss, and came back for more, provoking him.

A distant yell reached his ears but he didn't care. Someone whistled.

Jerking away from him, she faced the window. *"Merde."* She jumped up and hurried from the room. Several clansmen and servants stood outside, staring up at him with huge grins.

"Do you not ken how to give anyone privacy?" he yelled at them through the glass.

They scurried away.

"Aye, run now, you bastards." Now that they'd frightened Angelique away and ruined any chance he had of getting what he wanted most. His body was on fire with wanting her, his shaft standing stiff as a pike. "Saints!" He smashed a fist onto the desk and rose.

"Patience," he muttered, inhaling deeply. At least Angelique was starting to like and trust him a bit more. He must nurture that. Not much longer until their wedding.

So as to avoid the men in the great hall, he exited down the back stairs and strode to the stables.

"I saw you leading a white horse earlier. Whose is it?" Lachlan asked the young groomsman.

"The Lady Robertson arrived on it, m'laird."

"Aha. I thank you."

After looking the mare over and finding her strong and healthy, Lachlan found Chief Robertson standing before the fireplace in the great hall and asked him about the animal.

The tall, stout man was dressed in the Lowland style, and sported a full beard. "My wife would have my head if I sold her favorite mare." He grinned. "But we have two more white mares if you'd like to look at them sometime."

"Indeed, I would." A horse would be a wonderful wedding gift for Angelique, even if it was a few days late.

He would make her like him or die trying.

༺ ❧ ༻

Angelique stood impatiently in her chamber as the maids assisted in putting the many pieces of her wedding gown on her. Camille directed. The gown was scratchy, and a bit too large besides, requiring that portions of it be altered. After the maids had styled her hair with elaborate, coiled braids, Camille placed a wreath of wild white roses and dried white heather upon her head.

Unfortunately, Angelique was not enjoying this as much as she'd dreamed she would at fifteen. She had slept little last night as she'd overseen the final preparations for both the wedding and the feast. Even when she had gone to bed, nerves had kept her awake. Today the celebration had started early with breakfast for all the guests, then the dancing had commenced.

She was relieved in some ways that she and Lachlan had already married, otherwise she'd be far more nervous. But of course, she dreaded tonight when she'd have to deliver on her promise to sleep with him. Her breathing seized and she grew a bit lightheaded. *Put it from your mind and get through the day first.*

Minutes later, Heckie escorted her down the front steps and across the cobbled bailey. She was glad for his sturdy arm supporting her for her knees wobbled. *I must be strong.* She thought of the diamond pendant hidden beneath the dress, dangling between her breasts. This gift from her mother would give her strength. She imagined *Maman*, in her angelic form, gazing down and smiling. A slight calmness enveloped her.

They followed the Drummagan piper. The shrill notes of the bagpipes stabbed at her ears. Smiling clansmen and women, along with people from the nearby village, lined both sides of the pathway, bowing, curtsying, shouting out well-wishes. She plastered a smile on her face and nodded to them. Before she was ready, she and her escort entered the small stone kirk within Draughon's exterior curtain walls.

Her stomach knotted when she saw that every pew of the chapel was packed full. All rose when she stopped at the threshold. The huge stained glass window, which she'd always loved, glowed with brilliant colors in the sunlight. Lachlan stood before it in his Highland finery. But his belted plaid did not draw her attention; his smile did.

She knew what he was happy about... the marriage bed that she'd promised him this night. She lowered her gaze, her hands shaking at the very thought of lying naked with him. She had seen what he had to offer and she feared he would hurt her terribly when he forced his way inside her. She cringed, remembering the helplessness she'd felt when Girard had invaded her and taken away her right to choose.

Camille, standing up beside her as maid of honor, gave her a reassuring smile when she reached the front.

Lachlan took her right hand in his. "You're lovely," he whispered.

You are, too, she wanted to say, but could do naught but offer him a brief, wobbly smile. Her mouth was so dry she feared she would not be able to utter a word. Her white gloves prevented her from feeling the warmth of his roughened skin as she had during their first ceremony. She missed that small comfort.

As the minister recited the ceremony, Angelique grew more aware of the many Drummagan clan members and other clan chiefs behind them, witnessing their lives being bound together.

This time when Lachlan kissed her, she was ashamed to realize she welcomed his lips on hers and his tongue flitting into places it shouldn't with dozens of people looking on. If only the marriage bed involved kissing and not...coupling, she would be happy.

Smiling, Lachlan tucked her hand around his elbow and they rushed down the aisle toward the exit. Outside, pistols fired toward the sky in a salute and the kirk bells rang out. A cheer went up from the guests and grain showered down upon them as they raced across the stone courtyard. Angelique could not help but join in the happiness. Before she realized it, she was laughing.

Lachlan abruptly picked her up and kissed her again. Heavens! A brief but potent kiss. The crowd grew louder at this spectacle, with more shouts, whistles and laughter. She could not take her gaze from his smiling face as he carried her up the castle steps. At the threshold, one of the clanswomen gifted Angelique with a basket filled with bread and cheese. Lachlan then carried her into the great hall and set her in her garland decorated chair at high table, then sat beside her. Yes, he was having a grand old time, blast him. But so was she.

⟊⟊⟊

"M'laird, Kormad is at the gates, demanding entrance," Bryson whispered in Lachlan's ear where he sat at high table during the wedding feast.

The bastard had a lot of nerve. "You jest," Lachlan murmured low so no one else would overhear.

Bryson shook his head, his dark eyes most serious.

With the noisy celebration, music, and dancing going on, no one seemed to notice the interruption. "I'll be right back," Lachlan told Angelique, seated beside him, then followed Bryson to a more private area. "How many men with him?"

"About a dozen."

"Are they dressed for fighting?"

"Nay."

"Have Rebbie and Dirk meet me outside. Don't tell them why. And don't let any of the other guests nor my wife ken of this."

"Aye, m'laird."

"Send ten archers onto the roof."

Bryson nodded and hastened away.

Two of Lachlan's personal bodyguards followed him through the exit. He peered beyond the courtyard toward the gates. The sun was setting, casting Kormad and his party in silhouette outside the gates. Several Drummagan guards stood firm on this side.

"What's this about?" Rebbie asked, joining him. Dirk and the rest of the men filed onto the castle steps.

"We have uninvited guests." Lachlan nodded toward the gate. "Kormad, with a dozen men."

The chief of Clan Buchanan shouldered his way into the small space. "Is Kormad looking for trouble?" he asked in a gruff voice.

"We don't ken yet. They're not wearing armor."

"Appearances can be deceiving."

"Indeed."

Several more men joined them, Drummagans and men from the other clans, all carrying swords or pistols. En masse, they approached the gates.

"Kormad, how kind of you to pay us a visit," Lachlan said, staring hard into Kormad's malevolent dark eyes.

"MacGrath—er, I guess I should call you Draughon now since you're the earl—good to see you again." His sneer didn't pass for a smile. "I wasn't invited to your weddin' feast. I'm hurt."

"I didn't ken you were yet returned from London," Lachlan said, pretending he didn't know who had rained arrows upon them and injured Dirk.

"I posted some of my men here to keep the Drummagan clan and Draughon Castle safe until a new laird arrived. I'm wonderin' what happened to them. Are they in your dungeon...or dead?"

"Neither. I sent your men home to you with a message. Did you not receive it?"

Kormad was silent a moment, frowning, his gaze darting

about before landing on Lachlan again. "What message?"

"The leader of your men refused us entrance. I challenged him to a duel and won. But I let him live so he could tell you that if you wish to possess Draughon Castle, you would have to come and try to claim it yourself. Is that what you've come for?"

Kormad eyed Lachlan, then the men behind him—several powerful men including another earl, a baron, and three chiefs. Not to mention all their bodyguards and the armed Drummagans.

Kormad laughed, fake and loud. "Nay. Of course not. My men were acting under their own foolish notions. I never told them to keep you or Lady Angelique out, only outlaws so the castle wouldn't be looted."

"Well, I thank you for your concern. The castle is safe and in good hands now. You and your men are welcome to partake of the feast if you turn over all your weapons."

Kormad hesitated. "I thank you for your hospitality, but I must be on my way. I only returned yesterday and I have much work to do."

"I'm sure you do." *More plotting and conniving.*

"A good eve to you, Draughon. And congratulations again on your marriage."

"I thank you."

Kormad and his men mounted, turned their horses about and rode away.

"You should take one of his men or family members hostage. That would keep him in line," the Buchanan said.

"He doesn't give a damn about his men," Rebbie said. "I wager that's why they ran away when you sent them packing, rather than face him with failure."

Lachlan nodded. "Without doubt."

"That one bears close watching," Buchanan said and returned inside. Most of the other men followed.

Lachlan called Bryson aside. "See that all guards are at their posts. Tell me immediately if you see aught amiss."

"Aye, m'laird."

Lachlan mounted the steps.

"I'll stay out here and keep watch," Dirk said, standing by the portal, his left arm in a sling and a sword in his right hand.

"You'll do no such thing," Lachlan said. "You're still recovering from that arrow. Only last night you had fever."

127

Dirk cast a suspicious glance about in the gloaming and lowered his voice. "How do you ken you can trust all the Drummagans? You don't even ken what kind of men some of them are."

"I don't trust them. All we can do is be on guard at all times 'til they prove their loyalty." Nay, indeed, he suspected some of them were stealing from Draughon's coffers.

Dirk nodded. "Still, I'll stay out here a while. 'Tis too loud in there."

The wild, wary look in Dirk's eyes concerned Lachlan. "Do you ken something you're not telling me?"

"Nay. I just don't like the feel of the air."

৩৫ ৩৫

Trying to ignore Lachlan's large warm hand lying on her shoulder as they sat together at high table, Angelique tugged the red satin ribbon, releasing the bow of the tartan wrapped gift. Two silver and brass, jewel-encrusted daggers lay within, one large and one small.

"How lovely!" she said, running the pads of her fingers over the smooth rubies and emeralds studding the hilts of each. The sheaths were also decorated in the same manner.

"Rebbie, you bastard." Lachlan grinned. "I cannot accept my portion of this gift."

"You don't like it? Well then, 'haps I'll send it to Miles."

"Nay, 'twould be sacrilege! I thank you, Rebbie." Lachlan shook his friend's hand with much enthusiasm. "You are too generous by far."

She passed the daggers to Lachlan, then decided to keep her own. "*Merci*, Laird Rebbinglen. You honor us with this gift."

"My pleasure, *madame*. I thought you might need something to help fight off this rogue."

The men guffawed at that.

Angelique's face felt scalded and she wondered if they knew exactly how hard she had fought him off. And now feared her reprieve was over. Turning her attention to the next gift, she untied the bow around a carved oak box and lifted the lid. Two silver goblets rested inside on dark green velvet. "Oh." She removed one. An oval onyx stone and an engraved dragon decorated the side.

She had seen and touched this custom-made goblet before. In France. *Girard.* A sensation like ice water trickled through her body and she could scarce breathe. She glanced about the hall, skimming the dozens of faces. Where was he? Where was Girard?

CHAPTER NINE

"What's wrong?" Lachlan murmured in Angelique's ear.

The goblet slipped from her fingers and he caught it.

"Who is this gift from?" she whispered, her gaze darting into the back corners of the hall. No tall, vicious dark-haired man. No card or note inside the box.

"Who shall we thank for this lovely gift?" Lachlan asked the large group filling the great hall.

Murmuring followed and several heads shook. Some distance away, Camille's face paled.

Angelique's hands trembled and nausea rose within her. Lachlan took the box from her and passed it to a servant.

Mère de Dieu. Girard had come to kill her.

"What happened to the music?" Lachlan called, motioning to the musicians. "Dance, everyone. Excuse us." He rose and held his hand down to Angelique. "Come," he said to her in a low voice. "I'm thinking you need a break from all the celebrating."

She searched for Girard as Lachlan led her to the nearby solar. He lit candles and checked the room for guests. She had to speak with Camille immediately. Neither of them was safe.

"What upset you so much about the goblets?" Lachlan asked, stopping before her. His tone was compassionate, but his amber eyes fierce. "You turned pale as a banshee and looked terrified of a sudden."

As if he might see the answer in her eyes, she lowered her gaze and shook her head. "Nothing."

"Don't lie to me, Angelique. I promised I wouldn't lie to you, and I expect you to promise me the same."

She squeezed her eyes closed, fear climbing within her. "I cannot tell you."

"Why?" he asked, his tone harsher now.

She could not trust him with her deepest secrets. "I can only say... I have seen the goblets before. They were custom-made for a certain family. And the person who owned them is... not a nice person."

"Is he French or English?" Lachlan demanded.

"French."

"And you last saw the goblets in France?"

"Oui."

"What was this man to you?" Lachlan's voice was now that of a hardened warrior.

Her heart lurched. If she wasn't careful he would figure it out on his own. "I did not say this was a man."

"You also failed to correct me when I asked if *he* was French or English."

"I cannot tell you."

"Cannot or will not?"

She could not think what to say and wished only to escape this room and his questioning. During the silence, Lachlan inhaled a deep breath as if tired. Or perhaps he was trying to calm his anger.

"You can tell me anything, Ange," he continued, his voice gentler now. "I am your husband. We will have no secrets between us."

She shook her head, unable to trust anyone with her horrid secrets, save Camille.

"After I have protected you this long, you still refuse to trust me?" He sounded perplexed, perhaps even a bit hurt.

"I trust you to protect me," she whispered. Indeed, she did for he was a strong, skilled warrior.

Lachlan paced. "So, since the goblets are here, I assume that means this man who is not so nice is here in our home. Aye?" Pausing, he looked to her for confirmation.

"I did not see him; he might have sent someone."

"Are you thinking the gift is a message?"

"Perhaps."

"What does the message mean?"

She was silent. But inside, she was screaming. The message meant something too horrible to utter.

"Angelique, if you don't tell me what is happening, or what happened in the past, I cannot protect you and our clan. Is this man dangerous?"

"*Oui*, very dangerous."

"What has he done?"

No, she could not reveal that. At her continued silence, he sighed.

"Why are you making this so damned difficult? The whole clan could be in danger at this very moment."

Perhaps she could tell him a bit. "His name is Girard. Guy Laurent, *comte de* Girard... a very dangerous man."

"What does he look like?" Lachlan's gaze became piercing, like that of a golden eagle ready to strike a rabbit with his talons.

"Tall and thin with dark hair. He used to have a mustache and short beard." She moved toward the exit.

"What did he do? Why is he here?"

"That is all I can tell you... but indeed, he is extremely dangerous. He wishes to see me and Camille dead." She yanked open the door and ran to find her cousin.

Lachlan yelled a curse behind her. She dashed up the stairs to her sitting room where Camille waited.

"Where have you been?" Camille grabbed her arm. They raced into the bedchamber.

Angelique slammed the door and barred it from intruders. "Lachlan questioned me about the goblets," she whispered, her voice shaking.

"What did you tell him?"

Knees weak, she lowered herself to the settle. "That they must be from Girard and he is dangerous. I gave him a description. That is all. I cannot tell him about..."

"What will Lachlan do?"

"I do not know. Increase security, I assume."

"He will not give up until he knows the whole story."

Angelique's stomach pained her. "I know. But what if Girard is here? Either inside the castle or waiting outside the walls?"

Camille knelt before the hearth and stirred at the glowing fire coals with a poker, sending sparks shooting upwards. "We should have made sure the viper was dead when we had the chance." She almost growled the words.

"We are not murderers."

"No, we are not. But the bastard deserves to die. It would be justice."

.യുള ളൈ.

After Lachlan made sure Angelique entered her guarded chambers, he headed toward the great hall. He would find this Girard or his messenger. The bastard would not get away with invading his home and frightening his wife. Damnation, but she vexed him when she refused to reveal the whole truth to him. Why did she mistrust him?

"My laird," called a female voice from the shadows.

He halted, hand on his sword hilt, his gaze searching the dark corners of the corridor.

Eleanor stepped from behind a column and smiled. "Would you like to practice your swordplay skills?"

"What the hell are you doing here?"

"Surprised?"

"Aye. How did you gain entrance?"

She giggled. "Your guards were easily swayed with a glimpse of my noble cleavage."

He ignored the way she thrust her breasts toward him, jeweled pendants and necklaces dandling about them, her bodice barely covering her nipples. "Who did you travel with?"

"No one but my servants."

"You must go. I'm married now." He headed toward the great hall, determined to find out the implications of the mysterious gift and search for the French knave.

When he glanced back, Eleanor was gone. He despised it when the past came back to haunt him. He motioned to his friends and Bryson, then led them to the solar. Once they were inside, he posted a guard and closed the door.

"We have a problem," Lachlan said in a low voice.

"Another one?" Rebbie asked.

"Aye. Angelique and I have good reason to think a dangerous Frenchman is here, a nobleman named Guy Laurent, *comte de* Girard. Somehow he sent her a wedding gift, the goblets. And it could be a veiled message or threat. Angelique said the man wanted to kill her and Camille."

"Damnation! What does he look like?" Rebbie asked.

"Tall and lean with dark hair, perhaps a mustache and beard. He may be in disguise. I haven't yet determined why he is here, but he poses a serious threat to Angelique. We must protect her at all costs."

"If we find any Frenchmen, we'll detain them," Bryson said.

"Good. Increase security tonight. Allow no one else inside the walls. I want all the guards to watch the guests carefully. Tomorrow, the guests we do not know well will need to be sent on their way."

"Aye, m'laird." Bryson bowed, took the other clansmen and left.

"Rebbie, Dirk." Lachlan closed the door. "Eleanor is here."

"Who?"

"An English countess who does not need to be here. I don't trust her."

"Oh, a lady you dallied with?" Rebbie grinned.

"Aye. Angelique kens of our association. She's jealous, and I don't want Eleanor causing trouble between Angelique and me."

Dirk frowned. "What do you want us to do about it?"

"Distract her. Seduce her. I don't care so long as 'tis not a hanging offense. Tomorrow we'll send her away, as well, along with most everyone else."

"Are you thinking we want your castoffs?" Rebbie asked.

"You haven't complained before."

His friends scowled at that.

"Besides, she's a widow, deprived, eager, and quite adventurous in the bedchamber. She has dark hair, fancy clothing, jewels, and large breasts. You'll spot her easy enough."

"You take her," Rebbie told Dirk.

"Nay, you."

"You're acting like a couple of green lads. She is a wanton and she's looking for a man. Why are you complaining?" Lachlan passed them on the way to the door. "Now, by the saints, 'tis time for my wedding night."

"You'd think 'twas his first time," Rebbie scoffed.

"If you don't mind, please make sure Eleanor isn't hiding in my rooms. She had a habit of that in London."

Moments later, after a detour to the kitchens for a fresh bottle of Brabant, Lachlan knocked at Angelique's bedchamber door.

"Who is it?" Camille called.

"'Tis me. Lachlan."

Camille opened the door a crack and peered out.

"Is Angelique well?" he asked.

She glanced back.

Angelique whispered in French in the background. Something about telling him she was ill. While Camille was distracted, he pushed his way inside.

"You are unwell, Angelique?" he asked.

Her eyes wide, his wife drew back, further away from him. Was she frightened of him?

"Monsieur?" Camille's voice rose in concern.

"I wish to speak to my wife alone."

"Camille, stay." Angelique's voice was uneven, panicked.

Lachlan's glare shifted from his wife to her companion, and he hoped his meaning was clear. Besides, he would tolerate no more lies, about illness or aught else.

"Ange, pardonnez-moi. I shall wait in the sitting room," Camille said and hastened out.

Wise lass. He closed the door and barred it.

Angelique stood stiff by the fire, her face blanched. Fists clenched.

Just what he needed—someone terrifying his wife on their official wedding night. It would take every shred of his seduction skills to calm her now.

"You are ill? What is amiss?" he asked in a calm voice, glad to see she had changed into a lacy smock and silk wrap.

"My stomach is queasy and upset."

"I'm sure 'tis only nerves…and completely understandable. I have increased security throughout the castle. All the clansmen are guarding and looking for this Girard knave or any Frenchmen."

"Very good."

"I told you from the first I would protect you and I mean to," he said in what he hoped was his most soothing voice. "There is naught to worry about now. You're safe."

"Merci." She gave a stiff curtsey and watched him with suspicious eyes.

He placed the wine on a table by the settle, then slowly moved toward her and held out his hands. Hesitantly, she took them. He kissed her bare fingers, savoring the feel of her smooth, cool skin.

Too cool. He had to distract her from her fears.

"Come." He led her to the settle close to the fire. When she tried to sit on the opposite end, he tugged and she toppled to his lap. She tried to scramble away but he held her tight.

"Shh. All is well. We are not in bed. I just wish you to sit here for a moment so I can talk to you."

She perched rigidly on his lap, holding her breath.

"Take a deep breath, love, afore you pass out."

She flicked a glare at him but did as he asked, inhaling audibly.

"Good. Just relax. I'm doing naught but sitting here...and drinking wine." He uncorked the bottle of Brabant and offered it to her.

She took a delicate sip.

"More." He did not wish to get her sotted, but she did need the heat of it in her veins to calm her a wee bit.

Once she'd had three sips, he took a hearty swallow of the delectable honey and clove flavored wine, then returned it to the table by his elbow.

Taking his time, he feasted his eyes upon her beauty. Her flawless ivory skin was still far too pale, and her vivid green eyes too wide and fearful. Her lips, which he craved, were dark pink and lush. And her flaming ginger-colored hair remained in tight coiled braids, as it had been during the ceremony. He yearned to run his fingers through her silken curls and spread them upon a pillow. He almost cursed at the powerful arousal hardening his shaft and tensing his muscles, but he held his tongue. First, he would help her calm down and forget her troubles. 'Twas his responsibility to ensure she enjoyed their wedding night as much as he would.

"You were exceptionally lovely today, as you are now," he murmured, stroking her palm.

"*Merci,*" she whispered.

"And how do I look?"

Her expression moved from surprise to the beginning of a grin. "Lovely."

"Och. Lovely? I was thinking you might say handsome or dashing."

The hint of amusement in her eyes grew a fraction.

"What say you?" he asked.

"*Oui.* You are...handsome, my laird." Her skin now glowed pink in the firelight—far better than her earlier ashen color.

"Lachlan," he corrected.

She turned away. "*Oui*, Lachlan."

"What? I cannot hear you. Say it in my ear."

Guarded, she searched his eyes.

He tapped his ear.

"You are not deaf."

"Nay, but I like the way you say my name."

"Why?"

"You have a pleasurable French way of saying it, almost purring, with that *C* sound deep in your throat. Please, indulge me." He tucked his hair behind his ear and waited.

"You are full of nonsense."

"Och! My name isn't nonsense."

She shook her head and leaned toward his ear. "Lachlan," she whispered, her warm breath fanning his skin.

Mmm. Shivers of arousal coursed through his body, making his rigid tarse even harder.

"Very nice."

She pulled away slightly and his chest ached at her desertion. He wanted her to lie on him and whisper in his ear all night.

"Remember how your hair was the first time we wed?"

"A disaster."

"Nay, your fiery curls were loose about your shoulders, hanging near to your waist. 'Twas beautiful beyond measure." He was dying to see her that way again, but without a stitch of clothing hiding her creamy skin from him. But he must be patient.

Her only response was a distrustful glance, her blush still in evidence.

"In truth. Would you allow me to take down your hair now?"

Angelique knew what the seducer was about—leading her toward undress and the bedding, one tiny step at a time. Indeed, Lachlan was clever, but so was she. One thing he possessed, which no other man did in such abundance, was that damnable, disarming magnetism and charm. His relaxed, playful attitude conspired to make her the same, to melt away her defenses.

He wrapped one of her escaped curls around his finger. The gentle tug on her scalp sent a frisson of longing down her neck. Longing for what, she did not know, not the bedding. Perhaps another kiss, but that was all. What drew her attention more was his stone hard shaft beneath her thigh and thin layers of clothing.

Heavens! She did not know whether it intrigued her or terrified her. She only knew that part of his body was designed to hurt her, whether he intended it or not.

"Would you let me take the pins from your hair and unbraid it?" he murmured.

That was a question Girard would've never asked. He would simply have yanked the pins out, no matter her wishes.

"Oui." Parbleu. What was she saying? What was she allowing to happen?

"I thank you." Lachlan set about removing the pins with gentle fingers and dropping them to the floor. He appeared patient and didn't pull her hair overmuch, not enough to hurt. All the stimulation on her scalp showered down her body with an equal amount of yearnings and anxiety. He then unbraided the thick rope of hair and spread it in his big hands. Once her hair was loose, he combed his fingers through, and buried his nose in it for a deep inhale. "Mmm."

Mère de Dieu. He was far too sensual. Yet, strangely, she wanted to do the same to his neck perhaps even his hair, and breathe in his scent.

"Aye, 'tis the most bonny sight I have ever seen." He trailed his fingers from her hair to her neck and his attention shifted to her face. His eyes were the color of whisky in firelight and thrice as potent.

He moved his face closer to hers, his gaze dipping to her lips right before contact with his. She didn't know why she didn't jump up and run. His kiss was gentle, easy and tentative. Highly tantalizing. His tongue grazed her upper lip lightly. It was a dreamy kiss that snatched her rationale, like indulging in the most sinfully sweet dessert—honey and clove flavored. His tongue stole into her mouth, driving deep with sudden, compelling possession. Her nipples ached.

He slid his hand up the outside of her thigh, beneath the smock, higher and higher. His other hand rested upon her hip, holding her tight to his iron-hard shaft.

His kisses grew more passionate, his muscles harder, his embrace more tense.

Panic gripped her throat. She turned her face away, straining for breath, trembling with the realization of how far this had gone.

"Dear God, Angelique," he rasped. But he halted, his forehead resting against the side of hers, his breath harsh in her ear. "Mmm, you are delicious and…saints! I want you so bad I hurt with it." His voice was a fierce whisper.

Tears burned her eyes. She ached, too, her whole weakened body, the very core of her where he wanted to claim and possess her. But that ache would increase a hundredfold when he did take what he wanted.

She pushed at his shoulders but found them immovable, his arms locked around her, not painful but imprisoning.

"Do not," she said in a ragged whisper. She hated the tears dripping from her eyes.

"Angelique." He swallowed hard. "Don't do this. Please."

"No."

"You want me, too. I feel your desire. In your kisses, in your hands. You pulled me tight against you."

Her throat closed. She could do naught now but shake her head. She was caught, captured in his trap.

"Angelique." Her name was a pleading rasp. "Don't fear me. I won't hurt you. I swear it."

"You cannot help but hurt me…whether you mean it or not." He was not a woman; he did not know the pain of it.

He breathed deeply for a few moments. "You said you were not a virgin. Are you?"

She shook her head.

"Losing your virginity is what hurt, lass. After that, the pain is gone. There is only pleasure."

Maybe that was true for most women but… "No." She could not imagine pleasure, only the opposite.

"You think I'm lying?"

Perhaps not lying, but he simply did not understand her side. "You are a man like all others. I do not like coupling."

"Why?"

"It is painful…and demeaning." Heat and cold rushed through her.

"Who did you lie with before?" he asked, his voice harsher.

She could not tell him that. She could not say the name *Girard*.

"Or was that a made up story?" he asked in challenge. "Were you lying?"

She shook her head. "With a man I had planned to marry in France."

"Was he a bastard and didn't make it pleasurable for you?" Lachlan's breath fanned against the hair by her ear.

She shook her head.

"I'm not like him."

"Can you not understand? You have a very large...member. It could only hurt." Surely, rend her in two.

He let out a long breath. "Very well. We won't couple right now. I won't use my 'member' until you tell me to."

A bit of relief seeped into her tense muscles. "What will you do?"

"Give you pleasure," he murmured.

"How?" Her stomach knotted. How she wanted to relax and trust that he was telling her the truth. But in her experience, what a man saw as pleasure, she knew as pain.

"I'll touch your body with my hands and my mouth. Stroking you, kissing you all over." *All over?* Goodness! His voice was exceptionally heated, enticing.

"You will not receive any...satisfaction from that," she said.

"You don't know me at all, do you?"

She feared she did not. But she knew how men were; their desires sometimes overcame them. He might lose control. "When I least expect it, you will drive your shaft into me."

"Not until you tell me to, Angelique. Saints, at least trust me one time."

No. She could not let go. Already he was losing patience. She could not trust him enough for that. If he was lying, he would shatter her inside.

He stood, lifting her, and carried her toward the bed. Panic closed off her throat and the need to flee seized her.

"Non!" She struggled to escape him.

"Damnation, Angelique, I am at my wit's end. If you won't trust me, I'll have to prove it to you." He laid her on the bed, his big, hard body holding her down.

"Non! Arrêtez, bâtard!" She was trapped, suffocating beneath his weight. Her struggles against his strength were futile.

Camille pounded on the door. "Angelique?"

"Camille!"

"Be quiet," Lachlan said. "I won't hurt you." He shoved her arms above her head, quickly wrapping something around her wrists.

"Non!" She yanked at the bonds, but he had already tied the material, the belt of her wrap, around the headboard post. Stark terror paralyzed her.

"Don't look at me like that. I said I won't hurt you."

Scalding tears leaked from her eyes. Her throat constricted. Dear God, he was going to rape her.

He moved away for a moment, then came back with a wide ribbon. He wrapped it around her ankle.

Her senses returned and she kicked at him with all her might. But it was not enough; he secured her ankle to the footboard.

"Untie me at once, you brute! You are nothing but a vile animal," she said in French.

"I ken it well, m'lady." He sat beside her. She kicked at him with her one free foot but he caught it and removed her slipper. His lustful gaze lingered on her legs where her smock had ridden up. "Now what are you going to do, hell-cat?"

Any affectionate feelings she'd had toward him were now dead. She had known she could not trust the knave. "You will have to rape me, you bastard! Because I will never willingly let you touch me."

"Nay. I have never raped a woman, nor will I ever," he said in a calm tone. "You, on the other hand, will be begging me to make love to you afore 'tis over."

"Never! I'll kill you while you sleep," she said through clenched teeth.

"You're a bloodthirsty lass. I like that." He glanced aside. "You ken about the torture, do you not?"

"Torture?" *Mère de Dieu.* What was he going to do to her? Torture, then rape.

He moved to the dressing table, then returned to the bed. "Aye." Something stroked over her bare foot. A feather.

The tickle was a shock. She squealed and jerked away. "Do not!"

Holding her free foot in place, he slowly trailed the feather up the inside of her calf. He paused at her knee, caressed in a circle, then went higher, up the inside of her thigh. She squirmed and yanked at her bonds, wishing to escape the stimulation but could not.

She tried to make herself numb for indeed it was a twisted torture. Not painful, but she could not tolerate tickling. "I hate you!" She kicked.

He drew the feather down the length of her leg again to her foot, tingles scattering outward, then, feather forgotten, lightly traced his fingers along her calf. That did not tickle half as much. Some part of her liked his hands, while another part hated them.

She turned her face away, wishing to hide. Slowly, he ran his palms up the outside of her legs. *Bastard.* She clamped her thighs together and twisted her lower body sideways. No, she would not let him touch...

He slipped his hand up the back of her thigh, pushing the smock upward. Continuing, he ran his palm over her derriere. Shocked, she sucked in a sharp breath, turned onto her back again and kicked at him.

He crawled over her, holding himself above her in dominating mastery. Breathing hard, she turned her face aside. "Get off, you beast!"

"Am I hurting you?" he whispered, lightly stroking his lips over her ear. Some sensation she hated spiraled through her. Not fear, but arousal. He lifted himself and waited for her to look at him. When she did, he drew close to her mouth. She thought he would kiss her, but he didn't; he merely breathed upon her. Hungry for his mouth, she parted her lips, perversely craving his tongue invading and possessing, the sinful, addictive taste of him. *No, I do not!*

He brushed his cheek against hers gently, his beard stubble rasping. Again, his lips hovered less than an inch above hers. *Mère de Dieu, kiss me!*

No, do not!

Her breath caught and her eyes closed. Her body felt as if a trembling fever had taken it over. Surely, this was some horrid illness that caused delirium and lunacy.

He drew away, climbing off the bed. Where was he going? She glared after him through the mist of tears. Oh dear heaven, he was undressing, unpinning the brooch at the top of his kilt.

"Je te déteste," she muttered.

He unfastened his belt, removing his plaid. *"Non, mon ange.* You hate yourself for liking me."

"T'es goujat!" She yanked against the belt that bound her. "You could never be faithful to one woman."

"Do you wish me to be?"

"Wishing for that would be a waste of time. You could never do it."

"I've done many things others have said were impossible. Don't be underestimating me."

"Untie me!"

"Not until you trust me."

"Never! You think this will earn my trust? You are beyond insane."

He slipped the shirt over his head, leaving those burnished muscles bare, and climbed back onto the bed. His erection was massive, protruding like a weapon. *Mère de Dieu, non.*

While she held her breath, he pushed her smock up her thighs, clamped tightly together, his sword-calloused palms rasping over her, producing a shower of tingles. He exposed her mound completely.

How indecent! Humiliating. She closed her eyes, trying to hide from him...and herself.

Lightly, he touched the hair that hid her sex, combed his fingers through it. He paused at that most intimate spot. "Angelique, you're wet...extremely wet." His heated voice held a bit of awe. "Do you ken what that means?"

Squeezing her eyes tight, she turned away. *I do not want to know.*

"It means you want me. You desire me."

No, I do not! Yet she was paralyzed in this burning heat, unable to fight back anymore. Her body would not cooperate.

He kissed the top of her thighs, her hip bones. He pushed the smock further up, kissed her lower belly. He flicked his tongue into her navel.

Oh God, no! That burning hot, liquid sensation grew more intense. She ached in the core of her being.

Her body craved something her mind hated. And she was no longer in control of herself; Lachlan was.

A half moan escaped before she smothered it. Her body tightened, rigid like a bow, straining for something. She arched toward him, then forced herself to stop.

Slowly, he trailed kisses over her lower belly and down toward her mound. She tried to squeeze her thighs together but he had inserted his knee between.

Her legs trembled, her strength vanished. Pushing her knee up, he kissed her inner thighs, both of them, opening her to his view. She was utterly at his mercy.

"Oh." He was scandalous. She whimpered, praying it would not hurt.

"Mmm, you smell like heaven."

That most feminine part of her wept and ached...and yearned for something...he touched her there with his fingers, parted her female lips, blew his hot breath upon her, and licked between. "Mmm."

"Mon Dieu!" She gasped and her body did what it wanted, her hips thrust toward him, her legs widening like a wanton's, giving him complete access.

"Aye." He took full possession.

Her sole focus was on what he did, spreading her with his fingers, lapping with his tongue. He closed his lips around some part of her and drew on her, sucking. A sharp ache speared her. Not a painful ache, but one that yearned for something more. Not his member, no, she did not want it.

His tongue slid inside her, in and out. How could he do such a thing? Surely that was immoral and sinful...the most erotic thing she could imagine.

"Mmm, you are sweet as a plum tart," he murmured, his breath heating her skin.

A moan slipped out without her permission.

"You see? You like this."

She shook her head vehemently. "I hate it!"

"Liar. I love to hear you moan. Do it again." He slid his tongue inside, deeper, no...it was his finger. Before she could protest, he suckled at her flesh again, licked a most sensitive spot fast and hard. The sensations were blinding, mind-stealing. He would drive her to lunacy. Her body suddenly became possessed with something, taken over, bombarded and smothered with intensity.

Pleasure? No, something beyond pleasure.

His finger felt larger inside her, two fingers, stroking in and out. And she rode, hating him for making her crave it so badly. He tugged at her hair, exposing her more completely, licking faster, making the erotic sensation extend and magnify. She knew she was crying out, screaming, but was helpless to stop it. Her body clutched at his fingers, but wanted something more, something that wasn't there. Whatever invisible demon possessed her made her jerk violently beneath him, shoving her body more firmly to his mouth.

The possession released her and she felt she dropped back to the bed, her flesh tender and most sensitive. She wanted to draw away from him, fold into herself and hide completely.

"Mmm, Angelique. There you have it." Lachlan licked his lips, savoring her sweet, sensual flavor. Saints, that was the best sex he'd ever had and he hadn't even been inside her yet. Near to the edge of climaxing himself, he sat back on his heels.

Angelique sobbed and turned her head aside, crying into the pillow.

"Nay, don't cry." He stroked a hand over her hip. "Did you not enjoy that?"

"*Non. Va-t-en!* Leave." Tears glistened on her lashes.

He had seen women brought to tears during climax, especially their first, but not in this way. He was used to joyful tears of awe, or maybe an outburst of laughter. But not distraught as Angelique was. "Don't be afraid, lass. I wouldn't hurt you."

"I'm not afraid. *Que vous êtes brute!*"

"What's wrong, then?" He could not understand her, still hostile after such an obviously pleasurable release.

"Men. *Je les déteste.*"

So she hated men, not just him? "Why?"

"None of your concern."

"Did someone hurt you? Your first lover, the man you had planned to marry?"

She nodded slightly, surprising him.

Dear God, no. Why had he not realized? "Tell me his name."

"Girard," she whispered.

Poisonous jealousy and rage snaked through Lachlan, sickening him. "Girard? He was the man you had wanted to marry? The man who you fear is here now, threatening you? Why did you not tell me this before?"

"I did not wish you to find out," she said in a small voice.

"What else are you keeping from me? What secrets?"

"None."

What the hell have I gotten myself into? "Saints! What did the bastard do?"

She shook her head.

"Tell me. Did he hit you?"

She nodded but kept her eyes shut tight.

"What else?"

"C'est rein."

"Nay, I don't think 'tis naught."

Tears leaked from beneath her long lashes.

"Did he force you?" He tried to ask gently, but his voice came out a growl.

She turned her face into the pillow, her curls hiding her face.

"Ange, did the whoreson rape you?"

CHAPTER TEN

Damnation! Girard had raped her. Lachlan wanted to run the bastard through, nay, slit his throat and hack him to bits!

Angelique cried silently, her body shaking with the sobs.

Lachlan untied her hands and her ankle. Once free, she curled into a ball, and he covered her with the blanket. He knelt beside the bed and stroked a hand over her head, pushing the curls back from her face…trying to soothe her and make up for some of his own callous behavior.

"I will kill him," he said in a soft, rough voice. "By the saints, I swear it. When did this happen?"

Finally, she opened her eyes but would not hold his gaze. "A year ago, in France. The first time, after he asked me to marry him, he did not force me. I thought I was in love with him and, against my better judgment, agreed to become lovers. I hated the painful, humiliating act. Then I caught him with another woman, a serving maid. I told him I never wanted to see him again and this angered him. That is when he raped me."

A killing rage, nay, a dark bloodlust such as Lachlan had never felt speared him. He rose and moved away, fearing she'd feel the violence radiating off him. He wanted to smash something. "If I ever see him, I shall kill him. I swear it!"

She pressed her eyes closed and more tears leaked out.

Lachlan yanked on his clothes, imagining the hell she'd endured, trying to control his anger. No wonder she had not wanted him to touch her. And he'd tied her up. He'd terrified her beyond reason, probably made her think he was going to rape her, too. Though his only intention had been to give her pleasure, he'd been a bastard.

Once dressed, he again knelt by the bed and slid a hand over her hair, offering what comfort he knew how. "I'm sorry I tied you up. I didn't know."

"It is nothing."

"Nay, I was wrong to do it. I never meant to frighten you."

She remained silent. He knew naught else to say. How could he offer her comfort when his mere presence likely scared her worse?

"I hope you can forgive me. Sleep now, and I'll see you on the morrow."

He did not want to leave her like that. He wanted to crawl in bed beside her, pull her against his chest and stroke her, kiss her, 'til she felt better. 'Til she was happy. But that would not happen. Feeling helpless and in the darkest mood ever, he closed the door on the way out. In the sitting room, Camille glared at him with tear-filled eyes, her fists clenched at her sides.

"I didn't hurt her. I frightened her unintentionally...but I didn't hurt her." He stalked through to his own chamber.

The sounds of music and dancing carried up to him from the great hall, but he was in no mood to celebrate. Hell, he wanted to fight someone named Girard and seek vengeance for what he'd done to Angelique.

"Iosa is Muire Mhàthair!"

Lachlan had never encountered a woman who'd been raped before. The ladies who came to him enjoyed sex or wanted to; he knew not how to deal with one who hated it, feared it.

But he hadn't hurt her. In the end, she should see he wished her no harm.

After pacing about the room for a while, he knew he wouldn't sleep. He exited and descended the steps. He'd find that French bastard or whoever had brought the goblets.

ༀༀ ༀༀ

Angelique woke from a shocking dream such as she'd never had before. Her eyes were swollen and scratchy from crying. One candle and a glow in the hearth provided the only light. Had a dream or a memory wakened her? The heated, prickly sensation of Lachlan softly kissing her body, rubbing the slight stubble of his face upon her belly. He pressed her legs apart and kissed between, stroking her in forbidden places. Licking her and igniting a strange compelling fever within her. This was passionate arousal, the first she'd felt in her life…and Lachlan had provoked it.

He'd given her a climax. She'd heard women speak of it in France—*la petite mort*—but she had not imagined it to be so intense and all-consuming. She had thought perhaps it would be mildly pleasurable, but the climax grabbed her body and soul, something at the far edge of pleasure. Something almost frightening. Indeed, like a little death.

Her body ached again now. Images flooded her mind. She fantasized Lachlan returned to her, licked her and did all sorts of lusty, forbidden things to her.

"I do not like it," she whispered. *Or rather, I should not like it.* But somehow Lachlan had turned a distasteful act into a spellbinding one. She yearned for his magical touch in all her secret places. She pressed a hand against her crotch. The pressure soothed the ache slightly, but she was wet. He'd told her what that meant.

How could she want something she'd hated for the last year? Something that sickened her and gave her nightmares? Was it because Lachlan was an expert at seducing women? Or was it something more?

He hadn't forced her. He could have; she was tied up, helpless and at his mercy. Yet, he hadn't hurt her once. All her fear had come from herself, not from what he'd done. He'd even vowed to avenge her pain. Was Lachlan a man she could trust in every way?

The moist ache in her lower belly would not cease. It only grew stronger the more she thought of Lachlan. She didn't want him to bed her, did she?

When she imagined his honed, muscular body and his massive shaft, she should've been terrified…but she wasn't. No, this image increased her arousal tenfold. Though she knew his tarse would cause her untold pain, still she craved something about it. She wondered what it would feel like in her hand. Hard as stone, she knew. Would it feel hot? Smooth?

Or mayhap she only wanted to get the coupling out of the way. She had been dreading this so long. If she did it with him once, maybe the next time would not be so bad. And she did need to do her duty and have a child, an heir. She wished to get the act over with and appease this senseless arousal.

She slid out of bed and put on her wrap. When she tied the belt, an idea occurred to her. She would tie him up while he slept and seize control over him. She wouldn't fear him half as much if he was restrained.

Taking the lone candle from the mantel, she crept through the chill darkness of the sitting rooms to Lachlan's chamber. She opened the door, praying the hinges wouldn't squeak, and closed it back.

What am I doing? I have lost my sanity.

The flame revealed Lachlan in bed, asleep on his back, one arm thrown over his head. The counterpane covered half his chest. The bulging muscles of his chest, along with his massive shoulders and arms brought back that restless ache. Could a man be called beautiful? It made no sense...and yet, he was. A master should sculpt him or paint him, as he slept like this.

She moved forward and placed the candle on the bedside table. His breathing altered and she feared he'd awakened. She stared at him for a half minute. No, he breathed deep and even, eyes closed.

She removed her robe belt and wrapped it around his wrist near the headboard. Now, the hard part...she gently lifted his other arm. *Sacrebleu,* it was heavier than a tree limb, but she pushed it above his head and tied it with the remainder of the silk belt.

A snore escaped his nose. His chest rose and fell slowly. What would she tie his ankles with? She glanced about. Aha. She took his wide leather belt from the chair where it lay atop his *plaide*. She placed his big feet side by side, tightened the belt around his ankles, secured it to the footboard post, then slid the end of the belt back underneath itself at his ankles. Even a boar could not escape that.

She checked his eyes—still closed. Feeling a bit giddy, she lowered the counterpane, revealing twin ridges of muscles down his abdomen, an intriguing vertical band of muscle at each hip bone. A silky line of dark gold hair led in a trail from his navel down to the nest of hair his tarse sprang from. And it did indeed spring up, pointing toward his navel.

She studied his closed eyes again. He hadn't moved; his breathing was the same. She reached out a trembling hand and pressed her fingertips to his shaft. The skin was feverish hot. She jerked back.

Gathering courage, she touched it again—smooth as polished oak. No, smoother, the skin silky, but the flesh underneath like granite. The head was a different story. It was wide, forming a sensual crest. She slid her hand over it. It was firm but not as stone-hard as the rest, with velvety skin.

She must wake him. Would he be angry?

ೋ෴ೋ

Lachlan watched Angelique through slitted eyes and pretended to sleep, continuing his deep breathing. What the hell was she going to do to him? When she touched his shaft, it was all he could do not to groan aloud.

Did the wench honestly think a Highland warrior wouldn't wake with this much handling?

God's bones! What if she took a whip to him—or a dagger—in revenge for his earlier actions? He would regret letting himself get into such a vulnerable position, but likely he could rip the fragile material and escape if necessary. Considering the way she was petting and inspecting his erection, she had something else in mind entirely. Saints, he hoped! Something he could hardly believe, after learning what she'd endured the year before.

Her cool hand surrounded his tight flesh and squeezed. Pleasure ricocheted through him and he wanted to flex his hips. Stifling a moan, he pretended to be awakening. "Angelique?" He yanked on his bonds and discovered he could easily pull them loose and slip his hands free if he wished. The woman didn't know how to tie a knot. But he would indulge her.

"What are you doing? Why did you tie me up?"

"No talking." She pulled a piece of cloth from her pocket and blindfolded him.

"What are you going to do?" he asked.

"Something I will probably regret."

"God's teeth. I hope this has naught to do with a whip."

"I forgot my whip."

"Thank the heavens."

She stroked a cool hand over his chest, slowly as if exploring every inch. She dipped a finger into his navel and lust shot through him. When his erection jumped, she grabbed him again and squeezed gently. Pleasure wound through him and he growled. No indeed, this was no shy virgin.

Cloth whispered over skin and he imagined her disrobing.

Aye, please. He wanted her so badly he held himself rigid. Waiting.

Climbing onto the bed, she straddled his hips and lifted his shaft. The tip prodded something hot and moist. He growled. *Aye, take me, lass.* Holding onto the headboard, he tightened his muscles and felt himself hardening further.

She pressed down on him, impaling herself. He experienced the bliss of driving an inch or two into her excessively tight, wet sheath.

"Oh!" she near screamed.

He moaned and muttered a Gaelic curse. "Angelique?"

"I am sorry to do this, my laird."

"Don't be. My God, I want you." He gave in to the urge, tilted his hips and thrust. Oh, aye! Another inch. "Untie me and I'll show you how much."

She cried out, breathing hard, and levered herself up. *"Non. Arrêtez."*

"Take off this blindfold. I'm wanting to see you."

"Non. Be still." She pressed down, and he met her with another thrust.

He slid deeper still, her wet heat surrounding him, squeezing him, making him drunk with desire. "Saints! You're killing me." He turned his head side to side, dislodging the blindfold a bit so he could see her beneath it. She was a beautiful nymph, with slender curves and creamy, perky breasts that bounced slightly when she moved. What a nice mouthful one would make. He growled, aching to suck one of those pink nipples into his mouth and toy with it.

She placed her hands on his chest and lifted herself, then down again. What torture! Her long red curls swung forward, tickling his chest.

Her fast shallow breaths and her moisture told him of her desire. *Aye, ride me, Angelique.* He watched their merging bodies for a few seconds and he near lost control. What an erotic sight.

"I didn't ken you wanted this. I thought you were afraid."

"Shh. Do not speak." She increased the pace, riding him with her eyes closed. She was breathtaking with the impassioned frown, flushed face and parted lips.

This was a first. Never had a woman tied him up and had her way with him. Strangely, he was starting to love it. But her gentle, shallow thrusts were driving him mad. He wanted more, faster, deeper.

He tried to suppress the escalating desire and wait for her. "Untie me so I can give you pleasure."

"*Non!*"

"You'll not enjoy it as much this way."

"You will not have control."

Control? That's why she did this. At first he'd thought it was in revenge for when he'd tied her up. But nay, it was so he would be at her mercy. She wouldn't fear him if he couldn't touch her. Still, he wanted to hear it from her mouth. "Why are you doing this?"

"You desired a wedding night, so I am giving you one."

Ha. "Is that all?"

"I wish to know why the women want you in their beds. What is so special about you besides your *grand* tarse?"

He almost laughed, but controlled it. "I thank you for the compliment, but you cannot know what I can do unless you untie me. I like to use my hands. And my mouth."

"I know," she whispered and stroked a finger over his lips. Lifting his head, he opened his mouth and sucked her finger inside. Of course she knew, but what he'd done earlier was only the beginning.

Giving a short purr, she drew her hand away. Pressing her breasts against his chest, she kissed his throat while she continued to ride him. Her hard nipples rubbed his chest.

"Mmm. Kiss me," he said, craving some deeper emotional connection with her he didn't understand. Normally fast and furious sex was his specialty, but that was not what he craved at the moment. He wanted to explore all of her. He had not tasted her nipples yet; he desired touching her everywhere at once.

She leaned forward and nibbled at his lips, placed a small lick between. He opened, welcomed her inside. With her lifted up like that, he took advantage and thrust his hips, driving into her over and over, deeper. She gasped and accepted him, held still for him. He moaned. She near squeezed the sanity out of him.

"You push me to the edge, *mon ange*," he said.

"I am not your angel."

"Aye, you are," he whispered. "I'm inside you, love. By your own vow, you are my wife."

A burning tingle rushed through him. He tried to hold back the impending release and think of something unappealing. But he was too deprived, had wanted her too long.

His climax broke over him like a wave of happiness and all the best feelings on earth. His mind deserted him and he was drowning in a sea of pleasure. He shuddered and groaned with the enormity of it. "Ah, God!" His breaths whooshed in and out during the aftermath.

Angelique lay still on his chest. He wanted to pull his arms down and hold her close. After a moment she lifted herself, releasing him from her body and climbed off.

"Don't go. Untie me."

She quickly slipped on her smock and wrap. "I cannot stay."

"Why?"

"Now, maybe I will have a child," she said.

"What?"

"We need an heir to be the next Earl of Draughon, do we not?"

"Aye." Was that her only reason for riding him like a wild woman? Nay, she had wanted him intensely. She had been wet and aroused...still was. "Untie me." He could yank himself loose, wrap his arms around her and force her to stay with him, but...no. She should want to stay with him the night. It should be her choice.

She released one of his hands and before he could disentangle himself, she disappeared out the door.

"Angelique? Damn you," he muttered. This was the first time he had made love to a woman and not given her the pleasurable climax. But it was her fault.

He untied the belt of her wrap from his other wrist and then removed his leather belt from his ankles. After tucking the sheet about his waist he strode to her bedchamber door. He lifted the latch but found it barred. Why was he surprised?

He knocked. "Angelique."

"Time to sleep now, my laird."

"Let me in. I only want to talk."

"*Non.* You had your wedding night. *Là. C'est fini.*"

It was not finished by a long shot.

⁂

Angelique jumped into bed and covered her head, her body still pulsing with desire. She felt empty and cold. Her body craved his wrapped about her. Inside her. His heat. She did not understand it; though his hard member had initially hurt as she'd forced it into her, once she started moving something changed and he'd felt divine. Though coupling should have been a dutiful, onerous task, it was something incomprehensible. A secret pleasure. The absolute opposite of what Girard had done to her. Yet the same body parts were involved. How was this possible?

She had been shocked at herself for enjoying the act. Such feelings went against all rationality. No, she could not indulge herself overmuch and slide down that slippery slope of needing him or falling for him.

She was afraid she liked her husband a bit too much. He was trying to steal her heart and blind her to his true nature, but she was not so naïve as he wished her to be. Likely, he would find someone else, no doubt several women, to amuse him, whether now or later. Her own actions would not matter. So much the better if her feelings were not attached to him.

୬ଚ ୭ଚ

"And how was your long-awaited wedding night?" Rebbie asked Lachlan the next morn. He used a low voice so the many men around them wouldn't hear. They, along with Dirk, stood outside while the Drummagan clansmen readied the courtyard for the traditional chief's inauguration. Each clansman carried a stone to build a short pyramid while Heckie supervised. Lachlan glanced up at the gray sky, hoping the rain would hold off.

Rebbie elbowed him, then lifted a brow.

"Why can you not be more like Dirk and mind your own business?" Lachlan asked. In the past, he might have revealed certain details of his exploits with women, but his wedding night was not up for discussion.

"He wants to know, too," Rebbie said.

"But he's not asking."

"That bad, huh?" Rebbie grimaced.

"Nay, 'twas good." Actually, she'd given him the most amazing, earth-shaking climax of his life. He only regretted that she hadn't enjoyed it as much that time.

"Only good? Not magnificent?"

"Indeed, magnificent. But what's betwixt a husband and wife is private."

"I see," Rebbie said in a dry tone. "Lady Eleanor wished to share something private with you last night. I found her hiding in your bedchamber, as you predicted, when you were with Lady

Angelique."

"Hell, I forgot about her." He hadn't realized Eleanor would be so persistent in her pursuit of him. "I thank you for getting her out of there and keeping her occupied. Where is she now?"

"Still locked in the tower chamber, where I put her last night, alone."

"We must send her away from Draughon before Angelique finds out she's here. She is becoming too much of a problem."

Lachlan glanced back at Angelique, standing on the castle's entrance steps. So regal, she looked like a queen in her golden gown and bejeweled headpiece. Meeting her eyes, he winked and her skittish gaze darted away. Was that a blush?

He wanted to lick her head to toe and stay in bed all day, exploring every inch of her perfect body and each facet of her cunning mind. He would never grow tired of her. That realization struck like a punch to the stomach. God's blood! How could he know such a thing? He had no answer for himself; he simply knew. Facing forward again, he imagined the next time he'd get her alone.

"What the devil's so amusing?" Rebbie asked.

"Naught is amusing at the moment." Still, Lachlan couldn't hide his daft grin.

Dirk leaned toward them and whispered, "He's calf-eyed."

Lachlan scowled. "I prefer the word 'happy.'"

"Och. St. Andrew, deliver us," Rebbie muttered.

"This is an important and serious ceremony," Lachlan said. "And deserves my undivided attention."

"Aye. So stop staring at your wee wifey and pay attention."

"You blather on too much."

Lachlan tried to forget about Angelique and focus. He had been present at his brother's inauguration deep in the Highlands five years ago. The Drummagans had a similar tradition. He just hoped the pyramid of rocks, built to symbolize his elevated position as leader of the clan, didn't collapse once he sat on the chair atop it.

The Protestant minister said a prayer. Heckie, the *Seanachaidh*, recited the Drummagan genealogy back to the 11th century, then Lachlan's ancestry to the 12th century, which the older man had to learn from Lachlan in only a few days. Heckie then delivered a newly written poem in Lachlan's honor.

And he was honored. He still could not believe his great

fortune in receiving a title, becoming chief of this strong clan and marrying Angelique.

Though last night had surely been bizarre as wedding nights go, it was unforgettable. He had to make sure tonight was better for her, and hoped she had stopped fighting him.

As for the Girard outlaw, he had seen neither hide nor hair of the whoreson. And they couldn't discern where the goblets had come from.

꧁꧂

On her way to the great hall for midday meal, Angelique strolled along the dim corridor, passing servants and other clan members. She had not been close to Lachlan all day and must now sit beside him to eat. A sudden fit of nerves seized her stomach. What if he made mention of last night, either to her or to his friends? She would die of mortification. Yet, in another way, she looked forward to being near him. Too much. She could not let herself enjoy him and his charm too much.

"I am to take Lady Eleanor a tray of food," a female whispered.

Eleanor?

Angelique stopped and turned. "Wait."

The servants froze. "M'lady?"

"What did you say?"

The young servant lowered her timid gaze and curtseyed. "I have been instructed by Laird Rebbinglen to deliver a tray of food to Lady Eleanor, Countess of Wexbury, in the south tower bedchamber."

A hot torrent of fury raged through Angelique. "What is she doing there? When did she arrive?"

"I...I don't know."

Ignoring the fact she was supposed to be in the great hall for midday meal, Angelique continued along the corridor, toward the south tower. She would find out what the *putain* was doing here. Obviously, Lachlan knew of her presence if Rebbie did. But why had no one told her? Why had Lachlan allowed Eleanor to remain here? Angelique was afraid she knew the answer to that, though her heart railed against it.

A tall, burly guard, covered in thick leather armor and with a sword at his side, stood before the chamber portal.

"Unlock this door," she said.

"M'lady." He bowed. "I've been told not to."

"What do you mean? I know Eleanor is in there."

"My orders were to not allow you or anyone inside."

"Me? Who did your orders come from?"

"Laird Rebbinglen, m'lady."

"You do not work for Rebbinglen. You work for me."

"With all due respect, m'lady, Laird Rebbinglen said his instructions came from your husband."

A chill settled into her blood. "My husband?"

"Aye. His lairdship. No one is to enter or leave this chamber except for them or the servant who brings food."

Her icy rage spread. She would strangle someone—Lachlan. "Let me in or I shall relieve you of your duties. Your pay comes from my coffers."

The guard squirmed for a moment. "I must ask his lairdship."

"No. Now!"

"God help me," he muttered, unlocked the door and opened it.

Eleanor rose from the window seat. "Thank the heavens..." Her smile fell. "Oh, Angelique."

She forced herself to step inside the room. "What are you doing here? I do not recall inviting you."

Eleanor pressed a bejeweled hand to her huge bosom covered in rich fabrics, pendants and pearls. "What a horrid way to greet a friend."

"You are not my friend. You covet my husband."

Eleanor smiled—no, it was a malicious parody of a smile. "And I've had your husband. You are fortunate indeed."

Angelique felt as if she'd been struck down the center with a poleax. What did Eleanor mean? She'd had Lachlan since their marriage? She'd slept with him here?

"Oh yes, little Angelique. He is indeed an impressive specimen of a man, so seductive and commanding, is he not? Last night was breathtaking."

"You are lying," she managed to say in a seething whisper. Eleanor had to be lying, didn't she?

"Am I? Then how do I know the counterpane on his bed is green and that his window looks out over the courtyard and that a tapestry depicting Flodden hangs on his wall."

That bitch. "I shall kill you." She flew at Eleanor, her hands aimed at her throat. Before she made contact, someone grabbed her from behind and lifted her from the floor. She kicked and elbowed the male who restrained her.

"Angelique. Calm yourself." Lachlan's voice was a growl in her ear.

She redoubled her efforts to damage him bodily, her elbows and feet flying and bashing. But he carried her squirming from the room, down the stairs and along the corridor to the solar.

He kicked the door closed behind them.

"Let me go, you bastard!" she said in French.

"Not until you calm yourself."

She stilled, but inside a death pain sliced through her. "I knew I could not trust you. I knew men like you could never change."

He released her and she spun away from him, backing toward the opposite wall. Her eyes burned; her throat ached. *No, I refuse to cry.*

"I have done naught," he said, his tone defensive, hateful eyes glaring.

"Do not lie. I know you had Rebbie lock her up for your pleasure. So I would not know she was here."

"Rebbie locked her up to keep her out of my rooms."

"Because you cannot keep yourself away from her?"

"Nay! I have no interest in her."

"She was in your bedchamber last night!"

"But I wasn't there at the time. Rebbie found her, and that's why he removed her and locked her in the tower."

"You knew she was here before that, did you not? If what you say is true, why did you not send her away?" She could barely force the words out, hating her own damnable weakness and emotion for this bastard.

"I was planning to, but I forgot about her this morning."

"Forgot? You expect me to believe such?" How could he forget about the bitch who would destroy their marriage? "You were keeping her for your entertainment between ceremonies and meals and the chore of visiting my bed. And you forbade the guard to allow me inside the tower room. I will have her escorted to the gates. If you are determined to have a paramour, it will not be Eleanor." Angelique stalked from the room, forcing herself to appear strong, though she felt like a windflower tossed upon the ocean…sinking, drowning.

_ஒஇ இஒ_

"Angelique. That stupid little cow!" Eleanor, countess of Wexbury, waited outside the gates of Draughon with her trunks while her rented coach was brought out. She tugged her velvet-lined cloak closer against the chill Scottish wind. "I will not be treated as a fishwife. I shall have my revenge for this insult, this humiliation," she raved to her maid.

The young Englishwoman wisely kept her eyes downcast. The nearby guards stared straight ahead, avoiding her gaze.

It was the height of rudeness to throw out a peer, a member of the nobility. She would tell everyone she knew about Angelique's ignorance and viciousness.

A quarter-hour later, just as the fat drops of rain began, Eleanor's coach arrived from the stables. "Angelique had best be glad," she muttered and climbed inside. "We stop in the village, at the Breakstane Inn," she ordered her driver. While she sat inside the coach, her servants loaded her trunks then climbed on board.

As they'd passed through that little village yesterday, she had seen an inn which looked acceptable. Since it was about a half day from Perth, it was not too rudimentary. Eleanor was not yet ready to give up the pleasure of having Lachlan one last time...or several more times. He was the most splendid lover she'd ever had and she couldn't stop thinking about him, dreaming of him. He was so young, strong and virile. She didn't know a man could be so appealing, until him.

Thankfully, Eleanor had finally lost her elderly husband to natural causes, a man who'd been thirty-three years her senior, and she wasn't putting off enjoyment of life any longer. Of course, her father had forced her into the marriage with the old earl and she'd had no say in it. She'd endured his repugnant attentions for over ten years and bore him an heir. Now, finally, she could choose which men she slept with.

Angelique could never appreciate Lachlan and his bed-chamber prowess as she did. He would grow bored with his unfriendly new wife in short order and when that happened Eleanor wanted to be close by to fill his carnal needs, of which he had many.

She only hoped her associate had more luck in driving the two newlyweds apart. If not, she would pay Kormad a visit. Surely he would help her, if he thought he could get his hands on that estate.

CHAPTER ELEVEN

"Damn him." Angelique strode from the great hall toward her rooms. She'd barely held up her façade before the clan during midday meal while her heart splintered. She should've killed Lachlan last night while she had him tied up instead of bedding him. Now that he'd had her, he would pursue someone else. But not Eleanor; she'd made sure of that. Angelique was certain any woman would do, so long as she was still breathing. The selfish, lascivious whoremonger.

It should be a crime, what he did—forcing her to relish the shocking things he'd done to her with his mouth last night. But she was the imbecile for taking him into her body. She feared that act alone had caused her to take him into her heart as well. Or maybe it was the things that came before, the kissing, the sweet murmured words, his hands caressing. Even now, she burned for all those things, no matter that he would never be true.

"*Mademoiselle*," whispered a male voice in the darkened alcove between the great hall and solar.

She paused. The voice sounded familiar, the accent French. Not Girard…or was it? She backed away. "*Qui est-ce?*"

"It is I, Philippe." The young man she had once thought to marry stuck his head out.

She rushed to join him. "Oh, Philippe, what are you doing here?" she asked in French.

"I had to see you, *mon coeur.*" He grasped her hands and kissed them. "I love you. You must leave the barbarian."

She tugged her hands away from him, now realizing, though he was indeed her friend, he was little more than a silly boy. "What are you talking about?"

"There must be some way out of your marriage. You loathe him, do you not?"

Loathe? Indeed, she detested many things about Lachlan. Still, he was her husband. She had spoken sacred wedding vows and fully intended to keep them as long as possible. Plus, the marriage was now consummated, thanks to her rash, bold actions of the night before. She glanced behind herself through the shadows to make sure no one eavesdropped, then faced Philippe again. "No, the marriage cannot be undone. It is too late."

"It is never too late. I know some people, friends, who will help us be together. We can go back to France and live happily there. You love France. My father has written to me. He will give me a small estate in the country." Philippe's tone was rather desperate, as was his gaze. She did not like this aspect of him.

"Your father?" Last she'd heard, his father hated him and would not claim him.

"*Oui*, he is a wealthy nobleman."

"I cannot leave my estate and my clan. This is my birthright and my inheritance. At all costs, I cannot let Kormad claim it."

"But you are a lady. You need not concern yourself with the leadership of an uncivilized clan."

"That is your opinion, and I disagree with it. Besides, my clan is very civilized."

"I am sorry, *ma bien-aimée*." He knelt on one knee and she realized he moved her not at all. He was but a timid child compared to Lachlan.

"I beg of you, please consider going away with me," Philippe said, grasping her hand again. "I shall make you happy. You will not be happy here with that overbearing brute."

"Don't do this, Philippe. I am married," she whispered, resisting the urge to again yank her hand from his clammy one. She did not wish to hurt his feelings and hoped they could remain friends. "Do you not understand that?"

"Your mother left your father, her husband, and returned to her beloved France. You can do the same."

That was true but…this wasn't the same yet. She must bear a legitimate heir and do her duty; that much she would accomplish for her family and forefathers. And though it was the most extreme of follies, some small part of her prayed Lachlan would prove to be more honorable and faithful than she expected. She had no way of knowing if he was with Eleanor last night.

How dare Angelique dream he might develop feelings for her? Idiotic. Still, she couldn't help it.

"Have you never heard of annulment or divorce?" Philippe rose, releasing her hand. "You were forced to marry him against your will. I have friends who will help us."

"What friends?"

"What the devil is he doing here?" Lachlan's voice, almost like a growl, came from behind her.

Angelique jumped and turned. Her heart felt as if it would leap from her body. "Philippe has come for a visit…to wish us well."

Even in the dimness, Lachlan's cutting gaze was obvious. Deadly, when he observed Philippe. She had to sometimes remind herself the frivolous libertine was also a Highland warrior, skilled with the sword. He'd probably killed several people in battle.

"I see I shall have to fire my guards for allowing such vermin inside the gates." Lachlan captured her hand and pulled her toward the solar. "I will speak with you in private, *wife*."

Angelique's heart sped along. *Mother Mary, help me.* What would he do?

In the solar, he slammed the door behind them. "What were the two of you discussing?"

"Nothing of importance." Her head throbbed with sudden pain as she tried to remember every word she and Philippe had spoken.

"Plotting against me?" Lachlan demanded.

"Of course not, my laird." She backed away from his stalking advance.

"*My laird*," he mimicked. "You only call me that when you're hiding something. What is afoot?"

Her hands trembled and she could not think what to say. In his anger, he was irrational, like most other men, believing he had a right to his paramours, while she could not even have friends.

"Why is he here? What did he say to you?"

"I do not know why he's here and he said nothing."

"You are lying, *madame*! I heard part of your conversation. I understand French, remember?"

Mon Dieu. She was in trouble. What would he do, beat her? Force her to leave?

"In case you've forgotten, Angelique, he said something about an annulment or divorce. Then he said, 'You were forced to marry him against your will. I have friends who will help us.' Help you what? Are you thinking to leave me?"

Her shallow breaths rushed in and out, making her lightheaded. "No. I told him I would not do it."

"I didn't hear you say 'no.' You said, 'what friends?'"

"Before that, I told him no; it was too late."

"Tell him to leave or I will throw him out!"

She hated it when he became domineering, ordering her about. This was her home since she was a babe, not his. *"Non."*

"What?" he growled. "You're on thin ice, *madame*."

"No thinner than you are, *monsieur*. Locking your lover in the tower! This is my home. My friends are welcome if yours are. You had Eleanor come here."

"Wrong! I didn't invite her."

"You would not even tell her to leave; I had to. And I still don't know if you slept with her last night."

"I did not." His jaw hardened.

"How do I know? She said you did. It is your word against hers. Neither you nor she is reliable."

He blew out a laborious breath and tried to cut her down with his glower.

"You are a man controlled by your sexual appetite," she said.

"There is naught wrong with that! As I recall, your own sexual appetite was healthy last night, when you climbed on top and rode me as if I were a pony. Finally making use of your paid stud."

A furious heat inflamed her face. "You are no gentleman."

"What has that to do with it? I speak the truth."

Her thoughts were so mixed up, she could not think what she wanted to say next.

"Tell him to leave," Lachlan ordered. "I don't trust the puny bastard."

"Do not call Philippe a bastard. You are the bastard."

"Why do you defend him? I know you don't love the weasel!"

Angelique stood obstinate. How dare he tell her who she loved or didn't?

"Do you?" he asked.

"Mayhap."

"Very well, then. Take him to your bed! See if I care!"

"I will!" Angelique strode from the room, heat raging through her blood. She would pay Lachlan back for his cheating ways.

She found Philippe, looking sheepish and afraid, in the corner of the crowded great hall. No one seemed to notice when she slipped her arm through his and escorted him up the stairs. She would show Lachlan she was not afraid of him and that she would not obey his every snarl. She would call his bluff. If he could have lovers then so could she...or at least pretend to.

⋰⋱

"I don't care," Lachlan muttered as he stormed blindly out of the castle. Angelique could have her wee laddie if she wanted him that desperately. "This is a damned sham of a marriage anyway. Unfaithful, scheming, thorny bitch!"

When he reached the stables, a strong emotion struck him— battle rage, bloodlust. He turned on his heel and strode back through the great hall and up the stone steps, seeing no one and nothing save his destination. Fire pounded through his veins. He felt strong enough to topple a stone tower.

"Lachlan?" Rebbie trailed after him.

"Not now. I'm killing vermin." He drew his sword.

At Angelique's sitting room door, he used all his strength to kick the solid oak. The door swung back and hit something. He charged in. "If he lays a damned hand on you, I shall slice the bastard limb from limb!"

Angelique stood by the fireplace alone. Where was the whoreson?

Someone scuttled out the door behind him. He turned to see the retreating red cloak.

"Coward." Lachlan sprinted after him.

"Lachlan!" Angelique tailed him. "He did not touch me."

"You don't wish me to kill your lover?"

"He is not my lover! You dolt." She yanked at the plaid on his back but he did not stop.

By the time Lachlan reached the courtyard, Philippe was running for the open gates.

"Damned whoreson."

He hated the victory he saw in Angelique's eyes. It took all his strength to keep from throwing her over his shoulder and carting her back upstairs to give her a sound thrashing on the arse. She sent him a haughty look and disappeared back inside.

He motioned two of his guards forward. "Follow that lad, seize him and put him in a cell below," Lachlan said in a low voice. "Don't hurt him or let anyone know you've captured him. I'll question him later."

"Aye, m'laird." The guards mounted up.

Lachlan returned to the great hall where a couple dozen pairs of curious eyes watched him. He gave a brief bow. "Carry on." He took the stairs two at a time to Angelique's room. The sitting room door stood open. Her bodyguards remained at their post, staring into space as if Lachlan wasn't a mad fool. Aye, he knew he was, but he didn't care. Angelique was his wife and he wouldn't be sharing her. He knocked at her bedchamber door. "Angelique?"

"Go away!"

After she'd barred the door on him last night, he'd decided he would have no more of that and had removed the plank of oak when she'd gone down for breakfast.

He lifted the latch and pushed. Something sat before the door—a trunk—which he shoved out of the way.

"I will not speak to you, *monsieur*."

"Aye, you will and be glad for it."

"You, sir, are jealous!" Angelique gave him her back.

He slammed the door, placed the trunk before it again, and advanced toward her. "I am not jealous! I am your damnable husband. No man who is married to you will have a pleasant life. 'Tis a certainty."

"*Merci.* Nor will any wife of yours."

Grasping her waist, he turned her to face him and pressed her against the nearest wall. Taking her chin in his hand, he stared at her lips, lush pink. He would not share them. "Did you kiss that bastard?"

"*Oui,*" she said through clenched teeth.

"Liar." Lachlan crushed her lips beneath his, forceful, driving. A second later, she bit him.

"Och! Like biting, do you?" He nibbled her lower lip, caught it between his teeth, but not hard enough to draw blood. Fiery emotion burned in her darkened eyes, just as arousal burned inside him.

He released her lip and nipped her neck.

She sucked in a hissing breath, her whole body shuddering. Her hands fisted in his clothes and drew him closer. Aye, he loved her responsiveness. He tugged at her sleeve, baring her shoulder, and scraped his teeth over it, flicked it with his tongue. Her skin was smooth, hot and alluring. These blasted clothes were in the way. He yanked up her skirts and slid his hand along the silk stockings to the top, over the softest skin of her inner thighs.

She gasped. "Do not."

"Why not?" While looking into her hungry eyes, he gently stroked a finger over her wet curls. "Because I'll know how much you want me?"

"I do not want you," she said in a breathy tone.

"Nay?" He parted her swollen sex lips and her moisture drenched his fingers. "You're not good at lying, *madame*."

"It is Philippe that I want."

Ha, what a lie. "Is that right?"

"*Oui*. Just as you want Eleanor."

"God's blood! I don't want her. I only want you," he confessed. Indeed, that one truth stripped his soul bare.

"Now, who is the liar?" she said, near breathless.

"After last night, how can you doubt it?"

"I am not a naive child, *monsieur*. I know about men and their...desires. They want the woman they cannot have. They want many women because they like variety. They bore easily."

"You don't know me very well, then." Unable to imagine being bored with her, he stroked her with firm gentleness, that wee, sweet nub of flesh between her legs. She moaned, her eyelids dropping.

Aye. Over and over he caressed her, then slid a finger inside that snug passage. She whimpered but did not try to escape him.

He sensed the tension building within her, readying her for climax, and pulled his hand away. "Who do you want?"

Trembling, her breathing harsh, she glared at him.

He rubbed her inner thigh with teasing, light strokes.

"Touch me," she whispered.

"I want to do more than touch you."

"*Oui*. Do it." Her fingers grasped at his plaid.

Somewhere, he found a well of restraint and patience. "Not until you say you want me."

"I want you," she said in French, soft as a breath.

Saints! She was so lovely and passionate he wished to devour her like a juicy plum. "Say my name."

"Lachlan."

He took possession of her mouth, kissing her deep as shivers coursed through him. He must have her now. Lifting his kilt and her skirts, he anchored the material between them and picked her up. Urging her to wrap her legs around his waist, he positioned himself and slid into her. So tight she squeezed the control right out of him.

"Ah, saints, Angelique," he growled and halted a moment to savor her. So hot, wet and exquisite.

She buried her hands in his hair, fisting, pulling, and gave sweet little whimper-cries. "Lachlan?"

"Aye. That's good, hmm?" He moved, driving up into her gently but with persistence.

"*Oui*," she breathed.

Every stroke was pure heaven, even more so because of her enthusiasm. As he had suspected, she wanted him profoundly, as he did her. He was greedy! He never wanted this to end. The pleasure was absolute; climax teased him. Slowing, he fondled that sensitive spot with his wet thumb. She cried out, held her breath, wiggled on him.

"That's it, lass. Give it to me." When her inner muscles started to flutter and caress him, he drove into her hard. She screamed and rode him as her orgasm took over. He let go some of his control, allowing his own release to burn through him, so strong and all-consuming his conscious thought left him for a moment. He groaned, his face pressed into her hair.

"*Iosa is Muire Mhàthair.*" He had never felt anything so powerful. Legs weak, he carried her to the bed and laid her upon it. Still inside her, he rested a moment while gently kissing her lips. He didn't want to leave her. Not this time, not when she'd said she wanted him.

Her inner muscles tightened, caressing him again. He pulled out and stepped back to undress. When he'd shed his plaid and shirt, Angelique surveyed him with darkened eyes, her lashes a bit damp.

He could not think of that gut-wrenching feeling she inspired in him, not now. She was like a storm-tide at sea that would suck him under and suffocate him. He'd felt her pain and hated it when she thought he'd been with Eleanor. But Angelique refused to trust him. It cut him to the bone to realize how untrustworthy she saw him when it was the thing he longed for most. That and her devotion, affection.

He hoped she liked what she saw when she observed him for he was not quite done with her this day. In fact, he feared he would never be done with her.

She didn't resist when he loosened the ties and fastenings on her clothing. Soon he unlaced her corset, removed it, and she helped him pull the shift over her head. Sudden vulnerability softening her eyes, she crossed her arms over her breasts.

"You cannot be shy now. Too late." Smiling, he tugged her arms away.

After thoroughly devouring her mouth, he turned his attention to her breasts. "You have kept these luscious morsels from me too long."

"You do not..."

He placed wee cherishing kisses on one. "What?"

"They are too small," she whispered.

The uncertainty in her gaze flayed him. "Nay. Your breasts are lovely beyond words." With his tongue, he flicked her nipple, pink and scrunched hard, then sucked at it. "Perfect."

She whimpered and closed her eyes.

"Mmm." He switched to the other, savoring the feel of her fingers in his hair, holding him close.

He allowed his gaze to leisurely wander over her naked body, taking in each exquisite detail. Her breasts were not huge, true, but they were round and perky, in perfect proportion to her slim body. He did not lie; they were indeed the loveliest breasts he had ever seen. Her waist was slender and her derriere curvy and succulent. He wished to bite it, then lick and memorize every inch of her.

"Angelique. You're the most beautiful creation on God's earth."

"Do not speak." She placed a finger on his lips.

He kissed the tip. "Why not?"

She grasped his semi-erect shaft in her hand.

"Och." It was too soon. But as he watched her small, inexperienced hands stroking him, he hardened with gusto. "Mmm." He couldn't stay down long with her in control.

She rose over him, mounting him, guiding his shaft into her. He growled, loving her aggressiveness. A woman who knew exactly what she wanted and took it. She rode him for several blissful minutes.

He stroked her nipples, tweaked them gently, loving the simple act of observing his wife enjoying his body. A woman who had feared him and hated sex days ago. Giving her pleasure had become his primary goal in life. He was not sure when that had happened, but he burned to hear her cry out his name at the height of passion.

Before he could've expected it, her body shuddered around him in a climax. Screaming, she flopped onto his chest and he took over the thrusting as she squeezed him.

Still in complete control, he rolled her onto her back and rose over her.

Once she had calmed, he pulled her upwards. "On your hands." She lifted her upper body and held herself aloft on her hands, while he supported her hips. He drove himself into her and her head fell back on her shoulders.

"Lachlan," she moaned.

"Aye." A warmth of emotion rushed through his chest. He tugged her closer, placed her arms around his neck, brushed her lips with his. *I want only you. Do you understand? No other woman.* He wanted to say those words to her again, but they would only remind her of her jealousy. Would only make her ask, for how long?

He didn't know. Maybe forever. He could not imagine tiring of looking into her eyes, of driving himself into her hot, wet body. But he yearned to see more in her gaze—complete trust. Love. How could he gain such things? How could he decipher the secrets in her?

After another minute he detected a change in her breathing and loosened some of the control he held. They reached the height of pleasure together.

He lay her down beside him and pulled her close so they could rest.

"Angelique?" he murmured a few moments later, after his own breathing was back to normal, but she didn't respond. Asleep already? He kissed her cheek, quietly slid out of bed and dressed. While she napped, he would see what information he could extract from Philippe.

✣✣✣

Eleanor descended the narrow wooden staircase at the inn to dine in the common room. All heads turned to her as she and her maid entered. She prayed none of the men were thieves.

"M'lady." The stocky proprietor bowed before her. "I hope you will allow us to serve you supper this evening."

"Perhaps." If anything from his humble kitchen appealed. But she tried not to treat these poor commoners too badly.

"I've saved you the perfect spot." He escorted her to a private table in the corner by the window. Not that the view of a cobblestone street and livery stable was anything worth noting. Her maid and a footman stood nearby, if she should need anything. Being a countess could sometimes be lonely. How she wished Lachlan or some other member of the aristocracy was here.

Once Eleanor ordered and they'd served the wine, she waited while her gaze searched the faces of each person present. Commoners, all. Judging by their clothing, not even a lowly baron was present.

A tall, thin gentleman with black hair and stylish clothing descended the staircase. His dark brown eyes caught on her immediately. Well now, this one showed promise. He had to be titled or at least wealthy. She thought her eyes were playing tricks on her when she noticed one of his arms missing.

He approached and bowed before her. "*Madame, pardonnez-moi* for being so forward as to introduce myself. I am Guy Laurent, *comte de* Girard, at your service."

"A French count?" Indeed it was her lucky day.

"*Mais oui.*" Despite the paleness of his skin, his midnight eyes sparkled wickedly.

"Eleanor Stanhope, countess of Wexbury." She lifted her hand and he kissed the back.

"*Enchanté, madame.*"

"A pleasure. Join me, won't you?"

"*Merci.* Nothing would please me more." He pulled out a chair and seated himself across from her.

"Wine?" She waved her maid forward to pour him a glass. Eleanor had a most intense curiosity as to how he lost his arm, but minded her manners. "What brings you all the way to the wilds of Scotland?"

"Visiting an old friend." His French accent was very thick.

"And who would that be?"

"She is a countess, also. Perhaps you know her? Angelique Drummagan."

"Indeed, I do! We were ladies in waiting together for Her Majesty, Queen Anne. You wouldn't be...Angelique's former suitor, would you?" If this man would take Angelique away from Lachlan, then the Highlander would be free for her taking. What a brilliant circumstance.

"I am flattered. You have heard of me?" the *comte* asked.

"I only know she wished to marry a French nobleman but her Scottish father forbade the match. She did not reveal his name to me."

He smiled, but strangely, it did not appear a genuine smile. "You have found me out."

"I assume you've heard she is recently wed."

"Oui." He sipped the wine, then scowled at it and set it down. "What can you tell me of this fortunate man?"

Fortunate? Hmm, clearly he still had feelings for Angelique. "Lachlan MacGrath is a good man, a Scottish Highlander. The marriage was arranged by the king, you see, as a reward. But I fear it is a terrible match."

"And is this man brave, powerful?"

"Indeed, he is what one would call a warrior. Very large, strong and crafty with a sword. Also cunning. He saved the life of the king's favorite by uncovering an assassination plot."

"Aha." Girard leaned back in his chair, his expression turning frosty. "And his family?"

Eleanor was careful not to show her glee. Girard was clearly jealous. Perhaps he would kidnap Angelique. "The new Earl of Draughon is a second son, brother to an earl and chief. Lachlan is a formidable man. One would not want to confront him directly."

"Hmm." Girard lifted a dark brow, waiting.

"He has several guards and trained warriors who travel with him. If one wanted something he had, one would be wiser to steal it away while he wasn't looking."

"Indeed?"

Eleanor nodded, observing the scheming thoughts reflecting in the man's eyes. She did not want him challenging Lachlan. Not that he had a chance of besting him with only one arm. Still, pistols could be deadly accurate in the right hand.

"You have seen Angelique recently, no?" he asked.

"Yes, I've just come from a visit to Draughon Castle and the wedding festivities."

"And how is she?"

"Unhappy to have been forced to marry a man she doesn't love."

Girard snickered, his black mustache and neatly groomed beard lending him a devilish quality. "Poor little Angelique."

"Did you love her?" Eleanor prayed he did.

"Ah, *amour*. It is such a perplexing emotion, *non*?" The smirk appeared on his face again. Something about that was all wrong. The man was supposed to be jealous, angry, and wanting Angelique all to himself.

"I agree," she said. "Sometimes intense desire can masquerade as love."

"You are a wise lady, I see." His attention focused on her completely, delving down to that sensual side she tried to keep hidden, except before the right man.

Excitement charged through her. "I thank you." Oh, who cared if he had only one arm? The man was intriguing and debonair. With his slender physique, he could never measure up to Lachlan and his burly muscles, but he could keep her entertained in the meantime.

"Angelique took something from me," Girard said in a secretive tone. "Perhaps you would be willing to help me retrieve it?"

"Perhaps. If you will help me in turn. She stole something from me, as well...my lover. And I would like him back."

Girard threw back his head and laughed. Once he'd calmed, he lifted her hand and kissed it. "I think we have a deal, *madame*."

CHAPTER TWELVE

"Let Angelique sleep as long as she will. When she wakes, take the bath in for her," Lachlan told the servants. He must keep her occupied, after all. Hopefully, questioning Philippe wouldn't take long and he'd be back in time to share her bath before it was cold.

After taking almost an hour to bid their departing wedding guests farewell, he descended the steps to the dungeon. Rebbie and Dirk followed.

"We're here to see the French lad," Lachlan told the armed guard.

"Aye, m'laird." He led them further along the dank, underground passage and opened a wooden and metal door. Dirk carried a torch into the dark cell, Lachlan entered, unsheathing his sword and Rebbie followed.

Lachlan eyed the small fellow cowering in the corner, squinting at them. He might pity the weasel if he hadn't tried to steal Angelique. "What is your name?"

"Philippe Descartes, my lord." He crawled forward a few inches and remained in a submissive kneeling position.

"And why have you come here to Draughon?"

The boy's eyes were so wide, Lachlan feared they'd pop from their sockets.

"I am but an old friend of Angelique. I wished to congratulate both of you on your marriage." He bowed his head briefly.

"Humph. What a lie," Lachlan muttered, remembering the goblets from Girard. "Did you bring a gift?"

"A...a gift? Pray pardon, my lord, I did not. But I shall send you one if—"

"Nay, I mean, did you deliver a gift from someone else?"

"*Non.*" The boy's gaze remained steady for a few seconds, then dropped to the glinting blade of Lachlan's sword. Perhaps he told the truth, but who could tell? The gutter rat probably knew not how to be honest.

"Who did you travel from London with?" Lachlan asked.

"No one."

"I'll tolerate no more lies, laddie! I want the truth."

Philippe turned jittery, his hands trembling, gaze darting about.

"You traveled with someone or spoke with someone. Now, who was it?" Lachlan demanded.

"Eleanor, countess of Wexbury, my lord."

Rebbie muttered a curse, and Dirk sent him a concerned glance.

"I see," Lachlan said. Now what was that witch up to? "And who else?"

"Her servants and that is all; I swear it." The lad's voice broke, making him sound no more than a dozen years old, but he had to be around twenty.

"What has Eleanor said to you?" Lachlan asked.

"Sir?"

"I know you and Eleanor are plotting against Angelique and me. Planning to destroy our marriage. Tell me of these plans."

"There...there were no plans, my lord."

"You're lying again," Lachlan growled. "Would you like me to show you how dangerous lying is?" He lifted his sword before him, as if examining the sharpness of the blade.

Philippe trembled and gave his head a spasm-like shake. "She wished to...to visit with you. I wished to see Angelique one last time before I return to France."

"And what did she say about Angelique or me?"

"She has a most keen interest in you, my lord."

"Why?"

"I believe she has a great affection for you. Perhaps she loves you, though she did not say."

Rebbie snorted. And Lachlan felt like doing the same.

Eleanor wouldn't know love if it bashed her on the side of the head. Dallying with her had been one of the biggest mistakes of his life. "What did she tell you to do here?"

Philippe cleared his throat, his gaze darting from Dirk, to Rebbie and back again to Lachlan and his sword.

"If you tell me the complete truth, we won't harm you."

His breaths were so harsh as to be audible. "Eleanor wished me to…to lure Angelique away from you."

"I see." Lachlan had suspected the woman could be evil and cunning. "Do you suppose Eleanor went back to London when she left?"

"I know not…but I was to meet her at the Breakstane Inn in the village if we were separated."

"Do you know Baron Kormad?"

"I have seen him, but never talked to him."

"What about a French count named Girard?"

"I have never met him. I only know he asked for Angelique's hand in marriage but she refused to go through with it."

Lachlan kept his malevolent glower on the squirming lad several moments longer, hoping to frighten him one last bit. "I shall release you if you promise never to set foot here at Draughon and never approach Lady Angelique again. She is my wife and will remain so. My advice to you is to return to France and stay there."

"*Oui*, my lord. I shall. *Merci*." He bowed again, which put his face close to the floor in his kneeling position.

Lachlan and his two friends strode out. Near the top of the dungeon steps, Lachlan spoke in a low voice to the guard. "Release him but send two men to secretly follow him. See if he meets with a countess named Eleanor Stanhope at the Breakstane Inn. If so, see if they can find out what the two discuss. Have one man report back to me tonight."

⚬⚬⚬

"Where have you been?" Angelique asked when Lachlan entered her room minutes later.

He paused, observing her in the large wooden tub. Firelight gleamed off her wet, ivory skin. Her scrunched nipples flirted with the surface of the water. The sight arrested him, making him instantly hard.

"The remainder of our guests left." With much haste, Lachlan disrobed and dropped his clothing into a pile on the floor.

"What? I did not get to say good-bye." Angelique might have

176

been talking about guests, but her gaze devoured the more intimate areas of his body.

"I conveyed your good wishes and your gratitude." He knelt by the tub, observing her in closer detail. Her face was rosy, either from the hot water or a blush. Damp ringlets of hair teased at her neck, as he wished to do with his kisses. "How long have you been soaking in there?"

"Not long."

"Do you suppose there's room for me?"

"Perhaps." With a shy grin, she scooted back, lifting her upper body out of the water and drawing her knees up. He was pleased to see she was no longer shy about exposing her breasts.

He stepped into the tub, then sat. "Ahh, nice and hot."

"Oui."

"Come. Sit here between my legs."

Even in the dim firelight her blush was obvious.

"You're in no danger, I vow. We will refrain from coupling for now…if we can." He winked and sent her a wicked grin.

She giggled. If ever there was a sound he loved, that was it— Angelique being happy.

"We shall talk about other matters to distract ourselves."

A knock sounded at the door. "Your food, m'laird," the female servant called.

He took Angelique's smock from a nearby chair and covered her chest with it. "Come," he said.

Angelique sucked in a sharp breath, her blush deepening. "Why did you…?"

"I'm hungry. Are you not?"

The door opened and a middle-aged maid carried in a tray of food and drink.

"Place it here, if you would." He indicated a wooden chair near him, and she deposited it there. "My thanks," he said.

"M'laird. M'lady." The maid curtseyed and left.

"Mère de Dieu, that was mortifying," Angelique whispered.

"Why?" He tore off a bite of bread and threw it into his mouth.

"We are nude…together. And bathing."

"You are covered. The servants help you bathe and dress all the time. And she cannot see beneath the surface of the water with all this soap you've used. Besides, you are beautiful in the nude and should not be ashamed."

She blew out a breath. "You've surely gone daft."

He snickered and offered her a bite of bread. "If you'll come over here, I'll feed you well and proper."

"I thought we were bathing. Now we are eating a meal?"

"Indeed. We accomplish two things at once. It leaves more time for...other activities."

∽✦❀✦∾

A half hour later, the bath water started to cool. Lachlan and Angelique had helped each other bathe and wash their hair, in between sharing bites of food or sips of wine. Angelique found the whole exchange to be shockingly intimate but more fun than she'd had in years. Since Lachlan didn't try to couple with her, perhaps he'd had his fill of carnal pursuits, at least for now...even though he did have an erection half the time. This intimacy with a man was so new to her, she could not decide how she felt about it. She feared she was slipping beneath his seductive spell and enjoying him too much.

"Let us play hazard. What say you?" Lachlan asked when they stepped out of the tub. Droplets of water glistened on the finely wrought muscles of his shoulders and chest. He slowly dragged the piece of linen material over her wet body, sending delicious sensations along her skin.

"I do not know how. My mother would never allow me to play such gambling games." Shivering from the cool air, she picked up the clean smock from the foot of the bed.

He snatched the garment from her and flung it away. "Well then, I shall corrupt you." He winked. "Into bed with you now."

"That was clean!"

"You have no need of it."

She huffed but climbed into bed. Now what was he up to? She did not wish to lounge about naked for hours. Surely that was an activity more suited to a paramour than a wife. Then, she wondered if she could be both to him. What a daft yet exciting notion.

After he dried himself, Lachlan dug something from his sporran and followed her into bed, leaning back against the pillows and allowing the sheet to rest at his waist. His naked presence beside her in bed gave her more intense carnal thoughts and urges. His hard, hair-roughened thigh grazed her own, making her recall the erotic sensations of his legs sliding between hers. The grouping of three glowing candles on the bedside table revealed a few remaining drops of water sparkling on his chest. She entertained the mad idea of licking them off and brushing her lips over his chest, kissing every inch.

He jiggled something in his hand that clacked together. "Never played hazard?"

"No."

"'Tis easy. Whoever loses each toss of the dice must kiss the other person wherever they say. And we'll take turns."

"What do you mean...kiss...on any body part?" Had he read her mind?

"Aye."

"*Ma foi!* You are wicked."

His gaze turned sensual in the extreme. "And you like that about me."

Indeed she did, but she refused to let him know that. She hoped he didn't see her fiery blush. "You have played this before."

"Not for these stakes. Usually I only gamble for money, or weapons. Now, here are the rules. Choose a main—a number between five and nine, then roll the dice. If the number you chose comes up, you win. If not, different rules apply to each number. Ladies first." He dropped the dice into her hands.

"How will I know you are telling the truth about the rules?"

"You think I would lie? Whether you win or lose, I will enjoy the consequence."

She hid a mischievous smile and jiggled the dice much like he did. "The number I choose is seven." She rolled the dice and the number displayed was eleven. *"Parbleu."*

"You've won," he said.

"What? You're making that up. You said if I roll the number I chose, I win."

"Why would I cheat to allow you to win? 'Tis part of the rules. Ask Rebbie or Dirk if you don't believe me...later. Not now. Where would you like your kiss?"

Heavens! The man was truly daft, but the idea of a kiss from him did tempt her. "You may kiss my neck."

"Neck? Is that all?"

"*Oui.* What is wrong with that?"

"Naught. But I thought you would be more unruly...perhaps

a bit risqué." He leaned toward her. She tilted her head back and he pressed his lips to her neck. He nibbled, tickling, giving her chills, and she rolled away laughing.

He grinned. "My turn. Eight." He rolled the dice. "Five."

"You lose."

"Nay. I get to roll again."

"You are making this up, I vow!" she said.

"I have played this game since I was nine years of age. I ken the rules." He rolled the dice again and an eight came up. "Blast!"

"You have won. This is the number you first said."

"Aye, but if the main shows up on the chance, 'tis an out. You've won again."

She smiled and pointed to her shoulder. He gave her a seductive look and leisurely kissed her shoulder, stroked his tongue against it, then sucked at her flesh.

Shivering, she drew away lest he seduce her yet again, and so easily. Her nipples ached and yearned for his lips. The moisture between her legs tingled and itched.

His eyes gleaming with devilish seduction, he dropped the dice into her hand.

"Five." She tossed them.

He grinned at the three. "You lose."

"Can I not roll again?"

"Nay. Three is always an out."

"I intend to check with someone about these rules you are creating."

He nodded. "You should. But now I want my kiss." He pointed to his mouth.

She leaned toward him and placed a quick peck on his lips.

"Too fast. That didn't count."

"*Oui*, it did."

"Each kiss must last at least to the count of five."

"More rules you are making up?"

"Coward," he murmured, a taunting look in his eye.

Relenting, she leaned forward to give him a longer kiss. She must prove her bravery, after all. His firm, smooth lips moved against her own. She drew his heated breath within her and desire flared. Wishing to consume him utterly, she flicked her tongue between his lips.

"Mmm." The little moan came from him but he remained

immobile while his darkened, heavy-lidded gaze penetrated her. She forced herself to draw away. *Mère de Dieu*, she was too susceptible to him.

"Much better," he purred.

She lost the next round by tossing a two. He pointed to his chest and she kissed him there, taking a bit more time and brushing her lips over his hard muscles and sprinkling of hair as she'd imagined earlier. His male nipple was an erotic little sight. When she touched it with her tongue, breath hissed between his teeth.

Next, he chose seven as his main and rolled it. Grinning, he pointed to a spot just below his navel. The sheet still covered his erection.

Heavens, he could not be serious. "You are a beast," she said in French.

"Aye." When he lay back on the pillows, she leaned over him and kissed the muscle-hardened spot he'd indicated. That narrow line of hair on his flat lower belly tickled her lips and mesmerized her. She brushed her lips back and forth, then pressed her nose to him. His clean male scent tempted her, as did the thought of kissing him all night…and all over.

"Mmm." He handed her the dice when she sat back. "You best not lose this one, m'lady, or the penalty will be stiff."

Stiff? Her cheeks burned. "I know what you are thinking."

He lifted a brow. "Do you now?"

"Six." She nodded and rolled the dice.

When an eleven displayed, he hissed, then grinned. "Out."

"*Sacrebleu!*"

He chuckled and lay back on the pillow again, stacking his hands behind his head. "If you know what I was thinking, kiss me there. If you're right, I'll give you three turns. If you're wrong, I'll bite you on the arse, and it will hurt."

A laugh burst from her mouth before she could stop it. "How ridiculous. You are a lunatic."

"Aye, but you ken I'm good at gaming. I'll even write my answer down if you bring me that quill and paper."

"I'll not walk over there naked." She was covered from collarbone down in the sheet and wished to stay that way.

"I will then." He rose, his erection bobbing, and crossed the room. Goodness, he had not one speck of modesty.

Observing his broad shoulders and bulging muscles

everywhere, she sighed before she could stop herself. She had never dreamed she would enjoy staring at a naked man.

At the writing desk, he bent over, bringing her attention to his lean, manly arse, while he scribbled on the paper. What an intriguing sight.

"Make sure it is a word I recognize," she said.

"You ken this word." When he turned and strode back toward her, his erection was even larger. She forced herself not stare at it.

He lay down and covered himself as before but his tarse tented the sheet.

"You love gambling, do you not?" she asked, hoping to distract him.

"Aye. I usually win." He looked very pleased with himself. "And now for that kiss, *madame*."

She did not fear him anymore, but she was not entirely comfortable with him either. He had obviously written some word that meant his male member—probably tarse—and kissing him there would be scandalous. But…intriguing. She had heard women whispering of this in France and how intensely a man enjoyed it. Much in the same way he had pleasured her with his mouth the night before.

A dare lurked in his eyes and in his smile. He didn't think she would do it, she knew. He thought she was afraid.

She rose over him and pulled down the sheet to reveal his erection. *Ma foi!* Heat flamed over her when she studied his massive proportion close up. Leaning forward, she detected his scent was clean, musky and hypnotizing. She kissed his shaft once…twice. His skin was hot, silky smooth, and the flesh beneath, hard as stone. She flicked out the tip of her tongue for an experimental taste.

Lachlan stiffened and groaned.

She drew back, her gaze shooting to his darkened eyes, near closed in desire.

"Mmm." He hissed a few Gaelic words. "Very, very nice and I thank you." He blew out two long breaths, as if calming himself. "Any chance you might do that once more?"

"No, I will not!" At least not right now. Though she wanted to, she would not indulge his every carnal whim. He might think he had control over her.

"'Tis too bad." He bolted upright, flipped her face down onto the mattress and pinned her. "Because you lose again."

"What? That is what you were thinking. You wished me to kiss your tarse."

His brief growl and hot breath tickled her ear. "No matter how much I desire that, 'tis not what I wrote on the paper."

"You tricked me! You lout!" She squirmed, trying to free herself from his firm hold.

He gave a wicked chuckle. "I told you, I am good at gaming."

"Go get the paper and let me see."

"Again, you think I would lie?"

"Yes!"

"Very well." He climbed off the bed, retrieved the paper from the desk and held it up for her inspection.

"Elbow?" she demanded. "Why would you desire me to kiss your elbow?"

He grinned. "My elbows like to be kissed."

"You are a cheat!" And how bold and silly she had been, kissing his shaft. She would never live that down.

"I played fairly. Now I get to bite your sweet...little...round arse."

"No, it will hurt."

"You agreed to this bet."

"If it hurts, I get to bite you three times, hard as I want, anywhere I want. Are you agreed?"

"Och! You learn fast. That makes me proud. Aye, you may bite me...anywhere but my tarse. If you bite me there, it must be very gentle."

"*Très bien.*" Heavens, she could not bite him there, could she?

"Agreed, then." He winked.

"Write it on the paper and sign it."

"I don't understand why you refuse to trust me." He proceeded to her writing desk and drew up the contract. The sheet wrapped around her, she followed and read the paper when he'd finished.

"Now, bend over." He grinned like a big, hungry wolf.

She ran to the bed and leapt on it. He landed half on top of her, turned her onto her stomach and shoved the sheet away from her derriere.

"Mmm, 'twill be tasty." He first kissed it, grazed his teeth over it, then gently pressed his teeth against her skin. It was not a real bite and hurt not at all. He then proceeded to do the same to the other cheek. He brushed his beard stubble over it, tickling.

She giggled. "One bite is all you are allowed, *monsieur.*"

"I haven't bitten you yet."

"Yes, you did and it hurt."

"Liar! Does this hurt?" He licked her skin.

"No." Heavens, he had a wicked, delightful tongue. The itching moisture of arousal grew more intense between her legs.

"This?" He placed several kisses over her cheeks.

"No." A little ache speared her center, making her wish he'd put his erection to use.

Behind her, Lachlan spread her legs and crawled between. Angelique was more fun to play with than any woman he had yet encountered. The hellcat had sheathed her claws and become the purring kitten eager for petting.

When he widened her legs, she arched her back. So inviting. Placing a hand beneath her belly, he pulled her upward, parted her feminine lips and licked between. Her sweet arousal intensified his need. He flicked that tiny nub of flesh and she gasped.

She arched her back further, pressing firmly against him as if she wanted more. He gave her a thorough licking, until she was whimpering and crying out.

Kneeling behind her, he stroked the tip of his shaft through her generous moisture and between those delicate folds that reminded him of pink rose petals. He pushed just inside, her heat near scorching him. Keeping in mind she might be sore, he controlled his movements.

"Mmm." Thrusting in and out gently, he gradually went deeper each time.

She cried out. "Lachlan."

"Aye, Angelique. Are you liking that, then?"

"Oui."

Still fully inside her, he wrapped an arm around her below her breasts and lay down on his side, taking her with him. He aligned her back to his chest and breathed into her ear, nibbled on it. She made wee whimpering noises between those breathy French words. Just listening to her made him want to drive in harder. But he must not.

He stroked his hand from her breasts downward to brush over her mound, then lifted her leg.

As he thrust, he sucked at her earlobe and stroked her in a circular motion. Mindless, she cried out and pushed her hips back against him, meeting each thrust. Damnation, she fired his blood, made him want to take her with more forceful movements.

"Lachlan!" she cried out when her climax overcame her. How he had dreamed of that.

"Aye, you're so beautiful, lass." He held her tighter as pleasure exploded through him. He growled, relishing the way her body caressed his, milking him of his seed. Long seconds later, he regained his breath and kissed her neck, realizing each time with her was even better than the last. How was this possible? Usually he grew bored with a woman after a few times, but with Angelique, he grew more intrigued, more drawn under her spell with each bedding.

He turned her about to face him. His lips against her forehead, he drew her close and they rested, relaxing in the firelight, he knew not how long. He only knew he was happy and content, at home.

A knock sounded at the door, awaking him from a light doze.

"What is it?" Angelique asked in French, her voice groggy with sleep.

"I'll go see." He arose and covered her. After putting on his long shirt, he opened the door a crack.

"M'laird, Rebbinglen wishes to speak to you," one of Angelique's personal bodyguards told him.

"I'll be right out," Lachlan said, then closed the door. He returned to the bed, kissed Angelique on the cheek and picked up his plaid. "Rebbie wants to talk to me about something. I shall be back soon."

"It is late."

"Aye."

She remained silent while he dressed.

"You wish me to sleep here tonight?" he asked, observing her for reaction.

"*Oui*," she whispered in a vulnerable tone.

An aching thrill twisted through his chest. "'Twill be my pleasure." He gave her a lingering kiss on the lips.

Though he did not want to leave the room, he had to. Rebbie wouldn't interrupt them unless it was important.

He found his friend in the great hall with Dirk and one of the guards who had followed Philippe to the inn.

"Come." He escorted them to the solar and closed the door. "What news?"

The guard spoke first. "M'laird, the French lad did indeed go to the inn and meet with a richly dressed lady. We sat close but could hear naught of what they said. They whispered and drank wine. Later, they retired to separate rooms for the night."

"Now, tell him the most interesting part," Rebbie said.

"We stayed in the common room a while to see if either of them left. They didn't, but another man came in. A man with only one arm. This one was also a Frenchman—we figured out by his speech—but a more finely dressed one. Considering the way the proprietor bowed and coddled to him, we figured him of noble blood."

"Did you get a name?" Lachlan asked, almost holding his breath.

"No, we only heard his title mentioned. *Comte*. Count."

"God's teeth. 'Tis Girard, I'm certain of it," Lachlan said. Angelique's terror sliced through him again. He could only imagine the pain she suffered at the bastard's hand and body when he'd raped her. Lachlan should castrate the whoreson. "Our first priority is to protect Angelique. My concern is he will try to kill her or kidnap her. Why else would he be here?"

Rebbie and Dirk nodded.

"Anything else?" Lachlan asked the guard.

"Nay."

"I thank you. Excellent work. I will see you on the morrow."

When the guard left, Lachlan spoke to Rebbie and Dirk in a low voice. "You must not repeat this, ever, to anyone but you must know why Girard is so dangerous to Angelique. Do you swear?"

"Aye." Both men waited with troubled gazes.

Lachlan hated to even say the damnable words. "Girard raped her."

"Nay. The bastard," Rebbie growled.

Dirk's expression changed to lethal iciness.

"Aye." Lachlan said. "And I hope he gives me a reason to kill him outright." They knew what he meant. He had never killed a man in cold blood, nor would he ever, but his rage over this was intense and he yearned for justice. "If Girard tries to approach Angelique, I take that as leave to kill him. I protect what is mine.

186

Girard will never lay a finger on her again. Before first light, we'll leave for the inn."

CHAPTER THIRTEEN

A soft tap sounded at Angelique's bedchamber door. Her first thought was that Lachlan had returned. But no, he would not knock.

"Who is it?"

"Me." Camille stuck her head in.

"Enter." Angelique sat up in bed, the sheet and counterpane covering her breasts.

Her friend closed the door with a snap. "Well, I see you have been thoroughly bedded. Is he a skilled lover?"

Angelique's face burned. "Do not ask such a question." She could not discuss the profound things she and Lachlan shared. No words existed, in French or English, to adequately describe the astounding sensations and feelings he provoked within her. Too conflicting—wicked, yet divine. What she should find abhorrent was instead amazing and wonderful.

"I knew he would be by the way he moves…and the way he looks at you."

Angelique wanted to ask how Lachlan looked at her, but she already knew—with sensual, dark and lingering interest. His eyes communicated his sexual thoughts clearly. She shivered.

Camille sat by the fireplace, stirred the coals and added more wood. "He also seems very just and fair."

"I suppose." Angelique could not help but remember the silly games they'd played and how Lachlan had manipulated the outcome to suit himself…and her, too, if one considered the pleasure she received.

"Not only just, but almost lenient," Camille went on. "Though I feared he would kill Philippe in the dungeon, he released him instead."

A shock went through her. "Why was Philippe in the dungeon?"

"Oh, you did not know? He had Philippe held for a short while, went to visit him—I suspect to question him—then released him, free as a bird. Not many men would do that after someone tried to lure their wife away with suggestions of divorce."

"*Sacrebleu!* When did he capture him? I saw Philippe leave and run through the gates."

"After your ruckus, with all the chasing and yelling. What a lovers' spat that was." Camille giggled.

"Please tell me what you know."

"Lachlan had someone bring Philippe back. I suspect you were here being seduced at the time."

"That bastard!" She shoved herself toward the edge of the bed. "He manipulated me."

"As I said, he was lenient with Philippe; he did not harm him."

"He withheld the truth from me!" Angelique yanked her smock over her head, then slid on her wrap. "He promised to keep me informed about everything." And worst of all he had imprisoned her friend.

"If I'd known you would react this way, I would not have told you."

"What? You are my cousin. I thought you my friend."

"I am, but you cannot blame Lachlan for wanting to protect you. He is the best husband for you."

"You are as daft as he is," she muttered, though she could not imagine being married to anyone else.

"It is not my fault you refuse to see the truth. He would protect you with his life. If Girard returns, you will be most fortunate to have Lachlan for a protector."

That was likely true. She did trust him to protect her, as she always had, but…"I shall kill Girard myself."

"Like you did last time?" Camille's tone reeked of sarcasm.

"My aim will be better in the future. I must have you by my side, Camille. We protect each other, remember?" She sat down on the settle by her cousin.

"*Oui*. I am with you always, my friend."

"But Lachlan...I shall deal with him."

చ్ఠ ఆ౨

Awareness buzzed through Angelique when Lachlan returned an hour later, entering her room and removing his boots. "I thought you would be sleeping," he said.

"No." She sat by the hearth, watching the flames. "I awaited your return."

"Well then, you should've awaited me in bed, naked," he said in a teasing tone.

She refused to look at him, knowing that seductive expression would be on his face. Perhaps even a charming grin or wink. But she must stay focused on her anger. "You were to tell me of all your decisions that affect me and the clan."

"What do you mean?"

"You imprisoned Philippe without telling me." Not that she loved Philippe, but he was harmless. She often felt the need to protect him. He had been her friend back when few others were.

Lachlan sighed and dropped into the chair across from her. "There was no time to consult with you. I had to make a speedy decision. I had to find out what Philippe knew."

"You did not tell me because you wanted me pliable in bed." She sent him a sharp look, which he returned.

"I didn't force you. 'Twas your decision. You said, 'do it' and that you wanted me. I'm not one to refuse such an invitation from my beautiful, desirable wife."

So, he would seek to distract her with barbed compliments. "But if I had known you threw Philippe into the deplorable dungeon, I would not have wished to be in the same room with you."

Lachlan's eyes narrowed. "Do you want to know what your precious Philippe revealed to us?"

"What? Did you torture him for information?"

"Nay, I never torture. He is conspiring with Eleanor to break us apart."

"Eleanor? He would not. He doesn't know her that well."

"Apparently Philippe and Eleanor are fast friends. They traveled from London together."

"In truth?" If that was so, then Philippe was no longer her

190

friend. Anyone who conspired with Eleanor, she would not defend.

"Aye, but that isn't the worst of it. I believe Girard is staying at the inn in the village."

A deathly chill blew over her. She shivered. "*Non.* Girard?"

"I've been told a French count is there. He is as you described, tall and thin with dark hair. He has only one arm. Does that sound like him?"

"One arm? *Mère de Dieu.*" Her breath rushed in and out too fast. That was it. He would kill her. He desired revenge.

"Angelique? What is it? How did he lose his arm?"

Tears filled her eyes, burning. Her throat closed. And it was almost as if she were there again, on that bridge, a year ago in France.

Lachlan moved and sat beside her on the settle. He pulled her close and laid her head upon his chest. Stroked her hair. But he could not soothe her. No, Girard was plotting her murder.

"Tell me, Angelique. I must know so I can protect you and the clan from him. What will he do?"

"He will kill me...and Camille."

"Why?"

"Revenge."

"But why does he seek revenge? What I know about him is you wished to marry him and you were lovers. He cheated on you and you rejected him. He then raped you. Right?"

"*Oui.* After that, he stole the only thing of value my mother left me. A large briolette cut diamond pendant known as the Boehm Diamond. She gave it to me on her deathbed. Her lover had given it to her many years before and even stated in his will it was to be her property after he died. And that man was Girard's uncle. Girard said the diamond was part of his inheritance and that my mother had connived to steal it from his uncle. Girard is not so wealthy as he appears, you see. He's deeply in debt. After he raped me, he ripped the pendant from my neck and left. I refused to let him have the only thing my mother possessed, the only thing she left me besides the wedding gown. So Camille and I took the diamond back from him."

"God's bones, you're brave, lass." Lachlan's arm tightened around her, and with the opposite hand he stroked her cheek. The sweet gesture distracted her a bit, as did his dark, concerned gaze.

"We had to act quickly before he sold it. A few nights later, in disguise, we searched Girard's rooms but the diamond was nowhere. We hid and waited outside near his building. Girard and his friend Pierre finally staggered in from a night of drinking. Camille and I were both armed. We each had a loaded pistol and knives."

"You're always armed to the teeth," he said in a proud, serious tone.

"Only because I have to be." Nausea rose within her when she remembered how black the night was, how chill the air. "Girard knocked me down, discovered who I was and prepared to rape me again. We fought and I shot him. I missed his heart and hit his arm. His friend chased Camille with a sword. They struggled and Pierre fell from the bridge. He may have drowned in the river. It was never our intention to kill anyone. I took the diamond from Girard. Camille and I ran away and stayed with a cousin in Paris for a while. We did not hear anything from Girard until that gift arrived—the goblets. And now you tell me he has only one arm. Without doubt, the missing one was amputated because of the gunshot wound."

"I didn't know you were such a fearsome little warrior." Lachlan kissed her forehead, warming her. She felt safer in Lachlan's arms. Still, she feared even he couldn't protect her this time.

"He will want revenge for losing his arm and for Pierre, if he died. And he will want the diamond back," she said.

"Where is this diamond? I've never seen it."

"I keep it hidden at all times."

"Where?" Lachlan asked. "Surely you trust me enough by now to show me."

Despite being held in his protective arms, and enjoying it, something inside her would not let go completely. "I do...trust you, but you must understand...it is difficult after all that has happened to me. For more than a year, I have done nothing but look over my shoulder. And during that time, Camille was the only person I could trust."

"I know." Lachlan kissed her temple, and the affection in that gesture touched her deeply. "You don't have to show it to me now," he went on. "Only when you feel like doing so. Is there anything else about Girard you should tell me?"

"He is elegant but deadly. A viper. He smiles while he does

the vilest things. That smile can seem warm, charming and friendly, but it hides a heart of ice. Mayhap he has no soul. And yet, I did not know his true nature for a long while. You will stay away from him, *non*? You must not confront him directly."

Lachlan's eyes took on a predatory quality, again like a lion. "You confronted him; why would I not?"

"He is angered and perhaps desperate. He will blame me for all he has lost. And he may be even lower on funds than he was last year. He will not give up easily."

"Nor will I."

⊷⊶

Kormad watched the tall, one-armed man stride toward him across Burnglen's great hall. As a rule, he did not like Frenchmen but this one seemed eager to meet with him, considering the early hour. He doubted the gallant brought any men with him to reinforce Kormad's own small army, which he'd been building over the last few days.

"*Comte de* Girard, at your service, *monsieur*." He gave a deep, sweeping bow.

"Baron Kormad," he said by way of introduction. Though he was tempted to smirk at the man's posturing, he stepped forward and shook his hand. At least Girard's handshake was firm. 'Haps he would be a strong ally. "What can we do for each other?"

"I like that you arrive at the point quickly. I understand we have a common enemy, Angelique Drummagan and this MacGrath she has married."

"Who sent you?" Kormad demanded. If this was one of MacGrath's tricks, he would put an end to it quickly.

Girard raised a black brow, looking much like the devil himself. "The countess of Wexbury said you might be willing to help me."

"Eleanor Stanhope?" *Hmph*. The hoity-toity lady had always turned up her nose at him.

"*Oui*, apparently MacGrath was her lover and she desires having him back in her bed. I had to promise her we would not harm him."

Kormad would make no such ridiculous promise. MacGrath was naught but a whoremonger. Certainly not worthy to be earl. "You have my interest. Why are MacGrath and his new wife your enemies?"

"Angelique has stolen something that belongs to me. And I understand they have stolen land which is rightfully yours."

"Aye, they have!" A renewed spark of rage and determination lit within him. He would have Draughon.

"Perhaps we will help each other?" Girard stroked his sleek black mustache.

"In what way? Do you have men to add to my fighting force?" Kormad asked.

"*Non.* I have only one servant with me and he is not a soldier. I am not suggesting a battle, but something infinitely more subtle."

"Such as?"

"Subterfuge. Someone sneaks into this castle of theirs and destroys them from the inside."

"Aye, I like the way you think. But who would do this?" Kormad asked. A clever idea occurred to him. A distant widowed cousin of his lived nearby. Neilina Lockhart was both beautiful and sympathetic to his and Timmy's claim for Draughon because of their shared hatred for the late John Drummagan. Neilina and his sister Lilas had been the best of friends.

Burnglen's entry door burst open, interrupting Kormad's thoughts.

"M'laird!" MacFie trotted toward him.

"What is it?"

"MacGrath and his men rode by, headed toward the village."

"Well, don't just stand there. Prepare the men!"

જી જી

Wearing thick leather armor, Lachlan, Rebbie, Dirk and five more clansmen entered the low-ceilinged common room of the Breakstane Inn. Lachlan's gaze immediately landed on Eleanor, eating at a table by the window. She sent him a beaming smile and waggled her fingers in a flirtatious wave.

"Och. He is here no more than five seconds and he is summonsed to a woman's bed," Rebbie muttered.

"I'm going to question her. Watch for Girard." Lachlan approached her table.

"Oh, Lachlan, 'tis so nice to see you." Eleanor's voice oozed a sugary sweetness that near turned his stomach. Her gaze traveled down his body. "You appear to be dressed for a wild Scots battle. How exciting."

"If it comes to that."

"Won't you please join me? Oh, and congratulations on your marriage and your new title."

"I thank you." He dropped into the chair across from her. "I understand you traveled from London with Philippe Descartes."

Her smile disappeared. "Well...um...not *with* him precisely. We happened to be traveling to the same place, but for different reasons."

"Or for the same reason—to come between Angelique and me."

"No. Never." Her pout was even worse than the sugariness.

"Do you know a Frenchman named Girard?" he asked in a harsher tone.

She paled. "I wouldn't say I know him. I have met him."

"Here?"

"Yes, actually. He was here yesterday. I've not seen him today."

"Did he say anything about Angelique or me?"

Eleanor hesitated a second too long. "No."

So she was determined to lie to him. "Did he say why he was here?"

"I only spoke to him for less than a minute. We introduced ourselves. We did not state why we are here."

"And why are you here? Why were you at Draughon?"

"I but wished to offer you and Angelique my congratulations. I thought since we are friends, I might spend a bit of time in Scotland, but Angelique was far less welcoming than I expected."

What a load of horse dung. "Can you tell me anything else about Girard? 'Tis very important."

"I know nothing more."

He gave her a hard, threatening glare. "I think you do."

"I swear to you, Lachlan," she said in an intimate tone. "If I had more information, I would gladly give it to you."

He was wasting his time with her and her lies. He was not prepared to force the truth from her at knifepoint. But even her lies gave him information—Girard was here, he discussed Angelique with Eleanor, and he was likely now putting some plot into motion. "Very well, then." Lachlan stood and gave a brief bow. "I bid you good day."

"Wait! Would you perhaps like..." Her voice lowered to a whisper. "...some company today? I have the best room in this place, which isn't saying much but—"

"Nay. Thank you." He strode away from her and joined Rebbie and Dirk at a table on the opposite side of the room.

"I talked to the proprietor," Rebbie said in a low voice. "Girard is staying here, but he headed out somewhere very early this morn. He is expected to return."

Lachlan's stomach felt as if a lead weight landed in it. "He could be headed to Draughon for Angelique."

Dirk guzzled a hefty amount of ale and lowered the mug. "We didn't pass him on the road."

"If he is going there, he would not wish us to see him," Rebbie said. "Perhaps he traveled another way or hid when he saw our party coming."

"We need to head back. I'll leave a man to watch the inn," Lachlan said.

A quarter hour later, while on the road to Draughon, a flock of birds rose from the copse of bushes up ahead. A flash of steel glinted from among the shadows. The fine hairs on the back of Lachlan's neck stood on end. He motioned for the men to stop.

"They're waiting for us there." He pointed.

All his men pulled out weapons and readied themselves.

"Kormad!" Lachlan called. "I ken you're there."

Nothing, no movement.

Lachlan aimed his pistol. "If you're not there, then it won't matter if I shoot into the bushes."

Before he could pull the trigger, a shot exploded from the bushes and the lead ball whizzed over his head.

"Everyone, back!" He didn't want his men nor his horses injured. They retreated out of pistol range. "Anyone hit?"

A chorus of nays and curses went up.

"Come out and fight like men, you cowards!" Lachlan yelled.

A rustling from behind snagged their attention. Lachlan wheeled his horse about and came face to face with five men charging on foot, swords in hand. He fired the pistol, the lead ball catching one in the upper chest, near the shoulder. The man fell. Lachlan shoved the pistol into his belt and drew a basket-hilt broadsword to deflect the first blow aimed at him. The whoreson looked familiar; he'd seen him on the streets of London when they'd tried to steal Angelique's coach.

Clashes of steel, yells and curses filled the air.

Finally, Lachlan's blade sliced the other man's forearm. He screamed and ran away. Another warrior, wearing full leather armor including a helmet, rushed him. He looked familiar as well... the bald bastard who'd tried to throw Angelique from the ship.

ॐ๏๏ ๏๏ॐ

"Where is he, Camille?" Angelique stared through the distorted glass window in Camille's chamber toward the empty courtyard, praying Lachlan would ride through the gates on his big bay. "He should be back by now. It is almost noon."

"Will you please calm yourself and sit. He is a warrior knight. Not so fragile as you imagine." Camille's needle slid through the cloth over and over, effortlessly.

"He is a man, vulnerable as any of us." She strode to the other side of the room and back. "Girard is vile and devious. You can never tell what he will do."

"I believe you have fallen in love with your husband," Camille sing-songed.

Angelique snorted. "Nonsense. Just because I worry about his health does not mean I love him." She refused to love him. If she did, then she was the fool.

"What does it mean then?" Camille's blue gaze challenged her.

"It means I worry about my husband's health. I need a husband and he seems best suited for that role at the moment."

"Indeed he does. I'm glad you finally realize that."

"If he dies, I'll be saddled with another husband, one that might be far more dreadful."

Camille snickered. "'Far more dreadful.' You always did delude yourself, my cousin, since we were small children. I suspect Lachlan isn't dreadful in the least."

She refused to comment on that, though it was true.

"How was last night?" Camille inquired.

"Do not tease me." *Last night.* Angelique dared not think of the lovemaking, just as intense and passionate as their previous encounters. The indescribable carnal pleasures Lachlan gifted her with. Then he held her while they slept, snuggled and warm. How agreeable and cozy that aspect of marriage was. But he was gone this morn when she awoke. How dare he not even tell her good-bye before he went on such an important and dangerous mission?

Horses' hooves clattered in the stone-paved bailey outside. She darted to the window but couldn't recognize Lachlan's form through the wavy glass. "They are returned." She raced from the room.

Angelique ran across the great hall and outside. Rebbie dismounted, his arm and hand covered in blood. Other men were injured and bleeding. Her heart stopped.

"Where is Lachlan?" Her throat was so dry, the words came out a near whisper. Her gaze searched the men. "Lachlan?" *Please, Mère de Dieu, do not let him be dead.*

She spotted him emerging from the stables. She ran forward, scanning his body for blood and injuries, but found none.

"Lachlan, are you hurt? Are you bleeding?"

"Nay." He still wore that intense warrior expression.

Angelique launched herself at him. "Thank the *Bonne Mère.*"

He lifted her, holding her close while she kissed face, covered in stubble, sweat and dust—a most welcome feeling against her lips.

"I'm doing very well at the moment, thank you." Lachlan grinned, wondering what the devil had gotten into his wee wife. Whatever it was, he liked it. Her actions sparked instant, thrilling arousal in him. And happiness.

"Grâce à Dieu." She continued to plant little kisses over his face. How unusual, but sweet, her actions were. He turned his head aside and smiled at the teasing comments coming from the men. Best to take this to a private place, he decided, carrying her toward the entry steps. The men's calls, whistles and yells grew louder. Pride swelled through him that she would display her affection for him so publicly.

"I'm so glad you returned," she whispered.

"You're trembling, lass." He carried her across the great hall and toward the solar. No time for more steps to reach the bedchamber.

"I was afraid. I did not want you to be hurt."

His heart kicked about like a lunatic jester. "Why not?" Savoring her slight weight in his arms, as well as her admission, he closed the door behind them.

"You are my husband," she said in a breathy tone. Her darkened green gaze held his, communicating so many things…fear and desire. More—things he had never thought to see in her eyes. Trust and love? Was he imagining them?

"Aye, I am your husband. And glad for it." He set her on her feet.

She slid a hand around his neck and pulled his head down. He devoured her luscious mouth and grew hard as a pike. Her hand grazed him through the kilt.

He remembered the skirmish. "I should clean up before—"

She shook her head.

"Nay?"

"I want you now," she whispered against his lips. "I want you to make love to me."

Desire rushed through him, carrying something sharp and sweet to his heart, making it thump like a war drum. "With pleasure." At the moment, it seemed she accepted him completely, flaws and all.

He lifted her onto the table in the center of the room, removed the weapons from his belt, and shoved the skirts up her shapely thighs to the top. Her auburn curls covered the most feminine and arousing of sights he'd ever set eyes upon. "Lie back," he said, pushing her thighs wider. When she did, he dove in and tasted her. Oh, saints, she was wet and sweet, her lips swollen and dark pink. She gasped and cried out while he feasted upon her, slid his tongue deep. She arched, squirming, her hands clutching his hair.

He could wait no longer. Standing, he lifted his kilt, took his shaft in hand and trailed it through her moisture. "Mmm."

He tried to enter her gently, but that only lasted a trice. She was so very ready. Her body caressed his in a most bewitching way, wringing profound pleasure from him…no, something more than pleasure. Something strong he had not felt before. Something that made him tremble and his blood race. He growled, pushing deeper, thrusting harder while he watched her face strained in passion, her eyes dark beneath the fringe of her thick lashes. So beautiful.

She gasped, crying out.

"Aye, lass."

Sitting up, she clung to his neck. Murmuring and whimpering. *"Oui, s'il vous plaît, mon chéri."*

My dear one? She never called him that. Her words alone made him want to give in to his release, and with the added sensations of their bodies joining, gliding, he almost lost control.

"Ah, saints, Angelique!" He loved being inside her more than anything on earth.

Her cries of pleasure grew louder the closer she slid toward climax. He did not attempt to muffle those wonderful sounds, even though it was possible those in the nearby great hall could hear her. He wanted all the clan to know how much she wanted him. She displayed a cool façade before them. But his wife was a fiery angel when he touched her. He hoped that showed the clan her devotion to him and would help strengthen their loyalty as well.

He made love to her slowly but intensely, sliding deep; he wanted to draw every ounce of pleasure from her. At her climax, she screamed. He feared even those out in the courtyard could hear her now.

Lachlan's own release thundered through him. He was lost in the mad pleasure long seconds. When he became aware again, two guards burst through the door.

Angelique shrieked. Lachlan tried to shield her, though they were both clothed. "What the hell do you want?"

"Pray pardon, m'laird. We thought you were murdering her. Such bloodcurdling screams, we have never heard before."

He was too dumbfounded to laugh. "Does she look murdered to you?"

She hid her blush and mortified expression against his chest.

"*Le petit mort.*" Lachlan grinned broadly at the men. They chuckled and left the room.

Angelique smacked his arm. "Why did you tell them that? And I don't see why they came in here."

"You screamed, very loudly, during the height of your pleasure."

"I did not."

"*Mais oui,* you did, and I loved it," he said, more proud than he'd ever been of his lovemaking abilities, and his wife's desire for him.

Her blush darkened. "Why did you not make me be quiet?"

"I think that should be obvious."

She scowled. "You wanted them to hear me."

"I'm wanting them to ken how much my wee wifey likes me." He held back a chuckle, which he was sure she would not appreciate.

"I do not like you."

"Nay, I ken how much you dislike me, ma chérie." She could keep lying to herself if that was what she needed. He kissed the upper part of her chest. Her corset was so loose, he pushed it down a bit, yanked her smock out of the way and lapped at her nipples, just visible at the top. "Mmm, these are like sweet berries." His shaft still inside her, he felt her muscles flex, squeezing him. He grew tighter, hardening fully again.

Her breathing increased between whimpers. "Lachlan." She tugged him closer.

He withdrew and slid in deep again.

"Oui," she whispered. "More."

He held beneath her hips with one hand and pounded her harder and faster this time. Trapping her gaze, breathing her breath, he clenched his jaw against an intensity which seared him, body and soul.

Moments later, her keening cry near deafened him as she clutched at him tightly.

"Aye," he growled, and again lost his seed within her. Never had anything felt so astounding to him, as if the stars in the sky had tumbled into his body.

He gasped for breath, as did she. Thankfully, no one burst into the room this time.

An hour later, they were again immersed in a hot bath in her bedchamber, when someone knocked on the door.

"Can we see no peace?" Lachlan levered himself from the tub, held his shirt before him and opened the door. "Aye?" he asked the bodyguard.

"M'laird, a woman just arrived, Lady Angelique's cousin. She was attacked on the way here, near Burnglen, and one of her servants killed."

"God's teeth! Kormad."

CHAPTER FOURTEEN

Angelique rushed across the great hall to greet her second cousin and childhood friend, Neilina Lockhart. "Thanks be to God you were not killed in Kormad's attack!"

Neilina's clothing was ripped, dirty and askew, her auburn hair falling and tangled about her shoulders. "Angelique." Her breathing harsh, Neilina pulled her into an embrace. "I was lucky, but poor Jerome was not. They killed him and rode away with his lifeless body. No doubt they threw him in the river." She pulled back, her face scrunched, and sobbed into a handkerchief.

"*Mère de Dieu*, you poor thing. You must rest. The men will deal with Kormad." An arm around Neilina's waist, Angelique ushered her up the stairs and toward a guest chamber, then directed the servants to bring in her trunks.

Neilina's two maids straightened her drooping hair and poured water in a basin. "You must change m'lady. Your clothing is torn."

Despite the dirt smudging her cheek, Neilina was a woman of great beauty. Angelique remembered she had been pretty as a child, when they had played together during clan gatherings.

"Nay, I will be fine." Neilina waved them away. "I wish to give Cousin Angelique her gift."

"You are too kind to think of me in a time like this."

"Nonsense." Once the servants set down Neilina's trunk, she opened it and lifted out a carved box. "I'm so glad they didn't steal the wedding gift I brought you and your new husband.

202

Congratulations on your marriage." Neilina handed her the box and curtseyed.

"I thank you, but you should not have." Angelique didn't see how Neilina could maintain such self-possession, considering the violence she'd witnessed. She could've been raped or killed, for heaven's sake. But the women of her family were often considered strong.

Angelique opened the box lid to reveal a beautiful set of silver spoons displayed on red velvet. "Oh what an extravagant and lovely gift. I thank you." It truly was one of the finest things they had received.

"I'm so glad it pleases you."

"Indeed. Lachlan will love it, too." She closed the box. "I'm sure you would like to rest for a while and change. I shall see you at evening meal. And I do hope you will be staying with us for a while." Angelique said the words partly out of politeness, trying to be the perfect hostess, and partly because she truly would like to get to know her cousin again.

"Thank you. I would like that very much."

Angelique was certain she must have imagined the sly twinkle in her cousin's eye, for when she looked back it was gone.

⁘

At evening meal two days later, Lachlan glanced at those around high table in the great hall. Angelique's cousin's bold gaze met his and lingered. He had received such glances from enough women to know what it meant. He didn't want any woman interested in him except his wife who sat beside him. He lifted her hand and kissed it, hoping that said to Lady Neilina he was taken and interested in no one but his wife.

Angelique smiled at him.

He leaned closer and whispered in her ear. "I cannot wait to get you into bed again." He kissed her ear. Their last few nights together had been amazing.

Her cheeks flushed and she gently pinched the inside of his bare knee beneath the tablecloth.

Och! It took no more than that to make him hard? He wished she'd run her hand up his leg, beneath the plaid and find out exactly how she affected him. The quick rush of arousal near made him dizzy.

He placed her palm flat against his thigh. Saints! He was stiff as a ram's horn. Why couldn't he get enough of her? At this rate, he'd lift her from her chair and cart her off to the bedchamber before the meal was over.

"M'laird," one of the servants said behind his left shoulder.

"Aye?" He turned.

"A missive arrived for you."

Lachlan took the small folded parchment and broke the red wax seal. The message was from Chief Robertson. He invited Lachlan to his holdings to inspect the white mares and, if they met with his approval, choose one for his wife. Another buyer was interested in them as well, so Lachlan was to relay his decision forthwith.

Lachlan quickly refolded the paper, before Angelique could read it, and stuffed it into his sporran. The white mare was to be a surprise wedding gift for her. He was certain she would love it, especially after she'd mentioned having to leave her white horse behind in France. The Robertson's holdings were no more than two or three hours' ride one way. He could be there and back in one day, before Angelique even knew he'd left.

"Is something amiss?" she asked.

"Nay. All is well." He hid a smile, wondering if he might buy two horses. Indeed, two would surely make her twice as happy.

Angelique eyed him, suspicion written in her expression. But he could not spoil this surprise. He kissed her cheek, then whispered, "Come upstairs with me, now."

Her face turned bright red and she glanced about. But he did not care what the others thought.

"We must beg your pardon," he said to the table at large as he arose, her hand in his, and tugged her from her chair. Snickers and ribald comments ensued as they rushed from the great hall. Clearly, she knew if she didn't follow peacefully, he'd toss her over his shoulder. Or maybe her carnal hunger matched his own. Aye, he hoped that was the case.

"Lachlan," Angelique chastised him in a loud whisper once they were on the steps. "You are most uncouth!"

"Indeed I am." He chuckled.

⚬๑ ๑⚬

The next morn, as they were breaking their fast, Angelique noticed Cousin Neilina staring openly at Lachlan. At first, Angelique thought Neilina must want to say something, but quickly realized the woman's gaze held sensual interest. Had Lachlan noticed? He concentrated on eating, but did flick a heated look at Angelique and winked. Last night they had again shared an unforgettable and enthusiastic session of lovemaking. She was well and truly addicted to him now. Somehow, he had charmed his way into her heart and soul. He and his playful, seductive affection were the richest of ambrosia to her starved body and spirit. He filled her with expansive feelings of bliss such as she never knew existed.

Which was why Neilina's interested, furtive looks filled Angelique with a rage of concern so great she felt as if a battering ram slammed against her rib cage. There it was again—her cousin was devouring Lachlan with her eyes. Angelique hadn't expected such treachery from her own kin.

Mère de Dieu, Neilina was beautiful, more so even than Eleanor. What if Lachlan found Neilina attractive, irresistible? A cold fear arose within her.

Angelique tried to act normal as the meal ended and the people disbursed. But Neilina continued to peek briefly at Lachlan as he talked quietly with Rebbie.

The bitch. Angelique would strangle her.

Lachlan appeared not to notice her regard, but he had done that before. When he headed down a corridor, Neilina trailed behind. Angelique stiffened, then forced herself to follow silently and hid in the shadows.

"M'laird," Neilina said quietly.

After a few more steps, Lachlan paused and turned back halfway. "Aye?"

"'Haps I could meet you later in your chamber."

Poisonous hatred dripped into Angelique's blood, hatred for her vile cousin. Hatred that focused her attention and her vision. Her hands clenched in her skirts, craving a weapon.

Lachlan observed Neilina in silence for a long moment, but Angelique was so far away she could not see his expression. "The south tower room, just after sunset," he finally said.

Angelique froze, the blood pounding through her ears blocking out any other sounds. Her legs lost all strength. She slumped against the cold stone wall at her back, then slid down into a tiny ball. Nausea clutched at her. And a lance of despair smashed against her heart. The bastard! She'd known he would do this, yet she'd trusted him. Why had she let him through her barriers?

Neilina and Lachlan went their separate ways. Pushing herself up, Angelique forced her trembling legs to carry her to her bedchamber, where she blocked the door with two chests, crawled into bed and covered her head. Oh, *Mère de Dieu*, she could not breathe. Her corset compressed her lungs. Her throat felt as if a rope tightened around it. Slowly, she drew air in and the force of the devastation struck her. *Lachlan. No.* A sob tore from her body. *No. Do not! You are mine. You do not touch her!*

What was this horrid emotion devouring her from the inside out, like a vicious lion? Crushing her and sucking away her life like a great wave smashing upon her?

I do not love him. No!

But she did. Nothing else could be so painful.

"I am so stupid. Stupid, stupid!" She pounded fists against her pillow, hot tears gushing from her eyes.

She would kill Neilina...or confront her and send her away. But if she did that, Lachlan would only find another woman.

I will not go to the tower. I will not go there to witness his betrayal.

But she had to. She had to have proof. She had to confront him and tell him, see, you are not capable of fidelity, as I told you.

And her life would end in that moment.

◦◦◦

Lachlan met Rebbie and Dirk in the solar and closed the door.

"I have problems and I need your help," Lachlan said in a low voice. "I'm riding out this morn to Robertson Clan holdings to purchase a couple of white mares for Angelique as a wedding gift. Chief Robertson has another buyer interested, so I need to make haste. 'Tis a surprise and I want her to know nothing about it ahead of time. I'll take six clansmen with me to ride as guard. I want both of you to stay here and keep Angelique from knowing where I've gone and protect her in the event there's an attack. Also, I'm suspicious of Lady Neilina. She's just offered herself to me."

"What's so unusual about that?" Rebbie lifted a brow.

"I don't trust her. I'm thinking she may be Kormad's spy."

"But Kormad attacked her party, did he not?" Dirk asked.

"Supposedly. Or it could be a grand cover story so we would welcome her more openly."

"Ah. You may be right," Rebbie said.

"In any case, I'm not interested in her. I intend to be faithful to Angelique." Besides, he simply didn't desire any other woman now. Angelique had captured his attention completely, and he took his marriage vows seriously. "Dirk, I have a job for you, which I'm thinking you'll enjoy."

His friend scowled. "What?"

"I want you to pretend to be me, put on one of my kilts and meet Lady Neilina in the south tower chamber just before sunset. Make sure the room is dark so she can't see your face. We are of about the same size, and since she doesn't know either of us well, she shouldn't be able to tell the difference.

"Hmm, you're right. I could see myself enjoying that." Dirk grinned.

"Most importantly, find out what information you can from her," Lachlan said.

"Of course. 'Twill be my pleasure."

ംഔ ൧ം

Hands shaking, Angelique slipped along the passage and up the narrow steps of the south tower. She hadn't seen Lachlan all day. Undoubtedly, he was avoiding her because he had in mind to bed another woman. Whoremonger! The man had no ability to feel guilt. Her stomach ached from hunger and disgust. She hadn't been able to eat all day. Her world was about to shatter yet again. She sensed the impending doom. Why had she dared to dream?

She had waited too long and sunset had come and gone.

Pausing outside the door, she listened. Rustling came from within. Then a male groan. *The bastard. I will kill him and my whore of a cousin.*

Covered with cold sweat, Angelique quietly pushed the door and inched it open. He had been so stupid as to not even lock it, likely too excited to remember. A thick cloth covered the narrow window in the round stone room, further dimming the twilight. Their silhouettes were clear—a tall kilted man with long hair stood behind a woman, bent over a table, her skirts hiked. Gripping her hips, he serviced her from the back, moaning. The woman gasped and whimpered. "Oh, Lachlan. Yes!"

Severe nausea tore through Angelique. She fled down the steps, tripped at the bottom and crashed to her knees. Though she knew not how she found the strength, she shoved herself up and ran to her room. Once inside, she again sank to her knees and retched. But nothing came up.

I will not feel. I will not feel! He is dead to me.

Once her stomach settled, she arose.

"I cannot stay here." Her whole body trembling, she flipped open a trunk lid and crammed clothing into it.

"What are you doing?"

Angelique jumped, turning to face Camille in the doorway. "Leaving."

"Why?"

"Lachlan is swiving my cousin as we speak. The bastard! I knew he could not change."

"What? You saw this?"

"Yes, with mine own eyes. This morn, I heard him tell her where to meet him. Then, they were there when I arrived."

"The swine. I did not think he would do such a thing. He seemed besotted with you, cousin."

"Oh, he is most charming and deceptive, more so than Girard." Even Girard had not hurt her as much as Lachlan now did.

"Where are we going?" Camille asked.

"You are willing to come with me?"

"Of course. I go with you everywhere. How could you think otherwise?"

She had one true friend—Camille—whom she believed would never betray her or let her down.

"We go to London. I will seek a divorce."

"On what grounds? Clearly, the marriage has been consummated. Not impotence."

"That is not amusing. Incest."

"What?

"He is having sex with my second cousin who is now also his second cousin by marriage. Therefore, incest by affinity. If that doesn't work, I'll use the impotence plea. I'd love to see him prove his virility before the court."

Ha. She would love nothing. She was dead inside and never wanted to see Lachlan again.

"Where will you go after that?" Camille asked.

"I have not yet decided. If he leaves here, I may come back. If not, then France. We will go to Uncle Louis in the south of France. My mother and I visited him once a few years ago."

"But what of your castle here? Your clan?"

"What do I care?" Her throat tightened, but she forced the words out. "I do not even want to live. My clan hates me. They love Lachlan. He is their leader as I will never be. I do not fit in here as I had hoped. And I cannot abide an unfaithful husband and his whores."

"At least talk to him first. Angelique, I know you love him."

"No! I will never speak to him again. Have the grooms ready the coach in the stables so no one will know it's us within when we leave. Send some servants up to carry our trunks. And have them keep their mouths shut. No one will know we have left for a great while."

A half hour later, they slipped out the side door and to the stables under the cover of darkness. The coach was waiting with their trunks already loaded.

"We go into Perth," she told the driver and her two armed bodyguards. They nodded and climbed on board. One guard sat up front with the driver, and the other on the back. They needed protection passing Kormad's estate, and she was not so stupid as to forgo that.

The driver whipped the horses into motion and they rumbled through the gate which he'd had the guards open moments ago.

Sitting beside Camille, Angelique gazed back through the blackness at the glow in the windows of Draughon and the torches lighting the bailey. Her gaze found the south tower. Inside it, Lachlan had broken her heart a thousand times over.

I am just like my mother. Running from a heartache she would never escape. Though other men had loved her mother, she had loved none of them back. Not the way she'd loved Angelique's father.

Her throat constricted. "I shall never love again," she whispered. "I swear it."

"Oh, Ange." Camille moved to the seat beside her and pulled her into a warm embrace. "I knew you loved him. You should have confronted him."

Angelique shook her head. "No. I might kill him or his whore if given the least opportunity."

The lane became rougher. The driver slowed but they bounced back and forth. Outside the window, the night grew darker as clouds hid the moon and stars.

Nearby, riders on horseback, the many hooves thudding

against the ground, startled Angelique.

"Whoa!" someone yelled. The coach slowed.

"Where are we?" Angelique asked.

"The village?"

"No, we've not had time."

Angelique had forgotten to load her pistol. She drew a dagger instead.

⚜

Halfway home from the Robertson estate, Lachlan glanced back at the two white mares glowing in the twilight. Aye, indeed Angelique would love them. They were beauties, strong and spirited. Two of his clansmen led them. He had hoped to be home before dark, but the Robertson clan's hospitality knew no bounds. They had shared food, drink and lively talk too long.

A war cry sounded from the bushes. Horses galloped at Lachlan and his party of six.

"What the hell?" Lachlan drew his sword and charged them on horseback. Kormad again? The bastard!

His blade struck one of the attackers.

Pistol fire exploded, lighting the gloom for a second. A man cried out. Horses neighed and reared. In the melee and low light, it was hard to identify anyone. The men released the white mares and they galloped away.

"Don't kill him yet!" someone yelled. Kormad.

One man on foot grabbed Lachlan's horse's bridle, while two more came at him from the side. Before he could strike either, one latched onto his sword arm. A fist punched him in the stomach.

He struck out but could not free his arm from the clinging leech who near wrung his shoulder from its socket. Pain sliced through him. The bastards dragged him from the saddle. Once on the ground, Lachlan dropped the sword and closed his hand around the hilt of the dagger on his belt, better for close combat. Before he could withdraw it, something bashed into his head and blackness descended.

⚜

"If that is Kormad, why are my guards not shooting them?" Angelique whispered inside the coach.

"I don't know," Camille said. "What if it is Girard?"

Dread sank like a stone in Angelique's stomach.

"M'lady." One of her bodyguards opened the door. "Laird

Rebbinglen is here. He must speak with you." He moved back and Rebbie, holding a torch, took his place.

"Lady Angelique, what are you doing so far from Draughon this late?" Frowning, he ran his midnight gaze over her and Camille.

Angelique's lips seemed sewn shut. How could she speak the words, the truth, of Lachlan's betrayal?

"Lachlan has been captured," Rebbie said. "Kormad took him on his way back from the Robertson's."

"Robertson's? What do you mean?"

"Lachlan took a few Drummagan men, including the steward, and went to the Robertson's holdings this morn. On the way back, Kormad and his men attacked their party, killing one man. They knocked Lachlan out, made off with him, and sent word by the other men that they would hold him hostage until they had what they wanted. If they didn't receive it within a day, they would kill him."

"Mère de Dieu." Angelique's thoughts were a jumble. How could Lachlan have been gone to the Robertson's? She had seen him with her own eyes in the tower. Was this some kind of trick to get her to come back?

"The stable lad told us you'd left. I don't know what you're doing out here, or how you slipped past us, but you must come back to Draughon with us."

"Yes. We go back." No matter what Lachlan had done, she would not abandon him to Kormad. If he was indeed captured, she would help him.

The driver turned the coach, though it took several minutes. A short time later, they arrived back at Draughon.

"Where were you going?" Rebbie asked, once they, along with Dirk, Camille and Fingall, were in the solar.

"I do not wish to speak of it. It is between Lachlan and me," Angelique said, her stomach feeling queasy when she remembered what she'd witnessed in the south tower.

The room was silent for a long, tense moment.

"Why was Lachlan supposedly gone to the Robertson's?" she asked.

Rebbie and Dirk exchanged a glance. The sort of silent communication men do when they don't wish a woman to know a secret.

"He went to buy you a white mare as a wedding gift," Rebbie finally said.

"Two white mares," Dirk added.

"Is that so?" How long had it taken them to think up that story? And they couldn't even get it straight. Lachlan's two friends would lie and cover for him no matter what. They were loyal unto death and she didn't trust them to tell the truth any more than she trusted Lachlan.

"Indeed."

"So, Kormad has him. How do we get him freed?" she asked, trying to stay focused on the task at hand and not her mangled emotions.

"Kormad does not work alone. I believe you ken who Girard is."

The sensation of a chilling wind blew over her. "*Mon Dieu.* Not Girard. He is there, helping Kormad?"

"Aye."

She stared into Camille's terrified eyes. "God help us all. He will kill him."

"We're going to make sure that doesn't happen," Rebbie said, his voice stern. "Girard wants something he believes you have. Some sort of diamond pendant."

The diamond now hung suspended from a chain around her neck, the large icy stone lying between her breasts. It was no comfort at all. The thing was more like a noose.

"Yes, I will give it to him...if he will release Lachlan unharmed." She tugged the necklace from beneath her bodice and slipped it over her head.

"Very good. He also demanded that you deliver it in person, but we cannot put your life in danger. We'll dress up one of the smaller clansmen as a woman and he'll stand in for you."

She shook her head. "That will not work. Girard will know the difference. He is not an imbecile."

"Lachlan would never forgive us if we put your life in danger. We cannot allow you to be involved in this part."

"I will. I make my own decisions about my life."

"You are to stay here...with all due respect, m'lady." Dirk's tone was commanding, his expression fierce. "Lachlan will have our heads if you're injured."

"Aye," Rebbie said. "That he will."

Feeling powerless, she struggled for an answer. "But...I must help."

"You are helping by giving up the pendant. If you would allow me..." Rebbie held out his hand, palm up. She clasped the large diamond to her chest for a moment. The precious stone now represented two people she'd loved most in the world—her mother who'd gifted her with it and Lachlan whom she must relinquish it for.

She dropped the diamond into Rebbie's hand. "Very well," she said. "Bring him back alive...to me. Please."

৵৩ ৩৶

Lachlan has to live. "So I can strangle him myself," Angelique muttered to her cold, empty sitting room. He effectively knew how to rip out her heart.

She paced from one side of the room to the other, then stared out the window toward the River Tay. Burnglen was too distant to see because of the trees and the thick white mist that drifted like clouds fallen from the sky.

As a child, she had seen Burnglen Castle once and knew it was a hateful-looking ancient castle. Small as compared to Draughon, but gloomy and dark gray. She imagined Lachlan, in pain, perhaps unconscious deep in the bowels of the dungeon. Tears stung her scratchy eyes.

Mère de Dieu, protect him.

Rebbie carried her diamond in his pocket. He, along with Dirk and a dozen men, would make the exchange. What would happen when Girard and Kormad realized the young man dressed as a woman was not Angelique? She should have insisted on going.

When would they return with Lachlan? Two hours or more had passed.

Camille was asleep in her room. Angelique feared she would never eat or sleep again.

A thump sounded in the corridor and she approached the door. A man's groan. Metal clashed and more thumps. Someone had breached the gates and was taking out her guards? A chill slid through her. She ran into the bedchamber, threw on her thick cloak for protection, and armed herself with every weapon she possessed, hiding them in her secret pockets. She could not bar the door and the trunks were not heavy enough to block it shut.

The sounds of her sitting room door splintering reached her

ears. "Mother Mary, save us," she prayed in French, crossed herself, and drew a loaded pistol.

She peered around the edge of the doorway.

"I've killed the intruders, m'lady!"

"Fingall? Is that you?" A bit of relief swept through her.

"Aye." Her steward's voice echoed from the corridor. "Two masked men broke in and killed your guards. But I took care of 'em good."

"*Mère de Dieu!* My guards are dead?" She crossed herself again. Though she rarely thought of them by name, they had been her constant shadows for the past weeks and had protected her well. She hated for them to come to such a horrific end.

"I shall protect you myself, m'lady." Fingall stepped through the ruined door and into the room, a bloody dagger at his side.

"Do you think more will come?" Angelique kept her pistol pointed, not at Fingall, but at the doorway beside him. She still didn't know if the steward had stolen from them or whether he was trustworthy.

"I cannot rightly say if there are more. I hope not." He glanced from her to the door and back again, seeming jittery.

"What of the guards manning the gates?"

"I've not been out there. Lay down the pistol, m'lady, afore you hurt yourself."

"I will not hurt myself. I am well-trained with a pistol."

Running footsteps sounded in the corridor. Fingall rushed toward her. "Go into the chamber, m'lady! You'll be safe there!"

"*Non!* Do not touch me." She would take care of this problem herself.

The footfalls pounded closer. Her finger teased the trigger. Fingall grasped her right arm, shoved the gun upward and plucked it from her hand. His other arm went around her, capturing her.

"*Non!*" She kicked back into his shins, tried to twist away and escape, but he was stronger.

A giant, dark-haired stranger wearing leather armor appeared in the doorway. Who was he? Not one of her staff.

"Search her for weapons!" the stranger ordered.

"Fingall, how could you do this? You traitor!"

Lying on her stomach on the floor where he'd lowered her, she struggled against him, but he pinned her legs between his and held her hands behind her back. Next, he removed the daggers from her cloak pockets.

"Bastard! Stop!"

The stranger threw a blanket over her head, making everything dark. No! She must free herself. When Fingall levered himself off her, she twisted, turned and kicked. But the men were quicker and stronger. They rolled her up in the blanket in only moments, black, tight and suffocating. She screamed, attempting to thrust her arms and legs out, but the wool blanket held tight.

She gasped for breath in the tight space. *Calm. Breathe.Think!*

One at her head and one at her feet, the two men picked her up and carried her, she knew not where. The only sounds were their footfalls and a closing door or screech of metal now and then. They transported her, head first, down steep steps, bumping her against stone walls. The blanket loosened a bit and she slipped her hand into the secret pocket in her skirts where she had hidden the dagger Rebbie had gifted her with. *Grâce à Dieu.* The jeweled hilt slid into her hand. Her one comfort.

Why did no one stop these bastards from carrying her out of the castle? Surely the guards at the gates would come to her rescue.

"Help me! It is me, Angelique!"

Her hip slammed into a wall and pain shot through her. The giant bastard had done that purposefully. A loud clang sounded. The gates?

"Guards! Help me!"

The two knaves dropped her on the ground, jarring all the bones in her body. Ignoring the pain, she rolled, trying to escape the blanket. Her head came out. The hulking stranger approached two horses, while Fingall relieved himself near the low bushes. *Where am I?* She glanced back to see a small iron gate…the exit of the secret passages. She jumped to her feet and ran.

"Grab her! She's getting away!"

A moment later, Fingall snagged her skirts and yanked her back. She fell, her hands sliding over rocks. One smooth river stone fit her hand perfectly. When she was close enough, she smashed it against Fingall's head. He yelped.

"Imbecile!" Kormad's man shoved Fingall away and yanked Angelique's arms up behind her back. He breathed against her ear and ground himself against her derriere. "If that damned Frenchman didn't want you so bad, I'd take you right here. So don't tempt me. I like a wench with some fight in her."

Frenchman? *Mon Dieu*, he meant Girard. The bastard would show her no mercy. If it came to that, she prayed her death would be swift and painless.

"Keep your mouth shut or I'll cram something in it you won't like so much." Her captor kicked a pile of horse dung to get his meaning across. She tried again to wrest herself away from him, but he was too strong. He bound her hands behind her back, tied her feet and threw her over the horse.

She forced herself to breathe normally, and think of a plan.

"Fingall, are you coming?" he yelled.

"Aye."

She still had her dagger. If they released her hands, she could use it. And if Rebbie and Dirk had failed in their mission to rescue Lachlan, she would rescue him herself.

⁊๏ℰ ℰ๏

"Good work, Fingall," said a man behind Angelique.

She turned. Kormad's full black beard and evil dark eyes froze her bones.

The men had removed her from the horse and untied her. She now stood before the unholy entrance to Burnglen. All was gray, the heavily overcast sky, the stones making up the castle and its courtyard.

"Where is my husband?" she asked, placing a strong bite in her tone.

Kormad laughed and swept his hand toward the door. "You shall see soon enough. Welcome to Burnglen."

Dare she walk into such an evil abode, one she might never escape? Inside the hidden pocket in the folds of her skirts, she fingered the jewels on the hilt of her dagger, instead of her rosary beads, and whispered a prayer for strength and protection. With the right grip and stab, she could kill a man, if she didn't hit a bone. Her distant male cousin in France had taught her well.

Her first instinct was to attack Kormad, but he wore leather armor studded all over with metal. She had not the strength to stab her blade through that. Besides, the bailey teamed with armed guards.

"Take her inside," Kormad ordered the tall man who'd brought her.

"No!" she yelled.

He picked her up, flung her over his shoulder and carried her up the steps. Her stomach ached from his hard shoulder slamming against it, and nausea. What tragedy awaited her within these walls?

Grinning, Kormad followed them up the steps. *Bastards!* Trying to stab the giant who carried her would be useless, covered in thick leather as he was. She would save her attack until the right moment, when it would count. Maybe Girard would be the first one she killed.

Once inside the Burnglen great hall, the guard tossed her roughly onto her feet. Dizzy, she stumbled, but grabbed onto the long table. The stench of this place was horrid, rotten food and hound excrement.

"At last, we meet again, my sweet." The French words were delivered in a smooth, lethal voice.

She turned and met the devil-dark gaze of Girard.

CHAPTER FIFTEEN

Girard. Here to kill her...rape her. *"Mère de Dieu."* The sensation of ice claws latched onto Angelique's chest, cutting off her breath.

"I have missed you, *ma petite choute.*" He bared his teeth in the mockery of a grin; his pupils dilated. The missing arm amplified his malevolence...because of what it meant. She had done that to him. He would show her no mercy. She would rather die now.

Sucking in a breath, she tried to think normally. Dear God, to face a demon...*I will not faint. I will not faint.*

"Did you search her for weapons?" Girard snarled. His voice, an echo from her nightmarish memories, sent shards of dread through her.

"No need," Kormad said.

"You do not know our little angel, do you?" He sounded almost amused.

"You want her searched, do it yourself!"

Girard's gaze stabbed through her. "Where is that Camille bitch?"

"Not here," she managed in a strong voice. No, he would not see what he did to her. He would not see he had torn her apart, physically, emotionally, and that now she was but a patchwork, held together by thin threads.

"So, you will pay for her crimes as well as your own."

Angelique focused on survival, clasping the dagger hilt firmly within her pocket. She hoped he would attempt searching her. He wore no leather armor as the other men did. But if she killed him, likely Kormad would kill her.

What must I do? Lachlan. He would know what to do. A strong, warm protector, he was.

"I wish to see my husband," she said, barely pushing the words past her tight throat.

"Oh, you will." Kormad laughed. "'Haps you'd both like to be buried in the same grave? Together forever."

No. Lachlan could not be dead. She focused on the memory of his smile. Tears pricked her eyes.

"Oh, you love this husband of yours," Girard said.

She had not wanted him to see anything inside her. Already, he was breaching her defenses. "*Non.* He is a bastard like you."

One corner of Girard's lips quirked a fraction. "You will have a chance to say goodbye to him before I take you back to France."

"What? Back to France? *Non.*"

"She's not going anywhere!" Kormad growled. "Except a few feet beneath the sod of Scotland."

Girard speared Kormad with that devil glower. "We have a deal."

"That's not part of it."

"You promised her to me first." A bald man stepped forward. Who...? Dear God, he was the monster who'd tried to kill her on the ship weeks ago.

"Promised to you?" Girard said. "She is mine to do with as I please. I own her! Do you understand?"

They argued, growling and snapping like dogs, ripping apart her life as if it were a deer hide. Which one would sink in his teeth first? Angelique's legs trembled, and she dropped to her knees. She could not breathe. Dear heaven...rape, torture, death, her body used and abused by them. The blackness of oblivion would be better.

Get up; you are strong, some part of her urged...or was it a guardian angel whispering in her ear?

I cannot. I have nothing left.

Girard grasped her upper arms and jerked her to her feet.

Now, that defensive side of her shouted. The dagger hilt was firm in her hand. She shoved the blade up toward Girard's stomach. It bit through clothing and flesh. He shrieked and shoved her to the floor. Pain shot through her hip and elbow.

"You see!" Girard yelled. "You see why you should search her?" He tore at his clothing to examine the bloody wound. Not deep enough.

Kormad chuckled and snatched the dagger from her hand. "Take her to the dungeon and toss her in with MacGrath," he commanded the guards. Two yanked her up, one by each arm, painfully wrenching her shoulders. But she was glad to hear the name MacGrath. Was Lachlan alive? *I pray you, Mère de Dieu.*

"Wait, search her first," Kormad said.

Their meaty hands ran over her—her breasts, legs and hips. She almost gagged. "Cease!"

"No more weapons," one of the guards said.

"Take her below. We have more important matters to attend to. Have George saddle the horses."

The massive guard dragged her, stumbling, outside to another area, his cohort in front. Steps led down to a narrow stone passage, dark and underground. She tripped and would've fallen if this beast hadn't been holding her up. She could scarce breathe in this dank, foul place.

The cell door screeched as the guard in front opened it a narrow space. Her captor shoved her inside the blackness and the door clanged shut.

Gaelic curses resounded. "Angelique! How the hell did they get you?"

"Lachlan?" She turned, unable to see. "Where are you?"

"Here."

Relief surged through her, weakening her limbs. "*Grâce à Dieu,* you are alive. Are you hurt?" In the dark, she found him, her palms stroking over his doublet, up his arms to his shoulders. "Are you bleeding?"

"Nay." He framed her waist in his hands, then hugged her close, the most wonderful feeling in the world. "I have a devil of a headache, but I'll live." His voice was deep and husky against her ear. "Did Kormad hurt you?"

"No. Girard is here also. They were arguing about what to do with me—kill me or allow Girard to take me back to France. I will not go—"

"What the hell were Rebbie and Dirk thinking, letting you slip into the bastard's hands?" he rasped along with blunt foreign words.

"It was Fingall. He and Kormad's man killed my bodyguards, then stole me away through the secret passages."

"Damn Fingall. I had someone watching him and I had two guards posted in the secret passages at all times."

"Likely they are dead. I pray Rebbie and Dirk still live."

"As do I."

The warm possession of his embrace lured her, but his betrayal repelled her. She backed away. "I thought if they could not rescue you, I would myself, you miserable miscreant."

"I ken I'm a damned fool. If you die, 'tis my fault." His tone was tortured. "I couldn't even protect you."

"I did not need your protection."

"Well then, what did you need from me?"

Things too precious to verbalize. Finally, her eyes adjusted to the dark. The sliver of light from the small window in the door outlined Lachlan's tawny hair, the bone structure of his face, his broad shoulders. "What I needed, you cannot give, so it matters not," she said.

"Tell me."

"Fidelity."

"I gave you that, at least. 'Twas the only thing I gave you."

"Do you imagine I believe your lies?" How could he think she'd never find out?

"What lies?" he demanded.

"I know what you did yesterday."

"You're angry that I bought you two white horses?"

Her throat ached. "No! Neilina. The south tower. I am not an imbecile."

"God's teeth! That was Dirk with Neilina. We hatched a scheme so she would think 'twas me, but in truth 'twas Dirk pretending to be me."

Lachlan would never change. He likely believed his own lies. "You think I am exceedingly naïve, *oui*?"

"Nay. 'Twas a good hoax."

She turned her back to him. "How are we to escape this place?"

"Angelique. You cannot believe that was me. I was meeting with members of the Robertson clan to purchase two mares for you as a surprise, a late wedding gift. You can ask Dirk and Rebbie."

"If they live, I trust their word no more than yours. They are your loyal friends, so naturally they will lie for you.

"Ask anyone in the Robertson clan when I left their castle." He named the Drummagans who accompanied him. "Ask any of them."

"I won't have a chance. Kormad is going to kill us, you know. Bury us in the same grave…so we are together forever." A sob burst from her constricted throat.

"Come here." Lachlan pulled her into his arms, her back against his hard chest. His thick, strong arms held her tight.

She squirmed from his grasp. "No, you are a lecher. I believed in you. I believed you had changed and every word you said." The tears would not stop no matter how much she wished they would.

"I swear to you, upon my honor, I didn't touch Neilina. And somehow I shall prove it to you."

"But I heard you. You told her to meet you in the south tower at sunset."

"I did say that, but I didn't meet her. I never intended to. I had Dirk take my place so he could find out if she's Kormad's spy. I think she is."

"You…the man with her wore a kilt. Dirk does not wear a kilt."

"He wore mine. He pretended to be me!"

Did he tell the truth? She wished to believe him. It would be her fondest dream if he was honest, but some part of her refused to be naïve and trusting anymore.

"She moaned your name while…" At the image of Lachlan driving into another woman, nausea welled inside her.

"'Twas not me. I told you, you're the only one I want." His tone was low and fierce. He turned her and clasped her close, her face against his chest. And she allowed it. She but needed one moment of hope. The unique, appealing scent of him filled her nostrils, bringing back memories of the profound and sweet intimacies they'd shared. How she wished….

"I'm sorry you went through that, and believed it was me," he said. "Truly, love, I'm not lying. Dirk made her think he was me. It was necessary so she wouldn't know we suspected her of being a spy. How are you thinking I got captured out on the moor if I was in the south tower?"

"I do not know when you were captured. I left."

"What do you mean?"

"I left you." She shoved back from him. "I was going to London for a divorce when Rebbie and Dirk stopped my coach."

"Damnation." His voice held an icy edge as if she were the betrayer.

"I had every right!"

"You would do that without even confronting me. Just assume?"

"I told you—"

"You judge and sentence me all without my knowledge?" His voice echoed from the walls.

So the small pleasant moment was passed. No more deceiving herself.

"I knew this would happen when I married you. I knew you would have affairs and mistresses and whores. I knew you would draw me in with your charm, make me trust you, then that you would trample my heart like refuse. I should not have been surprised really, but I wanted to believe. My own folly. Why did you have to pretend...?" Why couldn't he have simply been honest about his intentions?

"I didn't pretend about us! I told you at the first I would never lie to you and I haven't." Lachlan glared at Angelique's back through the dimness. How could she believe such a thing about him? Had she learned naught about him in the past few weeks?

"I do not know what the truth is anymore," she whispered.

Her words stabbed like daggers into his chest. He had never been called a liar so much in his life. Unfaithful? Hell, he hadn't even been tempted to look at another woman since he'd married her. Strangely, she was all he desired. He didn't understand it, but she wasn't like other women. She was special in a way he'd never experienced before. He wished only to please her, protect her, and give her all she wanted.

But the thing that quelled his anger was the raw pain in her voice. She cared; she wanted him all to herself. That much, he liked. What sliced him to the core was her distrust, her doubts. Like everyone else including his father, she expected the worst of him. He was a worthless, faithless, ne'er-do-well and could not rise above it. What a fool he was. Their capture was all his fault.

He must prove the truth to her. How? The testimony of Dirk and Rebbie meant naught. No one else knew of their ruse with

Neilina. But plenty of men had seen him at the Robertsons'. None of this would matter anyway, if they couldn't escape. He had failed utterly at protecting her. What kind of husband was he?

"I have an idea," she whispered. "You will pretend to hit me. I will scream and cry, and the guard will come."

"I wouldn't have anyone believe I'd hit my wife."

"A ruse. He will open the door to separate us, and you hide behind the door and hit him."

"He will not likely come alone. And he'll be heavily armed if he thinks I'm violent."

"Do you have a better idea?" she asked in challenge but kept her voice low.

"Aye, you pretend to hit me and knock me down. He'll think I hit my head on the wall. My head already has a lump on it, so 'tis believable. You scream hysterically. They won't see you as much a threat. They'll think I'm unconscious or dead and come in. Then we'll disarm them. If there are two of them, you'll need to be careful."

"Very well."

"Let's get into a mock fight," he whispered. "Come on, throw a few punches."

Out of nowhere, her hand flew up. The slap cracked against his face.

"Ouch." His cheek stung and a resounding pain shot through his head from the earlier injury. "Do you have to be so damned enthusiastic?"

"You told me to."

"Not hard," he whispered.

"Weak lad!"

"Och. Come on, show me what you've got, wee wench."

She shoved lightly at his chest and he toppled backward in a controlled fall, though he tried to make it look real in the event someone spied through the opening in the door.

Angelique screamed, the deafening sound intense in the confined space. "I've killed him! I've killed him!"

"What the devil is going on?" The guard growled from the passage.

"I've killed my own husband! But he deserved it! The unfaithful swine."

That was a bit much. Lachlan watched the door through eyes

narrowed to slits. One guard entered, halting just inside the door, a torch in one hand, a dagger in the other, and his sword still in the scabbard. Angelique crouched in a corner, pretending to weep. "I did not mean to kill him. I shoved him. He fell and cracked his skull on the wall."

After wedging the torch between two rocks in the wall, the guard inched closer and nudged Lachlan with his foot. When Lachlan didn't move or even breathe, the man bent over him. Lachlan grabbed the guard's knife hand, shoving the blade toward his chest, and grasped the hilt of his sword at the same time. The guard jerked back, cursing, and dropped the knife. Lachlan took possession of both weapons.

"What's happening?" A second guard entered the cell.

Angelique sprang from behind the door and bashed the empty chamber pot against his head. He slumped to the floor.

The first guard backed toward the exit.

"Halt!" Rising, Lachlan motioned with the tip of the sword toward the back corner. "Over there."

When the man obeyed, Lachlan leapt over the other guard and joined Angelique in the corridor. She locked the cell door.

The first guard yelled. Lachlan closed the small opening at the top of the door, muffling his cries.

Footsteps and voices advanced toward them down the dim corridor lit by a lone torch.

"Hell. Kormad's men," Lachlan said.

"I am ready." Angelique held a dagger.

"Where did you get that?"

"From the second guard."

"Have a care." Damnation, what if he couldn't kill them all and protect her? Nausea clutched at him when he imagined the horrors she would endure if he died. Rape, torture, death. He simply could not fail.

Wielding the sword in one hand and the knife in the other, Lachlan confronted the first of Kormad's men. The large, leather-clad bastard charged him, sword slamming against Lachlan's. The impact traveled up his arm, clashing steel deafening in the confined space. Fortunately, the passage was so narrow two men could not fight abreast. He knocked the sword from the man's hand and quickly ran him through. Battle fury raced hot through his veins.

The second man stepped over the body and attacked. Once

he fell, Lachlan turned his attention to the next in line. He and two others hung back, their eyes wide in the dimness.

Someone charged in from outside, behind the men. A battle cry arose.

Rebbie? Indeed it was. And Dirk backed him. Clanging blades were a blur of motion.

Lachlan engaged the enemy closest to him. The man stumbled and fell. Lachlan smashed the sword's basket hilt against his head, knocking him out.

"Lachlan! You live." Rebbie slapped him on the shoulder. "Come!"

"How many outside?"

"None. We dispensed with them."

"I thank you." Lachlan took Angelique's hand, keeping her close by his side. "Where are the rest of our men?"

"Two or three were killed," Rebbie said. "The others, we know not what happened to them. 'Twas chaos. When we saw Fingall and the other man bring Angelique through the gates, we knew we had to act quickly."

Outside, Dirk held three of Kormad's horses.

Another guard charged around the corner. "Help her mount," Lachlan said to Dirk, then engaged in swordplay with the last man. He was fast and skilled.

More of Kormad's men poured down the distant castle steps. Where the hell did he get so many men?

"We must go now, Lachlan!" Dirk threw a stone at the man. It bounced off his shoulder, but that was enough to distract him. Lachlan's blade sliced his arm. Yelling curses, the enemy retreated.

Lachlan leapt onto the bareback horse behind Angelique and followed Rebbie's and Dirk's mounts at a fast gallop out the unmanned, open gates.

"Follow them!" someone shouted from behind.

❧ ❦ ❧

Hoof beats thundered behind them on the race toward Draughon.

"Damned whoresons!" Lachlan held Angelique tightly before him on the horse and glanced back. Two of Kormad's men gave chase.

Draughon's iron gates came into view. "Open the gates!" Lachlan yelled.

The guards moved quickly, obeying his orders. The horses galloped through and into the empty bailey. The gates clanged shut behind them.

"Where is everyone? Were all the men killed?" Lachlan leapt down and helped Angelique dismount.

"I don't know," Rebbie said. "We took a dozen to Burnglen with us."

Since the secret passageways had been breached, Lachlan didn't know what to expect. Drawing his sword, he ran up the steps and yanked open the door to the crowded great hall.

Kormad and Girard jerked around to face him, their eyes bulging.

"What the hell are you two doing here?" Lachlan's first instinct was to gut Girard, then Kormad. But caution froze him to the spot. "Who allowed them entrance?" This was his and Angelique's home, and these knaves stood here as if they owned the place.

"Get Lady Angelique out of here!" one of his guards yelled. "They have turned everyone against you." He sat in the corner, his face bloody, hands behind his back.

Kormad smashed the man in the jaw with his fist, and he keeled over. "Well, that's one of your last loyal men, MacGrath. I'll let you guess who the other one is." Kormad chuckled.

Another guard in the room, apparently unharmed and free, averted his gaze. What about the guard at the gate outside…also a traitor? Or loyal? Several Drummagan clansmen, guards, and those holding other positions, stared at him with hard, accusing eyes. Where was Bryson, his sword-bearer and war leader? And Heckie? How many had turned traitor?

Lachlan glanced behind himself to find Angelique standing before Rebbie and Dirk, safe for now, but wide-eyed and pale.

"You will leave now!" Lachlan commanded his enemies.

Kormad laughed. "The Drummagan clan kens of your misdeeds, MacGrath. 'Haps your wife doesn't know the whole of it yet. Murder. Rape."

"You thrice cursed whoreson!" Lachlan forced himself not to act on his impulses. He wanted to launch himself at Kormad, sword slicing. But they were greatly outnumbered. He backed toward Angelique.

"MacGrath raped these two women." Kormad indicated

Fingall's wife, mock weeping, and Neilina, who glared.

"You are insane!" Lachlan said. "I did not touch either of them."

"We have witnesses. Several, in fact. We know you killed the French lad, Philippe. We have proof."

Behind him, Angelique gasped. "Philippe is dead?"

"Aye, ask your husband about it."

"I know naught of it," Lachlan said.

"We found your dagger in his back," Kormad said.

"You took my weapons when you knocked me on the head and captured me."

"Angelique murdered a man in France last year," Girard said.

"More lies," Lachlan seethed, his hatred of Girard raged. It took all his strength not to lop the man's head from his body. "You are the rapist and I intend to see you pay."

"Not to worry, my friends." Kormad addressed the Drummagan clan. "I have sent one of my men to report their crimes to the constable and magistrate. Seize them!"

Lachlan stepped back, shielding Angelique. "Protect her."

Dirk and Rebbie raised their swords. Standing back to back, the three of them formed a triangle with Angelique at the center. Lachlan held her hand in his left.

"You wish to kill more innocent people, I see," Kormad said. "Things will go easier if you give yourselves up and admit to your crimes."

"We have committed no crimes. You and this damned Frenchman are the criminals—rapist, murderer and thief."

"'Twill do you no good to fight. I have already shown the clan the legal papers," Kormad said. "The former chief, John Drummagan, married my sister in secret and they had a son. Timothy, as the sole legitimate male heir of John Drummagan, is the rightful earl. I am his guardian and therefore will serve as chief until he comes of age."

"'Tis lunacy! Are you telling me you believe this man's lies?" Lachlan asked the Drummagan clan, men he thought loyal. Men he trusted. "You swore your allegiance to me. And yet you believe this outlaw's lies over your own chief?"

Several men of the clan dropped their gazes. Others glared at him, eye to eye.

"False papers are easy to draw up. False witnesses are easy to find if you pay them enough, aye, Kormad? I wager constructing this web of lies has cost you a large sum."

"It has cost naught, because 'tis all true."

"*Oui*, and I come to take this murderess back to France. She will have a trial." Girard's gaze on Angelique held an unholy gleam. Lust combined with deep hatred. Lachlan could not allow Angelique to fall into his hands at all costs. She would suffer more than death. The three of them could not fight Kormad, Girard, their men, and the whole Drummagan clan—not and keep Angelique safe. He should've kept the king's retainers a few more weeks. Now, aside from his two good friends, he had no men to help him fight.

"Rebbie, Dirk, we are going out the way we came in," Lachlan said.

"Stand aside!" Dirk yelled.

Slowly, they retreated through the front door. Lachlan and Dirk barricaded the castle door from the outside with several large stones they rolled from the side. "Hurry! To the stables. They'll follow."

Two of Kormad's warriors on foot rushed them, swords drawn—the men who'd chased them on the road. Rebbie engaged one; swords clanged. Dirk ran the other through on the second strike, then helped Rebbie.

"After you kill him, make sure the gates are open," Lachlan yelled. Angelique in his arms, he carried her toward the stables.

"I cannot believe how my kin has betrayed us," she said. "What must we do?"

"Angelique!" Camille trotted from the kitchen garden. *"Grâce à Dieu!"*

"Where have you been?"

"Hiding. Girard would see me dead."

"Saddle five fresh horses," Lachlan ordered the stable lad and set Angelique on her feet.

"I already have, m'laird." He led one from a stall. "I knew you'd be needing them when you arrived."

"Where will we go?" Angelique asked. She looked so small and pale, her big green eyes trusting, depending on him to keep her safe. Lachlan had failed so miserably, he didn't deserve her trust anymore, but he was glad for it nonetheless.

Determined to make up for his faults, he set about testing the saddles and strength of the girth straps. He would save her life if he did naught else.

"I wouldn't sabotage your saddles, m'laird. I ken Kormad is the biggest liar in all of Scotland. I shall be your eyes and ears whilst you are gone."

"I thank you. Stay safe." Lachlan turned to Angelique. "Can you ride alone?"

"*Oui.*"

He helped the two women mount, then did so himself. Once Rebbie and Dirk took to their horses in the bailey, they all galloped through the gates. He glanced back to see the clan pouring from the doors.

≈◌◖ ◗◌≈

"Where are we going?" Angelique asked Lachlan two hours later when they stopped, dismounted and allowed the horses to drink at a stream. Rolling fields and a few bushes surrounded them. All she knew was they were riding north toward the Highlands, toward the brown, rounded peaks of the Cairngorms she could see in the distance.

"MacGrath holdings. Kintalon Castle," he said. "The clan of my birth won't turn on us so quickly." Dried blood and golden brown stubble covered Lachlan's jaw. Dirt and blood smeared his shirt and plaid. But his expression bothered her most; the playful charmer had vanished, and in his place was this frowning warrior with a hard mouth and fierce eyes.

"Why did you not ask the nearby clans we have alliances with for their help?"

"If the Drummagan clan can turn on us so easily, so can any of the other clans if they believe Kormad's lies and false papers. But I trust my brother with my life and yours. 'Tis the only place I know with certainty you'll be safe."

He was most concerned with her safety? She could not look him in the eye after that. Her clan shamed her. She could not believe they had betrayed her and Lachlan so easily.

"Kormad and Girard are the most malicious men I have seen," she said. "I know one of them killed Philippe." He'd been her friend when few others had, and she would miss him. But he'd never possessed a piece of her heart as Lachlan did. Nevertheless, Philippe had never hurt anyone and didn't deserve to be murdered in cold blood. If not for her, he wouldn't have been in Scotland. So

230

in some small way, she blamed herself.

Lachlan observed her closely, his gaze almost cutting. "Greed, revenge—they are powerful motivators."

"What shall we do? We cannot simply allow Kormad to keep Draughon."

"And I won't. But first I must make certain you're safe. I cannot protect you and fight those two and their men at the same time. Besides, now that the clan is on his side, I have no fighting men. I am bright enough to ken when to retreat and gather forces. The MacGrath clan is larger than the Drummagan clan, and I wager, will be willing to come to our aid."

"I thank you for protecting me," she said in a low voice.

"You don't have to thank me for that." He strode away to wash his face and arms in the peat-tinged water of the nearby stream.

She was thankful they'd escaped Kormad's clutches, but what if she and Lachlan could never go home to Draughon?

༺ঙ৩ ৩ঙ༻

Before dusk, they arrived at a small derelict castle where, Angelique learned, an acquaintance of Lachlan and Rebbie, from their academy days, lived. This jovial baron fed them well, then Camille and Angelique stayed the night in a private bedchamber.

Lachlan, Rebbie and Dirk slept on the great hall floor with the rest of the men of the household. Though her bed was comfortable, she missed Lachlan's hard, hot body spooned against her back. They might never lie that way again. Sleep was elusive, and nightmares of Girard and Kormad plentiful.

Before daybreak the next morn, they quickly ate and set out on their journey, before Kormad and his men could catch up to them...if they were following. The baron provided supplies— blankets, tents and food—to see them through should they not have anywhere to stay the next night.

Lachlan looked better this morn, having washed up and borrowed clean clothing from his friend. Still, his expression remained shuttered, determined.

All that day, they rode hard. The mountains of the Cairngorm rose up around them. Through the mist, she glimpsed patches of snow at the tops of some mountains. She had never been this far north into Scotland and found the landscape both stark and beautiful. Black clouds gathered overhead and the north wind blew chilly.

Lachlan stopped and dismounted. He pulled a woolen plaid blanket from the collection of supplies, wrapped it around Angelique and covered her head. His touch was gentle but efficient, his mood distant.

"*Merci,*" she said.

"Tell me if you get cold."

She nodded.

"Can you wrap a blanket around Camille?" Lachlan asked Rebbie and returned to his horse.

Suddenly, she missed that intimate, lingering gaze Lachlan used to bestow on her. She did not even know why she wished to see it again from a man of his sort. This was just one more thing reminding her that her dreams of love were indeed foolish.

Once they commenced riding again, a thin misty rain sprayed through the air, making Angelique doubly thankful for the tightly woven blanket keeping out most of the dampness. Clearly, she was not a Highland lass, but Lachlan seemed in his element.

At sundown, the rain stopped but the cold remained. They dismounted in a sheltered area beneath trees, no castles or crofts in evidence anywhere.

The men unloaded supplies. In the dusky light, she and Camille gazed out toward mountains that seemed somehow welcoming but gloomy. Low, brown vegetation covered them, heather perhaps, but no trees. This was such a different world from the green, bushy Lowlands.

Footsteps approached. "Lady Angelique, could I have a word?" Dirk asked.

"*Oui.*" How unusual. He rarely said anything to her beyond a greeting.

Camille sauntered away.

Dirk's sharp blue gaze sliced through a person. He appeared most serious, but his cheeks were ruddy. "In truth, 'twas me with Neilina that evening in the south tower. Lachlan wouldn't be unfaithful to you."

Angelique had no response to that. Had Lachlan told him to say this, or had she indeed spied on this man in carnal relations with a woman? Her face burned. She wished he spoke sincerely, but she knew better than to take any man at his word. No, now her *naiveté* and innocence were dead. "I have no proof of that. Whoever

I saw looked exactly like Lachlan and...my cousin said his name."

Dirk frowned. "She did call me Lachlan, but I didn't correct her because I was pretending to be him. It was my duty to see if she was Kormad's spy. 'Tis clear she was. I've known Lachlan more than ten years and he has never taken to a lass as he's taken to you."

"He's married to me so he has to maintain a credible façade."

"God's truth, he is smitten with you, though likely he'll never tell you that. 'Tis all I wished to say. I bid you good eve." He gave a shallow bow and strode away.

That was the most Dirk had ever spoken to her. She didn't know whether to believe him or not. Lachlan smitten? How was such a thing possible?

Dirk joined Lachlan where he was setting up a tent, and spoke a few words to him. Lachlan then moved toward her, a solemn expression on his face. What were they scheming?

"I need to tell you something, Angelique." He pulled the plaid more tightly about his shoulders. "This is a hell of a time and place to do it, but I have little choice."

Panic rose within her. Was he going to confess his infidelity only minutes after Dirk tried to convince her otherwise? "What is it?"

He inhaled deeply, hesitated, then looked her in the eye. "I have two sons."

"What? Sons?" Surely she'd misheard.

"Aye, two wee lads. Orin and Kean. They live with the MacGrath clan at Kintalon."

"Mère de Dieu." The soggy Scottish soil had surely dropped from beneath her. "Are you sure that is all? Such a man as yourself probably has twenty children in every country you have visited."

He lifted a brow. "Are you trying to be amusing?"

Amusing? She wished to strangle him. She was the fool, the woman who did not know of her husband's sons.

"Why did you not tell me long before now?" Who was this man? Did she know anything about him at all? A stranger.

"I didn't tell you because I knew you'd be angry. And you are, aye?"

She was unsure how she felt at the moment. Like a woman being spun about in a whirlwind, everything beyond her control, out of her grasp. She didn't have her husband nor her estate—both in the possession of someone else.

"Were you married before?" she asked.

"Nay."

Just as she'd suspected, they were by-blows of his endless string of sexual liaisons. "What of their mothers?" Women he had given those same intimate and sensual delights to that he'd given her. Despite being his wife, she was not special; she was but one among hundreds. Well, she'd seen that back at Draughon.

"Kean's mother died tragically a few months ago in a fire. Orin's mother still lives in the village. I'm no longer involved with her, of course."

"Of course," she muttered. Whether or not he was involved with a woman hinged on a split second decision and how lecherous he was feeling at that moment. "You could have told me…about your sons." She felt defeated somehow. Lost. "I know you are only telling me now because we are going to Kintalon, where I'm likely to run into them. What if we hadn't? Would you have ever told me?"

CHAPTER SIXTEEN

The next evening, snow flew through the gray gloaming as the sweet sight of Kintalon Castle and its ancient towers appeared in the distance, the loch beside it like dark glass.

"Thanks be to God," Lachlan murmured, warmth spreading through his chest. He hadn't realized how badly he missed home.

He'd let Angelique down in a big way, but he intended to take possession of Draughon again. He would not be defeated in this. His stomach knotting, he glanced back at her, shivering in the blankets. Damnation, he had to be a much better husband to her.

"We're almost there," he called out, the icy wind carrying his words away.

A half hour later, they rode through the village and approached the gates. Upon recognizing him, one guard unlocked the gates while another ran for the castle—to notify his brother, no doubt. Their party passed through into the empty barmkin where a lone torch flamed, lighting the snow-strewn cobblestones.

His dark-haired, smiling brother emerged from the tower and advanced toward them. "Lachlan! You barely made it by first snowfall."

"Aye." After swinging down from his horse, he shook Alasdair's hand, but then pulled him into a brotherly hug.

Dirk and Rebbie dismounted and greeted Alasdair, whom they had met years before. Lachlan lifted Angelique down from the horse and wrapped an arm around her, sharing some of his warmth. She felt perfect next to him and he'd sorely missed her touch. "I'd like you to meet my wife, Angelique, countess of Draughon. Angelique, my brother, Alasdair, Earl of MacGrath."

"*Enchantée, monsieur.* Lachlan has told me much about you." She curtsied.

Alasdair bowed and kissed her hand. "A pleasure, m'lady, and congratulations on your marriage."

Dirk helped Camille dismount and Lachlan introduced her as well.

"Come inside. The snow grows heavy. A lad will see to your horses." Alasdair urged them toward the castle entrance. "Lachlan?" He hung back at the door.

Lachlan allowed Angelique to slip from beneath his arm and continue inside with the others. "Aye?"

Snowflakes lit on Alasdair's black hair, while his dark eyes gleamed with both curiosity and happiness. "When you wrote to me of your marriage I could hardly believe it."

"'Twas unexpected, to say the least. I must talk to you in private as soon as possible. I'm afraid this isn't a social call."

Alasdair nodded, clapped a hand onto his shoulder and ushered him up the steps.

"Did you wed Gwyneth?" Lachlan asked.

"Indeed." Alasdair gave him a broad smile. "I'm not letting her escape me again."

"I'm glad. Congratulations to you as well."

In the great hall, the smiling faces, warmth and light from the hearths, and the scent of fresh baked bread and mutton stew held a homey, welcoming appeal.

Gwyneth rushed forward, her middle a bit thicker than it used to be and Lachlan wondered if the next Earl of MacGrath had already been conceived. Lachlan smiled and kissed her cheek. "Gwyneth, good to see you. Please meet my lovely new bride, Angelique. Angelique, my sister-in-law, Gwyneth."

"'Tis a pleasure, *madame.*" Gwyneth curtsied as did Angelique. "I'm sure you're all frozen to the bone. Come, warm by the fire. The servants will bring food out in a few minutes. And rooms are being prepared. I'm so glad you've come."

Angelique watched in amazement as Lachlan continued to greet his grinning clansmen, all of whom shook his hand heartily or slapped him on the shoulder. Some of them teased him mercilessly. His arm around her, he proudly introduced her to all of them.

"I'm going to talk to Alasdair for a few minutes about the Draughon situation." He kissed her forehead and disappeared down a corridor. That brief affectionate action disoriented her for a moment, taking her back to those times she missed, of sharing his bed.

"You must be exhausted. Let's sit." Gwyneth escorted her and Camille toward high table, not far from the blissful heat of the fireplace. Servants bustled about, setting out food and drink. Gwyneth fussed over her and Camille as if they were a couple of children, serving their stew and pouring ale. "Whilst the men talk about...manly things, we shall eat." Gwyneth's aristocratic English accent stood out as unusual among all these Scots, and Angelique wondered how she'd met Lachlan's brother.

A lad of about six approached Gwyneth. She pulled him close and introduced him as her son, Rory. After a shy greeting, he scampered away to play with a group of children.

Gwyneth smiled. "We were so surprised and pleased to receive the missive about your and Lachlan's marriage."

Angelique wished she could be as pleased, but at the moment she didn't know what to think or feel. "Our marriage was as much a surprise to me. Arranged by King James, you know."

"I never thought Lachlan would marry," Gwyneth said.

"He probably should not have." *Sacrebleu*, why had she said that? Now everyone would know they were unhappy.

Flushing, Gwyneth frowned slightly and picked at her berry tart.

"Pray pardon. I did not mean to say that." The tears which had threatened for days now flooded Angelique's eyes. The exhaustion, fear and confusion finally overcame her.

"I must beg your pardon. I did not mean to upset you," Gwyneth said.

"Do not worry over it, my lady," Camille insisted, patting Angelique's arm. "It is only that Angelique and Lachlan have had a dispute."

"Forgive me. I didn't mean to pry." Gwyneth's worried gaze shot to the opposite end of the great hall. Angelique turned.

A young lad of about three or four sat atop one of Lachlan's broad shoulders. The child had the same smile as Lachlan. Blond hair. It was eerily like seeing a tiny version of Lachlan.

"One of his sons," Angelique whispered. Though she knew

about them, seeing one in the flesh was like a blow to her vitals. Forcing herself to breathe normally, Angelique found her gaze would not leave her husband and the lad, engaged in boisterous horseplay.

Lachlan held him upside down, the child laughing so hard he could scarce breathe. And Lachlan looking happier than he'd been in a while. Games. That was all he knew. He was more child than man, himself. And then she recalled the games she'd played with him in the bedchamber, the risqué version of hazard. Yes, he was a man full grown then. She had so enjoyed the play, but that was a thing of the past.

"I'm very tired. Would you mind if I lie down?" Angelique asked.

"Of course not. I'll be right back." Gwyneth hastened across the room and said something to Lachlan. He nodded, his gaze flying to her as he set the lad to his feet.

Gwyneth returned. "Please, follow me, both of you, and I will show you to your rooms."

Lachlan trailed behind at a distance, up the stairs to a dimly lit corridor. Gwyneth opened a door. "Lady Angelique, this is Lachlan's room and yours. Camille, your room is further along." The two women continued on.

Angelique paused, refusing to look at her husband when he drew near. "I wish a separate chamber," she said, needing to rest and release some of her emotions. She could not do that in Lachlan's presence.

"I must protect you, so we need to sleep in the same bedchamber," he said in a low, rough voice.

"It is but an excuse."

"Call it what you will. I'm your husband and we share a room, even if I do sleep on the floor."

"The floor. I agree with that." One part of her wanted to hurt him viciously as he had done her, while another part rebelled at the thought of him lying on the floor. No, that large poster bed with blue hangings of fine velvet was his.

He urged her inside the chamber and closed the door behind them. A thick white candle sat lit on the mantel and a cozy fire flickered in the hearth.

"That was one of your sons," she said.

His sharp, dark gaze shot to hers. "Aye."

"He appears to be a small replica of you."

Lachlan's lips lifted a bit. "Indeed. I hope you'll want to meet them."

Her mind felt overcrowded, too many thoughts and feelings squeezed into it. "Perhaps. But right now I'm exhausted. Would you mind if I rest alone for a while."

"'Tis exactly what you need." Lachlan turned down the covers and fluffed the pillow. "Would you like me to bring you anything else? Food, drink?"

"*Non. Merci.*"

"Well then, I'll return in a short while. I'll be in the library with Alasdair should you need me."

A knock sounded at the door. He opened it to Camille, bowed and showed himself out.

Lachlan strode away from his own bedchamber, the one he'd slept in most of his life, feeling as if it was no longer his. He had let Angelique down in so many ways. Mayhap those people who believed he would amount to naught were right. Maybe he was not capable of handling the responsibility given to him; maybe he had no potential at all.

"God's blood," he muttered. He would not be defeated in this. He would get Draughon back if 'twas the last thing he accomplished.

Upon entering the library, he found Alasdair by the fireplace, pitcher in hand. "Clarey?"

"Aye, thanks."

His brother poured wine into a pewter mug and handed it to him. "So, you—Seducer of the Highlands—are married?" Alasdair held his own mug aloft.

"Aye." Lachlan clanked his mug against his brother's in toast. "To our lovely wives." He drank a long swallow of the spiced wine.

"I never thought I'd see it." Alasdair smiled.

"Nor I. But I couldn't pass up the king's generous offer. And I had to protect Angelique."

"You like being married?"

"Aye." Lachlan couldn't prevent the grin that escaped when he remembered the few days of bliss he'd shared with Angelique. Making love during the day, or at night. The games. The way they'd laughed together. Would they ever be that close and harmonious again?

"I can see you care for her."

Lachlan nodded, staring down into his mug. His brother didn't know the half of it. But Lachlan wasn't going to enlighten him.

"I've heard a rumor that…you two have had a disagreement."

"Damnation. What did you—?"

The library door opened. Rebbie and Dirk strode in and closed the door back.

"Are we interrupting?" Rebbie halted. "Should we come back later?"

"Nay," Lachlan said. "We're done with that subject."

"I'm not so sure about that, brother." Alasdair grinned.

৵৶৩৵

Angelique crept down the dim, deserted stairway and toward the library where Lachlan was to meet with his brother. A chambermaid had been kind enough to tell her the location. Thankfully, Angelique encountered no one along her trek, though a murmur of conversation echoed from the great hall. She'd wished to sleep, but the restlessness would not leave her.

The library door was thick carved oak, but a slice of light escaped a narrow crack around the frame. If she held her head just right, she understood every word from within. The men did not keep their voices down. For a while they talked of the Drummagan clan and the problems at Draughon, then Rebbie mentioned Neilina.

"Who is this Neilina?" Alasdair asked.

"God's teeth, Rebbie. Can you not keep your mouth closed?" Lachlan growled.

"'Tis difficult."

Angelique awaited Lachlan's answer, a sick feeling coiling inside her. Would he admit his guilt?

"She's Angelique's cousin, and Kormad's. She was working for him, spying and trying to seduce me."

"You and your women," Alasdair scoffed.

"She's not my woman, never was. I sent Dirk to meet with her in my place to get information. She didn't even ken 'twas Dirk until after the deed."

"Then what happened?"

"She was furious," Dirk said. "Angelique believes 'twas Lachlan with her because I was wearing his kilt. We tried to tell her,

240

but she still thinks Lachlan is the guilty party."

"Can't say I blame her, given your habits, Lachlan," Alasdair said.

"To hell with you. I've changed my habits."

Alasdair chuckled. "So, you're faithful to your wife?"

"Indeed."

"Does he tell the truth?"

"Aye. He's not near as much fun as he used to be. No more carousing. He but obsesses over the wee lass," Rebbie grumbled.

"Do you love her?" Alasdair inquired in a smooth voice.

In the dark, Angelique could scarce breathe, afraid she would miss the answer. But more, terrified his response would be *nay*.

"Who?" Lachlan asked.

"Don't be daft. Lady Angelique."

"She is beautiful. I enjoy her. She enjoys me."

"You didn't answer my question."

"You ken I don't get calf-eyed over women."

"Has he gone calf-eyed?" Alasdair asked.

"Aye, that he has," Rebbie answered.

"To hell with you, too. Don't be putting words in my mouth."

"He will never admit it. Do you ken, he couldn't even bed his own wife until she made him go to the physician and get his tarse checked for the French pox."

"Damnation, Rebbie," Lachlan snapped.

The other men let loose an uproarious laugh.

Angelique's face turned scorching. Why had he told them everything?

Lachlan muttered curses. "Well, I'm healthy, officially, and completely free of disease."

"'Tis a miracle," Alasdair said.

"Some brother you are."

"So, how long has she had you cut off this time?" Rebbie asked. "A week?"

"I will not be discussing my intimate relations with my wife with you heathens."

"No lass was ever able to resist him long. So doubtless, his wife cannot resist him either," Alasdair said.

"Even if she wishes to kill him sometimes," Rebbie put in.

"A stormy relationship suits him, I'm certain," Alasdair said.

"Will you bastards cease discussing my marriage like a gaggle of fishwives."

"I think he loves her," Alasdair said in an astounded tone.

"He does. He can think of naught else but her."

"Did I not tell you 'twould happen?" Alasdair asked. "You've been bitten on the arse."

"No one has bitten my arse, I thank you."

"Cupid shot him in the arse," Dirk said.

They guffawed. Angelique fanned her burning face, wondering if what Rebbie said was true—did Lachlan love her?

"You're all daft." The abrupt noise of chair legs scraping across the floor sounded. "I'm going to bed."

"Nay. Come back. We're sorry." More laughter.

"He never could take teasing, though he likes to do it to others."

"His pride is as big as Ben Nevis."

"Will you stop talking about me as if I'm not here? A bunch of lasses, the lot of you. I thought we were here to discuss the Draughon situation. If not, I'm going to bed."

Angelique rushed away from the door and up the stairs. She ran into their bedchamber, closed the door, and jumped into bed, covering her head with the counterpane. Her hands trembled, as did her whole body.

Could any of it be true? Had he been faithful? Did he love her, though he would never admit it?

⁖ ⁖ ⁖

Two hours later, Lachlan entered his bedchamber quietly. He crept toward the bed. Angelique was asleep as he'd expected. Something about seeing her lying there in his bed struck him deep in his vitals. Her smooth ivory skin in the firelight, her flame-colored hair. She was so lovely he couldn't look away for long seconds. Saints! She had bewitched him.

Though he craved her, he would not touch her again until she wished it. He was innocent of the charges she'd hurled at him—innocent for the first time in his life—and he would not grovel at her gold-slippered feet. If she never believed him, never forgave him, he would suffer in silence. As long as he could.

What if they could never make amends? What if she never kissed him again or gave him that rare sweet smile he'd glimpsed a few times during their love-play? He would live in hell, that's what. Emptiness crept slowly over him. His skin ached for her hands on him. He remembered how she'd stroked her fingers down his chest, down his bare abdomen to the sensitive skin on the lowest part of his belly. She'd made him tremble with touching him there, so close to his shaft. Teasing him and making him yearn as he never had.

He grew hard now with the memory.

Releasing a harsh breath, he approached the fireplace and quietly added two more bricks of peat. He dropped into the padded chair and his gaze returned to her. Aye, what he wouldn't give now to strip naked and crawl between those warm sheets with her. Just to hold her.

But he did not deserve such bliss. He'd lost her estate, and he would not pursue his husbandly rights again until he'd earned them by reclaiming Draughon.

⋆⑩ ⑩⋆

Mid-morning the next day, Angelique opened the bedchamber window a crack to better see the view of the snow-covered Highlands. Bright sunlight gleamed off the white mountains and the shimmering loch reflected the blue sky, near blinding her. Tiny bits of ice and snow still flickered through the air. What a stark difference to the Lowlands of days ago.

It was a long way back to Draughon. Lachlan and several more men planned to leave two days hence. Imagining Lachlan being injured in a battle so far away from her wrenched her inside. What if he were to be killed and she never saw him again? She may as well die, too.

In the snow-whitened barmkin far below her, Lachlan stood talking to his brother. Secretly, she savored the sight of him. She had awakened this morn to find Lachlan sleeping in a chair by the hearth. He hadn't forced himself into bed with her—his bed, in truth. She was the outsider here. She felt vulnerable with a hundred questions hovering. How did he truly feel about her? She prayed he could learn to love her.

A woman, her belly large with child, ambled though the gates below. The lad of about five or six years broke away from her and ran to Lachlan. He picked him up, hugged him, and threw him over his shoulder like a sack of grain. The child's laughter was sharp in the crisp air. His older son, surely.

Alasdair walked away and the pregnant woman approached Lachlan. Angelique tensed, waiting for an emotional blow. But

243

Lachlan didn't touch her, even after he set the lad to his feet. He merely talked to her in a low tone for several minutes. He dug into his sporran, took something out and gave it to her. Coins. Dear Lord, that woman was carrying his child. Again.

Nausea rolling in her stomach, Angelique closed the window and pulled the thick curtain over it, making the room dark again. Who had she married? A man who wanted a harem? Angelique had done the most idiotic thing on earth and fallen in love with her rogue husband.

Several minutes later, she sat before the fire when Lachlan opened the door and entered the chamber.

"Are you well?" he asked.

She could not look at him; it was too painful. "*Oui*. Why would I not be?"

"Gwyneth said you were resting. I thought you'd be asleep."

"I do not take naps," she snapped, then realized she sounded like an irritable child.

"What's the matter?"

Her stomach knotted and a bit of her pain and rage crept out. "So, you are to be a father yet again?"

"What?"

"I saw you talking to her." She motioned toward the window.

"Och. Nay, the bairn she carries is not mine. I haven't been with her in years."

"Did you give her money?"

"Aye. For my son, and her. For clothing, food."

"And, of course, you have plenty of money now." She felt bitter and hateful even as she said the words. But it was true; he'd married Angelique for her money and estate.

He remained silent for a long moment. "Would you have them starve or wear rags?" His tone was not angry as she'd expected, but resigned.

She did feel sorry for them, other victims of Lachlan's irresponsible escapades. "Of course not." But did that mean her money should provide for them?

"I am bringing my sons home with us soon, once we have Draughon back."

"What?" She felt as if he'd struck her. Her gaze flew to him and his determined expression.

"Aye. I miss them. Kean's mother was killed. He has been

living here at the castle. Alasdair and Gwyneth provide excellent care for him, but I want to care for him. Both of them. I've never had the opportunity before. You wish me to be responsible, so I will be. I want to be."

She admired him for that. Still, for her to instantly be a mother of two children—her husband's bastards—what would people think of her, accepting them so easily? "You decide without even asking my opinion."

He moved to the mantel, stared at something upon it for several moments. "They will love you. And you will love them if you give them a chance. They are but innocent children. They have done naught wrong."

Tears burned her eyes and she stared at her lap. She knew that; she would never blame them for Lachlan's misdeeds.

"Kean asked me if you are a princess."

"Heavens. I do not know how to take care of children."

"We shall hire a nanny. 'Haps we will need one soon, anyway."

When she forced herself to look at him, he winked. Everything was a jest to him, was it not?

"Will your older son's mother not mind if you take him away?"

"Nay, 'twas what she was talking to me about. She fears she cannot watch after him once her new bairn arrives. Orin's a wee rambunctious, and gets into scrapes, as I oft did as a lad. But you don't have to worry; he listens to me."

"He looks so much like you." Indeed both his sons did.

"Aye, 'tis true." He smiled with affection. With love. He could love his children, but not her. She felt beyond ridiculous being jealous of her husband's sons.

"Angelique." He stepped in behind her and grasped her shoulders in his big strong hands, caressing deeply into her tense muscles. "I'm hoping you can understand. I'm sorry for my past, because of you. Because I ken it bothers you. But I'm not sorry I have children. Can't you see? They are like treasures to me."

She bent forward, trying to escape his hypnotic touch, trying to hide the emotion in her eyes.

He came around in front of her and knelt, took her forearms into his hands. "Angelique. What's wrong? Tell me."

She shook her head.

"When we have children, I will love them as much."

He could love her children, but not her. How foolish she was to care how he felt about anything. He wrapped his arms around her and kissed her hair, her temple. She loved the way he smelled, like soap and musky male, loved the feel of his strong body. He had not touched her in a while; she hadn't let him. But now he felt so wondrous, like she remembered. She wished to wrap herself about him tightly, skin to skin.

"We must have a son to be the next Earl of Draughon," he murmured. "Then, we must have a daughter, a wee lass who looks exactly like you."

How could he say such things? As if he might care. As if he wanted a true family with her. Tears pricked her eyes and she pressed her face against his chest.

"Shh." He rocked her and stroked her hair. "We shall get Draughon back. Never fear."

"I hope you are right." Yes, let him believe she worried she would never possess Draughon again, when in truth she feared she'd never possess him.

⚬ઉ૨ ૭ર⚬

After evening meal, Angelique sat by the fire in the great hall. Lachlan had convinced her earlier to meet his sons. He now brought them forward and knelt between them.

"Kean, this is my wife, Lady Angelique." Lachlan whispered something else in his younger son's ear.

"M'lady." His wide-eyed gaze locked on her, then the tiny lad bowed.

Angelique's throat tightened. "It is a pleasure to meet you, Kean."

The lad beamed at her, his light brown eyes and endearing smile so like Lachlan's it near broke her heart. What an adorable little cherub he was.

"And this is Orin." Lachlan stood and placed his hand upon his older son's shoulder.

"M'lady." Though only five, he gave a dramatic bow as if he'd been practicing a while.

She couldn't help but smile. "Orin. It is so nice to meet you."

Orin did indeed have Lachlan's light hair and facial shape, but his eyes were clear blue.

Kean inched closer to where she sat, staring at her intently. "You're pwetty," he said.

246

"*Merci.* I thank you. What a little charmer you are." Smiling, she touched his baby-fine blond hair. He took that as leave to climb onto her lap and snuggle.

With no idea what to talk to such a small child about, she looked to Lachlan for help. The grinning scoundrel only winked. She placed her arms around Kean to hold him, and some emotion struck her she had never felt before—a warm, maternal feeling. She and Lachlan might one day have a son much like Kean, yes, some part of her wanted that intensely.

Outside, in the barmkin, men shouted, giving her a start.

"Stay here," Lachlan said and moved toward the entrance along with his brother and several more men.

Two guards entered and talked quietly with Lachlan and Alasdair.

Lachlan returned to her side. "Kormad, Girard and their men are outside the gates."

CHAPTER SEVENTEEN

"I never suspected Kormad and Girard would find us," Lachlan said to Alasdair as they donned studded leather armor in the armory. Rebbie, Dirk and the MacGrath clansmen prepared themselves in a like fashion, choosing weapons.

"'Tis better this way," Alasdair said. "We shall defeat them here. On our home sod we shall have the advantage."

"How many men with them?" Lachlan asked.

"About two dozen."

"I hate to see any of the Drummagans killed. I'm supposed to be their chief."

"Aye, but if they ride with Kormad, they're traitors. You don't want a man in your clan who isn't loyal."

Lachlan knew it was true. Still, he'd failed them. Why hadn't the Drummagans trusted him? Why had they turned against him so easily?

Once they had their weapons and targes, they headed outside into the snow and icy wind. Evening descended, casting the barmkin in gloom.

"Hand him over!" Kormad demanded when Alasdair and Lachlan were some twenty yards from the closed iron gates. "He is a fugitive wanted in Perth for murder and rape."

"Trumped up by you," Lachlan said.

One of Kormad's men fired a pistol through the bars.

Alasdair and Lachlan dove for cover behind a wall. The MacGrath archers on the battlements rained down arrows onto

Kormad's men. Amid shouts, more pistol shots exploded from both sides. Another volley of arrows flew from above, all landing outside the gates.

"You bastard, Lachlan MacGrath," Girard yelled in French.

The mere sound of his voice lit a fuse of rage within Lachlan. "I shall kill that craven whoreson if 'tis the last thing I do!" He had already told his brother in confidence what Girard had done to Angelique.

"Is he the man with one arm?"

"Aye, she got a bit of revenge. Shot the bastard's arm off."

Alasdair sent him an unholy grin. "Both our wives have a bloodthirsty streak."

"We are fortunate." Lachlan peered from behind the wall and a shot whizzed over his head. He ducked. "God's teeth!"

He lay on the ground and aimed at the whoreson—one of Kormad's hired mercenaries—and fired. The man jerked and howled. Lachlan slid behind the wall again. His comrades fired in retaliation.

Kormad's men shot flaming arrows toward the windows and roof of Kintalon. Good thing Alasdair had ordered all the shutters closed. Moments later, some of the flaming arrows flew downward again from the roof to strike at the men who'd lit them.

"Retreat!" Kormad ordered. The men disappeared from the gates.

Alasdair rallied his men and moments later, they all rode out on horseback, making sure the gates closed behind them. Several guards remained to defend the castle.

"Capture them if you can," Alasdair yelled.

⋄⊙⊙⋄

Through a crack in one of the shutters, Angelique watched the MacGrath men give chase to Kormad's and even members of her own clan—those who'd turned traitor. In the evening light, she picked out Lachlan's figure; he rode at the head of the men beside his brother. Her stomach aching, she crossed herself. *Mère de Dieu, protect him.*

She glanced aside to find Gwyneth with her eyes closed, her face white. Then with watery blue eyes, she met Angelique's gaze. "Every time Alasdair rides out on that black warhorse…" Swallowing hard, she shook her head.

Angelique knew. Life was incredibly fragile, even that of a

249

trained, armored warrior. "I am so sorry to have brought this trouble to your clan."

"'Twas not your fault. And I can see you're worried about Lachlan."

"*Oui*. He takes too many risks. Thinks he is immortal."

"All men do."

Angelique nodded, remembering how Lachlan was a free bleeder and prayed he would suffer no injuries.

A while later, moonlight reflected off the snow and the riders returning, shouting. Hooves clattered on cobblestones in the barmkin. Angelique's pulse spiked. Where was Lachlan? Through the window she could not tell who was who in the darkness, despite the few torches. She and Gwyneth ran down the steps to the entrance.

When Gwyneth opened the thick door, icy cold pierced Angelique's clothing. She had not thought of a wrap or cloak. They peered through the cracked door. The MacGraths unloaded bound men from the horses and shepherded their prisoners toward the far corner of the castle.

"They're taking them to the dungeon," Gwyneth said. "Listen." She let out a breath. "That's Alasdair talking, giving orders. Thanks be to God. There he is with Lachlan." She pointed.

A man with light hair separated himself from the mass of teaming men and horses. She recognized his stride. Angelique whispered a prayer of thanks. In her heart, she now believed he had not betrayed her. She was afraid she had fallen foolishly in love with him. If only he would feel the same.

∞⊙෧ ෧⊙∞

A half hour later, Lachlan followed the other men into the great hall, the heat from the two hearths welcome on his cold skin. With Kormad and Girard captured, they were halfway to his goal of reclaiming Draughon. His eyes scanned the large room for his wife.

Someone tugged on his arm and pulled him into an embrace. Red curls filled his vision. Angelique pressed herself to his chest and her lavender-rose scent filled his senses. Unexpected excitement buzzed through him. Not just sexual excitement either, which surprised him. He could only describe it as happiness.

"Angelique?"

Taking his hand, she pulled him into the less crowded stairwell, slid a hand around his neck and reached up for a kiss. What had he done to deserve this? He tried to tease her and hold back. But her breath upon his lips was sweet torment. He moved closer and she pressed her lips firmly against his. A thrill shot through him. She was hot, alluring and delightful.

He kissed her as he'd yearned to for days, deep and lusty, the sweet taste of her going to his head, bewitching him. She must have forgiven him. When she tried to climb higher, get closer to him, he picked her up, pressing her into the corner of the stone wall, giving her another thorough kiss.

Two MacGrath clansmen passed on the steps, whistling and making sounds of bawdy encouragement.

Everyone did love to tease him. Grinning, Lachlan set her down and shielded her from their view. After making sure they were gone, he observed his wife, her eyes dark, her lips parted and red. He had an erection that wasn't likely to leave soon.

"What was that for?" he asked.

"I worried for you. I am glad you are well." Her voice was breathy and feminine, her accent more pronounced. Just like the other time he'd returned from a skirmish with Kormad, she was extremely affectionate...and likely aroused. Saints! The things he wanted to do to her, if only he could get her alone. But now was not the time.

"Indeed, I'm well. I have to go back into the dungeon to question the men we captured. We must get to the bottom of these false papers and charges against us. 'Twill likely take several hours."

⚜⚜⚜

Later that night, a sound woke Angelique. Water splashing. The fire burned low but revealed Lachlan's naked form across the bedchamber where he washed himself at the basin. His body glowed like sculpted bronze in the firelight.

"What did you learn?" she asked.

He turned. "I thought you were asleep."

"I was." She'd tried to stay awake and wait for him but must have slept a short time.

He finished bathing and dried his face, arms and the rest of his body with a cloth. Without even trying, he seduced her with his raw sensuality, his confident movements and those delicious muscles. His shaft was relaxed but starting to grow larger as he approached the bed and sat on the edge. "I'm glad I woke you, then."

"Why?" Though she wanted to ask him about the prisoners, she wanted to touch him more.

"Because." He lifted her hand and kissed the back of her fingers. "You're more fun awake."

Without thought, she turned her hand, her fingertips brushing the prickly stubble of his cheek, her thumb stroking his full lips. He had a mouth designed for sinful kisses and she trembled in some deep part of herself with the need to taste his lips and drink in his breath. His gaze burned into her with dark gold flame. His brows lowered; his jaw clenched. He kissed the sensitive pads of her fingers, her palm. Oh, such tingly heat...it raced from her hand, up her arm, to her breasts, then spread down her body. His tongue touched her palm, producing a sharp ache within her.

She sat up and quickly pressed her lips to his. Her heart leapt. *You are mine, Lachlan.* "You are mine." A noise escaped her, halfway between a cry and a gasp. She had not meant to say the words aloud.

"Aye, lass, I'm yours. And you're mine," he breathed against her lips.

"I did not mean—"

"Shh." He took possession of her lips again and urged her to lie back on the pillow.

Her mind would not function while his mouth seduced with hot licks and possessive thrusts of his tongue.

She took great handfuls of his hair, twining the silken strands around her fingers to better hold his head while she feasted upon his mouth. No matter his sins, no matter if he shattered her heart again tomorrow, she could not deny herself this moment of bliss.

Between kisses, he murmured and whispered to her in a language she knew not. *What...what are you saying?* But no words would emerge from her. She craved air, and his breath. All over, her skin tingled, needing his touch. He untied the belt of her wrap, pushed up her silk smock, stroking his rough palm over her thigh and hip. Hot shivers coursed through her. She arched her back and allowed him to remove her garments.

"Och, Angelique, you are so lovely." He fastened his lips onto her nipple, both his hands supporting her back. He devoured her, licked and sucked, his beard stubble rasping her breasts during the overwhelming pleasure.

Lying down beside her, he returned to her mouth with the consuming kisses, his big hand now cradling her derriere, sliding down to lift her thigh. He aligned her to his body, his muscles unyielding to her soft flesh, his stone-hard shaft pressing against her lower belly. Insistent, demanding. Just inside, she yearned for him, aching for him to impale her with that male weapon.

He was everywhere at once, his heat, his hardness, his sensual mouth. She released a gasping cry of frustration, of wanting what he would never give her. Not just his body but his heart. "Lachlan, damn you." She seized his shaft in her hand, firmly, his skin fever-hot and silky, the flesh beneath like steel. She wished to possess him, body and soul, so he would never look at another woman. Never know another woman existed. No one but her. She stroked him up and down. He growled more of those foreign words, his hips flexing, jaw clenching.

He twisted abruptly, escaping her hold and pinning her beneath him. Between her thighs, his hand explored her hidden places. His fingers slicked over her, and she knew she was very wet for him, craving that he drive himself as deep as he could into her, without mercy.

"Mmm." He bit his lip. His eyes, staring into hers, reflected dark lust, his lids lowered. She imagined those terse Gaelic words rolling off his tongue had sinful and sexual meanings. Or was their meaning more emotional?

She thrust her hips toward him. Surely her need was clear.

He trembled—she thought—as he pushed her thighs wider and rose to his knees. He took his shaft in hand and stroked it against her burning, tingling flesh. She gasped and thrust her hips again. *Yes, do it.*

She held her breath when he pushed inside her, that invasion she obsessed about. At first shallow, making her yearn for more, but with each stroke, he slid deeper. More and more, he challenged her limits with his size. It was not pain she felt, but an erotic stretching sensation that soon gave way to pure blissful pleasure. His broad, muscled shoulders above her fueled her need for him. So delicious was he, she savored everything about him. His gaze, locked on hers, communicated things no words of any language could express. Connection, emotion, intensity.

He dropped over her, an elbow beside her head, and brushed his lips against hers. Losing control, she cried out with each sensation he propelled through her body.

Then his breath burned against her ear. She stroked her palms over his beard stubble, his sweaty face and into his hair, pushing it back. His finger teased her magical spot just above where his body joined with hers. The tingles became a maelstrom too intense to bear. Something propelled her off the edge of the world, shattering her with that euphoria only Lachlan knew how to draw forth from her.

He ground into her hard, shuddering with deep growling sounds and foreign words. Seconds passed as time seemed suspended.

His breaths came in great gasps as he withdrew and dropped to the bed beside her. "Saints! Angelique," he rasped. "You'll be the death of me with that kind of bedsport."

While he held her, she lay with her forehead against his upper chest. Oh, the things she wished for...that he be hers alone, forever. That they share this intimacy every night and every day. That he might grow to love her. That she could love him without fear he would shatter her heart on a whim.

⁘

"He's acting all 'happy' again," Rebbie muttered to Dirk as they strode across the snow-covered barmkin the next morn. "So, all is forgiven?"

"What do you speak of?" Lachlan asked, taking a moment to enjoy the clean icy air and heated memories of last night.

"Don't pretend to be daft. You're smiling like a lunatic."

"Am I?" Lachlan wanted to laugh but held it in. "Well... indeed, she believes me now—that I wasn't with Neilina."

"Why?"

"Came to her senses?" Lachlan opened the door to the dungeon, unsure exactly how or why Angelique had warmed to him. All that mattered was that she had. "And she accepted Orin and Kean." When she had held wee Kean on her lap, showing his motherless son affection, Lachlan's chest had tightened. Angelique had the softest of hearts, which she kept hidden behind thick steel armor.

Rebbie snorted. "You're the luckiest bastard I've ever seen."

"Nay, just canny."

"Pah!"

They entered the low-ceilinged underground room where his

brother and a few other men waited, including his cousins, Fergus and Angus. Several candles and a torch lit the room.

Alasdair motioned for Lachlan to join him at the table in the center of the room. "Bring them in," he told one of his guards.

Moments later, the guard returned, leading a bound man, one of the Drummagans Lachlan had never grown close to. A quiet man with steely, suspicious eyes.

"What can you tell us about the false documents Kormad had drawn up?" Lachlan asked.

"I ken naught of it." He set his determined jaw. This was likely a man who would not even crack under torture.

"Do you know where the papers are now?"

The man shook his head. This was a waste of time.

After they'd questioned two more men, both with lips sealed tight, Lachlan said, "Bring in Bryson."

The guard nodded and shoved the uncooperative man out the door.

That his sword-bearer had turned against him surprised Lachlan most and sickened him. He had truly thought Bryson loyal above all others, except maybe Heckie. And he had no inkling where Heckie was at the moment. Safe, he hoped.

Moments later, the guard pushed Bryson into the room. He stood before them, his hands tied behind his back.

"Bryson, I am most disappointed to find you riding with Kormad," Lachlan said.

The stocky, dark-haired man glanced at the closed door. "I'm not with him," Bryson whispered. "I'm still loyal to you, chief."

Lachlan studied the man's dark eyes, unable to read the sincerity. He didn't know the man well enough. Damnation, he was an idiot for trusting so easily. And now, what if this was a lie? "You sure as the devil fought hard against us last night. Why should I believe you?"

"I've come to help you defeat Kormad and that Frenchman, but I don't want them to know. They'll kill my family if they find out."

"They have threatened your family?"

"Aye!"

"Do you know where the false papers are? We searched Kormad and they were not on his person. Nor were they on his horse."

"They're back at Burnglen, hidden. But I don't know where exactly."

"How many men did he leave there to guard?"

"Three that I know of. He left more to guard Draughon."

The bastard. "How many Drummagans turned traitor?"

"About twenty men. They locked the others up in the dungeon."

Lachlan was glad to know Kormad hadn't killed the rest. Still, they might be injured. He needed to see them released and safe as soon as possible. "I thank you, Bryson. Are you willing to travel back to Kormad's estate with us and help find the papers?"

"Aye." Bryson knelt on one knee much as he had done when he pledged his loyalty the first time. His gaze was dark but respectful.

A bit of the pressure lifted from Lachlan's chest when another Drummagan vowed his loyalty, agreed to help and was released. Alasdair set guards on the two men and didn't allow them any weapons. Lachlan's plan was that three dozen of them, mostly MacGraths, would leave early the next morning for Kormad's estate. Lachlan would lead them while Alasdair would remain behind to guard Angelique and the others. Once Lachlan had the false papers, they would reclaim Draughon. Now, he but had to tell Angelique his plans and hope she didn't fight him on it.

•◦◑ ◐◦•

Kormad ground his teeth and cursed. He hated this despicable, dark and cold dungeon. Pike and several of his men waited in this cell with him. What was taking Bryson so damned long? Kormad had told him what to do two nights ago, pretend loyalty to Lachlan MacGrath and get them out of this hellhole. He had chosen Bryson for this task for three reasons. One, since he was MacGrath's sword-bearer, MacGrath would be more likely to trust him. Two, Bryson was highly skilled. And, three, he had a family. If Bryson didn't obey orders, the man's wife and son would die. Kormad would make sure of it. He had them detained in the dungeon back at Draughon with orders to one of his guards, if he didn't return by a specified date, to kill them.

Kormad had always heard Highlanders were ruthless, but he was starting to doubt it. This MacGrath chief hadn't even tortured any of them for information. He was so soft and lenient, Kormad was sure he posed no threat if only they could get these cells unlocked.

A door in the distance opened and closed, then running footsteps sounded.

"I think he's coming," Kormad said.

His men stood, breaths held. A lantern appeared.

The cell lock clicked and the door opened. "Hurry, 'tis almost dawn." Bryson waved them forward.

"Ah, Bryson!" Kormad said. "I kenned you could do it. Release the rest of my men." He motioned to the other cells.

One of the other Drummagans, a friend of Bryson's, helped him, no doubt for the same cause, to save Bryson's family. Kormad might even let them live.

"Where shall we find weapons?" Girard asked, exiting one of the other cells. "I need at least two loaded pistols and a knife."

"Wait in line," Kormad growled. This Frenchman was trying his patience, and if he wasn't careful he would find himself downed by a stray lead ball.

"I have five of the guards' weapons hidden. They were heavily armed," Bryson said.

"How did you kill them?" Kormad loved stories of triumph, as well as pushing a man to do desperate things.

"During the night, when most were asleep and no one was looking, we silently took out our personal guards and hid the bodies, then we removed the dungeon guards, one by one, by jumping them when they least expected it and slitting their throats."

"You impress me with your skills of war, Bryson. You'll have a high position once we return to Draughon. Now, I have just one more job for you. I need you to go in and fetch that little Angelique witch. Don't kill her, but feel free to kill anyone who gets in your way."

"I can hardly wait to have her in my grasp again," Girard said, grinning like a maniac.

৵৶৻ ৶৻৵

A knock sounded at Angelique's bedchamber door. Lachlan had insisted she bar it when he arose before dawn.

"Who is it?" she asked near the door.

"'Tis me, Lachlan," he said in a low tone.

Good, she must see him before his departure to Draughon. She could hardly bear that he was going to fight a battle, and with her so far away. She prayed he would not be injured.

She opened the door but Lachlan did not wait outside. Girard and Bryson stared back at her. Sharp chills paralyzed her a moment. She shoved the door to close it, but the two men forced their way inside.

"No!" She screamed. "Help!"

Girard shut the door. "Hold her. Cover her mouth," he told Bryson and the man obeyed. "You will not escape me this time, whore."

She screamed behind Bryson's dirty, bloody hand. How could the man who'd been her own father's sword-bearer turn traitor? She kicked and twisted, dislodging his hand, then screamed again.

Girard slapped her hard across the cheek. Everything went black and numb for a few seconds, then she found herself face down on the floor beneath one of them. Pains shot from her elbow and knees where she had fallen on them. The side of her face burned and ached.

"Bastard!" If only she could reach her dagger, strapped to her calf, but Bryson was too strong. Despite twisting and kicking, she could not escape his iron-like grasp.

"Gag her with this," Girard commanded.

Bryson shoved a thick piece of material into her mouth and tied it behind her head.

"No, damn you!" she tried to shout, but it sounded like a moan.

"Bind her hands."

"You said you wouldn't hurt her," Bryson said.

"I said I wouldn't kill her. At least not now. But Kormad will kill your wife and son if you do not obey me. Besides that, you have just murdered five MacGrath guards. What do you think the rest of the MacGraths will do to you if we turn you over to them?"

Angelique emitted muffled shouts as Bryson tied her hands so tightly the thin rope bit into her wrists. Why had she not thought to take out her knife before opening the door?

Lachlan, where are you?

One of the men yanked her to her feet and threw a cloak around her shoulders. Dizziness overwhelmed her and she swayed. *Sacrebleu!* She had no chance of reaching her knife now. What would they do to her?

Girard poked his head into the corridor, then motioned them

forward. Bryson guided Angelique out and along the passage to what must have been the back servants' stairwell. Very narrow. Glancing around, she saw no one about. She tried to scream or yell for help, but the sound only sounded like a loud moan.

"Quiet," Girard growled and shoved her toward the stairwell. Her feet tangling in her skirts, Angelique fell into Bryson, in front of her. He turned, catching her, and hauled her to her feet again, wrenching her shoulder. *Mère de Dieu!* She was going to die. Girard was finally going to get his revenge.

Stop crying, damn you. Think! But she could hardly see for the tears burning her eyes. She only stayed on her feet in the stairwell because of Bryson holding her up. How would she get out of this? She'd been in worse fixes. Or maybe not.

When they reached the kitchen, Girard waved a pistol before him. The women servants screamed and backed away. Bryson dragged Angelique, stumbling, outside into the snow of the kitchen garden, then around the side of the castle toward the barmkin and stables. The shock of an icy wind buffeting her snatched her breath. A shiver convulsed her body and stiffened her muscles. Bryson shoved her forward, keeping hold of her upper arm.

Where was everyone? She glanced wildly about for a familiar face, for someone who might help her.

They approached Kormad and the rest of the traitorous Drummagans, waiting in a protected corner, their clothes blood-spattered. *No!* It appeared they'd fought a battle already. How had they escaped? Two MacGrath guards lay on the ground nearby, their blood melting the snow. Nausea arose and icy tears burned her eyes. *Mère de Dieu, where is Lachlan?*

Kormad's gaze lit on her and he laughed.

Bastard. I will kill you.

"Now we go," Girard said.

Her legs were so stiff she could scarce walk. She stumbled and slipped on the icy cobblestones but Bryson kept her upright. The wind flung her cloak back, chilling her despite the wool dress. Through the blur of tears, she watched a few older MacGrath clansmen and lads scurry back wide-eyed as the force of Drummagans moved toward them.

"MacGrath!" Kormad yelled from behind her.

She twisted, tried to jerk away. A strong hand tightened on her arm, securing her in place as a shield in front of them. The cowards.

Lachlan and his brother appeared in the castle's portal.

No! Go back, away from danger, she wanted to shout. Then she wished Lachlan would kill both Kormad and Girard.

Kormad chuckled. "He looks very surprised."

"You damned bastards, release her now!" Lachlan demanded and drew his sword.

"Why would we be doing that?" Kormad's tone was unnaturally cheerful.

"If you hurt one hair on her head...." Lachlan spoke through clenched teeth. His face was dark and his gaze as sharp as the blade he gripped in his fist. He eased forward.

"Stop there," Girard said. With his only hand, he pressed a cold pistol barrel against her ear.

Shivers shot through her, making her teeth chatter. She clenched them together so hard her jaw ached. *Mother Mary, I pray you....*

"What do you want?" Lachlan growled.

"I think you ken," Kormad said.

"Release her and take me instead," Lachlan said.

Angelique shook her head. *No, no!* They would kill Lachlan sooner than they would her.

"I like that plan." Kormad snickered. "All of you MacGraths, lay down your weapons."

Lachlan murmured something to his brother, just behind him, then lay down his sword.

"Any daggers, dirks and pistols, too," Kormad commanded. "Tell your brother to back away and call off the men."

Non, Lachlan, imbecile!

She would rather die than lose him now.

Lachlan held up his hands in surrender and eased a few steps forward. "Release her." A blast of harsh wind carried his sharp words away and flung his hair back from his face.

"Not until you're over here."

When Lachlan drew closer, one of Kormad's men rushed out and grabbed Lachlan. He didn't fight, his eyes riveted on Angelique. "Release her!"

Something in Lachlan's face turned wild, the untamed warrior, and he broke away from the man holding his arms. He launched himself toward Angelique. A blade materialized in his hand, aimed at Girard. The quick movement knocked Girard's pistol aside. It fired in a deafening explosion by her ear. Lachlan landed on top of her on the ground. His hand cushioned her head, and his weight covered her so completely she gasped for breath.

More pistol shots exploded, swords clanged around them, shouts echoed. A battle. Her hearing was distorted, muffled. She tried to see what was happening, but Lachlan's hair curtained her face.

Mère de Dieu, please let him be well.

She screamed through the gag, but the sound emerged as a pathetic groan. Lachlan's body was a dead weight upon her. She prayed with all her might, since that was all she could do.

A moment later, Lachlan rolled off her and she inhaled great gulps of cold air into her burning lungs. But no, someone had rolled him and now dragged her by an ankle. *Girard!* The bastard. She tilted her head to look at Lachlan again. He simply lay on the ground, eyes closed, the warriors slashing with swords over him. Blood soaked his light hair. Was he shot in the head?

Mère de Dieu. Please, no!

She had to help Lachlan. Her bound hands lay beneath her hips and back, being raked over the cobblestones. The rope loosened. She yanked hard and tried to make her small hands even narrower so she might pull one through the ropes. Girard dragged her into the stables and closed the door against the chaotic noise outside.

Her fingers ached and burned, scraped horribly and near frozen but she didn't care. One hand slid free.

Girard attempted to yank her to her feet, not so easy one-armed, and he was no longer a strong man.

"Get up!" he demanded in French.

Pretending to pass out, she collapsed forward into a crouch. She slipped a hand beneath her skirts and drew the dagger from her calf.

When he pulled at her arm again, she rose and stabbed the blade upwards into his gut with far more force than the last time she'd attempted this move on him. Though her aching hands shook, she shoved the blade deeper.

"Aaahhch!" He staggered away from her, yanked his doublet open, and stared down at his belly where blood bloomed over his white shirt. "You bitch!" He surged toward her.

She scrambled to her feet and backed into the corner of a stall, straw beneath her feet.

The big portal to the stables opened. "Angelique!"

Lachlan? Through the crack, she saw him, his hair bloody, but could only emit a moaning sound behind the gag. *Watch for Girard!*

She yanked at the tightly tied strip of material, unable to slip it from her mouth.

"You bastard. Where is Angelique?"

A shot exploded, deafening. Lachlan's arm jerked and a red stain appeared. He rushed Girard, sword in hand. Blades clashed. She eased forward, trembling hands clutching her dagger grip, slick with Girard's blood. Lachlan made two strikes, one against Girard's sword, flinging it aside, and the next to Girard's throat. Blood spurted from the wound and he fell, clutching his neck. His eyes, full of hatred, sought out Angelique. He had looked at her thus before, in France. But this time he would never open his eyes again.

Lachlan turned, his wild gaze finding her. "Are you well?" He rushed to her, took the dagger from her stiff hands and cut off the gag.

She locked her arms around him. "*Oui.* But you are badly hurt." She pulled back and observed his bloody hair and shirt. "You were shot in the head?"

"Just a graze I think."

Blood soaked his torn shirtsleeve and dripped from his fingers like wine.

"Girard shot you in the arm. *Mère de Dieu,* you are losing a lot of blood!"

"Aye, but I shall live." His face looked far too pale.

"We must get you to a physician."

"Gwyneth is a healer." His voice sounded raw and breathy. He blinked his eyes hard and, with his good arm, caught at the stall door. "God's bones." He sank toward the floor and closed his eyes.

Panic clutched at her throat. "Lachlan!" She dropped beside him and ripped his sleeve. Heavens, such a hole blown in his upper arm and him a free bleeder. She found the discarded gag and tied it above the wound. She had heard this would slow bleeding.

The outside door thumped. Kormad, bloody and evil-eyed rushed toward her.

Her dagger lay by Lachlan's limp hand. She seized the weapon and drew back.

"Aha," Kormad howled. "I shall kill you if 'tis the last thing—"

She flung the dagger. It stabbed into the target—Kormad's throat. He went down, clawing at the knife, pulling it out, but blood poured from the wound.

He growled, crawling toward her a few feet, then he sank into the straw.

Shaking, she snatched Lachlan's sword, intent on protecting her husband with her life. Kormad didn't move. She examined Lachlan again. His breath was warm against her hand, and the bleeding less. "*Mère de Dieu*, help me."

Men rushed into the stables. Her heart slammed into her throat. Not more Drummagans.

"Where's Lachlan?" Alasdair asked, bloody sword in hand, his clothing spattered red from the skirmish.

"*Grâce à Dieu*. Here! He needs help. He has lost a lot of blood."

"See to them," he told the MacGraths following him and motioned to the two dead men on the floor. He knelt by Angelique and held his hand before Lachlan's nose.

"Fergus, help me with him." The two large, dark-haired men lifted Lachlan and carried him across the windy barmkin littered with bodies and into the great hall. She followed, in a fog, not trusting her trembling legs but she remained upright.

"Gwyneth!" Alasdair called.

"Oh, dear heavens." She rushed forward, glancing at Angelique. "You are well?"

"*Oui.*"

The men lay Lachlan before the fireplace on the floor. Gwyneth ordered the servants about like a small army of her own. They already had boiling water, herbs and whisky nearby.

All Angelique could do was pray and wipe at her own tears, her hands and clothing covered in blood.

"I'll need to remove the lead ball, then we'll have to cauterize the wound," Gwyneth said.

"Aye, let's do it," Alasdair said.

"Are you hurt, Ange?" Camille suddenly stood before her, touching her face.

She shook her head, her whole body starting to tremble.

"Come, I will help you clean up," Camille urged.

She shook her head again. She could not take her eyes off her husband. His pale, still face. *Wake up, Lachlan!*

Unable to hold herself upright any longer, she sank to her knees. Kneeling by her, Camille clutched her in a fierce embrace and murmured comforting words in French.

When Gwyneth removed the lead ball, blood again ran from Lachlan's wound.

"No, he cannot lose more blood! He is a free-bleeder," Angelique cried.

"Help her upstairs," Alasdair murmured to someone.

"No! I must be with him."

"Shh. We shall clean you up." Camille and two other women forced her toward the stairs. When she resisted, someone lifted her, a dark MacGrath warrior, and carried her up the steps to her bedchamber—no, Lachlan's bedchamber. The man lowered her into a chair before the hearth and left. Camille talked fast to everyone. The servants brought a basin of water.

Camille knelt beside her. "Heavens! Look at your hands, Angelique."

They were scraped, raw and bloody. "It matters not." No, nothing mattered if Lachlan did not open his eyes.

Camille washed her hands in warm water and soap that scalded like lye against her skin. She ground her teeth but said nothing. It was but a small punishment for the stupidity of letting herself be captured and used to draw Lachlan out.

While another woman wrapped bandages around Angelique's hands, Camille stroked a wet cloth over Angelique's face. Her hot tears streaked down the cool, damp skin of her cheeks.

"Shh. He will be well, Angelique. They know what they are doing."

"He must live," she whispered. "Pray, Camille."

"Yes, we shall pray."

"I cannot lose him."

I love him and I did not tell him yet.

֍֎֍

The next day Angelique sat alone by Lachlan's bedside. She stared at his ashen face, her eyes scratchy from lack of sleep and the salty tears. The bleeding had stopped yesterday once they'd cauterized the wound. He had not even awakened during that horrible pain. Gwyneth had redressed his wounds this morn and done all she could for him.

Angelique moved to the side of the bed and sat by his hip. She touched his face, willing him to open his eyes. Their golden whisky color and his teasing expression she yearned to see above all else. His beard stubble had grown scratchy during the night. She relished even this small sign that he lived. His breath puffed softly against her hand.

"Stay with me," she whispered in French. "I am sorry for not believing in you. I was wrong about you. You are the best of men, honorable, faithful and noble."

He remained unmoving.

"*Je t'aime*. I love you."

Still no response.

"Do you hear me? Wake up." She jiggled his good hand as she squeezed it. *Mère de Dieu*, how could she fall in love with him, only to lose him in the next instant? How could fate be so cruel? She pressed his hand against her face and burst into tears. Great wracking sobs. What was wrong with her? She never cried like this. All the pain in her life had gathered behind her eyes and in her throat, almost choking her.

"Dear heavens, what's happened?" Gwyneth bent over Lachlan to examine him.

Though Angelique wanted to stop crying, she couldn't. She dropped to her knees by the bed and tried to pray silently despite her tears.

Sweet Mother Mary, I love him. Do not take him from me, I beg of you. I have done much to be sorry for in my life. But I pray you, let him live.

The talking around her became louder, but she did not want to face them.

"Ange." Camille hugged her and helped her to her feet. "Did you see? Lachlan grimaced."

Angelique swiped the tears from her eyes. In the blur, it seemed his lips moved.

"He's trying to say something," Gwyneth said.

Alasdair moved forward. "Aye, brother?"

"Angel," Lachlan whispered in a raspy dry voice.

She could not breathe for fear she imagined it.

"Angelique," he murmured, this word clear. His head moved, and his eyes opened a crack.

"Je suis ici." Her throat closed as she took his hand and pressed it to her lips. She feared he would say something to her and die. "You must get well."

"Aye."

"We must get him to drink some herbal tea," Gwyneth said. Alasdair lifted him into a sitting position.

Lachlan groaned.

Gwyneth pressed a cup to his lips. "Drink."

Lachlan took a sip, then grimaced. "You trying...kill me?"

Gwyneth smiled with tears in her eyes. "'Tis an herb to help rebuild your blood. You lost so much."

After a few sips he turned his head aside. "Enough," he rasped. They let him lie back.

"Are you in much pain?" Alasdair asked.

"Could use...whisky." He inhaled a deep breath and opened his eyes, his gaze traveling over those around his bed. "Don't look so worried. I'm not that easy to kill."

His gaze stopped on Angelique and he reached for her hand again. She savored the warmth of his skin on hers.

He is alive. He will live. A sparkling rush of relief and gratitude filled her, fresh tears pricking her eyes. Tears of happiness.

"Why don't we let him rest a while?" Gwyneth suggested. "I'll be back in a short time with broth."

Rebbie, Dirk and several MacGrath men filed out of the room, leaving Angelique alone with Lachlan. She leaned forward and kissed his cool forehead.

"What was that for?" he whispered.

"Because I love you and you must live and stay with me."

"Och. Angelique." He observed her a long moment, strong emotion and a smile in his eyes. "I love you, too, lass."

His image blurred and her eyes burned. "Do you mean it, truly?" she whispered. "Or is this just...?" She could not force the rest of the words beyond her constricted throat.

"Aye, I mean it. I've never said those words to another woman. I didn't ken what they meant until I tangled with you, my wee hellcat. Besides, I told you I would never lie to you." He observed her in a serious manner. "I haven't been a good husband to you because I didn't protect you and your inheritance, but I promise to from now on."

"How can you say this?" She frowned. "You almost died

because of me, to save my life. I can never repay you for your heroic deeds."

"You blather on too much. I told you I would kill Girard, and I did. He hurt you. Anyone who hurts you shall suffer, I vow. What of Kormad?"

"Dead." She could not quite bring herself to admit she'd done the deed. "Along with several traitors of our clan. Bryson and a few others live. The constable is going over the evidence and testimonies." Rebbie had found her diamond pendant on Girard's body and returned it to her, but Lachlan was her only treasure now.

"I'm sorry I questioned your honor and fidelity. I know you have been true to me," she whispered.

A grin quirked his lips. "Indeed, I have."

"I believe you."

"You are the only woman I can see now. I am blind to all others, and it has been this way since I met you. I don't understand it, but there 'tis. Come, lie here with me." He gently tugged her closer to him.

"No, you are not well. We cannot…"

"Shh." Though it seemed to take a great deal of effort, he lifted his good arm and stroked his fingertips over her face and into her hair. "Did you say you love me?" His eyes fierce and golden, he observed her closely.

"Yes, I love you."

"How much?"

"More than I've ever loved anyone. More than the amount of water in all the oceans. More than the number of stars in the sky."

He swallowed hard. "'Tis a lot. But, I vow, I love you more." He drew her closer and pressed his lips to hers in a warm, gentle kiss of pure emotion.

EPILOGUE

A week later, when Lachlan was well enough, they had a feast in honor of the two brothers and their new brides. Lachlan sent Rebbie, his cousin Fergus MacGrath, and several others to straighten out the problems at Draughon, find the false papers at Burnglen and meet with the Perth officials and the constable.

Two weeks after that, when Lachlan was strong enough to sit a horse for several hours, he, Angelique, Camille and Dirk prepared for departure. A dozen MacGrath guards and cousins would escort them.

"I wish you'd stay until spring," Alasdair said, his breath fogging in the crisp morning air.

"Much as I'd love that, I must see to Draughon," Lachlan said, observing his brother's dark frown. "I'm fine, mother hen."

"Take care of him," he told Dirk.

"As if he needs it," Dirk muttered, then sent a smirk to Lachlan.

"I've sent messengers ahead to some chiefs and friends along the way who will give all of you a night's lodging."

"I thank you, brother. And we'll see you again soon. In the spring, aye? We'll return for Orin and Kean, and I'll get to meet your new son. Or daughter."

"Indeed." Alasdair shook his hand, hugged him and slapped his back as if trying to knock something from his windpipe.

"Och." Lachlan would show no weakness or he'd be stuck here another fortnight. He turned to his mount. Aye, he could sit in a saddle, but mounting was the problem with a sore arm. Alasdair and Dirk grabbed him and hoisted him onto the horse's back.

"Damnation. Warn me when you're going to do that."

"He appreciates naught," Dirk grumbled. Lachlan knew he was teasing but maybe it was true and he didn't show his appreciation enough.

"I thank you, friend."

Dirk tried to hide a grin as he mounted.

Lachlan turned his attention to Angelique on a bay mare not far from him. He winked, drawing a secret smile from her. Indeed, he had much to be thankful for, especially his adorable wife. The past three weeks she had cared for him like a bairn and near spoiled him. A few days after he'd awakened—once he'd convinced her he would not die—they had indulged in lovemaking such as he'd never imagined. He had not known such depth of feeling was supposed to accompany the bedding. Now he understood why Alasdair had been willing to move heaven and earth for Gwyneth. He would do the same for Angelique.

They traveled slowly south but the late autumn weather did not cooperate. They waited out a snowstorm at another castle, midway, before they could continue. It took over a week to reach Draughon.

At last, they rode through the gates of their home. Rebbie descended the steps to meet them in the courtyard.

"'Tis about time, you slackards. I was tempted to send out a search party."

"What news?" Lachlan dismounted, then helped Angelique, glad to feel his arm growing stronger.

"All is well. Naught to worry over," Rebbie assured him. "We found the false papers at Burnglen and were able to prove to the constable the signatures were forged. Some of the lying witnesses were arrested and others ran away. We found your loyal Drummagan clansmen locked in the dungeon and they testified against Kormad."

"Heckie?"

Rebbie grinned. "Aye. He is well and ornery as ever."

Lachlan slid his arm around Angelique's shoulders and they entered Draughon's great hall, the rest of the party following.

"M'laird. M'lady." The servants and clansmen bowed respectfully, then a cheer went up.

269

Lachlan thanked them, shaking hands all around, a bit sad that only half the clan remained. But he was fairly certain these were the people he could trust.

"Who is this?" Angelique asked.

A wee lad stood near high table. Something about him looked familiar, not just his green eyes and red hair but his facial shape and expression.

"This is Timmy," Rebbie said. "We found him at Burnglen with his nanny. Lady Angelique, he is apparently your…natural half-brother."

"*Mère de Dieu.* In truth? My father's son?" She crept forward.

"That's the rumor. Even I can see the family resemblance."

Angelique knelt. "Good day, Timmy."

He ran and hid behind a woman's skirts. His nanny.

Lachlan watched while Angelique gently coaxed him out and even convinced him to talk in a whisper. He was so young, no more than four summers. Soon, he would no longer remember much about his uncle Kormad. Timmy would grow up here at Draughon with Orin and Kean, Lachlan decided. A good start to their family.

Rebbie joined Lachlan and Dirk. "I need to talk to both of you," he said quietly.

They proceeded into the library.

"What is it? Has something else happened?" Lachlan asked.

"Nay. I but wanted to tell you, when I arrived here a few weeks ago, Eleanor had taken up residence."

"You jest! She had that much gall?"

Rebbie chuckled. "Aye, but I sent her packing back to England soon enough. Hopefully, she will leave you and Angelique in peace."

"I thank you for taking care of that debacle."

"About the two white mares you purchased for Angelique's wedding gift, they are in the stables whenever you wish to present them to her."

"Och. I wondered where they went." Lachlan looked forward to seeing the happiness on Angelique's face when he gave them to her.

"When the horses were released the night of your attack, they returned to the Robertson's. The chief then sent some of his men to return them to you."

"I'm relieved."

Rebbie opened a drawer on the desk and took out what appeared to be a missive bearing a red wax seal. He handed it to Dirk. "This arrived for you."

"For me?" He frowned.

"Aye, it bears your name."

Dirk broke the seal and unfolded the paper. Standing by the window, he read in silence for a few moments.

Lowering the paper, he muttered, "Damnation."

"What is it?"

"I'll tell you later." Taking the letter, he strode out the door.

"Hmph," Lachlan grunted. "I wish he wouldn't do that."

"He's the most secretive person I know. 'Tis vexing."

"Well, given your prying skills, I'm sure you'll find out soon enough," Lachlan said, opening the door.

"Och." Rebbie frowned.

Lachlan smiled. "In the meantime, 'tis time for my beautiful wife and me to retire for the evening." They had much rest and lovemaking to catch up on.

Entering the great hall, Lachlan found her talking to Timmy's nanny. Taking Angelique's hand, he kissed the back.

Her wide-eyed gaze flew to him. When he pressed another kiss to her satiny skin, a pink flush moved over her face.

He drew near and whispered in her ear. "I think 'tis time for a long, hot bath. What say you?"

She grinned and glanced around at the people observing them, her blush darkening. He had no worries about who watched or if they knew he desired—and loved—his wife. He scooped her up into his arms and headed toward the stairs amid many snickers and chuckles from the clan, along with a few bawdy comments.

"Lachlan," she scolded quietly. "Your arm! It is not yet healed. You will injure yourself."

"Nay. My arm is growing stronger. Besides, you weigh no more than a bluebell blossom."

"But everyone is watching," she said in a scandalized whisper.

"I don't care if they know how much I love my wife," he said, trying to nibble on her chin or neck. If only she would stop squirming.

"But...." she sputtered, finally growing still as he quickly mounted the steps. Her emotion-filled eyes locked on his.

Aye, indeed. How could she argue with that? He grinned.

"I love you, too, my wild Highlander," she whispered. At the top of the stairs, she took his face between her palms and kissed him eagerly. Lachlan's heart melted because he would never tire of hearing those words. Nor would he tire of trying to please his wee hellcat.

๑ଇ ୨ର

Look for *My Brave Highlander*, Dirk's story, next in the series.

Camille's story is *Stolen by a Highland Rogue*, first in the Scottish Treasure Series.

๑ଇ ୨ର

ABOUT THE AUTHOR

Vonda Sinclair is the USA Today bestselling author of award-winning Scottish historical romance novels and novellas. Her favorite pastime is exploring Scotland and taking photos along the way. She especially loves ancient castle ruins! She also enjoys writing about hot Highland heroes, unconventional ladies and the healing power of love. Her series are the Highland Adventure Series and the Scottish Treasure Series. Her books have won the National Readers' Choice Award, the CRW Award of Excellence, the Winter Rose Award of Excellence in Published Romantic Fiction--1st Place Historical, and an EPIC Award. She lives in the mountains of North Carolina where she is crafting another wildly romantic Highland adventure.

Please visit her website at: www.vondasinclair.com.

The Highland Adventure Series

My Fierce Highlander
My Wild Highlander
My Brave Highlander
My Daring Highlander
My Notorious Highlander
My Rebel Highlander
My Captive Highlander
Highlander Unbroken
Highlander Entangled

⚬⚬⚬

The Scottish Treasure Series

Stolen by a Highland Rogue
Defended by a Highland Renegade

Printed in the USA
CPSIA information can be obtained
at www.ICGtesting.com
LVHW040313291023
762458LV00007B/119

9 781478 337638